The Ways of Light

Mystic Haven Dimensions book 1

This book is part of The Codes of Creation Multiverse

Arlie Sheelin

---

1. http://www.dennisdotywebsite.com/editing.html%20

2. https://www.arliesheelin.com/

Dedication

TO ALL THE READERS and Writers of Mystic Haven Origins, past and present.

READERS: Whether you are there to read the stories, for community, for laughter, or just because you want to know what those crazy bastards are up to: We, the writers of Mystic Haven, are so glad you found us and read our stories. Each of us, as writers, have brought our own unique take and style of writing into the mix. We are so glad you enjoy our stories. Thank you. You are the reason we do this.

WRITERS: We've always been a crazy bunch of misfit rebels, and I've loved that about us. Whether you write as a hobby or dream of writing books: Your stories have inspired and delighted me for years. I hope you never stop writing. Your stories are important. Thank you for being a part of Mystic Haven Origins.

Author's Note

BAYLEN'S JOURNEY IS about darkness, and loss, and grief. It's about bad choices, anger, bitterness, and soul-deep pain. It's about being lost.

It's also about courage, strength, resilience, and hope. and it's about the light that overcomes the darkness.

It's about seeking the light and finding your way. It's about being the light so that others may find their way.

Please be aware that his story deals with abduction, sexual abuse, violence, murder, loss, grief, anger, vengeance, stalking, evil, and sexual situations that include BDSM. If you are sensitive to this kind of subject matter, please be mindful of your mental health. I wish you well in your own journey of courage, strength, resilience, hope and finding your way through the darkness.

Special Acknowledgement

TO MY DEAR FRIEND COLEEN Smith who is the creator and writer of Micah Thallan, Adler Llewellyn, Etan Llewellyn, Helio MacConaill, Arion Aossi, Janie Valeska, Nerys Daenala, Shade, and Reef, in the Mystic Haven Origins online RP group. Thank you for all the years we have written together. Thank you for our wonderful friendship. Thank you for believing in me and allowing me to introduce Micah and your other band of rebels in The Mystic Haven Dimensions series.

To my readers: All of Micah's parts and all Coleen's band of rebels in this book have been a collaboration between me and Coleen. She is wonderfully creative, infinitely inspiring, and incredibly patient with my crazy brainstorming sessions. We have spent many hours writing together, crafting the world of Mystic Haven Origins. And now she has joined me in the creation of the Mystic Haven Dimensions book series. Stay tuned, you will see much more of Coleen's writings as this series progresses.

Acknowledgements

THE CREATION OF THIS book would not have been possible without these people. They have contributed a lot on this crazy journey. Thank you for your steadfastness, and your belief in me.

To my beta readers: Brandy, Andrea, Cara, Ann, Michaele, Nicole, and Dirk. Thank you for your patience and eagle eyes. My books are made better by your skills and the conversations we have had about this story.

To my editor Dennis Doty, who steadfastly tells me that he gets caught up in my stories and must go back and edit. That makes me smile. Thank you, Dennis, for so clearly hearing my voice and seeing my vision for these books. Thank you for encouraging me to walk my own path. Thank you for all the work you do to make my stories shine.

To Steven Novak, thank you for this beautiful cover. You've captured the essence of Baylen Knight perfectly.

Dear Reader

WELCOME TO MYSTIC HAVEN Dimensions, the third series in The Codes of Creation Multiverse. The Ways of Light is the first book in the Mystic Haven Dimensions series. It takes place in Dimensions three, two, one, and Dimension nine million, seven hundred thousand, two hundred forty-one of the multiverse.

This book is an urban fantasy novel with sci-fi elements and a secondary spicy romance. The Fae in this book are a combination of mythology and my imagination. They are unique. Expect the unexpected and don't expect the expected. There are also many other types of Superhumans in the Mystic Haven Dimensions series.

These three books happen concurrently in this multiverse series. There is no reading order with these first books.

Please note that The Way Maker, book 1 of The Zemyneah Experiment Series, contains a prologue that is important to all the books.

The second book for The Zemyneah Experiment series will be released next.

The three series are the beginnings of a vast multiverse of sci-fi/fantasy stories. I hope you enjoy the adventures, and misadventures of my heroes and heroines. Just watch out for the dragons.

One more thing. I'm Canadian, therefore you will find that I use Canadian spelling and grammar. Thank you for your understanding and kindness.

~Arlie

https://www.arliesheelin.com[1]

---

1. https://www.arliesheelin.com/

Prologue

DIMENSION ONE
Tuatha Star System

LIGHT SHINES AND THE darkness cannot overcome it. A simple matter of physics. A truth that cannot be denied.

They were the bearers of light. A powerful race of Fae, and they fought the darkness.

Their lineage was not royalty but the ordinary, everyday citizens who made up the multiverse, as diverse as the snowflakes that fell from winter skies. Their genetics were mixed, their species of origin combined and recombined, they were few and they were unique. When the final component was added to their own, they became more. So much more. For Fae blood was powerful and dynamic. It united all the parts. It was the glue, the bridge. It was the final piece of a long-forgotten code—And it ignited an explosion of light.

They were the peacekeepers, the negotiators, the innovative thinkers. The ones called on to resolve problems, to prevent wars—and they were the ones who ended the wars. Light bearers. Darkness Slayers. Changeling Fae.

Part One

Black is the void

Chapter One

ARACSNA, DARK FLAME Star System
    Stardate: 19490.04.03
    Earthdate: 932 AD

ASH MORANA THE FIRST, and most feared of all the Fallen. The owner and creator of Hell, The Dimension of Shadows, The Abode of the Damned, The Carnage Ground, Triu'qira, The Lake of Fire, Ceanex, or his personal favorite—Eternal Darkness. In the end, it didn't matter what you called it. It was simply a container for the souls that he'd captured. A beautiful, artistic nightmare of pain and suffering. A cruel smile edged his lips as he turned his attention to the creature who'd given his report. "What do you mean there is an anomaly with the subject's DNA, Adan?"

Adan glanced up at his Lord and Master, briefly meeting his eyes. "I have studied this Fae being for several months. I know you wanted to know their weaknesses, but this anomaly is highly unusual. Never have I seen DNA like this before. Not once, Lord Morana. Not in any of the beings you have brought to me. I thought it was important to inform you."

Ash studied Adan curiously. The creature was from a race he himself had created. A secret race, made for one purpose—to destroy the Fae whom Rune and Eliana loved so much.

His first attempt to create life had not exactly failed. In fact, the demons that he commanded were, in his opinion, a success. They were vile creatures with the ability to take possession of any mere mortal being. Personally, he found that a useful trait. He could command huge armies of demon possessed mortals. How he loved their suffering. His demons also had outstanding abilities, killing in the most sadistic ways possible, or torturing with a creative passion he had not expected.

Of course, these mortals were Rune and Eliana's creations, and they did not take kindly to their creations being harmed. They'd been so upset that they'd kicked him out of the Angelic Realm and taken away his ability to enter The In-Between where they dwelled. *Ah well, who needed them anyway.* They were, of course, afraid he would become more powerful than they were. He smiled a deeply secretive smile and turned to admire his creation once again.

The V'ran were one of the many creatures he had created since he'd struck out on his own. They were humanoid in appearance. Grey skinned, jagged toothed beings of incredible power with a fondness for consuming Fae energy. He was proud of that little attribute. "You've done well, Adan."

Adan grinned, his gleaming jagged teeth showing. "Thank you, Lord Morana. The answer to your original request is far simpler. The V'ran are more than capable of destroying the Fae. Our world, Aracsna, orbits a neutron star in the Dark Flame Star System. As you planned, it is the perfect habitat for beings who need to be strong enough to kill the Fae."

Ash smiled coldly. "I want them to suffer. No, fast, easy death for Rune and Eliana's favored beings."

"It's quite excruciating to the Fae subject when I consume some of his energy."

Ash nodded. "We shall attack in three months' time. I need a sample of the Fae subjects' DNA."

Adan handed Lord Morana a small vial. "I thought you might. May I consume the subject now?"

"No. I have a few more experiments to run. Be patient, Adan." *He wanted every V'ran to be starving when they attacked.*

Chapter Two

TUANTHA STAR SYSTEM
 Stardate: 19490.07.21
 Earthdate: 932 AD

EVEN THOUGH HE WAS Fallen, Ash still retained the angelic capability to create the chaotic wormholes that would instantaneously move him through dimensions, time, and space. The Angels and Creators called them vortexes. He didn't care what it was called. The importance was in its existence and his control over it. He opened a vortex and stepped inside, glancing down at himself as the vortex closed.

Normally, he took on the appearance of an elegant well-dressed leader of whatever species he was dealing with, but today was the beginning of a war. A war that would be a decisive, demoralizing, first strike against his enemies. That required something special. His shoulder length blond hair he wore loose, his goatee trimmed neatly, and his black feathered wings shone. He wore the practical black leather of a warrior with two swords crossing over his back. Several illegal Angelfire blades were prominently displayed on his person. He'd made sure to have his image recorded. It would find its way to the people who wanted him to fail.

When they saw the image, they would know the Angelfire blades he so boldly displayed were blades he had taken after slaughtering their owners. Sure, he could no longer wield them as they'd been intended. He grinned. *Ah, but the damage they now caused in their corrupted state was far, far more deadly.*

He stepped out of the vortex and onto the bridge of a sleek blàck battle destroyer, a ruthless Fallen Angel in all his glory. The vortex disappeared instantly. "General Gatlin, it's time to begin the attack."

Opening a second vortex large enough to encompass the battle destroyer and the entire fleet that accompanied it, he anchored the end in the heart of the Tuatha Star System. "The vortex will bypass the early warning systems on their outermost planet. Make sure you knock out all communications with the Star Initiator as soon as you leave the vortex. It will appear on their sensors as a coronal mass ejection.

"The Tuatha Star System is made up of seven worlds and an asteroid belt. Start with the Changeling Fae on Aelrindel and its moons. The Changeling Fae are powerful. Hit them hard. Hit them fast. There can be no survivors to warn the other planets.

"After you've finished with Aelrindel, you need to release multiple squadrons to hit every planet simultaneously. They must release their payload high in each planet's atmosphere. The higher the Electromagnetic Pulse bombs are released the better. It's vital that all electronics be destroyed.

Once the V'ran are on the ground they will need to establish webs. Do not underestimate the Seelie and Unseelie Fae. They are different from the Changeling Fae, but they are still powerful.

"On the planet Erendrial, the first target is the Fae king and his Trium. I do not care how you get to him. Kill him and his Trium. If you don't take out the Royal Trium fast you will fail." Ash's eyes filled with icy hardness. "Failure is not an option."

Part Two

An Ancient Darkness

Chapter Three

EARTH DIMENSION THREE
Vancouver, B.C., Canada
Over a thousand years later

WISTERIA ABITAL HAD found the murderers of her people—The prey who thought they could be predators. Now she needed to find her pawns. Those she could control. This was not her world, and these were not her people which made her task so much easier. She smiled, a cruel twist of her black lips. Studying the people who inhabited this area of the planet, from the safety of the shadows that hid her grey skin, Wisteria began to shift her appearance. By the time she entered the ferry terminal she was a young adult human female. She boarded the ferry and set out for the island that contained the energy signatures of her enemy. She would dine well this day.

Chapter Four

BAYLEN KNIGHT WAS PURE Fae, although he laughed whenever someone said that to him. He'd never known a *pure* Fae in his life—But he was one hundred percent Seelie Fae. His parents were both Seelie Fae, and his grandparents and his great-grandparents. In fact, his family line could be traced back hundreds upon hundreds of years.

He'd joined the Fae Air Force at eighteen, like his father and his grandfather. Fae had a thing for flying. Yes, they could fly without the machines, but come on, who didn't want to have control of a powerful machine capable of flight and mass destruction.

The Fae had never been the creatures of whim and whimsy that humans told tales of. They were a race of powerful alien beings. Honor and integrity ruled them. They tried hard to contribute to this planet that they'd adopted as their own when their worlds were lost to a terrible enemy. Yet they fully understood the dangers their abilities brought to this world of fragile humans.

The rare white dwarf star this planet orbited was the key component for the Fae. If a Fae overexerted their powers, they experienced a condition called Flame-Out. Flame-Out was a dangerous fatigue that could kill if not treated. Though treatment was simple. Sunlight. Days of sleeping and resting in the sunlight. Basically, the Fae needed solar power the way a handheld device needed to recharge. Hell, it irritated the shit out of him.

Flying was a natural ability, but it was also a skill that took a lot of damned hard work to develop properly. Most Fae flew the way most humans went for a walk around the block. It was nice to get out in the sun, and it was good for your health.

The other problem with flying was the risk of being seen. Fortunately, when the Fae found earth, humans were not the only inhabitants. Superhumans had evolved alongside their human cousins. Secret sanctuary cities were scattered across the earth, their presence well hidden.

Humans believed they ruled the earth, and they did not believe in Fairies, or Elves, or any other mythical creatures. Hell, they hardly believed in aliens.

Baylen pushed away the history lesson running in his head. Right now, he was on leave and not due to return to the secret Fae military base for another week. He fully planned to re-enlist, after his leave. It had been eight years, not all of it easy, but deeply satisfying. He figured he would be a lifer like his father.

He rolled out of bed, pulled on jeans and a tee shirt and ran his hand through his long dark curls before heading out to the patio to join his parents and brothers for breakfast. It seemed an ordinary morning, spent in the first light of the day, eating and laughing with his family. It was something he had come to appreciate as a man who flew dangerous missions to help protect the world.

The sunshine was warm, energizing him and renewing his strength. After breakfast, he started to help clean up, but his mom laughingly shooed him out of the house, telling him to go and enjoy his time off. He kissed her cheek, grabbed his backpack, and headed out to hike up into the mountains intending to stop at the hot springs.

Yesterday, he'd met a beautiful tourist on the docks and told her about those hot springs. She'd looked him over and he'd looked right back at her. They'd spent the day together and most of the night and agreed to meet at the hot springs today.

Chapter Five

EARTH DIMENSION THREE
Mystic Haven, B.C., Canada

PARKING HIS MOTORBIKE in the designated parking spot, Baylen set out on the mountain trail. After hiking for a good hour, he stopped to drink from the water bottle he'd packed. His Fae instincts twinged, and he glanced around, listening carefully, but there was nothing but the birds and insects. He turned in a slow circle unable to shake the feeling. Nothing. He shook his head, ruefully running a hand through his long dark hair, then took the sunglasses he'd hooked into the neck of his t-shirt and slipped them over his dark brown eyes. A smirk curved his lips, and he shook his head. Fae instincts were dicey at best in, his opinion. Yeah, his ancestors had needed them to survive, but they had evolved a helluva lot since then. So, he ignored the strange feeling and continued to the hot springs.

There she stood, Wisteria Abital. She waited for him, all lovely, with tanned curves, and big brown eyes—and not wearing a stitch of clothing. He gave her a slow grin, lust burning like a wildfire through his veins. *The things he planned to do to that lush body.* Tearing off his clothes, he jumped into the water with a wild shout, hauled her into his arms, and took her mouth in a rough kiss—And that's when his nightmare began.

There are dark things in the universe, things that should never see the light of day. This day, Baylen faced an ancient darkness.

He was used to being in charge, and surprised by her aggression, he drew back and found himself staring into a face he did not recognize. He jerked away as he took in the black eyes, sharp teeth, and grey skin. Shock seeped into him. *No. No. They were all dead.*

She looked at him and laughed, leaning forward slowly, clearly intending to kiss him again. He tried to lift his hand to keep her away from him and discovered he could not move. He exerted more energy, his teeth clenched, sweat beading on his forehead. She drew closer and his skin crawled. Pressing her black lips against his, she whispered to him. "Poor little Fae, what's wrong? Don't you like the truth? Did you think you were invincible? Do not worry, young one, you are not my prey. You're only the pawn." She pressed more kisses to his mouth, licking at his lips with her blackened tongue.

How the fuck did she know he was a Fae? Sickened, he tried desperately to move, to turn his head. His efforts becoming more frantic as with dawning horror he realized that she was feeding from his energy, from his life force.

"My prey is so much more than you can ever realize, pretty Fae." She stood up, water running down her perfect body and strode from the pool, and he followed her, helplessly, a puppet in her hands.

With everything in him, he tried to stop himself. Fought to stand still, commanded his feet not to move, but it was futile. She turned once and frowned at him. "Stop wasting your energy. I will need it later."

He stopped resisting her even as his brain screamed at him to fight.

They walked into the forest, deeper and deeper. His feet cut and bleeding, but he could not stop. Pain filled every step. Time lost all meaning. He struggled to use his powerful Fae abilities. Every desperate telepathic mind link slammed into concrete walls of emptiness, and he realized how alone he was. He was alone with an enemy that the Fae race believed dead.

Eventually, she came to a halt, and he was faced with the horror of the creature that controlled him. Before him was The Ward created by his people, a powerful sentient being designed to detect evil and destroy it. The Wards' normally golden energy was the color of thick tar, it roiled and writhed like it was in terrible pain.

Wisteria grabbed him and shoved him into The Ward, and he was struck by a blinding wave of dark energy. He fell to the ground, screaming in agony as the energy tore through him, wrapped around him, until he was utterly entangled in its web.

Chapter Six

EARTH DIMENSION THREE
Mystic Haven, B.C., Canada

WHEN HE REGAINED CONSCIOUSNESS, Wisteria stood gazing down at him, a small cruel smile on her lips. "Fae." Her voice was mocking. "I need your assistance."

"Go fuck yourself, bitch."

She laughed, "Your hatred, it's so—arousing." With a wave of her hand, she compelled him to stand before her.

He glared at the creature before him, a thousand murderous plans running through his mind. He would kill her.

"Kneel." Her voice was a dark compulsion that he fought until blood ran from his nose. Fought harder even as his knees gave out and he found himself kneeling in the cold dirt. A thousand fruitless plans left his fists clenched and hatred burning in his soul, as with a horrifying sensual smile, she demonstrated exactly how much control over him she had.

Chapter Seven

EARTH DIMENSION THREE
Mystic Haven, B.C., Canada

HE LAY ON HIS SIDE fighting not to throw up as she reclined, facing him, idly stroking his hip. "You are good, Fae. I think I will keep you around for a long time. You are much, much better than the two before you."

With those words and a casual wave, the dark energy rolled back. An ugly stench filled his nostrils until he was desperate for pure clean air, and he found himself staring in horror at two rotting corpses. Somehow, he managed to tear his gaze from the dead bodies. "What have you done?"

"It's simple Fae, this quaint little Ward has become my web. I will rule this island from here. The people of Mystic Haven are simply here to feed me. To feed my power, while I conquer this backwards little world you inhabit. It's the perfect revenge, and I shall glory in every moment until I have drained this world dry." She studied him with a faint smile. "I hunger, and soon, someone will answer the call."

Tracing a line up his side with her nail, she continued. "The Fae will be my power source, the others...." A cold smile edged her lips. "They are food, my pet. Don't worry, I will share. After all, you are an amazingly strong source of power, and I don't want to drain you too quickly. The others were a disappointment. Old men who had clearly lived past their usefulness. The first one lasted only minutes, the other maybe an hour."

Chapter Eight

SHE STOOD AND MOVED away from him to the edge of The Ward. The sound of someone walking through the forest, reached his ears. He shouted to warn them, and she laughed. "They cannot hear you. My voice calls them, my power sings to them. They want nothing more than to please me."

A young couple came into view, holding hands and walked straight toward them without looking around.

Oh, Goddess, they were shifters. "Run! Fucking Run!"

But they continued forward, coming closer and closer. She laughed at him, and returned to crouch beside him, stroking his hair. "I love all this wild passion you possess. It tastes so good. Fae energy is difficult to harvest these days. We gorged well when we were released on your worlds. Of course, we were starving so none of us had the forethought to farm your species. Imagine my delight when I came across this world and found your people's hiding place. Fae enough to last me a lifetime. It's a tragedy, I am one of the last of my kind. What a glorious party it would have been if we'd discovered this world a millennium ago."

"Gods." He stared at her. *She was— No, that wasn't possible. It couldn't be possible!*

"We were enemies once, Fae. My people and yours. Your people were destined to die at our hands. We were destined to feed from all your glorious power. We were destined to rise and take all that you had."

"V'ran!" He choked out, horror in his every breath.

She smiled. "You didn't really think you could escape us, did you? We are relentless."

"No. The V'ran are dead. They were destroyed!"

"Your king tried, Fae. He and his warriors found our home world. He destroyed our nest. We had no place to return. So, we did what we were created to do. We hunted the Fae across the universe until we thought they were finally extinct. Our destiny was complete, and my people began to die. Until only a small remnant remained.

Now, I have discovered my purpose, why I remain. Destiny was not finished, but now, it will end here, with me," She looked at him, and he saw the evil in her eyes. "And you. Finally, my people will be avenged. We will be victorious when I kill every last Fae on this island. On this planet. But first," She laughed. "I will drain the Fae of their precious power. I will use their weak, pathetic, goodness to destroy them. I will make them watch as every person here becomes my food. As I wreak havoc on this little piece of paradise that you all mistakenly thought was your sanctuary.

At some point, your king and his Trium will come." She rubbed her hands together. "I long for that battle, my pet. I will gorge on your people's strength. I will twist and weave the Fae's golden energy into the pure darkness of my people's energy. I will use it to give me the strength I need to kill a Fae king and his Trium.

"Don't worry though, I will keep you alive, to see it all. You will stand at my side, as my consort. Betrayer of your own people."

He cursed her with every foul word he knew, struggling to stand, struggling to draw on his power.

With a mere wave of her hand, she allowed him to rise to his feet, a mocking smile curving her lips. "Did you know that my people are distantly related to a tiny creature on this planet? I think you call them Arachnids. Spiders. Do you know what some female spiders do with their mates?" Wisteria leaned in close. Her breath whispering over his lips. "She eats him." A soft feminine giggle. "It is a glorious calling, Consort." Her voice was a gentle sound as she stroked her hand down his abs.

"Remember," she whispered.

His mind filled with the ancient history of his people. Her voice narrating the brutal war with the excruciating details that only an eyewitness could have. The battles, the screams of the dying, the desperate flight to protect their race from an enemy who saw them only as food to be gorged upon. When she finally released her grasp on his mind and walked toward the couple who had stopped at the edge of the Ward, he fell to his knees retching over and over again.

A terror filled scream rent the air.

He jerked his head up. She had the male in her arms allowing him, and his mate, to partially surface from their trance. He could feel their terror sweeping across the Ward, and it writhed in agony. Shards of glass piercing his skin. Gritting his teeth, he rose unsteadily to his feet. He had to save them. Had to stop this evil. His only hope was that she was distracted with the male who had managed a half shift and was fighting her. She laughed as the male's blood flowed red down his chest. Her fingers tipped with lethal black claws slashed again and more blood flowed.

Drawing on the Fae energy of his people, Baylen charged her, and slammed to a stop mere inches from his target. She turned her head to look at him and laughed. "Pet, I know you want to help, but it is too late for these two. I've tasted the sweetness of his blood and learned the power of their bond. Whatever manner of creature they are, they are delicious with all their terror and fury."

Baylen could do nothing. He shouted, he raged, he struggled with every ounce of his Fae might, but he could not break through the powerful energy web that she'd cast over him.

In desperation, he attempted to shift time, something he'd never been good at. If he could just save one of them. Give them a few seconds to escape. Somehow, he broke through. Barely.

Time froze as the shift took hold. The monster and her prey froze in a moment of unending terror. "Run! Fucking Run!" He screamed at the female.

Instead, she attacked the creature, in a wild attempt to save her mate.

"No! No! Creators No! Run! Get help!"

Suddenly, time snapped back to normal, and Wisteria sneered at the female shifter before ripping her throat out with a single swipe of her clawed fingers. The male let out an enraged roar and rushed the monster who had killed his mate. He died seconds later.

Baylen closed his eyes fighting the burning behind his lids. "Fuck! Fuck! You stupid bitch! You killed them. You killed them! Why didn't they run?" He sank to his knees, not even realizing that she'd released the web. "Why didn't they run?"

She suddenly grabbed his hair in a punishing grip and yanked his head back. Hot liquid poured over his mouth. He flung himself backwards in horror, as blood washed over his face and down his throat.

Swearing hoarsely, he wiped his mouth with his arm, even as a metallic taste flooded his mouth. Lifting hate-filled eyes, he stared deeply into the black gaze of this creature who held him captive. "I swear on every Fae who has ever died at your people's hands that I will kill you! With your death, the existence of your race will finally be forgotten. It will be as if you never existed!"

Shrieking, Wisteria launched herself at him. The gouges she tore out of his chest were deep. Blood spilled down his body, but the pain only reminded him that he lived, and he had a chance. A chance he was determined not to waste. He swung a fist at her and she fell, sprawling on the ground. She struck back, her power a vast crash of black energy that left him screaming in agony.

She rose to her feet and sneered at him. "You will kill me? You? A weak pathetic Fae. There is not even the remotest possibility that you could succeed. You will die, along with all the others of your kind. Food for a superior race." With a look of contempt, she strode away, leaving him writhing in the agony of her energy web.

Part Three

When there is only darkness, we will be the light.

Chapter Nine

EARTH DIMENSION THREE
Mystic Haven, B.C., Canada

HOURS LATER, HE LAY panting in the dirt. She'd released him from the agony of her web, but every move he made caused him to lose his breath.

She'd left the Ward, with a promise to return in the morning, and a jaunty wave of her hand. Strolling away through the forest as if she was simply going for a walk.

It was quiet, so quiet, and dark. The night, an inky blackness pressing in on him, making it impossible to see even a few feet in front of him, and he was glad. Because he could not bear to look at the bodies strewn about The Ward, as if they were so much garbage.

Time crawled by and he tried to think of a way to stop this monster. *There had to be some way to defeat her.* He shook his head, as the soft sound of an ancient lullaby filled his mind. *Ah fuck!* He was losing his mind. Shaking his head again, he tried to think, forcing his tired brain to consider every possibility.

The lullaby played softly again, and he closed his eyes. He was so damn tired. He desperately wanted to sleep, but he was so deep into flame-out that if he did, there was a real possibility that he would never wake up. He was all that stood between his people and a creature from the deepest pits of hell. The soft tinkling notes of the lullaby played again, and he opened his eyes.

The music was close to him, coming closer all the time. He glanced around, worried. The ancient words that were taught to all Fae children, from the time of their birth began to flow through his mind.

If the darkness should arrive,
Let the light be your guide.
Even one small glimmer of light
Pierces the blackest night
When there is only darkness,
we will be the light.
Light remains.
Seek the light,
Find your way.

He always thought it a strange lullaby, but it was a Fae tradition and who was he to argue with that? The words flowed through his mind again and he realized the words were coming from somewhere else, someone or something was sending him the lullaby. It was like a mind link but different, foreign to him. He lay still, and a broken energy brushed against him. The Ward. It hadn't been fully destroyed by her black twisted webs.

He sent the lullaby back using the strange path and it came back to him, stronger and clearer. The Ward was attempting to communicate with him. Was it possible there was a message in that lullaby? Could his people have ensured that the way to defeat this enemy was passed down from generation to generation?

He could sense The Ward's pain and determination. He thought The Ward was dying, that she'd defeated it. *But if it was communicating with him...was that correct? Was it possible that the blackness of her energy could not defeat the light of the Ward? The light of his people. Oh, gods. The Ward was the light. Energy. She used a black energy, but his people used golden energy. What did the lullaby say? Even one small glimmer of light*—He stared into the darkness, and wished he had a fucking match so he could see something, and that was when he realized exactly what the lullaby meant. No matter how dark it was, light always vanquished the darkness.

He thought about The Ward and the day his parents had brought him and his brothers to visit it when they were nine years old. *His mother's voice whispered around him. "Do you see that golden glow? That is Fae magic recognizing goodness. Your hearts are pure. The Ward is an energy field, but it's so much more. It's aware. It's sentient. It's intelligent. Do you understand boys? It will communicate with you if you listen. Please remember that goodness strengthens The Ward. But also remember that The Ward will destroy evil. That is its purpose.*

"When the island was first settled, all the Fae and the Fae king gathered to create The Ward. It was a dangerous thing to do because if even one of them had been evil, The Ward would have destroyed them all. They did it to protect Mystic Haven. To turn this beautiful island into a refuge for all superhumans in need. Remember, true power comes from goodness, compassion, and courage.

Baylen lay in the dirt, naked, covered in the blood of innocents, and the wounds inflicted upon him by that creature, and he was stunned. He knew what he had to do. Gathering what little remained of his strength, he knew he was long past flame-out. He didn't know what the hell was keeping him going, but suspected it had to do with The Ward. There was no way he would survive what was to come.

But he would do everything in his ability to ensure that his people lived. He drew a deep breath and linked to The Ward, calling it to him. "I am of the light, filled with the golden energy of the sun, taste my goodness. Come to me and be strengthened." He kept his voice pure, soft, and he let go of the human glamour that every Fae wrapped themselves in. His ears resumed their natural pointed shape, and his immense energy wings appeared.

The Ward slid along his skin, and he forced himself to remain calm, even as he shared The Wards' agony. The blackness she'd forced into the energy being came into contact with him. He groaned, at the feeling of a thousand razor blades piercing his body. Forcing himself to lay still, he breathed deeply. The Ward wrapped all around him, and he flung open his natural shields. Agony raced down his spine. He writhed as The Ward suddenly discovered the goodness of his Fae soul. The split second that it took for The Ward to fully merge with him was a dark torment. The blackness of the diseased Ward encased him, began to pulse and twist. He fought his screams, choking on his agony as tiny pinholes of golden light appeared and the blackness began to dissolve.

Baylen could feel the energy of every one of the Fae who had carefully crafted this unique entity. He could feel their determination and courage. Hell, he could feel The Ward. It was infuriated, incensed by the torture it had been subject to. The killings within its field had driven it to the point of madness.

Baylen whispered soothing words and tried to pour healing energy into the damaged being —but he had so little right now. The immensity of The Ward's injuries caused despair to rise within him. *It was so broken —how could he heal it?*

The agony of the black energy was stunning. Its alienness, its darkness was a horror his soul had never known. He closed his eyes and gritted his teeth. He did not know how much time he had, but it was imperative to get The Ward healed before she returned. He could not fail. *Fuck! He. Could. Not. Fail.*

His brothers. He swallowed, fought the grief, at the sudden image of them that shimmered in his mind. He'd shared a womb with them. They were tied together in inexplicable ways. He couldn't save himself, but by the Creators, he would save them!

Concentrating he poured all his energy into healing The Ward, driving the blackness back. But for every inch the darkness retreated it crept back in another area. He could not defeat it this way.

Frantically, he reached for The Wards' mind, needing its knowledge. The Ward responded with images of all the Fae that had created it, Baylen groaned. Hell. How did he make The Ward understand? More images poured through his mind, and with them came a sense of urgency. So many images of Fae. So many that he was overwhelmed. *"Stop!"*

The Ward paused, waiting expectantly.

He heard her. She was returning! She called his name in that sweetly evil voice. "Baylen, my pet, I know what you are doing. You cannot succeed. My power is too great. Stop wasting my energy this way!"

Fuck! Fuck! He wasn't ready! He was not fucking ready! Suddenly, her cold hands slid across his chest. "Pet, you really must stop this." She scraped a claw along the point of one ear. "Pretty golden Fae. You smell delicious. I wondered if my leaving would entice you to reveal your true form. Do you not understand that you don't contain enough power to stop me? Accept your fate. Embrace your destiny."

He stared into the inky blackness of her eyes, and everything inside of him rebelled. There was no way in hell he would ever accept the future she described. No way he would allow his people, to be destroyed, his brothers—fuck no!

With a roar he flung open his soul, seeking all the energy he could find, from anywhere he could find it. Seeing a faint golden line of energy, he grabbed onto it with the last of his power. Carefully he drew it to himself, absorbing its bright energy, and fed it out to The Ward. The draw became fiercer, and faster as The Ward began to recover. Whatever the hell he'd tapped into was an incredibly vast supply of energy. He was burning up, becoming brighter and brighter. At first, the creature laughed with delight. "For me, Pet? You are a darling." But as soon as she attempted to feed off the energy radiating from him, she shrieked. "What have you done!"

She rose to her feet, screaming, enraged, and she slammed a bolt of pure black energy into his body!

He arched in agony, but the draw of golden energy flowing into him was vast. She slammed more and more of her corrupt black energy into him, the pain was beyond anything he had ever experienced, but there was nothing that could stop the golden light.

Some still functioning part of his mind realized that he had tapped into the impossible. The essence of all the Fae that had gone before was streaming into him. The energy from every single Fae who had ever lived, from the smallest Fae to the greatest warriors and kings was flowing into him—and he channeled all that energy into The Ward.

Whatever this phenomenon was, however, it had come into being, it was not done with him yet. The Fae—every single Fae alive—on this island and from all around the world began to add their energy to the immeasurable force pouring into him. The night was driven back as The Ward began to glow.

The creature screamed and yanked a black bladed knife from her belt. "No! No!" She shrieked. "You will not succeed. You will not win against me!" With all her strength she plunged the blade straight into his heart.

It was like a match set to a powder keg. The ground shook with the force of the explosion. There was a blinding flash of white energy that incinerated everything in its path. A hot searing wind blew across the island, huge waves crashed against the shores, and the night grew as bright as the day.

Baylen lay on the ground. Blood ran from his ears and nose. He was dying, and he knew it. His ears rang, and his skin was raw. He could not see. He lifted a hand, let it fall. He listened for her, but there was only the ringing in his ears and the sounds of wind blowing through the trees. Then the gentle brushing of The Ward against him. *"It's finished. You are safe."*

The words whispered in his mind. He closed his eyes, relief rushing through him. "Thank you." He whispered, not knowing if he was thanking The Ward, or all the Fae, those who remained and those who had gone before—and returned to fight with him, against an ancient enemy.

He took a slow, painful breath and tried to rally enough strength to send a mind link to his brothers. *"Jarek, Riot... Tell mom and dad... love you all."*

"Baylen Effing Knight, you will not die! Do you hear me!" Jarek, second born of the triplets, his fury and pain a tangible thing even through the distance that separated them.

"Baylen! Hang on we're almost there. Do you think you can turn down the damn light? It's damned hard to see!" That was Riot, the youngest of the three.

Moments later he heard running footsteps and swearing. His father reached him first, then Riot and Jarek. His hand trembled as his father grasped it. "Son, we've got you. We're here. You hang on. Doc Brody is on his way. You're going to be okay."

Baylen hung on to his father's hand. "Dad? You found me? Is she dead? Please tell me she's dead!"

Zander Knight stared at his son, and it took everything in him not to cry out at the sight of his injuries. "There is no one here son. The forest for a mile around you has been incinerated. Nothing survived that blast." Baylen nodded as more voices joined them, and he heard Dr. Brody yelling for a helicopter.

# Part Four

Seek the light, find your way

Chapter Ten

EARTH DIMENSION THREE
Mystic Haven, B.C., Canada

EVERYTHING WAS FUCKING different now. How could it not be? He'd fought and won a terrible battle with an alien creature. It took him weeks to get his eyesight back. More weeks for his heart to heal from such a grievous injury.

He decided against re-enlisting. Mastering Fae magic was his obsession. Every Fae skill he'd ever known of, and a few he'd never. The power that flooded his system, during that horrific struggle changed him, altered him in ways that there was no going back from. He had more power than any Fae in existence, he had memories that went back to the most ancient of days, and even his physical appearance had changed.

He refused to look in the mirror and ignored any reference to the changes. He knew. Hell, he looked more Fae than anyone had ever looked. His ears had sharper points. His eyes almost glowed with the unrestrained energy coursing through his blood. Even his wings were different, pulsing with energy, they easily carried him anywhere he wanted to fly. It was like his Fae genetics had been supercharged, and now, he was literally the Fae'est Fae that had ever lived.

His father had done some research and suggested that he looked much like the first Fae who had existed in a distant galaxy, a hell of a long time ago.

He remained connected to The Ward, aware of every Fae that went to pay homage to it, positive that every single Fae on the island had visited The Ward.

His family was determined that he was going to be okay. They kept reassuring him that everything would go back to normal. But he knew in his heart, that was not possible. What had happened to him was irrevocable, but he was going to survive.

Chapter Eleven

EARTH DIMENSION THREE
Mystic Haven, B.C., Canada

HE'D NEVER KNOWN HOW long it could take a Fae to recover from flame-out. Three months after being released from the hospital was a fucking long time, and it annoyed him. Yet here he was again sitting out in the sun, absorbing the life-giving rays. This time, he'd chosen the beach, because his mom was driving him crazy with her worry and constant check-ins. By all that was holy, he was a grown-ass man.

He settled a pair of sunglasses on his face and glanced down the beach. His eyes widened. A big-ass bear was lumbering toward him. *What the fuck? Natural or Shifter?* He stood up cautiously allowing his wings to appear, preparing for a fast take off. The bear chose that moment to shift in a shower of sparks, and there, before him, stood his air force wingman, Rhys Bjorn.

The next instant he was wrapped in a huge bear hug by a naked monster of a man. Talk about fucking trauma. He hugged his friend back then shoved him away "Get some fucking clothes on man."

Rhys smirked. "You love my sexy body. Jealous cause you can never hope to pack the package that this bear does?"

"In your dreams, Bear. I got fucking Fae skills. Your package…" He whipped off his sunglasses and cocked his eyebrow. "Has no hope of even coming close."

Rhys roared with laughter and dragged on a pair of sweats he'd had in a backpack. A backpack that Baylen failed to notice when he had seen the bear.

"What the hell are you doing here man? I thought you were going to re-enlist."

"Re-enlist when my effing partner did a disappearing act? I don't think so. I was sick of all the orders about two days after I enlisted the first time. Been re-enlisting to keep your ass out of trouble, and the first time I take a damn leave by myself, you went and got yourself into a heap of trouble. Listen Knight, you need to pay better attention to when I am around to pull you out of shit. You think you are superhuman or something?"

Baylen started to laugh. "Well, honestly? Yeah."

"Bloody Fae, always think they are superheroes." Rhys looked at him seriously. "Are you okay, man? You're looking a little primal right now."

For the first time in months Bay roared in laughter. "Oh man, you hit the nail on the head." *Primal Fae. What the fuck?* But, oh man, did it ever resound with him. It fit. He was a fucking primal Fae. There was power in that image for him. *Better than the Fae'est Fae.* He gathered his glamour back around him, which now meant that his wings disappeared, but nothing would ever hide his ears now, or the sharpness of his features. He was a primal Fae. "This is it, Rhys. The most I can hide now."

Rhys looked at him and shrugged. "I think it's an improvement. You never were as handsome as me."

Laughing, Baylen flipped off his friend. "What are you doing here, Rhys? You really want to follow me around, saving my Fae ass? I always figured you had a thing for it."

"Fuck you." Rhys snorted and shuddered at the visual image that assaulted his mind. *I need some mind bleach.* He sat down on a rock beside Bay and stared out at the ocean. "I think, if we are going to be staying on Mystic Haven, we need to build an airport and start a charter service. That ferry ride was brutal. I do not like boats. Especially when they float over bottomless bodies of water with giant fish in them. Who knows what kind of monsters are circling underneath just waiting for the opportunity to rip the bottom out of it? You getting me? We need an airport here and a charter service, and since we are pilots, we're the perfect ones to do it. We'll make a killing, man. Get rich. Besides, the ladies love pilots. You know we're chick magnets. Let's go somewhere and talk. I need a coffee, and I have plans I want you to look over."

Chapter Twelve

EARTH DIMENSION THREE
Mystic Haven, B.C., Canada
Six Months after the Wisteria Encounter

HE FIGURED HIS PARENTS had been relieved when he and Rhys came and talked to them about their crazy plan. They got on board so fast he'd been stunned. They helped wade through the mountains of paperwork, they helped scout out a spot, and his father used his contacts to help find the right builders. He worried about the money. It was an amount that scared the hell out of him. The banks didn't even blink. They okayed the loans.

The next day, Baylen was standing on the land that they planned to buy for the airport debating if the whole thing should be called off. It bothered him that the banks had been so fast to approve those massive loans.

His senses suddenly on high alert, he looked up and watched warily as the Fae king and his Trium landed. "Hello, Baylen Knight. I'm Ryder dé Danann, and this is my Trium. Blade Maddox, Protector, and Maxen Ransom, Healer."

As if he didn't know the Fae king and his Trium. Everyone knew them. Everyone. He eyed them and crossed his arms. *What the fuck did they want with him?*

Finally, after the King raised his eyebrow, Baylen nodded, once. "Hello, King dé Danann. What can I do for you?"

"I believe that you have done more than was expected already, Baylen. We are here to thank you. The moment the ancient energy of our people began to rise, we knew something terrible was going on. It was over by the time we arrived. To discover that our nemesis had found us, was..." Ryder shook his head and gazed up at the sky before looking back at Baylen. "It was as if the unspeakable had happened. We thought we had destroyed all of them. Can you confirm the creature's death?"

Baylen shook his head. "There was an explosion, and she was gone. I don't think she could have survived. Everything, for a mile in every direction, was incinerated."

Ryder nodded. "We examined the blast site. I would feel better if there had been some remains." He rubbed the back of his neck and looked at his Trium.

"I would too." Blade Maddox spoke up. Baylen regarded him and nodded. He understood the Protector's concern. "She talked like she was the last of her species."

Blade nodded. "Even one is exceedingly dangerous."

"I found that out."

"You survived. Something that is unheard of. Would you agree to a meeting where we could discuss the details? We would like to add to our knowledge base. In case there is ever another attack."

"I can do that."

"Thank you, Baylen Knight." Blade nodded and stepped back.

"Baylen, you have done the Fae a great service. Now, we are informed that you wish to help Mystic Haven even more by opening an airport with a charter service. I arranged for the banks to okay your loans." Ryder held up his hand when he saw the storm clouds gathering in Baylen's eyes. "Mystic Haven is as much a sanctuary for the Fae as it is for all superhumans. What you are doing is a good thing. It is not unusual for the Fae to back important developments and enterprises. We merely backed the loan. We have no say in your business, or how you develop this airport. The success or failure of it is on you and your partner. I wish you luck and good fortune." Ryder turned to his Trium. "Ready?"

"Not quite." Maxen stepped forward. "Baylen, here is my business card. I am very interested in the physical changes you've experienced. If you ever are ready to discuss your experience, I would be happy to meet with you."

Baylen took the card and nodded, knowing full well that he would never be ready.

Part Five

Even one small glimmer of light, pierces the blackest night

Chapter Thirteen

EARTH DIMENSION THREE
Enceladus, moon of Saturn

ASH FLEW OVER THE MASSIVE ocean on this small frozen moon. Enceladus the humans called it. It was time. He lifted his hand. The icy surface 30 to 40 kilometers thick began to crack. Ash's lips twisted with a wry humor. It was like cracking an egg. There was life under the icy shell of this moon. Life that he had carefully created. Life that he had cultivated. Life that he had refined to cold blooded perfection. A blast of blue Angelic power and a hole opened on the frozen surface. Carefully he enlarged the opening before landing. He walked over and peered down into the depths. Holding his hand over the expanse, he smiled as the water began to rise. He stepped back and waited. Within a few moments the water stirred, and his latest creations began to surface. They were exquisite. A carefully crafted species born of captured female Mer from the planet Earth Dimension Three and his demon's. For hundreds of years, he'd practised patience as his creations incubated and reproduced under the ice. Now, they would fulfill their purpose. He opened a vortex. "You are Demon-Mer. Fierce, Dangerous, Cunning. You do not possess the weaknesses of other species. I have eliminated compassion, and mercy from your species. Together, with my other armies, we shall conquer my enemies. You are The Cold-Blooded Army!

He opened a vortex that would take them to the time and place of their victory.

Chapter Fourteen

EARTH DIMENSION THREE
Far beneath the Pacific Ocean

THEY WERE CALLED THE Cold-Blooded Army, and they were every bit as dark and terrifying as their name implied. They had one purpose—and only one purpose. To kill and destroy on the behest of their master. Their creator. They were the Demon-Mer and they had been promised victory today.

With military precision they surrounded the scattered Mer cities deep under the oceans that covered seventy percent of the planet Earth. Their targets had no chance. A whole species isolated from the rest of the planet. Help was not coming.

Chapter Fifteen

EARTH DIMENSION THREE
Mystic Haven, B.C., Canada

THE TIGER PADDED SILENTLY through the moonlit forest, his white coat and black stripes blending seamlessly with the vegetation. Midnight darkness, the mist rising from the forest floor winding around the trees, and the light of the full moon all came together to give him the perfect camouflage. He was invisible, a deadly predator stalking his prey. There would be no warning, no mercy. His quarry had run out of time, his life forfeit.

Crouching down on the edge of the meadow, he waited patiently, his tail swinging back and forth. He looked at the beautiful scene painted in the black and whites of the moon's light and thought only of the kill he would make. The silver of the stream, the white lilies blooming along its banks, the stars in the sky were merely the backdrop to what would happen here in this peaceful forest glade.

A deer stepped cautiously from the forest and made its way to the stream to drink before continuing on its way. A few minutes later he caught the faint scent of the wolf shifter, and he crouched lower waiting patiently. He'd stalked his prey for weeks. Finally, it would end. He watched the shifter step into the clearing, and he felt no fear, no rage, and no compassion. He simply waited for the perfect moment.

When the wolf sat down and lifted his head to howl his song to the moon, the tiger leapt. Some inner instinct warned the wolf and he turned, but too late. The tiger hit him hard, a terrible roar sounding through the silent forest.

Twisting, the wolf tried to avoid lethal claws. He failed, the tiger slashing through his thick coat, tearing great bloody furrows down his side. The wolf yipped and rolled, coming back to his feet with an enraged snarl. A menacing growl rumbled through his chest as he crouched low and leapt. Two heavy bodies crashed together, vicious growls and roars filled the silent glade. Wicked claws ripped through heavy pelt as the tiger tore into the wolf again.

The wolf stumbled, and the tiger was on him with a savage roar. Deadly curved fangs tore through skin and bone, crunching down on the wolf's skull, crushing it.

Stepping back, sides heaving, the tiger watched coldly as the wolf's body shifted into the form of a man. A man who'd already killed a young woman on the mainland before he followed a teen home to this island, stalked and terrified her.

No, he had no compassion and no mercy for any creature that tried to turn his people into prey.

The golden light of The Ward glided into the clearing, and wrapped itself around the tiger, in a tangle of energy and light. The tiger chuffed and lay down. Moving away from the deadly predator with blood splashed fur, The Ward approached the slain shifter.

Thunder roared, a flash of lightning lit up the dark glade, and slammed into the body. Silence, thick and heavy, as wind rushed through the trees, scattering the ashes until nothing remained.

The Ward glided back to the white tiger laying in a patch of glimmering moonlight and wrapped itself around the beast. Sparks lit the darkness, and Caden Brody, his body stained with blood, stood wrapped in The Ward's embrace.

"Justice," the Ward whispered into his mind and swirled around him until it called his Fae forth, until his runes lit up proclaiming the arrival of the Guardian. *"Justice."*

Chapter Sixteen

EARTH DIMENSION THREE
  Mystic Haven, B.C., Canada
  Two years six months after the Wisteria Encounter

"MAYDAY, MAYDAY. THIS is flight Charlie, seven, seven, niner, Bravo, Kilo. I am going down. I repeat I am going down. Mayday! Mayday!" The alarms became more strident, and the radio went dead. "Fuck!" His mind filled with images of his beautiful mate, Jadeah, and their new babies. Gods, he was never going to see any of them again.

The helicopter impacted the ocean with enough force to send a giant wave high into the air. The blades bent, one snapped off and hurtled across the sky. The body of the helicopter slammed around onto its side and threw Baylen violently around the cockpit. The world was a tumbling blur filled with pain and the deafening roar of the helicopter breaking apart. Glass shattered and icy water poured into the fuselage.

The water was fucking cold. He fought with the seat belt release. Gods he hurt!

Hands grabbing him, attempting to unbuckle him. He couldn't see who was helping him. *What the fuck?* He hadn't seen any boats in the area before he crashed. He looked for the boat but there was only water as far as he could see. Water rising over his head. He held his breath, trying to create a bubble of Fae energy around him but he couldn't summon enough power. He was running out of air. His eyes met another set of eyes. Green, his hazy mind supplied. A braid of long blonde hair over a feminine shoulder. Another person. Dark hair. Neon-blue eyes. Male.

He was out of air!

A knife flashed, and suddenly, he was free of the harness that held him in the wreckage. Agony as he was dragged out of the twisted cockpit. Sunlight glinting through the ocean highlighting the water tinted red with his blood. He tried to kick urgently needing to get to the surface. Bone slid against bone. He gasped and water filled his lungs. A black vortex hovered, threatening to suck him in. Two sets of hands lifted him to the surface. Cold air slapped him in the face, and he coughed, gasping and groaning at the pain in his ribs. Two people bobbed alongside him. "Boat?" he asked between violent coughing fits that caused him to throw up the sea water.

The blonde shook her head and exchanged a look with the dark-haired man. "We'll get you to safety. There is a small island close by."

The woman put her hand on his back and warmth began to pour into him.

"I hope that helps. I'm sorry I can't do more until we are on the island."

Chapter Seventeen

EARTH DIMENSION THREE
Mystic Haven, B.C., Canada

CHIEF OF THE MYSTIC Haven Police force, Caden Brody, hung up the phone after speaking with the coast guard and Mystic Haven's search and rescue teams. Ships and aircraft were deploying in a search for Baylen Knight.

He stood up, a tall dark-haired man with hazel-green eyes. With his glamour firmly in place, very few understood that he was part Fae, part White Tiger Shifter. His mind on the need to get down to the wharf, he opened his desk drawer and took out his gun, putting it in the holster attached to his belt.

He was going to be aboard one of the boats that were part of the search.

A knock on his office door. "Come in."

His sister, Tori, one of the two dispatch officers, opened the door. "Caden, you have a visitor. She said it's urgent." Tori moved back, and a blonde woman with green eyes stepped forward.

"Hello, Chief Brody. I'm Riley Muirgheal. I must speak to you about an urgent matter." She kept her eyes on his, not about to show any reaction to the dangerous aura of this Fae halfling.

Caden nodded and mentally swore. When it rained, it poured. "Walk with me." He was already assessing her energy trying to figure out what species she was. Nothing that he had ever come across before, that was for sure. "How can I help you?"

"We saw a helicopter come down in the ocean. We managed to pull the pilot from the wreckage, but he was badly injured. We had to get him to the nearest island to save his life. He requires healing that I cannot provide."

Caden stopped and faced the woman. "Where is he now?"

"We took him to a small island, about thirty-two nautical miles west of Mystic Haven."

"Why didn't you bring him here?"

"We didn't have a boat, and he wouldn't have survived the swim."

Caden's mind was racing. "You were thirty nautical miles out in the ocean without a boat?"

The woman nodded. "It was closer to thirty-five. We are Mer."

"Mer?" Caden re-assessed the woman. It was possible. "Not a myth after all."

Riley nodded once. "Not a myth, but we have stayed away from land dwellers. Unfortunately, that left us vulnerable to an unknown enemy who destroyed our civilization. We are seeking a place of safety to rebuild."

Caden studied the woman for a minute. "Let's get Baylen home. After that, we can discuss your situation."

"Agreed."

Chapter Eighteen

THEY TOUCHED DOWN ON the island and shoved the doors open. Jumping out, they ducked and ran over to the man on the far edge of the island. He was leaning over a prone figure on the ground, attempting to protect him from the wind the blades of the copter stirred up."

"Finn Gallagher. Caden Brody." Riley said as they crouched down beside Baylen. Caden nodded, taking note of the man's scars and hard neon-blue eyes. A man brought a stretcher over and crouched down beside them. "I'm Dr. Maxen Ransom. I'm a Fae Healer. I need to assess him."

Finn moved back.

Minutes later Finn stood beside Riley as the land dwellers' helicopter took off. "Are you sure, Riley?"

She looked at her second in command and nodded. "If we are to survive, Finn, we must have help."

Chapter Nineteen

EARTH DIMENSION THREE
Mystic Haven, B.C., Canada

THE HELICOPTER LANDED on the hospital helipad and shut down. The medical staff rushed to the aircraft.

Darkness. Gods, he hated darkness. Sounds filtered through the blackness. Voices. *Where was he? What had happened?* An enormous push of healing energy filled him moving through his body. *Maxen.* No other healer had the immense power of the Royal Healer

He wanted to tell him to stop, to not waste his energy. It was far, far too late, but suddenly his vision filled with the most beautiful person in his world, Jadeah. He tried to lift his hand to touch her, horrified that she should see him so broken. He did not want her to have to face this, to have her last memories of him as this broken shell of a man.

Maxen's voice. "Jadeah, you need to hold him to you. Don't let him go."

Jadeah's voice pleading with him to hang on. Grief struck him, his life slipping away. He did not want to leave her.

Darkness swirled around him. She called him, and he fought the darkness to find her. She was the whisper of everything good in his life. He tried desperately to hold onto their dream, but it kept slipping through his fingers like wisps of mist.

Stillness settled around them, so profound that he tore his desperate gaze from Jadeah. A figure strode into his view. His heart began to pound. The Healer. Why was the Royal Healer here? He frowned. No, that wasn't right. Maxen? He turned his gaze to the man pouring enormous amounts of healing energy into him. Who was the other man? Confusion rose at the stranger's words. "Baylen Knight, you will not die. Your people have a great need for you. Your children have a great need for you."

Children? His vision clouded, and the cries of babies filled his mind. His heart sighed. *His babies. His triplets. Jadeah's and his.* A vast energy so boundless he had no way of understanding it, entered him and there was only blackness.

Chapter Twenty

EARTH DIMENSION THREE
Mystic Haven, B.C., Canada

"MAY I ENTER BAYLEN Knight?"

Baylen glanced up and recognized the stranger as the mysterious man from the helicopter. He damn sure wasn't Maxen Ransom. But... he was The Royal Healer. This wasn't making sense, and he began to get a bad feeling. "Of course, you can enter. You're the damn Royal Healer. No one is going to say no you can't come in."

The Healer chuckled and strode into the room. He was tall with short dark hair and brilliant purple eyes. Most people would have thought he was a badass, with his tight jeans and leather jacket. He pulled up a chair.

"Alright, Healer." Yeah, there was a slight sarcastic edge to his voice. "What the fuck is going on? You only attend the king and his family. Why are you here?"

The Healer leaned back in his chair, his smile enigmatic. "I'm Striker Barron, Baylen Knight, and you know my duty. The current king, and his Trium, have served the Fae people for over a millennium. His time is over. The calling passes to another. But—Your Majesty," the Healer grinned. "I am going to enjoy the show."

Baylen's mind was going a million miles an hour, until he had a stunning thought. "Wait a minute. Wait one damn fucking minute! Majesty? Ah, fuck no." Another horrifying thought rushed through his mind. "This means—you are going to send for the new Royal Protector! Fucking hell. No." Baylen shook his head. "I'm not doing this! Go find yourself someone else to bother."

The Healer regarded him with a raised eyebrow.

He was definitely smirking. Baylen growled.

"Baylen Knight, I would say, of everyone I know, you are the most in need of protection. I have sent for The Protector already. Jett Sidhe is heading to your home to set up safeguards."

Baylen swore long and hard, and The Healer grinned.

"I am the last person that should ever be called. I have no interest in kingship."

"Yet, you have been called, Baylen Knight, and you know this. The Fae crown is not passed down from father to son. It is passed down through the immortal essence of our people, who have passed to the other side of the veil. You don't make that choice. There is no turning back from this."

Part Six

When Darkest Comes

Chapter Twenty-One

EARTH DIMENSION THREE
Mystic Haven, B.C., Canada
Earth Date – Three years after the Wisteria Encounter

BAYLEN SHUFFLED THROUGH some fucking dumb-ass royal protocol paperwork crap in his office when his Fae instincts kicked in with a vengeance. A powerful rush of dread swept over him. In an instant, he jumped up and headed for the garage at a dead run. Jumping onto his motorbike and pulling on his helmet, he tore out of the garage like the very demons from hell were after him. All he could think of was Jadeah. His beautiful Jadeah. She had a small but busy plant shop down on the main street that she adored. He sent her a mind link needing to know she was alright. *"Hey Babe, how are you doing?"*

"Bay. I'm good. It's pretty quiet here. The lunch rush has passed. I'm going to have a coffee."

"Jadeah," He hesitated. *"I'm on my way in. I'll see you soon. Just... be careful, Babe. I love you."*

Her warm laughter over the link, a rush of wild passion and love. *"Maybe we can sneak into my office for a... 'conversation.' Love you, too."*

He shifted gears and opened up the throttle. Something was wrong. Something was very fucking wrong.

Filled with a terrible urgency he sent a mind link to his Trium, Jett and Striker. *"Something is wrong! Fuck! Guys, something is wrong!"*

He pulled onto the main street of Mystic Haven, weaving in and out of the traffic. Cutting dangerously close to the other vehicles, he took the corner way too sharp and just about laid his bike on the pavement before he regained control. Slamming to a stop outside Jadeah's pretty little shop, he yanked off his helmet and ran.

Chapter Twenty-Two

EARTH DIMENSION THREE
Mystic Haven, B.C., Canada

CADEN'S FAE INSTINCTS were driving him crazy, but he couldn't get a clear read on it. Irritated beyond belief, he strode out of his office. "I'm going for a coffee. I'll be back in an hour."

Deciding the walk would clear his head, he rounded the corner and lifted an eyebrow as Baylen Knight came screeching around the corner on his bike. *What the hell?*

Baylen damn near lost control, but at the last second got it back. Frowning, Caden shook his head. *Fae king or not, he was getting a ticket.* Glaring, he watched Baylen park illegally and toss his helmet as he ran for his wife's shop. Two tickets. The hotshot Fae king was getting two tickets.

Chapter Twenty-Three

EARTH DIMENSION THREE
Mystic Haven, B.C., Canada

HIS HEART RACING AS he yanked open the door, Baylen saw Jadeah sitting at the counter with a coffee. She glanced up at him, and her whole face lit up. He took a step forward, another, his heart pounding. A stranger rushed into the shop, throwing his coat on the floor and yelling. Bay's glamour dropped away, his protective instincts surging. The man had explosives strapped to his chest!

His eyes met Jadeah's as he drew an enormous amount of Fae energy and sent it flying in a supersonic pulse toward the man. *Too late. Too fucking late!*

The world exploded in a flash of red-hot flames. A split-second later Fae energy slammed into the explosion! Rebounding it smashed back into him, the combined shockwave picked him up, threw him backwards through glass and brick. A fireball of heat and magic roiling through the air, consuming everything in its path. He crashed into something hard, and a ragged snarl tore from him as heated metal pierced his back. Instinctively, he recognized the deadly magic enveloping the ruins of his wife's shop! He reacted, frantically throwing out a time shift, thinking only to contain the black magic he could feel rising up from the

71

explosion. A deadly magic that had the potential to destroy the whole island. He staggered to his feet, and horror was everywhere around him. "No! No!"

With his bare hands and telekinesis, he began to throw aside anything blocking his path. Using his Fae energy to stamp out flames, he fiercely held onto the time shift. He had to get to Jadeah!

"Jadeah! I'm coming! Hang on. Please, Babe, please!" Grimly ignoring the silence of their bond, determined to find his mate he refused to even entertain anything but finding her safe and bringing her home to their babies.

Chapter Twenty-Four

EARTH DIMENSION THREE
Mystic Haven, B.C., Canada

CADEN STAGGERED TO his feet gasping for breath, the world spinning. He stared in horror as fire and smoke billowed upward from the rubble that had once been Jadeah Knight's little store.

He took two steps and went to his knees, his body protesting. Wiping a trickle of blood away from his eyes, he forced himself back up, ignoring his injuries and keying the mic on his shirt "Explosion! Mainstreet! Jadeah Knight's shop! All available officers respond! We need fire and ambulances!" Smoke and ash filled the air. Taking a hoarse wheezing breath, he ran toward the decimated shop, staggering as a nearly impossible time-shift filled the air over the smoldering ruins.

Baylen was alive! He was the only Fae capable of that kind of feat in the midst of a disaster.

Chapter Twenty-Five

EARTH DIMENSION THREE
Mystic Haven, B.C., Canada

THE SIRENS THAT FILLED the air only added to the surrealness, to the horror of what he was facing. Shifting aside a massive slab of brick wall, Baylen froze for a moment at the sight of a body. He swore violently. The man who was responsible for this. *Creators, he was so young. How was his body even intact? It had to be the black magic.*

He checked the time shift. It was holding, but he added what energy he could afford to spare to the field. "Jadeah!"

Grief welled up inside him, the emptiness of the mating bond leaving his soul in tatters. He pushed it away—his mate was alive! She had to be alive. He grabbed a huge chunk of debris and threw it out of his path. He would find her!

Chapter Twenty-Six

EARTH DIMENSION THREE
Mystic Haven, B.C., Canada

AS CADEN DREW CLOSER, his runes lit up. *Evil.* The smell of black magic filled the air. Seeking the source, he was appalled and relieved to see the black magic was contained by the time shift energy field the Fae king had erected.

Goddess, he had to get to them! The sheer immensity of the task horrified him. His glamour dropped away as he began using his telekinesis and the power of his shifter side to move through the wreckage. "I'm coming, Baylen!"

Chapter Twenty-Seven

EARTH DIMENSION THREE
Mystic Haven, B.C., Canada

BAYLEN GLANCED UP, his eyes wild when someone grabbed the section of the roof, he was straining to lift. Caden. They forced the heavy metal back, their muscles screaming in agony—and his world ended.

He stumbled, falling to his knees. Tears burned his eyes and blurred his vision. Death marked her beautiful face, and his soul screamed in agony. Reaching with trembling hands, he gathered her to him. "Jadeah. Babe. Please." His voice broke. He desperately pulled Fae energy and directed it into her body in a flash of golden light. He could heal her. He would heal her. "You can't leave me, Babe. I need you. Our babies need you. Please, Babe, breathe." He pushed more energy into her broken body, harsh sobs tearing from his throat. "You have to live!"

His grasp on the time shift slipped but Caden threw up his hand, the Guardian's Fae energy spilling over the dark magic that threatened to unleash death and destruction across the island.

Anguish crushed him, stole his air. "Jadeah. Babe." The roar of his grief filled the heavens, echoing throughout eternity.

Part Seven

The darkness you embrace

Chapter Twenty-Eight

EARTH DIMENSION THREE
Mystic Haven, B.C., Canada
Four years after the Wisteria Encounter

BAYLEN STARED AT HIS computer, his face grim as he read the heavily encrypted information. "Fuck! Fuck!" Standing up, he raked his hand through his long dark hair. "Fuck!" He took a calming breath, poured himself a whiskey, and downed it. He had to get a hold of himself. He paced the room and, in an instant of fury, hurled his glass at the wall. Glass shattered everywhere. He shook, vibrating with rage. He caught a glimpse of himself in a mirror on the wall and paused, fucking fae'est Fae ever. A dangerous beast clothed in the body of a being of light. He turned away from the image that reminded him of the darkness he carried inside, of the monster he'd become.

Stepping out onto the balcony of his office, he stared into the night as he weighed his options. He'd sent one of his best intelligence agents hunting for information the day after the explosion. It had taken over a year, but he finally ran those bastards to the ground, and no one but his agent and he knew about this. Baylen's man would never tell anyone, his loyalty absolute.

He strode down the hallway to check on his kids. They were sound asleep. He stood staring down at them for a long, long moment. So innocent. Finally, he nodded at the nanny and walked out.

Stepping outside into the immense gardens at the back of the castle, he dropped his glamour fully, growling when Jett moved out of the shadows. "Leave it alone, Jett. I need some time. I am perfectly able to look after myself, especially in this mood. Any fool who dared to approach me tonight would never make such a mistake again."

The Protector crossed his muscled arms over his chest and regarded him silently, finally nodding and stepping back into the shadows. Baylen stared after him for a moment before launching himself into the night sky. Filled with violent angry energy he soared high, feeling the cool air rush over him.

He flew a long way, needing to get some kind of hold on the hatred that burned deep inside him. *It was his decision if they faced justice.* His heart grew icy cold, but his fury was white hot. Ruthless determination filled him. Those sons of bitches were going to pay for what they had done. They would pay for murdering Jadeah. Before this night was over, blood would flow.

That twisted circle of dark wizards had no clue what they'd done when they set their evil loose. One thing was certain. They were about to come face to face with the monster they had created. By all that was holy, those spawn of the devil wizards were going to die! Every fucking one of them.

His target was a small remote island far to the south of Mystic Haven, the coordinates firmly locked into his mind. An island was good. There would be no avenue of escape.

As he approached, he sent his magic out seeking any traps or alarms that the wizards might have placed around their hideout. It didn't take him long to unravel the few warning spells that he encountered. The wizards were too complacent, too arrogant, obviously believing that they were safe here. Too fucking bad they had gone after the king of the fucking Fae.

He circled the island, taking his time to make sure he was not walking into a trap. When his phone gave a soft beep, he glanced at the caller ID and shut off the device. Charli. The woman he'd just started dating. He could not speak to her right now.

Slowly, deliberately, he made his way over to the large house he'd seen in the middle of the island. Headquarters to the 'Pure Earth' Wizards.

His lips pulled back, baring his teeth. Blood pounded in his ears. Adrenaline rushed through his body filling him with an edgy, twitchy sensation. He wanted them dead. Every last one of them. They'd destroyed his light, and he could feel the darkness within him rising. He would avenge his Jadeah. His children would never have to fear an unknown enemy, because that enemy would no longer exist.

He watched through a window as the inhabitants moved around, silently counting them. It did not matter to him how many there were. By daylight there would be none. There was no mercy, no guilt. They had killed that part of him when they had murdered his queen.

He lifted his hand and magic flowed, Fae energy spreading in an impenetrable golden bubble that separated this house from any others. When the seal was complete, he drew upon the energy that surrounded this world, it flowed through him filling him to an excruciating level. With violence in his heart and death in his eyes, he sent all that energy hurtling toward the home of his enemies. The blast shattered the windows of the circle's headquarters. It blew open the doors and collapsed a wall.

The Wizards rushed outside, magic gathering around them. Baylen stared at the miserable excuses for superhumans. A snarl twisted his face. "You thought, you could mess with the Fae king and survive?" Contempt edged his words. "You thought, I would fear your pathetic powers? The stench of your corruption and evil can be smelled everywhere. I sentence you to death. There will be no peace for you."

"We are not afraid of death, Alien." An older wizard with long grey hair and beard stepped up to him. His eyes shone strangely and were filled with violence and hatred. "You have no right to our world, to our sanctuaries. We are going to take it all away from you! If the death of your alien queen whore was not enough, we will kill every Fae we find. We will kill your children and your friends. Every one of them will die!"

Baylen absorbed the hate filled words and everything inside of him went still. His natural Fae glow began to grow. His eyes became deep pits of blackness, and he struck without another warning. Blood colored the landscape. Screams rent the air. They had created a monster, and it was the monster they faced. The monster that exacted the cost of his creation.

Part Eight

Darkness enshrouds my soul

Chapter Twenty-Nine

EARTH DIMENSION THREE
Mystic Haven, B.C., Canada
Five years after the Wisteria encounter

BAYLEN FLIPPED THE switch releasing his load of fire retardant. "Knight One to air ops. Airdrop at two hundred feet." He spoke into the mike attached to his helmet as he battled the turbulence buffeting his helicopter. The winds coming off the fire roared as his copter shook, and he fought to keep the aircraft level. "Looks like we have a blowup on the southeastern flank."

The air tactical group supervisor came on the air. "Knight One we have a crew one klick from your position, extraction needed asap."

"Roger, air ops. Proceeding to extraction point." He eased the stick forward and grimly rode out the bumps. "Fucking wind," he muttered as he kept his focus on flying. The smoke was bad, visibility was low, and he was flying fucking close to the tops of the trees. He was going to need a beer when he got done with this day. He sure the fuck hoped that Rhys was not having the same kind of turbulence, but he knew it was a remote hope.

Spotting a flare, he began a cautious descent to the rough cleared helispot. The moment he touched down, the

84

crew ducked and ran to the helicopter. They piled into the craft and the door slammed shut. He glanced over his shoulder at them, and they gave him the thumbs up sign. He nodded once and took the helicopter back up. "Air ops, this is Knight One. I have the crew, and we are heading back to base."

"Negative Knight One. We need you to hold the line on the blowup. Divert to Gray Lake and fill up your Bambi. Three thousand liters. Copy?"

"Roger air ops. Diverting and will hold the line." His voice was grim as he looked back at the exhausted firefighters. "Sorry guys, you're in for a bumpy ride. We've been ordered to hold the line until they can get ground personnel up here. Make sure your seatbelts are on."

He'd dropped three Bambi's on the front line of the fire before he was able to land at base helispot and refuel. Rhys was there, refueling too. He walked over to talk to his friend.

"Don't know if you heard, Bay, but they evacuated a hundred and thirty-seven properties. Sent them over to the castle. This fire has estimates of being over twenty-one thousand hectares, and with this blowup, it's only going to get worse." Rhys rubbed his neck tiredly.

"Fuck." Baylen pulled out his phone and saw that Charli had sent him a text saying she had everything under control and not to worry. He looked at Rhys. "The fire won't get past the Wards, but after the 2018 fires, we put in deep ponds that feed right from an underground river. Jett is probably already having the whole area sprayed down." They talked for a few more minutes as the refueling finished up, then climbed back into their helicopters and flew out to take their turns holding the line.

He'd lost track of how many times he'd flown to the lake to refill his bucket. Hell, he wasn't even sure if it was day or night in this godsdamned smoke. He brought his helicopter in low, keeping an eye on the altimeter. He needed to be two hundred feet above the treetops not sitting in them. A hard gust of wind slammed into his copter, and he swore, but brought it back under control, the bucket swinging wildly by its cable. "Knight One to air ops." He flipped the switch releasing the water, it fell away in trails of white to the raging fire below. "Airdrop two hundred feet."

The words no sooner left his lips, and the wind slammed violently into his helicopter. His copter tipped and bucked with brutal force. Alarms started to blare. *Fuck. Fuck. Fuck.* He fought the controls. "Knight One. Mayday!"

Shit! He was not crashing this bird. He strained to keep it in the air. A tree flashed by, and he hauled back on the stick, forcing the chopper into a climb. Another gust of wind slammed into the side, and he growled.

"Knight One!" The air tactical group supervisor came on the air. "What is your emergency?"

"Fucking wind gusts off this blow up!" Alarms were still blaring as he fought to bring the helicopter back into control, and he knew everyone at air operations could hear them. The entire situation with this firestorm had become incredibly dangerous for the helicopters fighting this fire. "Get the other choppers out of the air!"

"Roger Knight One. Closing down air ops. We have you on radar. You are at three hundred feet and climbing. Level out."

Swearing, he grimly worked his controls, fighting the wind every fucking moment. He leveled out and pushed the helicopter farther from the fire. The alarms began to fall silent one by one, but he could tell something was off with the way it was flying. "Knight One to air ops. Returning to base with damaged bird."

"Roger, Knight One. Look to your left. Bjorn One is flying a perimeter to eyeball the damage. How is your saturation level?"

"Roger, air ops. Saturation is high." He was no fucking idiot. He knew he was task saturated, and it could be a big fucking problem. The only smart thing to do was to keep air ops informed of the situation.

"Knight One, this is Bjorn One. You have wind damage to your tail. Let's get this bird to base."

"Roger, Bjorn One." He carefully eased his 'copter into a turn. "Air ops, about three klicks from base. Tail damage. Have emergency on standby."

"Roger, Knight One. We'll be ready. Safe flight."

He looked out his window again and saw that Rhys was flying alongside at a safe distance. The man was a fucking worrywart, but damned if it wasn't a relief to see him still there.

Those three klicks were a slow eternity, and he was fucking glad to see the helispot when it came into view. It took every skill he had to set that bird down safely, but he got it done. Carefully, he went through his checklist as he shut down the helicopter. When the blades stopped turning, he stepped outside, and Rhys was standing there.

"By the sonofabitching goddess, Baylen! What are you trying to do to me? I don't need grey hair yet!"

"You roar like a damned mother bear, Rhys. I'm fine." He was shaking like a fucking leaf, but hell if he was going to admit to that bullshit. He turned and began to walk around the helicopter even as the emergency crews swarmed over it to make sure there was not any danger of fire. He could see the damage and it was extensive. The bucket had managed to wrap its cable around the tail and through some stroke of luck had not become entangled with the rotors. There were dents and torn metal, but fuck if it had not got him back safely. He patted the machine and turned to Rhys. "Give me a lift home?"

Rhys nodded. "Charli is going to have your ass."

Baylen narrowed his eyes, glaring at his friend. A heavy sigh escaped him. "Yeah, pretty much."

Rhys smirked. "But that make up sex...."

Baylen started laughing. "Right. Gotta look at the positive."

Chapter Thirty

EARTH DIMENSION THREE
Mystic Haven, B.C., Canada

IT HAD TAKEN WISTERIA years to retrace her journey to this dimension. Years of her life and once she finally arrived, the first thing she saw was her consort, with another woman and three little brats that looked like him. *How dare he! How dare she!*

There would be consequences.

Silently, using her abilities to camouflage her natural appearance she followed them to a massive castle. A castle surrounded by powerful Wards that she could not penetrate.

Her rage knew no bounds, but she'd learned from her last foray on this island. This time she would use stealth, she would use her cunning. She would invade his life so silently that he would never know she was there until it was too late. Oh, the punishments she would mete out. But first, she needed a pawn.

That part was relatively simple. A trip to an airport with a flight destined for Mystic Haven. She used their archaic computer systems to study the passenger manifest. Her target chosen, she walked into the women's bathroom to wait. Sure enough, the pretty dark haired Fae woman came in before she headed to the airplane. She was lovely. As lovely as Baylen Knight. Perhaps she would have two consorts. But there was time for her to decide that later. After all, this woman would be hers to enjoy while she taught the Fae king a lesson he would never forget—And while she got rid of that bitch, Charli, who thought she could claim another woman's property.

"Hello, Ciara. I'm Wisteria. Your new mistress." She struck! It had been intense, arousing, and dreadfully frustrating, because she had a plane to catch with her new puppet.

Chapter Thirty-One

EARTH DIMENSION THREE
Mystic Haven, B.C., Canada

SHE WAS GETTING IMPATIENT, even though she had enjoyed the weeks with her new toy. It was such a shame that her people had not taken the time to discover all the ways a Fae could be used. She smiled down at her naked slave, enjoying the woman's pain and fear. "Today is the day, my dear. I am finally going to be rid of that woman and those brats. I think you will enjoy knowing my consort. Baylen is truly lovely, and he's so strong." She smiled remembering his struggles. "I always enjoy a good challenge. You've also been delightfully challenging. If Baylen enjoys you as much as I do, then I believe a reward is in order for you." She watched with malicious delight as Ciara curled in on herself. "I'll be back soon."

Chapter Thirty-Two

EARTH DIMENSION THREE
Mystic Haven, B.C., Canada

CIARA'S EYES SNAPPED open. She was lying on the floor, naked. Cold. Everything hurt. She lifted a trembling hand. In the grey light she could see the dirt and blood on her fingers. Her nails were broken and ragged. She pushed herself up, gritting her teeth against the massive headache that threatened to leave her huddled in a ball of agony. *She had to find a way out.*

The monster was not here now. She could feel the emptiness of the room. She hissed a breath when her left hand brushed against the wall. Wave after wave of pain engulfed her. She clutched it to her chest and could feel the odd angle of the bones in her arm. Her body burned with the sting of a multitude of cuts and scratches. Her face hurt, and she could barely see out of one eye. A tear trailed down her cheek. She had no idea where she was or how she had gotten here—but she was damn sure she was not staying.

Chapter Thirty-Three

EARTH DIMENSION THREE
Mystic Haven, B.C., Canada

CADEN WALKED AROUND the house searching for a way in. No one answered his knock, and the doors were locked. He released a Fae Orb into the air to give him light as he carefully peered into windows, but what he could see only increased his uneasiness. The house looked empty, and the young woman who'd purchased it had not been seen since she'd moved in. Something wasn't right here. He should have waited for Maverick and Josef, but his Fae instincts had been going crazy since the call from the woman's concerned grandparents.

It was in the backyard that he spied a basement window that was only partially covered. He crouched down, and peered in. The floating orb gave him just enough light. *Fuck!* He ran to the backdoor and kicked it open.

Chapter Thirty-Four

EARTH DIMENSION THREE
Mystic Haven, B.C., Canada

IT WAS EARLY EVENING as Wisteria stood in the tree's watching a woman called Charli walk toward the small cottage that she painted in. She'd thought the woman would bring the brats, but maybe this was better. She could focus all her attention on her upcoming feast of Fae energy with no distractions. It had been no small feat to arrange for the Fae king and his Trium to be off the island today. The bodies she'd left for them to find should keep them busy for many hours.

Chapter Thirty-Five

EARTH DIMENSION THREE
Mystic Haven, B.C., Canada

CIARA WAS PURE FAE, incredibly dangerous in her own right, now, injured and cornered, she was deadly. Her appearance spoke of how terrible the injuries she'd sustained were. Her golden energy was flickering and fading. Her energy wings were ragged and limp—but she still managed to throw an incredibly powerful energy blast straight at this new threat. The only thing that saved the man who suddenly burst in was the fact that he was The Guardian.

Caden staggered. *Shit that hurt.* But he remained on his feet, talking softly to the wild, terror-stricken creature in front of him. "Ciara. I'm a police officer. My name is Caden Brody. We met a few weeks ago, before you bought your home. Before you moved here. Remember?"

His words penetrated her terror. Caden. Police officer. She lowered her hands, swaying on her feet. Staring at him. "She will—come back. Hurry. Monster—" Her voice a rasping broken whisper, her flickering energy clearly showed the dark bruising around her throat. "We must not— be found—here."

Shrugging out of his jacket, he stepped towards the woman. She flinched and backed up a step, but he continued to speak quietly to her, offering her his jacket.

She took the jacket, understanding on some elemental level that he was a very powerful Fae. He moved suddenly and scooped her into his arms. She gasped, her hand clenching on his shoulder. Blackness colored her vision as her broken arm pressed against his chest. She cried out in pain as he swept her up the stairs and out the door.

The fresh air cleared her mind enough for her to realize that everything was a muddled-up mess in her brain. She'd left her home. Got to the airport. She was sure she had gotten to the airport. It must have been when she went to the washroom that she'd met her. The monster. It was all a mess after that. Blank spots, blackness, and too many terrifying memories of pain. She clutched her head as agony roared through her brain. No! She would not flame-out! She would not lose consciousness. She had to stay awake! It was not safe! Her eyes widened as she remembered something important. "Caden! Stop!" She struggled out of his arms and staggered a few feet. Where were they? Where was it? She turned. There. To the right. Her new house, full of sunshine and light. She'd hoped it would be her forever home. Instead, it had become her prison. A place of nightmares and evil. There was something—important. She stumbled and Caden grabbed her. She stared at him, horror in her eyes, and pulled away. Limping, wavering she made it to the edge of her property and dropped to her knees ignoring the pain of the small pebbles that cut into her.

Caden crouched beside her. "Ciara. Are you alright?" He put his hand on her shoulder and instantly became aware of a massive current of Fae energy streaming into her. "What are you doing Ciara?"

She had to concentrate. She had to finish this. She had to stop the monster. Surviving no longer mattered—destroying the evil, her only focus.

She drew more Fae energy into her broken body, stifling the agonized sounds. More energy.

"Stop! Ciara, stop!"

She couldn't contain the broken cry. "Can't." She panted, and her pain filled eyes met Caden's. "Baylen. Charli. The Monster." She could not stop. She would not. She had to try. The night's darkness was driven back by the golden glow coming off her as she drew every bit of Fae energy she could contain. More than she could contain—and in a moment born of excruciating agony, she thrust all that energy at the house that anchored a monster in a realm it did not belong in.

Chapter Thirty-Six

EARTH DIMENSION THREE
Mystic Haven, B.C., Canada

WISTERIA WAITED A FEW minutes before walking up to the cottage now lit with soft golden light showing through the windows. She knocked on the door. When it opened, she smiled into the face of the pretty young woman her consort was fornicating with. "Hello, Charli. I can't say I blame you for falling for my consort. Baylen is lovely. But he's mine."

Her hand shot forward and wrapped around the woman's neck. She lifted Charli off her feet and began to squeeze as the woman kicked and clawed at her hands, her wide brown eyes panic stricken. She smiled as Charli desperately tried to gather her Fae energy. "Ah, how lovely. Thank you my dear." Wisteria began to feast on the energy flowing from the woman, drawing more and more of it as her life began to drain away.

Chapter Thirty-Seven

EARTH DIMENSION THREE
Mystic Haven, B.C., Canada

THE NIGHT SKY LIT UP. The roar of thunder crashed through the air, and a brilliant flash of supercharged energy slammed into the security Wards that had once protected Ciara's home. Wards that the monster had systematically twisted and distorted.

"Ciara. Stop!" Caden didn't dare try to interfere. She'd pulled so much energy that it had to be discharged, or she wouldn't survive.

She ignored him. This was a place of evil. It had to be destroyed. With a whoosh, the energy went white hot, and her house exploded into a fireball.

Caden grabbed her, The Guardian side of his nature coming fully alert. Instantaneously, a golden shield of Fae energy snapped around them, protecting them from the backlash that would have burned them alive.

Chapter Thirty-Eight

EARTH DIMENSION THREE
Mystic Haven, B.C., Canada

TOSSING THE BODY AWAY, Wisteria looked around the little cottage, regretful that this had ended so quickly. She should have toyed with the little bitch. She began to take notice of the decor in the little cottage. It was apparent that this was more than an artist's studio. It was also a love nest. She gazed at the big wrought iron bed, and a smirk lifted her lips. Turning, she lifted the body of the woman and stripping it naked. Carefully, she arranged the body on the bed. Next, she took a paint brush and dipped it into the blue paint that lay open and she painted —Baylen belongs to Wisteria—on the body. Laughing, she stepped outside into the night and a scream left her lips as the anchor that held her to this dimension, began to quake. No! No! She was not done! Baylen! No! The anchor shattered.

Chapter Thirty-Nine

EARTH DIMENSION THREE
Mystic Haven, B.C., Canada

CIARA LOOKED AT CADEN. Everything inside her was used up—gone. Even breathing was hard. It was not as scary to die as she had feared.

Caden growled and snatched the woman into his arms before she passed out. "Ciara!" *How the hell had she even had that much power left in her?*

"Destroyed her web. Web was—the anchor. Baylen. Charli."

"Don't you die on me!" He shot up into the air as he sent a mind link to his partner, Josef. *"Find Baylen and Charli Knight! They're in danger! Be careful!"*

"Ciara, hang on. You hear me? Hang on!"

Part Nine

Light Shines through the darkness

Chapter Forty

EARTH DIMENSION THREE
  Mystic Haven, B.C., Canada
  Six years after the first Wisteria Encounter
  One year after the second Wisteria Encounter

JUAN ESTEBAN SWORE bitterly in Spanish as he heft-ed his worn backpack and made his way to the foot passenger exit ramp. Mystic Haven, his last stop. He had tracked those motherfuckers to this area. He knew they were not here. Not in this sanctuary for his people, but close. He also knew he had to get help. He was a therapist, not the policía, not a soldado. Though he knew how to fight and more than hold his own. A leopard shifter was no easy target.

As he walked off the ferry and stepped onto the island, he pulled a worn business card from his wallet. Caden Brody. Chief of Police. He headed into the town, stopping long enough to ask directions.

Caden looked up at the knock on his office door. A moment later, Tori peeked in. "Hi, Caden, this is Juan Esteban. He needs to have a conversation with you."

Caden put the report he'd been reading away and rose to his feet. He studied the man for a moment, taking in his tired features and wrinkled clothes. From his scent the man was a leopard shifter. "Welcome, Juan. Have a seat. Let me get you a coffee." He walked over to his coffee maker and poured them both a cup, before going around his desk and taking his seat. "What brought you here today? Are you in danger?"

Juan looked into the man's eyes for some kind of confirmation that this man, this Caden Brody, was the man of honor he had been told about. Finally, his leopard chuffed deep inside, and Juan knew he could trust Caden Brody. So, he began his story.

"My brother, Ricardo, and his sweet mate, Emilia, have been after me for a few weeks to come for a visit. I am a psychologist, and the last few months at my job were difficult—so many hurting people." He stared at the police officer behind the desk, and the man nodded. "I needed a little time to regroup. I cleared my calendar for a week and set off into the Colombian jungle to my familia's home.

"I left my small apartment in the early hours of the morning, in my leopard form." Juan shook his head remembering the sounds of the animals that inhabited the rainforest. It had been a beautiful symphony to his ears. He had run for many miles, his leopard in charge and needing the freedom it had been denied for months.

He finally stopped to drink at the stream a few miles from his old family casa, enjoying the icy cold water that ran down from the mountains.

"About a mile from my family's casa, I stopped, my leopard suddenly on alert. The jungle around me was utterly silent as if holding its breath. I crept forward and froze again as I realized the scent of blood hung heavy in the air.

That mile was the longest mile I've ever run in my life." He stared at the man sitting across from him remembering how everything had kicked into slow motion and his breath was loud and harsh in his ears.

"When I finally burst out of the jungle I stepped into a scene of unimaginable horror. My brother was dead in the yard. Brutally murdered. His beautiful wife was broken and dead in the kitchen of their home." Juan stood up and walked over to stare out the window as he fought for control. "My niece, Jazmin, was missing."

He turned back to Caden. "I was crazed, desperately searching for her, for her scent. She's only seventeen years old. She's still in school." He could imagine her terror, and it drove him close to the breaking point, until his leopard forced his mind to the task of tracking the ones who had done this. "I found their scent, and the scent of my niece with them." He'd followed —a deadly predator on a mission. His leopard filled with a killing fury.

"I missed them by mere days. No matter how hard I ran, no matter how little sleep I got, they were ahead of me, and I could not catch up. Finally, they reached a city, and I had to shift back to my human form. I had remained a leopard for weeks, but I could not easily move around a city as my cat. I managed to obtain clothes and went directly to the policía." He shook his head and gave Caden another look as he sat down again. "That was a mistake. The human policía had no interest in my missing niece. They suggested I forget it all." His eyes became the green of his cat as he fought to contain the growl that wanted to erupt from his chest. "It was no suggestion. It was a barely veiled threat."

Caden nodded, his expression serious. He was not surprised. The human police in some South American countries were not exactly on the side of the law.

"I walked out of that police station and headed directly to the docks. Searching desperately for some hint of scent, some clue that they had come this way, and praying to the gods that they had not. How would I find her if they had boarded a ship?" He stared down at his hands and swallowed the lump in his throat. "As I walked along the dock, I caught wisps of her scent. Small fragments. I stopped and breathed deeply searching for more of her elusive scent, and the sunlight glinted off something along the edge of the dock. I picked it up." His hands shaking, he took the small jeweled compact and set it on Caden's desk. "I gave this to Jazmin, the last time I saw my family."

Caden picked up the small mirror and examined it. Noting the delicate filigree and tiny jewels, he turned it over, and it was engraved.

To Jazmin love from Tío Juan.

Juan shook his head and turned his agonized gaze to the man he hoped would help him find his niece. "I could not even stand. I was in despair. My leopard was savage, his rage a thing of violence." He swallowed.

Caden studied the man before him. "What did you do, Juan?"

"I—I captured the Harbour Master. The bastardo was up to his bribe filled eyeballs in this human trafficking ring!"

"How do you know that?"

"Jazmin's scent was in his office along with her captors."

He had done the unimaginable. He tortured the man, until he finally broke and told him what boats had departed in the last twenty-four hours and their destinations, and which one had a load of humans. Humans they were going to sell. Perhaps his leopard had been in charge for too long, or perhaps he had hidden darkness deep inside himself. He didn't know, and he no longer cared. When he left that man badly broken and bleeding, his only goal was to find his niece. Nothing else mattered. By the gods, if they had harmed one hair on her head, he would kill them all! Every one of them.

Caden could well imagine what had gone on in that man's office when Juan found him. He knew full well what he would have done if someone had stolen one of his sons, and it sure wouldn't have been pretty. "What did you find out?"

"The only boat that could have hidden the humans with their captives was headed to a remote island off the Canadian west coast." Juan looked at the cop, his jaw clenched. "I knew there was a superhuman sanctuary close to that island. So, I came here to get help. Will you help me find my niece, Caden Brody, and will you grant her and I sanctuary?" He braced himself for a swift death. Instead Caden studied him silently for a moment, then nodded.

"We'll find her, Juan Esteban, and we'll bring her home."

Chapter Forty-One

EARTH DIMENSION THREE
Mystic Haven, B.C., Canada

CADEN HAD NO IDEA OF the chaos that was about to enter his life. He wouldn't have run because he'd come to the reluctant conclusion that chaos was his life, but he might have thought about it while he drank a large black coffee for fortification.

He glanced around with hard eyes as he pressed against the small shack where the hostage was being held. Hostages, he corrected himself. The TWS technology that they'd used had clearly shown there were several children and adults inside. His eyes lingered on a large tree, he couldn't see the man hidden in the foliage, but he knew that Micah Thallan was there, his high-powered sniper rifle ready, waiting for his signal. Giving the go signal, he kicked down the door as the first sniper shots rang out. Bursting into the small building, weapon drawn, he shot the armed guard and turned, his eyes gone tiger in the dim interior. Ignoring the cries, he swept the room for other targets. Outside he heard more shots as his men took down guards.

Four superhuman women, two superhuman teenagers, and five superhuman children the youngest of which was a baby. The women were in bad shape. They needed urgent medical help. He couldn't help but wonder how the hell they'd been taken. An Angel, a Mer, a Sprite, *and* a Shifter. He inhaled. Cougar. A dangerous, dangerous shifter. This should have been an impossibility. He scanned the children—Bruises and scrapes. A male Elf in his late teens, with wild brown hair and violet eyes, who looked like he had a broken arm and was in need of some moonlight. A half-grown female leopard curled up against the Elf, Juan's niece.

"*Clear.*" He sent the mind link as he lowered his gun.

"*Clear.*" Micah.

"*Clear.*" Maverick.

"*Send in Juan.*" Caden looked at the hostages. "Mystic Haven Police. I'm Caden Brody. You're safe." A sound at the door had him lifting his gun. Juan stepped in.

Caden nodded to him. "The guard was human. Do you have medical training?

Juan nodded, his eyes sweeping the room for his niece. Hearing a small growl, he glanced over and saw a half-grown leopard leaping at him. He automatically opened his arms. "Jazmin!" He caught her and hugged her fiercely.

A wild looking Elf suddenly stood in front of him. "If you hurt her. I will kill you."

Caden narrowed his eyes, edging closer in case there was a problem.

Juan stared at the Elf in surprise. "I am her Tío. What is the word? Eh, Uncle. Who are you?"

The young man stared at him through violet eyes that had seen far too much, his posture stiff, his chin lifted. "I'm Khiiral, and she belongs to me."

Juan frowned and inhaled the scent of the young male as the leopard sprang from his arms to nudge at the Elf's leg. Swearing silently at what he scented, he sighed. "Let's get somewhere safe. All these things can be discussed then. Sí?"

When the young man looked as if he was going to argue, Juan put his hand on his shoulder and gave a gentle squeeze. "You have done well to protect her. Now, it's time to look after you, too, and the others. Let's get them out of here, to a safe place, Khiiral."

Khiiral nodded and reached out to the leopard shifter. She chuffed and fell into place beside the Elf as he turned to the children. "This is Jazmin's uncle. They are here to help us. We can go with them."

Caden's heart clenched at the sight, and he nodded to Juan before turning his attention to the children. His heart turned over as he saw a tiny white-blonde Fae girl holding a crying baby dressed in a dirty pink sleeper.

He crouched down by the little Fae girl doing her best to quiet the baby. "Can I help? I promise I won't hurt her. I have five little sisters, and twin sons. I'm pretty good with babies." Reaching out, he gently took the baby and cuddled her close, purring softly. She relaxed into his arms and molded herself against him. Her tiny arms reached up, circled his neck, and he lost his heart. "I've got you sweetheart. I won't let anyone hurt you." He patted her back, then reached out and gathered the little Fae girl close to him. Goddess, so many kids. How the hell could any being hurt children? He kept his fury firmly in check and noticed two red-haired Pixies, peeking at him from their hiding place behind a small Bear Shifter who looked to be about twelve years old. He saw the boy had his claws out, ready to defend the little ones behind him. *Good boy.* He was impressed. *"Let's get out of here."* He mind linked Maverick. *"Contact the hospital and let them know we are on our way there."*

Chapter Forty-Two

CADEN WATCHED AS JUAN, Jazmin, and Khiiral, his arm in a black cast, all got into Josef Drake's SUV. His second in command had invited them to stay with him and his mate until they could get housing arrangements sorted out. Cassandra would fuss over them and help them get settled. It was a good call.

With a nod to Juan, he turned back to the kids standing so quietly on the sidewalk behind him. They'd been released into his care. The bruises and scratches would heal without medical intervention.

He hadn't expected to be taking them all home with him. But they were superhumans and could not go into a human foster care system. The superhuman social worker they had called in felt that the kids should not be separated at this time. They'd lost too much already and formed bonds with each other. The fact that he had a large home with lots of room was a big part of the equation. Maybe he shouldn't have volunteered, but the kids had stuck to him like glue since their rescue. To the point where his Da had taken him aside.

"Caden, these kids need you. I know you have your hands full with Gunner and Chance, but I think you should consider becoming their guardian. Maybe even adopt them."

He'd looked at his father in surprise, his mind boggled by the idea of having seven children, then looked down as a little hand slid into his. It was the little Fae girl, Pandora. "Could we have pizza for supper, Daddy?"

He'd blinked and his heart had done this funny little thing. Fae Intuition swept through him with a clarity that shocked him. These kids were his. A fierce protectiveness surged through him. He had to do right by these children. He'd looked back at his father. "I need to try to find their families first."

He shifted the baby in his arms and watched as Pandora took the hands of the young Pixie twins, and Benjamin, the bear shifter, hovered protectively. "Come on kids, my SUV is right here. I've got a big house with lots of bedrooms, and I have twin sons, just a little younger than you, Ben. Let's go home."

Chapter Forty-Three

EARTH DIMENSION THREE
Mystic Haven, B.C., Canada

CADEN HAD BEEN INVESTIGATING the people behind the human trafficking ring for months. Hell, it wasn't a human trafficking ring. It was a superhuman trafficking ring, and that fact was beyond comprehension. Superhumans had skills and abilities that should have kept them safe from such things.

These bastards had targeted their most vulnerable. Children, and a few of their women who were hurt or otherwise in a position of vulnerability. Women who, in normal circumstances, would have killed any who dared to come after them.

He knew, with a bone deep certainty, that he still didn't have enough of the puzzle. Why were they targeting superhumans? Humans, by and large, did not know of superhumans. They remained hidden for their own protection and that of the humans. The rare incidents in the past where humans had discovered small groups of superhumans, had never had outcomes that were good. Superhumans had been tortured and killed. Humans had died. No, it was far better for them to remain hidden. Unknown. Myths and legends and Fae tales.

The women he'd interviewed shed some light, but not enough, far from enough.

The man in charge of the traffickers had been arrogant. Talking in front of the captives as if he thought they were no threat. A dangerous assumption, considering that even young superhumans had powers and abilities. A fact that was no doubt driven home to the leader when Khiiral Darkfire, a nineteen-year-old Elf, had turned a man to ashes, for daring to touch one of the children. By then it was far too late for the arrogant asshole leader to change what had happened. The captives had heard every plan.

What they'd heard had been horrifying.

The children had been specifically targeted. The common link was the fact that each of them came from a small family unit where there were no living relatives. Each target was investigated and watched for months to ensure the information was correct. Their mistake had been when they targeted Juan Esteban's seventeen-year-old niece.

Maybe they had not known of Juan, or maybe they arrogantly thought that he was a male leopard and would not care that his brother had died. It was a fatal mistake.

What the captives had not heard, though, was why. Why had they been taken? What did the captors want? Caden understood, of course, that the men they captured had only been the hunters, the delivery men. They had no knowledge of why they had been contracted to carry out this mission.

He swore again and got up to pace to the window of his office that overlooked the busy downtown core of Mystic Haven.

They'd questioned the one man that survived the rescue. The information he gave them was pitifully small. He was a guard, a human with a history of small-time crimes. He'd been recruited when he got out of jail the last time. Every name he'd given them had been a dead end.

This operation was obviously financed by people who had extremely deep pockets and access to technology that could keep them hidden. Well hidden. It was as if they had disappeared into thin air. Not something any human was capable of doing.

He would find them. It was only a matter of time. He'd put feelers out in all the superhuman underground refuge cities and boroughs right across the globe. His contact was looking into the secrets that were hidden deep within those boroughs. Somewhere, someone knew something.

Chapter Forty-Four

EARTH DIMENSION THREE
Mystic Haven, B.C., Canada

CADEN DOUBLE CHECKED to make sure that he'd packed everything before shrugging into the backpack. "Come on kids. We have exploring to do. Make sure you have a jacket on and a bottle of water and some snacks in your backpacks." He settled Dakota into a rugged stroller meant for hiking, gently smoothed her multihued hair, and handed her a bottle of milk. In the months since he'd brought the kids home, they'd all learned how to be a family. It hadn't been easy. Not with the trauma they'd endured and not with him being a single parent. There'd been many times when he wondered if he was completely insane, but he wouldn't change a damn thing. "We're going to the stream in the forest." A small stampede rushed past him and out the door.

Grinning, he followed them, pausing to release the protection Wards that guarded the backyard. Protection Wards were a necessary thing when you owned four full sections of forested land that bordered the ocean, and you had seven kids who naturally leaned toward mischief and adventure.

When they got to the stream, after many pauses to examine flowers, insects, and a few frogs, he had them all sit in a circle under a large tree.

"Today we're going to discover a little more about each other." He lifted Dakota out of her stroller as his glamour fell away. Dakota babbled happily and reached up to pull on his pointed ear. He laughed and blew a raspberry on her neck, then set her on the ground at his feet. "I would like each one of you to let your glamour go or shift." Glamours were a simple bit of defensive magic that all non-shifter Superhumans learned to utilize. It allowed them to appear human, thus protecting both them and their human cousins. Shifters of course, were either human in appearance, or they were their animal. Mystic Haven, along with the other Sanctuary cities spread across the planet, had strict laws regarding the tourists that sometimes found their way to these superhuman communities. If an unsanctified human was present, then glamours were mandatory. Warnings were always sent out through community mind links to prevent mistakes.

The air filled with sparks as the three boys shifted into a bear cub and two tiger cubs. Dakota clapped her tiny hands and crawled over to climb onto Benjamin's lap. He carefully wrapped his paws around her so she wouldn't tumble off his lap. At twelve, Ben was a serious boy who was passionate about protecting his younger siblings. His fur was the same deep cinnamon brown color as his hair, and his eyes were a dark brown with golden striations.

Dakota was a coyote shifter, but it would be at least another year before she experienced her first shift. She growled playfully at Chance who growled back and nudged his twin. Gunner padded over to Dakota and licked her face until she dissolved into a fit of giggles. Both boys had dark hair and amber eyes.

Caden grinned. Damn, he was so proud of his boys. Gunnar and Chance had been through hell when their mother, his mate, had died in a car accident. The boys had been four when he met Santana and into all kinds of mischief. He'd had five beautiful years with his mate. Gunnar and Chance were eleven now, and full of a helluva lot of mischief. He would never forget the day he brought home five more kids. He'd been worried they would be angry with his choice. Instead, they'd embraced the idea of having a large family. "We almost have as many kids now as Grandpa and Grandma did," they'd exclaimed proudly, and he'd had to laugh. His parents had been very prolific. They'd had five daughters after he was born, and a few years ago they'd had a set of twins, and finally, he'd gotten a brother. He was terrified to ask if they were done yet.

He looked over at Pandora and smiled. She had full control of her glamour at five years old which wasn't unusual for a Fae child, though errors could still happen. Fae parents normally held glamours for their children from the time of their birth until they learned to take over, usually within six months. Pandora released her glamour and a slight glow appeared around her. Her white-blonde hair was braided, revealing her tiny, pointed ears. Her purple eyes brimmed with mischief, and her energy wings shifted intensity with the pulsing of the energy field that made them. She floated up a few inches and hovered off the ground. Fae were born with wings and learned to fly soon after they learned to walk.

Marisol and Macen were sitting on the ground beside Pandora, and he blinked a couple times when he saw them. He was just never going to get used to that blue. In their natural form, Pixies were light blue, had pointy ears, and larger slightly tilted eyes. His pixies were adorable—Their dark red hair and bright green eyes a startling contrast to their light blue skin. He grinned at them and winked. They giggled and glittery pixie dust fell around them in a sparkling cloud. As adults, they would learn to control that, but children could not prevent their pixie dust from appearing and he, for one, was thankful because trying to find a child that could shrink to three inches in height was damned hard.

Scooping up Dakota, he cuddled her, smiling when she patted his cheek.

"Dada, Dada."

He grinned, his heart mush at her words. He brushed her soft hair back, the sunlight playing over the many shades of blonde and brown, and she captured his hand. "Ouch! Dakota!" He pulled his hand away. Two fang marks had broken the skin. He tilted his head and looked at her again. She grinned at him and beside her two tiny front baby teeth were fangs. Tiny baby coyote fangs. *What the hell?* "How did you do that, Babygirl?"

She chortled, a few tiny sparks filled the air, and the fangs disappeared.

"You're a very smart little coyote shifter." He grinned at her, and she giggled again. She'd managed to do a partial shift. Pretty impressive stuff for a baby shifter.

He sat down beside his kids and began to hand out the root beers and sandwiches that they had brought with them. When they were finished eating, he carefully took a bakery box out of his backpack and set it in the middle. "Gunnar, Chance, and I have an announcement to make." He opened the box with a dramatic flair, and his kids gasped at the small chocolate cake with mounds of fluffy icing. He set a stack of unbreakable small plates beside the cake, along with forks and a cake knife. This afternoon they were having their own private celebration. Later this evening, his family and friends would descend upon them, and they would really party. Reaching back into his backpack he pulled out a large envelope. "Come here, Gunnar and Chance." His sons traded a conspiratorial grin with him. He gave the boys the envelope. "Hand these out please." When the documents had been handed out, he looked at his oldest son. "Ben, what does it say?"

The twelve-year-old studied the paper, his face slowly changing from confusion to astonishment. He looked at Caden. "Dad?"

Caden swallowed against the lump in his throat. This was the first time that Ben had ever called him that. He nodded.

"We're a family? A real family?"

"Yes. It's final. We're a family."

"I'm Benjamin Brody?"

Caden nodded. "If you want to take my name."

"Whoo hoo!" The boy shot to his feet and ran over to Caden. He dropped to his knees and wrapped his arms around him in a huge bear hug. Caden laughed, hugging his son back. All the kids suddenly surrounded him, hugging, laughing, and pronouncing that they, too, were Brody's. And they were.

Part Ten

Do not war with darkness. Bring in the light

Chapter Forty-Five

EARTH DIMENSION THREE
Mystic Haven, B.C., Canada
Eleven years after the first Wisteria Encounter

BAYLEN LAY SPRAWLED across the bed fast asleep. The covers had been shoved away as he tossed and turned restlessly. He shifted again, a low groan escaping as his mind betrayed him yet again, dragging forward the memories, the emotions that he refused to acknowledge. The memories morphed and became a distorted echo of reality as they reshaped themselves into dreams—and nightmares.

Baylen paused as he automatically checked to make sure the door was locked. It was dark here. Wherever the hell here was. He glanced around trying to identify this place, and his heart started to pound. Jadeah's shop. He'd entered through the back. Before his eyes, the scene morphed, and he found himself with an armful of a lush woman. His head lowered, and he took her mouth in a long slow kiss. Fire seared him with each stroke of her soft hands. Her scent filled his senses, and his dick hardened.

Closing his hands over her hips, he lifted her and set her on the desk. His mouth found hers as he thrust deep inside her. Her pussy was paradise, warm and slick. He wanted to stay buried inside her forever. He began to move his hips, thrusting deep and pulling back. Again and again, her gasps, urging him on.

Golden Fae energy raced down his spine, and he growled as he lost his glamour. His thrusts became harder, faster, urgency curling around him as his heart raced. He lifted his head and his eyes stared into the face of his first mate—a woman long dead. Her long platinum blonde hair spread out on the desk, her eyes a stunning silver grey not found on this world. She lifted her hand, and her fingers seemed to trail fire over his skin.

"Jadeah." His voice was an anguished breath of sound.

"Baylen. Please." Her body tightened, and he groaned, unable to resist her plea. He moved his hand between their straining body's and rubbed his thumb over her clit. She cried out and convulsed as her orgasm rushed over her, the wet rhythmic pulsing of her pussy dragging him over the edge with her. A harsh groan tore from his throat—His heart aching. Wild pleasure shuddering through them, sweeping over them. Tears stinging his eyes.

Suddenly, they were falling, and his passion-fogged brain kicked back in. He flipped them over and crashed onto the floor. Her slight weight landed on top of him, and his breath rushed out of him in a loud umph! Soft laughter filled the air, and he lifted his eyes to meet the brown eyes of the laughing brunette with paint-stained fingers. His cock throbbed and she smirked. "Round two, Baylen?"

"Charli?" Fresh grief burned through him as papers rained down on them from the desk. His mind stumbled to understand how Jadeah had become Charli. Rage and grief

filling him. He fought the tears, and his hands shook as they rose to clasp her head. "Oh, gods. Charli. How?"

She stared at him quizzically, and he remembered her death at the hands of the deranged creature, Wisteria. The second woman who had loved him unconditionally. A mate he never dreamed he would have after losing his Jadeah. A mate he'd had so little time with. A second mate he lost. Grief. Anguish.

He roared his pain as he snapped out of the dream, sweating, shivering, his heart racing as he gasped for air. Slowly, he sat up, swung his legs over the edge of the bed and leaned forward, his elbows resting on his knees, his fists pressed against his forehead. His long sweat-damp-ened hair hung around his face. *Gods. Gods. Gods.* He took a deep breath. Another. He swiped away the moisture from his eyes. *Why tonight?* There was never an answer to that question. His demons haunted him at their will.

He rose and stared out into the darkness. The dawn would be here soon, and he would face his other demon with its rising—The one that had haunted him since his first encounter with the evil that was Wisteria Abital.

The Fae celebrated the life-giving sun, joyously greeting its rising everyday. But what happened to him during the rising of the sun had nothing to do with his Fae.

It was the darkness, itself. The darkness that ran through his veins warning him of the coming dawn. It woke him most nights, in the darkest hours. He would lay there hearing its siren's call, knowing that evil resided inside him.

He shoved his hair back, bracing his hand against the glass patio door, allowing the coolness of the glass to center him. Patiently, he waited for the sun to rise, waiting for it to reach the point when its life-giving rays would flood across the castle grounds. There. He stepped out onto the balcony, naked. The sun burst over the grounds, and its rays poured over his skin. He stood stone still, his muscles clenched in agony. The golden rays that, at one time in his life were a loving embrace, now seared their way over his skin.

It took him years to develop the control that prevented a single agonized cry from leaving his lips. He clenched his jaw and turned around allowing the searing rays to reach every inch of his skin.

The darkness in him howled and retreated. But he grimly continued to stand in the morning sunlight, even as he knew blisters were forming along the scars that marked his body.

They would leave quickly, healed by his Fae power, when the sunlight burst fully over the horizon. It was only this first touch of the light that burned him.

He rose daily, willingly enduring his punishment, where no one would witness the sunlight rejecting a Fae.

Chapter Forty-Six

EARTH DIMENSION THREE
Mystic Haven, B.C., Canada
Eleven years after the first Wisteria Encounter
Earth Date: June 17th

ALIORA AURELIUS HURRIED down the street. Today above all days, she wanted an iced caramel macchiato. Her medieval lilac dress swirled around her ankles revealing her favorite cinnamon brown, flat-soled, leather boots. She adjusted the point on her right sleeve as she dodged a group of schoolchildren with backpacks. "Ali. Ali!" they called out to her. She smiled and waved, sending a gentle mist of golden sparkles to sprinkle over them, before hurrying on, the music of their laughter filling her heart with gladness. Her aquamarine eyes with their striated bronze and gold rings, widened as she noticed the new bookstore. *Oh.* Its name was perfect! Another Dimension! *Oh, my goodness! Maybe they had the new fantasy book she'd been wanting to buy.* She took half a step toward the brick building before the scent from the darling little coffee shop she attended religiously caught up with her. *Oh! Coffee first! Then books!* She turned and came face to face with Caden Brody, Chief of the Mystic Haven Police, as he exited the coffee shop.

"Careful, Ali," Caden said with a grin as he steadied her and took a sip of his extra-large black coffee. "Ah, the best way to start the day. What is your poison today?"

Ali smiled at his obvious enjoyment and blinked at his choice of words. *Poison?* No, no. It was her energy potion. "Iced caramel macchiato."

Caden shuddered. "How can you do that to coffee?"

Aliora smiled sweetly. "I don't do it. I just drink the magical energy-giving elixir."

"I don't think we can handle a more energized you, Ali." He started down the street. "I'm going to warn my officers."

Laughing, Aliora opened the door to the Chicco di Caffe. Arianna Tyrrell stood behind the counter, and Ali gave her a happy smile. "How are you, Arianna? Busy morning?"

Arianna smiled back. "Very busy. Are you having your usual this morning?"

Aliora shook her head, the natural mix of bronze, copper, and strawberry blonde in her hair glinting in the sunlight that poured in through the large windows. "Iced caramel macchiato, please."

Arianna paused and stared at Ali. "Are you sure, Ali?"

Ali nodded. "It's my day off. I'm going to the new bookstore and the beach. I need energy. Lots of energy. Please brew my magical elixir."

Arianna laughed. "Alright, Ali, one iced caramel macchiato coming up. Do you want a muffin too?"

Ali bit her lip and looked at the selection of muffins and other goodies. Why were there always so many that she wanted? "Uhm. I'll have a Blueberry scone... No. Wait. The lemon poppy seed loaf. Uh, I'll have both, and one of those bacon cheese stick bread things—For the protein."

Arianna grinned and went to work on her order. Aliora took her canvas Star Wars Rebels backpack off her shoulder, and when Arianna handed her the paper bag with her food, she tucked it inside careful not to squish it. She did up the backpack and swung it over her shoulder, grabbed her drink, turning quickly as she called out a happy thank you. *Bookstore next*—she collided with an extremely solid male chest, and two things happened at once. Golden sparks of magic filled the air and ice-cold caramel macchiato burst out of the cup, splashing down on her and the fierce looking male Fae she had crashed into. She gasped and gasped again when she saw his long dark hair was now covered in sticky sweet coffee and golden sparks of magic. She blinked as she saw her reflection in the store window. Heavens. She was as soaked and sparkly as the man she had run into. Who would have thought there was that much coffee in her cup? Who would have thought she would lose control of her magic like that? Her startled eyes met his. "I'm sorry!"

"Ah, fuck!" The man glared at her and she could see his glamour starting to slip. He was glowing. He must be really angry. His dark eyes blinked once, and she forgot to breathe as he slowly looked down her body and back up. She blinked twice. *Had he? He couldn't have. What?* At five foot four and one hundred and fifty-four pounds of curves, she had never ever experienced that kind of look from anyone. Her cheeks grew warm, and she tucked her hair behind her ears, revealing their points. "I— I'm terribly sorry. I didn't realize you were behind me! Why are you swearing? Oh! Are those your children?" *She was babbling. Somebody, please, stop her.* She smiled at the three dark haired kids standing behind the man. They peeked at her and she waved to them. "What are your names? I'm Aliora." She ignored the growl from the man.

"I'm Falcon." The boy spoke up. "These are my sisters Aurora and Jewel. We're in grade three."

"Are you triplets?"

The trio nodded in unison, and she grinned. *So cute!* "That's exciting! Are you enjoying grade three? Do you trick your teacher by trading names?"

Another low growl had her glancing up at the glowering male. His eyes locked with hers. *Oh dear.* She turned to Arianna who had already made her second iced caramel macchiato. "I'll pay for their drinks, give the kids each a cake pop for their lunches and..." She paused and glanced up at the grumpy man. "You better give him at least a couple of those bacon cheese thingys. He seems hungry. He probably missed breakfast and his morning coffee trying to get his tribe ready." *Still babbling, shh Ali!* Using her magic, she floated her debit card over the machine ignoring the stream of swearing coming from the man.

Taking her coffee, she carefully stepped to the side, winked at the kids, and risked a brief look at the man who was glaring daggers at her. Nope, she was not going to say it. She took a step past him. She was not going to— "You should not be swearing around your children."

Arianna made a choked sound. The man seemed to forget where he was and released his glamour completely. *Wow.* His wings were amazing! She lifted her hand. Realizing that she'd almost touched a complete stranger's wings she dropped her hand. Her eyes met his again, and she swallowed at the look in his eyes, clutched her coffee more securely and rushed out the door.

She didn't stop until she stood in front of the new bookstore. Thank goodness she caught a glimpse of herself in the window. She took a deep breath, and a sip of her coffee, trying to calm her frazzled nerves. Glancing around she saw that no one was paying attention to her and lifted her hand, sparkling golden magic spilling from her fingertips. A second later she was dry and clean.

Opening the door, she stepped inside. The smell of books, paper, and some other exotic spice lingered in the air. Oh, she could get lost in this store. She glanced over at the blonde woman behind the counter and smiled. "Hello. Are you an Angel? I've only met one or two so far."

The woman laughed and nodded. "Hello. Yes, I'm an Angel. I'm surprised you could tell. My name is Amara Zayas."

"I'm Aliora Aurelius. I'm sorry. That was rude of me."

Amara laughed. "It's alright. It's not a secret. Is there any particular book you are looking for today?"

Ali nodded and asked about her book. By the time she had browsed her way through the bookstore, she had a whole stack of books in her arms. She frowned, but they were books. She needed books as much as she needed her coffee. After paying for them and stashing them in her backpack, she stepped from the store. Next stop, the beach.

Chapter Forty-Seven

EARTH DIMENSION THREE
Mystic Haven, B.C., Canada

SHIRINA SÍTHEACH PARKED Rosie and climbed out, patting the pink vintage Volkswagen van affectionately. "You got us here, Rosie. I'm going into the store to get groceries. Be good and don't flirt with that SUV beside us. His gas consumption is off the charts, even if he is pretty." With a final pat, she strode off to the big warehouse store humming softly. A cool rain-scented breeze tugged a few strands of silvery blonde hair from her messy bun and swirled the flowing skirt of her teal flowered dress around her ankles.

Reaching into the small, leather purse slung diagonally across her chest, she found her membership card and grabbed a cart, her bracelets clicking against each other quietly. She showed her store membership as she walked in, slipped it back into her bag and adjusted the silver rings on her fingers. Making a beeline to the pet food section, she began to load her cart. Two giant bags of cat food, three giant bags of dog food, a bag of lizard food, fish food, and mouse food. That done, she walked over to the pet toy area and found something special for each one of her fur babies.

Her next stop was the gardening area. The forecast had promised another rainy day in Mystic Haven, but she really wanted to get a new house plant, something bright and cheery. In the end she bought three. Then on to get groceries, her original reason for coming to this store. After getting the essentials she went over to the baking aisle and started loading up on baking supplies.

Humming happily, she got the ingredients for several of her favorite varieties of cookies. Her house was often the gathering place for the ancient Fae, and she liked to be prepared. The cart was heaped well over the top when she finally had everything.

She paused to double check her phone list. Chocolate. She had almost forgotten her chocolate. She wheeled the cart around and headed directly to the candy aisle. That's when the shopping got serious.

A few minutes later she was standing in the lineup for the cashier and replying to a message from Caden Brody, asking her to check up on The Ward. She frowned and texted him back.

All of the Wards?

The line slowly advanced as she texted back and forth with him, her fingers flying over the keys. By the time she got to the cashier she had ascertained that Caden was simply being cautious.

As she wheeled her cart forward, she tucked her phone into her purse and smiled at the cashier. Twenty minutes later she pushed her cart out of the store, her mind whirling with ways to help the cashier who was a single mom and worried about affording her rent.

On the way to her van, she used her telekinesis to hold her phone to her ear so she could call her foundation and give them the name of the young woman. They would look into the situation and make recommendations back to her.

Opening the tailgate, she turned and carefully scoped out the parking lot. No one was close by, which was why she had chosen the farthest parking spot from the store to begin with. She smiled and with a gentle movement of her hand, her groceries began to load themselves. It was good to be a Fae.

Groceries loaded, she climbed into her van, started it, and patted the dash. "You're a wonderful van, Rosie."

Placing her phone on the wireless charger in her console, she spoke to her onboard computer. "I'm heading home, Luna." She owned a huge piece of ocean front property about an hour away from Mystic Haven. It was her sanctuary.

"The normal route will take you approximately one hour and ten minutes if you proceed at the posted speed limits. Traffic is light today. There were no attempted security breaches to Rosie while you were in the store. However, the owner of the gas guzzling SUV almost scraped the front driver's fender as he pulled out. Would you like me to send his information to the police?" The husky feminine computer voice asked.

Shirina grinned. "No thanks, Luna. I'm sure it was an accident. Please start my playlist." Luna was her favorite upgrade to Rosie, and she'd thanked Nerys Daenala many times. That woman was simply amazing with technology, and of course, centuries ahead of anything here on earth, but that was to be expected. After all, they'd traveled the stars to get here.

Her beloved pink van filled with the sounds of her favorite pop music, and she smiled. "Thank you, Luna. Please call Baylen Knight and bring up a current map of the Wards and all the Ward readings."

Rosie's front windshield filled with glowing blue information. Shirina tapped her nail on the steering wheel for a moment, considering the information on the screen. "Luna, you better drive while I talk to the king."

The phone rang once, twice, before it was answered. Having a direct line to the King of the Fae came in handy. "Hi, Bay. It's Shirina. How are you and the kids?" She chatted with him for a few minutes, listening carefully to his answers before she finally got down to business. "Have you noticed anything strange with The Ward?"

"No, but I was thinking that it's been a while since we had a gathering at The Ward."

"That's true." She made a note and looked at the information lighting up her screen. "All my readings seem normal. Caden requested a general check up on all the Wards. I figured I'd start with you and see if you had any concerns. I'll check the Forest Ward when I get home, and over the next week I'll check the Castle Ward and the Protection Ward that guards our borders. I'll also put in a call to the Mer and ask them if they will allow me to check their Ward. Give your kids a hug for me. Take care, Baylen."

Pulling into her property, she parked Rosie in the garage and walked over to unlock her house, followed by the parade of groceries she'd bought at the warehouse store.

Her three dogs came bounding up to her from wherever they had been playing on the property and she laughed bending down to hug and pet each of them. Not that she had to bend far. Her dogs were huge. "Argon, Elvis, and Gypsy, were you good while I was gone?"

Gypsy stared at her like she was crazy. The black pure-bred Borzoi had more than her fair share of personality. Shirina laughed and rubbed Gypsy's silky fur. "I know the boys probably were busy, Gypsy, but I don't see any messes."

Argon, a Great Pyrenees, barked, and Elvis, an Old English Sheepdog, stared at her. "Boys, I'm sure that Gypsy did not mean to get you into trouble."

An annoyed meow filled the air, and Shirina looked over to see her five cats lined up watching her, impatient for their turns. She crouched down and stroked each of them in turn. "Hello my beautiful felines. I've bought you all a treat and a toy."

A squeak and she looked to the large custom-made mouse cage stationed in her living room. Gus-Gus, Whiskers, and Matthias impatiently waited for their share of the attention. "Hello my small friends. You need to be patient. I'll get your treats as soon as I can." She reached into the cage to give each of them a gentle rub on their tiny heads before turning to peer into Spot's cage. Her leopard gecko crouched on a branch and stared back at her. She grinned and straightened up.

"Alright everybody. I'm just going to put away the groceries, give you your treats, and feed our fish, then I need to go to work for a bit."

Elvis woofed in his low, deep way and Shirina smiled. "Yes, Elvis, Argon, Gypsy and you can come with me. We all know The Ward would be very offended if I left you behind, and we can't have that."

Chapter Forty-Eight

EARTH DIMENSION THREE
Mystic Haven, B.C., Canada

BAYLEN WOKE WITH A roar already on his feet beside the bed. His breaths shuddered out of him as if he'd run for miles. His fists opened and closed, his dark hair a tumble around his shoulders. His head was bowed, lips curled in a grimace of agony that turned his whole face into the mask of a dangerous predator. His eyes glittered in the darkness as dark memories of golden sparkles lingered. Anguish filled every breath in—as sharp as the deadliest dagger. Bitterness tore at him with every breath out—his grief a torment of thorns tearing through him, leaving only a fragmented, broken man, steeped in the blackest of nights. His darkness knew no end.

Bare minutes after checking in with his hunter, names and addresses secured, he soared through the night, a deadly hunter seeking his prey.

The gunshots were still resounding through the alley on the mainland when he landed. He took in the scene at a glance. A woman's broken body lay on the ground. As ice cold darkness filled him, the men who'd attacked her looked up and he saw the horror in their eyes. He did not fucking care. He was a terrifying sight to most humans, with his massive energy wings, his pointed ears, and sharp chiseled features, he looked alien and dangerously power-ful. Those fuckers had a right to their terror.

His eyes hardened to obsidian and with a wave, their guns flew from their hands and clattered to the ground, broken into a million pieces. He stalked forward, death in his eyes and when they rushed him, he grabbed the first bastard by the throat and threw him. The man's head bounced as he hit the brick wall and he dropped like the sack of refuse that he was.

Baylen ignored the fallen man and continued walking toward the man running toward him with a length of pipe in his hands. The man was big, scarred, tattooed, and dead-ly. "You should have kept going, you weird piece of alien shit! I'm going to kill you. You think you are some tough hero come to save the day? You're nothing. Nothing. You hear me, motherfucker? You are going to die."

Baylen struck with deadly accuracy. His fist slamming into the man's mouth. Blood flowed. His other fist smashed into the man's ribs. The man stumbled back, the pipe clattering to the ground, curses falling from his bleed-ing mouth, but he didn't go down. Twisting, the man threw a wicked hard punch that hit Baylen on the jaw, snapping his head back.

A cold half smile curved the Fae king's lips, and he stepped forward, his right fist lashing out to drive a solid blow to the man's ribs again. He sidestepped, and the punch aimed at his nose grazed his ear instead. He could end this fight in an instant. One blast of pure Fae energy and this human would be dead, and he deserved to die, but

Baylen was not in a benevolent mood. There would be no swift, easy death for this man. There would be violence and pain, and a full knowing that he was about to meet his end at the hands of the Fae king.

Baylen blocked the next punch and hammered a shockingly fast blow to the man's ribs again, they cracked under his fist. The man gasped and lunged forward, landing two solid strikes to Baylen's face, jolting him. His lip split, and warm blood slid down to drip from his chin, but still the Fae king advanced, ignoring his own pain, to rain blow after blow to the man's body.

The man stumbled back, evading the next blow, and reached into his pocket. In a heartbeat, he had a knife in his hands and a half-crazed glint in his eyes. He leaped forward, swinging the weapon. Baylen jerked back as the blade grazed his stomach, throwing a hard right he connected with the man's jaw. The man staggered. Caught himself. Then he rushed the Fae king.

Their bodies crashed together, and Baylen began to pound his fists into the man, intent on his destruction. A searing pain streaked through him as the man plunged the knife into Baylen's side. A terrible growl filled the air, and the Fae king backhanded the man, sending him reeling back.

Baylen was on him, slamming him to the ground and hammering him with brutal strength, the damage inflicted with ruthless intent, without remorse, without mercy. When Baylen stepped back, the man's breath was a death rattle in his throat. He stood over the man watching him die and he felt nothing.

A slight noise reached him. He whirled around as the first man sat up, his eyes large with terror. Baylen growled, and advanced. The man shrank. Contempt filled Baylen's gaze. "Your friend died at the hands of the Fae king, take that message back to whoever the fuck you answer to. If you ever return, I will be waiting."

The man fled, Baylen's growl following him down the dark alley. Turning, Baylen crouched down beside the woman. She was bleeding badly, but she was alive. Scooping her up, he shot up into the air, streaking toward the nearest hospital. As he landed, he wrapped a glamour of invisibility around him and the victim. Silently he negotiated the halls of the hospital and set the woman on a gurney in the emergency room. He glanced around, his dark gaze hooded. Seeing a nurse, he allowed her to see him, using his powers of compulsion to direct her to the woman. As the nurse shouted for a doctor, he wrapped his invisibility back around him, and walked out the nearest exit.

Chapter Forty-Nine

EARTH DIMENSION THREE
Mystic Haven, B.C., Canada

CADEN DROVE ALONG MARINE Drive, enjoying the beautiful ocean views over the high cliffs, and thinking about the weekend. Yeah, he took the long route home, this time, thankful for his family who'd stepped up to watch his horde of children. They knew his job, and no one would worry if he was a little late getting home. Today's reluctance to get home had nothing to do with his kids, and every-thing to do with trying to make sure he was in a better state of mind when he got there. His kids deserved his best. They deserved his focused attention, and he was determined to give them that.

He was thinking about whether to order Chinese for supper when he saw the oncoming car swerve. He swore as he realized the vehicle was out of control. He glanced in the rear-view mirror. Hell. Too many cars coming up be-hind him. Flipping on his red and blue lights, he spun the steering wheel of his SUV, tires screamed as his vehicle slid sideways into the path of the out-of-control vehicle. At the same time, he threw a time shift at the oncoming traffic, but there was nothing he could do about the out-of-con-trol vehicle except brace for impact.

The car slammed into the side of his SUV, rocking it, and he grunted as air bags detonated, and his seat belt tightened. Then swore as the out-of-control vehicle careened over the cliff. "Shit!"

Ripping off the seat belt he yanked open the door and jumped out. Sprinting over to the cliff edge he saw the car floating in the ocean, its front end beginning to sink.

"Josef! I'm on Marine Drive. There's been an accident! We need fire and rescue!" He sent out a yell for help over mind link, before he dove off the cliff and into the ocean, praying his time shift would hold until help arrived.

The water was icy cold, and it snatched his breath away. Surfacing, he swam to the car aware of the unraveling time shift. He sure as hell hoped the drivers behind him were supers who understood a time shift had a hold of them. They would have time to brake when that time shift let go, and that was the best he could hope for. Reaching the sinking car, he peered in the driver's side window. A young woman was behind the wheel and unconscious, in the back seat was a wide-eyed baby.

Cursing, he drew back his fist and using his shifter strength, slammed it into the driver's window. Glass shattered and he poured Fae healing energy into the mother even as he used his telekinesis to try to keep the vehicle from sinking any further.

"Wake up!" He ordered the woman, his voice the rough growl of his tiger. "Wake up! Now!"

His glamour flickered and winked out, his wings moving to lift him higher in the water. With a frustrated growl, he looked around to assess the situation better. *Shit.* The car was still sinking. Fury swept through him, and he roared as he ripped the door off the car with the combined strength of his tiger and Fae. Claws burst out of the tips of his fingers, and he slashed the seat belt holding the woman in place. He dragged her out of the vehicle and wrapped her in a bubble of Fae energy praying it would keep her afloat as he climbed into the sinking vehicle.

The baby was howling and honestly, he sure didn't blame the little one. The water was damn cold. He climbed into the backseat and slashed through the shoulder straps of the baby car seat and lifted the baby out. Cuddling the child against his chest, he slammed his foot into the rear door of the car. "Come on! Come on!" He slammed his foot into it again, and again until finally the door gave way and he jumped out of the vehicle, holding tight to the baby. His wings lifted them clear of the car as it tilted and sank beneath the waves. He spun around searching for the mother and saw Josef, in full out dragon mode, lifting her from the ocean in his massive claws. Relief swept through him, and he nodded at his partner, thankful for his swift response.

Hearing sirens screaming as police, ambulances and fire trucks responded to the emergency he turned and flew to the cliff top. He landed as the first ambulance screeched to a stop and the paramedics sprinted towards them.

Josef set the woman down and began to shift as the paramedics loaded the woman on a stretcher. A second team of paramedics took the baby from Caden.

He took a step thinking he was going to stay close to the baby, and flame-out swept over him in a staggering rush. His knees went out from under him, and he ended up on the hard ground. He lifted a bloody hand and shoved his hair back as he panted, trying to catch his breath. This was not how he'd wanted to start the weekend.

Part Eleven

Light shines, and the darkness does not understand it

Chapter Fifty

EARTH DIMENSION THREE
Mystic Haven, B.C., Canada

CADEN STOOD STARING up at the sky, his instincts going crazy. Dropping his glamour, he soared up, searching for the cause of his unease. The runes that covered his chest and arms, marking him as a Fae Guardian, moved and he swore.

The sky roiled and rumbled ominously, clouds so dark grey they were edging into black, piled high. A light seemed to hover under them casting them in a strange neon blue glow.

He soared higher trying to get a better view of what was causing the glow, but the only thing he could tell was that it was moving at a high rate of speed. He put on a burst of speed intent on catching up with whatever the hell was flying over his island. As he drew closer, he saw The Ward keeping pace with the object, matching it move for move. Shit.

The stillness of the Guardian moved through him as he drew close enough to the glow to make out the shape of a being with immense black wings. A Fallen Angel.

Caden opened his mind to The Ward and a rush of information flooded his mind.

"*Danger!*" The warning was a sharp thrust of urgency followed by images of the Royal Fae Trium launching into the sky and rushing toward him.

The knowledge that The Royal Trium was heading toward him didn't change the fact that he was the closest, and there wasn't a chance in hell he was waiting for anyone, not when The Ward was this agitated.

"You have no business here, Fallen One."

The Angel turned and stared at him. "Fallen One?" He laughed, the sound a harsh bark of amusement. "You have no idea. I'm in a generous mood. Leave and I will allow you to live."

"This is my island. I'm the Guardian and protector of these people. You have no chance of entering Mystic Haven. You will die if you attempt to breach The Ward."

The Fallen Angel smiled. "My name is Ash. Ashtar Morana." His voice was gentle, and Caden felt the compulsion. He crossed his arms, immune to that bullshit. He knew that name though. Ash Morana was a Fallen Angel of legendary notoriety.

"Caden Brody." He supplied his own name. "You need to move on, Morana. There is nothing for you in Mystic Haven."

"Ah, you see, that is where you are wrong, Brody." The Fallen Angel shrugged eloquently. "A slaveling that I was particularly attached to, a thousand years ago, has found refuge on your island. She is mine, and I want her back."

"A slaveling?" Caden's voice carried his disgust. "Life lesson, Morana. We don't always get what we want." Caden stared hard eyed at the Fallen Angel. "There is no one on my island with your mark, and even if there were, there is no chance I'd hand them over to you. Move on."

Ash Morana laughed. "Brody, your reputation precedes you, and I see that it's correct. You are a hard man." He tilted his head and smiled at the cop. "But I am the Ashes of Death, Fae. Shall we dance?"

Caden spun to avoid the blast of energy that accompanied Ash's words. It burned past him, flashing white hot in the grey of the sky. There was no hesitation in Caden's response. The energy blast he sent hurling toward the Fallen Angel was quickly followed by two more. They soared high in the skies over Mystic Haven, a being filled with evil and one dedicated to keeping evil from touching the lives of those who called Mystic Haven home.

The fight was savage and merciless, brilliant flashes of tainted angelic power and Fae energy colliding and exploding in the towering clouds. The crash of two bodies slamming into each other, throwing punches backed by superhuman power.

The fighters broke apart, breathing heavily, blood dripped, and Ash wiped the back of his hand across his lip. "There is more to you than a simple Fae." He watched the superhuman through hardened eyes, as he wiped another bloody drip from his mouth. "It's as good a day as any for you to die, Cop. I will enjoy plundering this island that you protect. Do you have family? A wife? I'll make sure I add her to my personal collection."

Caden studied him, silently weighing the next round. His ribs had taken the full force of that tainted angel power along with more than one rock hard punch. He was hurting, but there was no way in hell this creature was getting on his island. No chance. He drew a careful breath, and threw a punch backed with the power of the Guardian. There were no rules for this fight, no holds barred, no quarter asked or given. This was a brutal bloody battle, fought with fists, superhuman powers and the grim determination to win.

They battered each other. Punch after punch. Superhuman powers smashing into hard bodies. Blocks thrown up as one or the other dodged an attack or reeled from the undiluted power that slammed into them.

Caden saw his opening and took it, hammering blow after blow into Ash. The Fallen Angel faltered and Caden pressed his advantage, determined to end this. He threw a punch aimed for Ash's jaw and the burning agony of an Angelfire blade entered his chest. He gasped. His eyes met the Fallen Angel's who smirked. "Ashes of Death." The being whispered and shoved Caden back.

He was falling, and there wasn't a thing he could do about it. He struggled to fill his lungs with air, hearing the wheeze as the last of his breath left him, blood trickling from his lips as the wind rushed around him.

Chapter Fifty-One

EARTH DIMENSION THREE
Mystic Haven, B.C., Canada

EVEN FLYING AT IMPOSSIBLE speeds that only The Royal Fae Trium could attain, they did not get there fast enough. Baylen saw the Guardian fall as Striker's voice shouted over their mind link.

"Caden's down!"

Jett saw Caden falling, but he also saw that there was not just one enemy. *What the hell could take a Guardian out of the skies* "Baylen, Striker, we have targets!"

"Striker!" Baylen's voice, loud over the mind link, as he motioned towards the falling Guardian.

"On it." The Healer banked, arrowing toward Caden.

A lone man with black wings was pointing to The Ward and Jett suddenly had a bad feeling. *Shit!* "That's Ash Morana. That bastard is the head of the biggest superhuman crime syndicate on the planet." *What the hell was he doing here?*

Baylen studied the group of men he saw behind Morana and a sick feeling grew in his gut. A dragon, several fallen angels, and at least one vampire. *Fuck!* Why the hell hadn't his intelligence force seen this coming? They should have had warning! Cursing, he blasted out a mind link to all the Fae. *"Prepare to evacuate! Fae warriors! Protect The Ward. If it comes down, fight with everything you have! Protect Mystic Haven!"*

Chapter Fifty-Two

EARTH DIMENSION THREE
Mystic Haven, B.C., Canada

"CADEN." Striker reached out through a mind link as he dove. His arms at his side, his wings held tightly to his body, he'd wrapped himself in Fae energy to shield from the heat and the friction as he streaked across the sky trying his damnedest to reach the man free falling towards the Earth. Grimly, he went over the facts in his mind. There was a strange blue glow trailing Caden. He knew only one thing that could do that. An Angelfire blade. The longer it remained embedded in Caden's chest the more damage it did. *"Caden."*

Chapter Fifty-Three

EARTH DIMENSION THREE
Mystic Haven, B.C., Canada

BAYLEN FLEW STRAIGHT for the bastard who seemed to think he was king of shit hill. *Let's see how he and his band of assholes deal with the Fae Trium.* The wind blew Baylen's long dark hair back, revealing the primal Fae that he was.

Ash turned toward him, his eyebrow lifting as he saw a Fae whose genetics were pristine. As if he was the first Fae who'd ever existed. As if thousands upon thousands of years of evolution had not occurred. Power was in every breath of this Fae. Ash narrowed his eyes. No matter what else happened in this battle, he needed to get a sample of this Fae's blood.

Baylen hovered in the air. "These are my lands. These people are mine. Leave."

Ash let a smile lift one corner of his mouth, calculation entered his eyes, and he started to spin his lies.

Baylen's gaze was ice cold. "There is not one gods-damned thing you have to say that I want to hear." He sent a blast of Fae energy so powerful that the Fallen Angel was thrown backwards. He crashed through his men, scattering them as they fell.

The sky was a dangerous place to fight even when you had wings. Laying down blast after blast, on Ash's crew Baylen had no mercy. They were in his territory now. Fucking bastards were going down.

Morana recovered from the fall and rose, his wings smoking. Several of his men were falling from the sky, burned beyond recognition.

Baylen did not fucking care. "Get the fuck away from Mystic Haven or we will destroy you."

Ash shook out his wings, and with a nod, his remaining men surged forward. "As I told Caden Brody, it is a good day for you to die, Fae."

Chapter Fifty-Four

"BRACE, CADEN. I'M COMING in fast." Striker spoke calmly even though what he was going to have to do was incredibly dangerous. *"That's an Angelfire blade. I'm going to have to remove it as soon as I have you and push a helluva lot of Fae healing energy into you to cauterize the wound. Don't fight me."*

Chapter Fifty-Five

EARTH DIMENSION THREE
Mystic Haven, B.C., Canada

JETT BLASTED A VAMPIRE, burning a hole right through the place where the bastard's heart would have been. Jett wasn't sympathetic. If you were foolish enough to come after their island, you had no one to blame for your demise but yourself. Or— His eyes landed on Ash who was engaged in a violent battle with Baylen. *Or really bad leadership.* Why the hell was Morana doing this shit? This wasn't adding up.

Chapter Fifty-Six

EARTH DIMENSION THREE
Mystic Haven, B.C., Canada

BAYLEN FIRED A GOLDEN blast of Fae energy direct-ly into the body of the Fallen Angel he was fighting, and the being growled and slammed tainted Angelic power in-to his chest. He cursed and slugged the bastard in the stom-ach. They were too close. His punch didn't have enough power. He shoved the black winged angel back, swiped the back of his hand over his bleeding lip, and drew Fae energy from the sunlight.

Chapter Fifty-Seven

EARTH DIMENSION THREE
Mystic Haven, B.C., Canada

STRIKER REACHED OUT his arms closing around Caden, as he beat his wings hard fighting the drag *"I have to get that blade out!"*

"Acknowledged." Caden's mental voice was a whisper of pain. *"We're falling too fast."*

Striker grinned wryly. *Count on the Cop to notice their speed, even when he was hurt. "You can't ticket me for speeding. I'm trying to save your damn life."*

Chapter Fifty-Eight

EARTH DIMENSION THREE
Mystic Haven, B.C., Canada

"LOOK OUT!" BAYLEN YELLED as a dragon swooped past him heading directly toward Jett.

Jett blasted the dragon shifter and kept blasting until the great beast roared in rage. Swearing, Jett soared higher in the air dodging through the clouds, trying to avoid the fire being blasted at him, and find the right angle for a killing blast of Fae energy to take this dragon out. A stream of fire swept toward him, and he wrapped his wings around himself, for once glad for the strange characteristics of the Royal Protector's wings. He still got singed, but it could have been a hell of a lot worse. In an instant, the dragon was on him, and he found himself staring down a maw of sharp deadly teeth. He delivered a hard punch to the sensitive skin of the monster's snout, even as he threw another volley of Fae energy with his other hand. The Dragon roared and clamped down on his arm. Jett shouted in agony as the Dragon bit through flesh, tendons, and bone, before shaking him hard.

But the dragon had been seriously injured in the battle and he faltered, his huge body turning slowly as he began an uncontrolled tumble out of the sky.

Swearing Jett began to fire round after round of Fae energy at the beast's soft underbelly, his shots going wild as they plummeted from the sky.

The hell he would die like this! He began hammering punches into the dragon's face. "Open up you asshole! Open. Up!"

They somersaulted again before the dragon heaved a mighty sigh, his mouth falling open as his dying breath rushed out of him.

Cursing, beating his wings, and drawing on the power of the Trium, Jett twisted, feeling the flesh on his arm tear as he managed to free himself from the dagger sharp teeth. Blood flowing, he shot up into the air.

Out of danger, he hovered, breathing hard and staring down at the falling dragon as it slammed into The Ward and instantly incinerated. Glancing at his arm he could see bone through the mangled flesh, there was no doubt that it was broken. He grimly brought the arm against his chest, fighting to contain the shout of pain that forced its way out of his throat. Panting, he poured as much healing energy into his arm as he could, but it was barely enough to stop the bleeding. *"Striker."*

Chapter Fifty-Nine

IGNORING THE FACT THAT they were free falling through the air, Striker wrapped his hand around the glowing blade. *"One."* He began to shove pure Fae power into the polluted blade even as he heard Jett's voice in his mind.

"Get into the Sunlight, Jett. That's a bad break." He began to funnel another path of powerful healing energy through the Trium bond, and straight into Jett.

"Two." The blade began to heat in his hand cauterizing the wound. Caden arched against the pain.

Chapter Sixty

EARTH DIMENSION THREE
Mystic Haven, B.C., Canada

JETT FLEW HIGHER, BREAKING through the clouds into the early morning sunlight. Power flowed through him, the sun's energy wielded by a Royal healer. Before his eyes, the bone knit itself together and his flesh closed. *"Thanks."* He turned to go back to the battle, aware that Striker was still in a desperate battle of his own to save the Fae Guardian.

Chapter Sixty-One

EARTH DIMENSION THREE
Mystic Haven, B.C., Canada

"THREE!" Striker yanked the blade out of Caden's chest, throwing it across the sky and slamming a hard burst of Fae energy into it. The deadly blade exploded into a mist of steel dust carried away by the wind.

Chapter Sixty-Two

EARTH DIMENSION THREE
Mystic Haven, B.C., Canada

JETT DOVE BACK INTO the battle, the power of the Trium flowing through his body. It was a godsdamned free for all. They could not afford to lose this fight.

Chapter Sixty-Three

EARTH DIMENSION THREE
Mystic Haven, B.C., Canada

ALIORA RUSHED OUT OF her house and onto her private beach, when the island alarms began to blare. She knew what that meant. They wanted everyone to evacuate to the emergency caves. Caden had told her all about the emergency system they had in place when she first arrived on the island.

Staring up at the sky, she could see The Fae Ward was in trouble. The normally shimmering gold energy creature was showing deep reds. Deep reds in any Ward were a bad thing.

But what was frightening to her was that away from the main battle, she could see several non-corporeal beings attacking The Ward. She was Fae enough to have heard the Fae king's call, but she also understood that even he did not know of the other beings. She paced the small strip of beach in front of her home. She had to do something! Going to hide with all the other vulnerable citizens was not an option.

Taking a deep breath, Aliora called an air current to her and stepped onto it, gliding up until she could get a better view of the unseen beings attacking The Ward. She almost fell off the current when she saw that they were Fallen Angels in their non-corporeal state. Oh, this was not good. Quickly, she reversed the glide, and once she was safely on the beach again, she began to build a Ward.

Chapter Sixty-Four

EARTH DIMENSION THREE
Mystic Haven, B.C., Canada

SHIRINA TOOK A PAN of chocolate chip cookies from the oven, her mouth watering at the delicious aroma, when the piercing sound of alarms filled the room. She set the pan on the stovetop, slammed the oven closed and ran into her home office. "Luna, show me what is happening out there!"

A clear pale blue holo-screen opened. Shirina began to swipe through the information streaming in. The Ward was under attack!

The Fae king's voice filled the common Fae mind link. *"Prepare to evacuate! Fae warriors! Protect The Ward. If it comes down, fight with everything you have! Protect Mystic Haven!"*

Chapter Sixty-Five

EARTH DIMENSION THREE
Mystic Haven, B.C., Canada

STRIKER GRIMLY PUSHED more and more Fae heal-
ing energy into the Guardian as he finally managed to bring
them to a full stop in mid-air. He directed more healing energy to where it was needed most and heard Caden gasp.
Noticing the stripes appearing on Caden's skin, and the
dangerous claws that had emerged from his fingers, he sent
a mind link to the halfling Guardian. *"Caden, I know this
has got to hurt like a bitch. Don't shift on me, your tiger
would not like falling from this height."*

A rough pain-filled laugh in his mind. *"Tiger's under
control. Just get this done."*

Chapter Sixty-Six

EARTH DIMENSION THREE
Mystic Haven, B.C., Canada

"LUNA, START ROSIE. Feed all the information to her computers!" Shirina quickly deactivated the protection Ward from her hidden safe and grabbed a small high-tech blaster. A wave of her hand reactivated the Ward. She strapped the blaster to her hip and ran outside. Rosie was parked, its engine running, outside the door.

"Woof"

She looked around and saw her three large dogs. "Not this time. It's too dangerous. Protect the house." She climbed into Rosie. "Luna, get me as close on the ground, to that fight as you can. I'm going to need to help The Ward." She pulled out onto the road and the windscreen filled with information from the battle taking place in the skies over this sanctuary island. "Luna, please drive while I sort out what is going on."

"Affirmative. Oven shut off. GPS shows the best access is Mount Faeir. Coordinates locked in. Navigating to the target."

"Thank you, Luna. I forgot about the oven. Map view of the battle please. Launch drone." The windshield became a glowing green map as a panel in the van's roof slid back and a high-tech drone arrowed up into the sky and was gone in the blink of an eye. "Mark the Royal Trium with Purple. Mark the attackers with black."

Three purple lights appeared.

"Guardian Brody has been injured and is being attended midair by the Royal Healer."

A golden light appeared by one of the purple lights.

"How bad is it?" Shirina could not help but ask, her healer's heart aching to help.

"Difficult to assess fully. There's a lot of Fae healing energy in the air."

Shirina swallowed. *Bad then.* She forced her focus back to the map as black lights began to fill the screen. "There are so many." Shirina whispered.

"Affirmative."

"Can you identify the enemy, without losing the drone?"

"Affirmative. Fallen Angels, Dragons, Vampires."

Shirina paused in mid swipe. "Superhumans?" She shook her head and got back to work sending information to other Sanctuary cities and boroughs on the mainland.

Chapter Sixty-Seven

GOLDEN ENERGY FILLED sparkles and iridescent colors flowed from Aliora's fingers and she began to weave Fae energy as sea water lapped at her toes. Each weave layering in color, power, and consciousness.

As she worked, mist began to rise around her. The mist grew and grew sweeping out across the ocean, a shimmering iridescent vapor. Neon blue began to light up the ocean wherever the mist contacted the water, and still it grew.

"You are a sentient being, you have free will, and you have the ability to learn."

The mist swirled around her.

"You are unique, and powerful, and a protector of good."

The newly created Mist Ward sent her feelings of happiness and love. Aliora smiled and returned the feelings. A pause and the Mist Ward whispered into Aliora's mind. *"Danger."*

"Yes."

"There is one like me, but... different. It fights evil. I must help."

"Thank you."

The Mist Ward began to rise, higher and higher, spreading across the sky. Aliora watched, worried about how The Ward would react to this new entity, the Mist Ward.

Chapter Sixty-Eight

EARTH DIMENSION THREE
Mystic Haven, B.C., Canada

SHIRINA MONITORED THE battle and The Ward when a new light appeared on the transparent computer screen. "What is that, Luna?"

"The birth of an unknown Ward."

"What?" Shirina sat straight up.

"It is growing exponentially." The light on the screen was blinking faster and faster.

"Are you sure it's a Ward?"

"Affirmative."

"A Fae Ward?"

"Negative... and positive. There is a Fae energy signature. Other energy signatures are also present."

"Is it a danger to The Ward?"

"Unknown."

"We need more information! Track its origin. Get me to where that Ward started!"

The van started driving. "Unknown Ward is rising toward The Ward."

"Faster Rosie. We need to get to whoever created that Ward!"

"Engaging hover-hypersonic drive." Luna replied. "Rosie is not able to perform sentient actions."

"Sorry, Luna. I know that Rosie is not self aware like you are."

"Acknowledged. The Unknown Ward has made contact with The Ward. Shields engaged."

Chapter Sixty-Nine

EARTH DIMENSION THREE
Mystic Haven, B.C., Canada

SHIMMERING GOLD AND iridescent colors layered against The Ward and Aliora held her breath. A flash of light and power, and the invisible non-corporeal Fallen Angels became corporeal. A blaze of lightning and the boom of thunder filled the air. The Fallen Angels who had been attacking The Ward, disintegrated into ashes. Aliora released her breath, the Mist Ward had been accepted.

Chapter Seventy

EARTH DIMENSION THREE
Mystic Haven, B.C., Canada

A MOVEMENT CAUGHT JETT'S eye and he saw three Fallen Angels appear out of thin air and make a run for the island. Before his eyes, the three superhumans slammed into The Ward. Thunder roared, and ashes drifted away on a slight breeze.

He shook his head and looked at Baylen. The Fae king shrugged, his eyes hard. There was no way for evil to cross The Ward.

Chapter Seventy-One

EARTH DIMENSION THREE
Mystic Haven, B.C., Canada

"DRONE, SHOW ME THE Ward!" Shirina shouted as she swiped through screens, touching and moving different lights and images. A loud crash of thunder shook the van as lightning flashed. "Report!"

The screen changed and Shirina could see The Ward hovering in the air under the battle, against it lay a shimmering iridescent layer that she had never seen before. "What the hell?"

"Language." Luna responded. "The Ward has joined with the unknown Ward. Hidden targets revealed. Targets eliminated."

"Hidden targets? Oh, my Ancients. What in the universe is going on?" Shirina shook her head and restarted the video. "How is that even possible?"

"Unknown. We have reached our destination." The pink van came to a stop by a small house on a remote section of beach.

Chapter Seventy-Two

EARTH DIMENSION THREE
Mystic Haven, B.C., Canada

"CADEN. I'M ALMOST FINISHED. I need to get you to the hospital."

Thunder roared and lightning lit up the air. The Ward. Striker cursed.

"No hospital." Caden's agonized mind link came through loud and clear. *"I need to get back into that battle."*

Striker poured more healing energy into him. *"You need time and more healing, Caden."* The immense power of the Guardian rose steadily, and he could feel it pushing at him.

"We cannot lose the Trium. I need to get back in there."

Striker concentrated on healing as much of the wound as he could. This was field surgery at best, Caden's injuries too severe to be fully healed in this setting. He did the best he could before he cut off the flow of healing energy, knowing he could not stop the Guardian from going back into battle. *"Caden, I don't like this, but you are a Guardian. I will treat you as part of the Trium, healing power will continue to flow into you while you fight."*

Caden drew a deep breath and shot up and back toward the battle at a speed that should not have been attainable. Striker rushed to catch up.

Chapter Seventy-Three

EARTH DIMENSION THREE
Mystic Haven, B.C., Canada

SHIRINA GOT OUT AND followed the path that led to the beach. She saw a woman sitting in the sand watching the battle in the skies. "Hello."

The woman turned to her, and she was unlike anyone Shirina had ever seen. From her long multihued copper hair to her unusual aquamarine and bronze eyes. Her energy signature— what in the world was she? "I'm Shirina Sítheach. I'm the Fae Ward Expert.

Aliora studied the woman before her. Long platinum hair, purple eyes, the tell-tale trademarks of a Fae Healer. "Hello, I'm Aliora Aurelius. My grandfather's mentioned you."

"Who's your grandfather?"

"Edge de Fae."

Shirina laughed. "Don't believe his stories."

Aliora laughed. "He said you would say that. What can I do for you, Shirina?"

"Did you create that Ward?"

Ali bit her lip. "Oh. You've seen it? I saw the incorporeal beings that were attacking The Ward. It needed help so I created the Mist Ward."

Shirina blinked, staring at the woman in open astonishment. "What are you? How did you create a Ward of that power by yourself?"

"I'm a superhuman, like you. Caden invited me to Mystic Haven a few years ago. He said there was darkness, so he was bringing the light."

Shirina tilted her head. "Light. I think I understand. Welcome to Mystic Haven, Light bearer."

"You smell like chocolate chip cookies."

Shirina blinked. "Uh, I was baking cookies when the emergency happened."

Aliora nodded, "That makes sense. I must try to find a recipe. I think I would like to bake."

Arching an eyebrow, Shirina waited.

Finally, Aliora sighed. "Yes, I can make Wards. They are not like The Ward that protects the island. I've never made one as big as this before. But isn't she beautiful?"

She? Shirina looked up into the sky and saw the iridescent Mist Ward working alongside The Ward to incinerate any of the enemy foolish enough to attempt to breach them. "Your Ward is female?"

Aliora tilted her head to the side, her eyebrows coming together. "Well... The Ward is male, so I created a female entity to balance him."

Shirina tilted her head. "It is? Wait. Wards don't have gender."

Aliora stared at the slender female in front of her. "Perhaps you should ask The Ward, next time you visit it."

Shirina started to laugh.

Chapter Seventy-Four

EARTH DIMENSION THREE
Mystic Haven, B.C., Canada

BAYLEN SENT AN EXPLOSION of energy soaring toward Ash followed by rapid fire blasts. Ash faltered, and Baylen pressed his advantage only to be caught by surprise as Morana suddenly flew directly at him.

They slammed into each other. Baylen grabbed the bastard by the throat and poured molten supercharged Fae energy directly into him.

The Fallen Angel shouted in agonized fury and slammed a hand against the Fae's chest. The power of his blow would have killed a lesser superhuman. Growling, infuriated by the pain of the burning energy pouring into him, he struck a second time.

Baylen held grimly to the son of a bitch, ignoring the pain radiating from the powerful blows. A sharp gasp and a curse escaped him as the Fallen Angel, thrust a dagger into his back and twisted it. *Fucking bastard!* He could feel numbness spreading through his arm, and cursing, he picked up the whoreson and hurled him into the trio of Fallen angels that were flying to Morana's rescue.

Reaching back, he yanked the knife from his back and stood his ground, his teeth bared, bloody dagger in hand, daring that fucker to come at him again.

Ash Morana righted himself, ruthlessly throttling his rage. He was going to kill the Fae king. Movement caught his attention and he saw the Guardian approaching.

He took a deep breath. Not today, however. He'd found out what he needed to know. He looked at the three Fallen Angels, all that remained of the team he'd gathered for this mission. It was time to retreat. He turned, a smirk on his lips and faced the Fae who'd come close to killing him. "We shall dance again, Baylen Knight." With a burst of angelic power, he threw open a vortex, and an instant later, they were gone.

Chapter Seventy-Five

EARTH DIMENSION THREE
Mystic Haven, B.C., Canada

SWEARING AND CURSING a blue streak, Baylen turned to Caden. "You're looking a little pale."

"What happened with The Ward?"

Baylen shook his head. "I have no fucking idea."

They turned to face The Ward. "That's not right." Caden said as he flew closer. "The Ward has never had that iridescent shimmer."

"The enemy is no longer in the area. We will remain on alert."

"We? What happened to you?"

The Ward was silent. Growing concerned, Caden mind linked Shirina. *"What's happened to The Ward?"*

"You're never going to believe this Caden."

"Try me."

"Aliora happened."

"Aliora?" Caden paused. *"Aliora?"* he asked again, just before he faltered.

Striker grabbed him. "Time for us to go to the hospital."

Chapter Seventy-Six

EARTH DIMENSION THREE
Mystic Haven, B.C., Canada

ASH LANDED ON THE HIGH tower of his castle fortress in Europe, and stalked through the door, his wings disappearing as he began to snap out orders to the man who was waiting. He ignored the warriors limping in after him. "Get a healer, run me a bath and bring a good meal. Make sure my men are seen too."

"It did not go as expected, Sir?"

"There were some unexpected issues but overall, it went the way I expected it to. As I said when we left, it was a long shot but worth a try. Having control of Mystic Haven would have made what is coming, much easier. Notify my generals that we will proceed with the plan. I also want all the intel on Mystic Haven updated. That Guardian is a powerhouse. But so is the Fae king."

The man turned to the hovering servants and dispatched them to the tasks he'd already known would be assigned.

"I should have been able to take the Guardian down, and every one of those Fae." Ash began to remove his fighting leathers. "The information we have about the ancient Wards is incorrect. Get that updated." He pulled a small vial containing the Fae king's blood from his pocket. "Take this directly to my lab. I want a full analysis."

Chapter Seventy-Seven

EARTH DIMENSION THREE
Mystic Haven, B.C., Canada

IT HAD BEEN A WEEK since Caden had been released from the hospital and he was ready to tear his hair out. His kids were bouncing all over the emotional scale, happy he was home one minute, fighting with their siblings the next, or crying and clinging to him when it was time to go to school.

Every night, one by one they trickled into his bed. By morning they were all exhausted because, while his bed was king sized, it was never meant to hold seven restless wiggly little bodies and one still recovering adult. He had no idea how many times he woke up with Dakota's feet in his ribs. His still very sore ribs, and every time he turned around Pandora was trying to heal him and wearing herself out in the process.

Marisol and Macen were running ragged between all their siblings trying to make them feel better. He knew that it was the Pixie way to try to heal emotions, just as he knew it was Pandora's Fae nature that was driven to heal his injuries, but there was no way in hell they could go on like this.

This morning he'd had to wade into the middle of a vicious fight with a shifted bear cub and two shifted tiger cubs while his coyote toddler sat in her human form on the sidelines howling her little head off.

No more.

While the kids were at school, except for Dakota, he began to load up his extended cab pickup truck. He used his telekinesis to move his mattress into the box of his truck. Then he sent out a parade of blankets and pillows while he carried a cooler and handed Dakota her favorite stuffy. He buckled his youngest daughter into her car seat and gave her a sippy cup filled with milk as the school bus came down the long driveway.

It was a sullen group of Brody children who exited the bus. He shook his head and told the kids to get into the truck. Ben had a mutinous look on his face and Caden wasn't having it, he folded his arms across his chest and stood right in Ben's path. "Get in the truck, Ben."

Once all the kids were seat belted into the rear and front seats, he handed out sandwiches and juice boxes. Climbing into the driver's seat he started the truck and headed out on the bare dirt trail that led across his property. Fifteen minutes later he parked on the top of a huge hill and got out, watching as his horde of children spilled from the vehicle. The kids all grouped together silently watching him and waiting for direction. *Well, hell. This was not his wild bunch of hellions.* He sighed. Normally, they would've been running all over the place and exploring as soon as their little feet hit the ground. "You can do whatever you want, just don't wander off too far. And Macen..." He gave his youngest son a look. "Stay out of the trees." The kids just looked at him. *Okay...* He turned, grabbed a large blanket, and using his telekinesis, spread it out on the ground and floated the cooler over to the middle of it. "We're going to spend the night out here. Go and play for a while then we'll have supper." The kids didn't move.

He frowned, shoving a hand through his overlong hair. *Gods he needed a haircut.* He decided that his ribs had healed enough to handle a shift. Without a word he shifted into his tiger and crouched down to growl playfully at his kids. They looked at each other wide-eyed and he chuffed, stalking closer.

Dakota blinked and laughed, her little hands clapping and suddenly the rest of the kids ran laughing and shrieking to evade him.

Hours later, as the slender crescent moon rose, he helped the kids climb into the box of the pickup truck and get comfortable with pillows and blankets. The stars spread out in a breathtaking display of sheer unearthly beauty. As they lay there, he told them the story of his ancestors who had braved the dangers of the unknown to make their way to Earth. The kids had so many questions. He answered what he could and suggested that they visit some of the ancient Fae this summer and find out more about that journey. The kids were enthusiastically excited about that idea, and he smiled.

That was better.

Suddenly, the tension that seemed to fill them all, broke. They spent the rest of the night looking at the stars, talking about what had happened, and making plans for the rest of the summer. Plans that included a lot of coming out here to look at the stars.

Healing took time, and he was determined that his family would take that time together to heal. Under the starry sky seemed like the perfect place to do it.

Chapter Seventy-Eight

EARTH DIMENSION THREE
Mystic Haven, B.C., Canada

ASTERINE SKYFIRE WALKED into the police station and glanced around. This was not something she looked forward to. Officer Drake saw her and came over. "How are you, Commander Skyfire? Is there something I can help you with?"

She shook her head, her red hair tumbling around her shoulders. "I need to speak to Caden. It's important."

Josef Drake looked at the renowned ancient Fae for a moment. "Come this way." He led her to an office down the hall and knocked on the door before opening it and ducking his head inside. "Caden. Commander Skyfire is here to see you."

Caden turned from where he was standing, his eyebrow raising. "The Commander Skyfire?"

Josef nodded.

"Send her in."

Josef stepped back and Asterine stepped in, the door closing behind her. Caden smiled. "Welcome Commander, what can I do for you? Would you like a coffee?" He gestured to his coffee station set up on a side table along the wall. When she nodded, he poured the coffee and brought the filled cups over to his desk. "Please, have a seat."

Asterine sat down and took the cup Caden offered her. She took a sip and set it on the desk. "Call me Asterine. Was it Ash Morana that attacked a few weeks ago?"

Caden nodded, his eyes sharp. "You know of him?"

"I—" she hesitated. "I knew Ash."

Caden set down his coffee. "How?"

"The asshole calls me his 'pet.'"

"He did mention a slave."

Asterine sighed. "Caden, I met him shortly after the Fae arrived on earth. I was in a bad place, like many of us were. Grieving, and struggling to come to terms with what had happened to us. I left the Fae settlement and traveled through some human cities. I met Ash. I'm embarrassed to admit this, but I fell for his nice guy routine. He has a castle in Europe. At the time, it was a new castle. He invited me to visit him there and I went. Turns out that he was more interested in sharing me for profit than having a relationship with me."

Caden swore. "I'm sorry Asterine. That is a terrible thing to experience."

Asterine nodded and picked up her coffee. She took a sip before setting it down again. "It was a terrible experience, but I survived, and I rebuilt my life. I won't allow him to control me again."

"You feel he will make a serious attempt to take you again, even after he was defeated? I don't believe he can get past The Ward."

"From what I observed of that battle, he has no chance to get past The Ward, but for a being like Ash, that is a challenge he won't be able to resist. He'll be back."

"That's my assessment too." Caden leaned back in his chair, his mind racing. "I believe the safest place for you right now is—"

Asterine was already shaking her head. "Right here in Mystic Haven. At this point he can't get past our Wards. Believe me, I'll have so many damn ancient warriors camping out at my place every night, vying to protect me, that I'll probably want to kill them all."

Caden laughed. "You're one of the Fae's most celebrated heroes, Asterine. I've heard what you did to save our people in the Tuatha war."

Asterine shrugged. "I was doing my job."

Caden nodded, understanding her response. "You're still the only one who ever flew a Star Talon, Red Star." He deliberately used her call sign. "You're the one who had the courage to disobey the king and test a highly experimental technology that made the exodus from the Tuatha Star System possible. You're the one who flew the Fae through uncharted space to reach Earth."

"Nerys deserves the full credit for that technology, and she flew that mission with me." A grin curved her lips. "I can tell you that Ryder was not too pleased with us."

Caden laughed, glad to see the shadows leaving her eyes. "I can imagine."

"I can give you information on Ash. Maybe it will help."

"Thank you, Asterine. Would you be willing to join our task force working on the Ash Morana problem?"

"Yes. I want to take that bastard down."

Chapter Seventy-Nine

ASTERINE STEPPED OUT of the Police Station and took a deep breath. She was glad she'd talked to Caden, but she hated discussing her past. It still drove her crazy that she'd fallen for that asshole's lies. *She'd been a damned warrior for creator's sake! You didn't become an elite fighter pilot without learning how to fight. How could she have been so stupid?*

Movement by a large tree caught her eye and she stiffened. A man with short dark hair, wearing a perfectly fitted black suit stepped out onto the sidewalk. *Adler Llywelyn.* The sexiest man she'd ever met. Well, deity actually.

"Hello, Asterine"

"Adler. What are you doing here?" She kept a tight hold of her glamour as she walked up to him.

His dark eyes searched hers as he stepped closer and opened his arms to her. She stepped in and he pulled her into a hug, holding her tightly. She closed her eyes and held onto him just as hard. *Creators, he smelled good.* She was the one who stepped back first. Not because she wanted to, but because she knew he would hold her as long as she needed, no matter how long that was.

"I heard that Morana attempted to breach Mystic Haven's defenses." His eyes burned with fury, his voice was dangerously low, and the things it did to her should not be legal.

"Yeah. I was just talking to Caden about the bastard. He—Ash said he was looking for his slaveling." *Creators, she hated that word. Hated that he'd called her that with a tone of possessive affection.*

"I promise you that he will never get his hands on you again, Star." His gaze held hers—a promise that felt sacred. He wrapped his arm around her shoulders. "Walk with me, Mo cheann chothaímid."

My cherished one. Asterine swallowed the lump in her throat and nodded, her whole body relaxing. *This.* She'd needed this. She'd needed time with the one who'd seen the worst and still saw her value. The one who'd always made her feel safe.

Chapter Eighty

EARTH DIMENSION THREE
Mystic Haven, B.C., Canada

ASH STOOD ON THE TOWER roof, leaning against the parapet as he surveyed the land that spread for miles in all directions. The sun was about to rise, and he was not eager to greet this new day. A few weeks ago, he'd gone into battle with clear goals and the knowledge that he would most likely not take Mystic Haven.

What had he learned? That he needed to get eyes on that island. That truth was clearer now than it had ever been.

The sun began to rise, and he stood watching the amazing color display playing across the sky. It was a thing of beauty. He'd seen thousands upon thousands of sunrises on many different worlds, and they never ceased to amaze him. It could, of course, be broken down into scientific facts. The planet's rotation, molecules in the atmosphere causing light to scatter, and clouds catching the rays of the sun and reflecting this light to the ground. Those facts took nothing away from the sheer magnificence of the dawn. Eliana had once called him a monster, and she was right, but even a being as terrible as he could appreciate beauty.

His thoughts turned to Eliana, and it fed the flames of his anger. If she had listened to him the multiverse would have been so much better off. He stared broodingly at the sky. She was to blame for so many things. An unkind smile began to slowly spread across his face. Perhaps she should bear the brunt of his displeasure. After all, she had an unhealthy fixation on a certain era of this world. He paused. No, not this Earth. The signature of her presence was barely a trace in this dimension compared with Dimension Two. She was fascinated with Dimension Two's Earth, and he knew the exact timeline of that fascination. He opened a vortex and stepped into it, changing his clothing to suit the fifth century.

Chapter Eighty-One

EARTH DIMENSION TWO
Caerleon, South Wales
Fifth Century

ASH STEPPED OUT OF the vortex in the second dimension of Earth, fifth century, at Caerleon, South Wales, and before him stood the great Camelot. Castle of King Arthur and his legendary Knights of the Round Table. Eliana's obsession.

He moved easily through the people, his clothing and the fine sword hanging at his side, proclaiming him to be a nobleman. Their thoughts filtered through his mind, and he began to search for references to Eliana and who she met with when she came here. It did not take long to find who he was looking for. There was a tournament yesterday and the winner's name was on everyone's mind. Dagger Marrok, King Arthur's bodyguard. He made his way to the training grounds where he could observe this knight. The man was tall with dark hair and unusual amber eyes. He was sparring with a partner and did not wear armor. His muscles flexed as he moved, and it was apparent he was a man of great strength. Ash considered if Eliana had slept with him yet, and immediately dismissed the thought when he read the man's mind and saw that it was occupied with his wife and sons. Ash stored their images as he began to see the possibilities. He dug a little deeper into the man's thoughts and saw his memories of Eliana. Ash smirked. The man was definitely attracted to her, but he also saw her as some kind of princess. A gentle and kind woman that needed his protection. He went deeper, looking at the man's motives and his dreams. What he found annoyed him. Marrok had only good intentions toward 'Princess' Eliana. He followed a strict code of chivalry. He considered himself her champion. Ash wanted to throw up. He started sorting through the man's dreams, and that's when he found it. An erotic dream of the lovely princess Eliana. A dream that filled Marrok with agonizing guilt. Ash smirked and wondered what this Marrok would think if he knew who Eliana really was. Would it shock him if he knew that Ash had fucked her? He smiled. The plan was evolving. He left Marrok to his training and went to seek out Marrok's wife, Lady Aalis. He found her in the garden of Marrok's fortress, complaining bitterly to her maid about Marrok's lack of wealth. Ash's eyebrow rose and he glanced around at the beautiful fortress. The building had every amenity of its time. The woman's clothes were finely made, and she looked healthy. Yet she complained. Ah a woman after his own heart. A woman he could manipulate into doing his bidding, and all for a few coins. There was a name for women like her. His eyes drifted over her slender figure and his cock hardened.

Chapter Eighty-Two

NEPHARA, DIMENSION 9,700,241
Earth Date: Present Time

WITH A GRIN ASH RETURNED to the vortex and stepped out into a time and dimension far removed from the one he had been in. The planet's name was Nephara and here he had built a private fortress. It was the place he came to plan. Everything about this place could be called decadent. From the naked servants of all genders that served his every need, to the finest of foods, lavish furnishings and every other want he could have. Even the underground labs and holding cells were the best that could be built.

He walked into the marble and gold building and was immediately greeted by his servants. "Hello, Rome. Hello, Lavender." His eyes drifted over the muscular silver haired man, a dangerous hardened warrior, and the dainty woman with long pink hair who he knew to be gentle and kind. They were opposites and he found it amusing that his housekeeper had put them on duty at the same time. Another time he might have been interested in the why of that, but now he had work to do.

"Follow me." He led the way to his office on the top floor. The room was huge, with floor to ceiling windows, chandeliers, marble floors, fireplaces, and a bed on a dais at one end of the room. He absentmindedly waved a hand at the two servants. "Rome, fuck Lavender while I work. I find the noise stimulating."

Lips pulling back, teeth bared, Rome fought to contain the fury that swept over him. *That Whoreson.* His fists clenched as he struggled to contain the guttural roar that threatened to erupt. Taking a deep breath, he willed the red that had washed his vision to go away.

Ash watched Rome with interest, and when he heard Lavender gasp he smiled. He hadn't forgotten she was newly married to a man she loved with all her heart. In fact, he'd introduced them. He'd encouraged them. He'd been kind and caring, playing matchmaker until he wanted to throw up.

Now, there was just one other move to make, because he had never forgotten the other piece in this game. He poured himself a Timarian whiskey and sat on the corner of his desk, crossing his feet. Waiting for the perfect moment.

He glanced over at Lavender, his eyes cold. "Is there a problem?" Her tear drenched grey and purple eyes met his, realization and terror flashed across her face. He lifted his eyebrow, and she shook her head. "Proceed."

Rome clenched his hands. "There is a problem." His voice was a low rasp. He kept his face expressionless, willing the ice that was forming in his heart to show in his eyes. *He should have known that Ash would pull this drakshit.* He knew Ash well. Knew the cruel games he played. Knew the bastard delighted in the pain he caused others. If he granted you a favor, there would be a cruel price to pay for it later, and the favor he'd granted Lavender and her husband Relic, would have a steep price. His eyes moved to Lavender, and he wanted to warn her. He swallowed the words that would only cause more harm and silently willed her to hide her pain.

Ah. Was that a crack in the ice that normally encased his top warriors' emotions? Ash smiled. "What is this problem, Rome?"

A low growl filled the air. "I will not take her."

"Why not? She's beautiful. I've seen you watch her. I've seen the look in your eyes. You want her. Consider it a perk of the job. Consider it a bonus. Consider it my way of saying that I am pleased with you."

Rome glared at Ash, his teeth bared. "She's married."

Ash smirked. "Such honor. That has always been your problem, Rome. That was your father's problem too. In fact, it was the problem of your whole species. That's why they died." Ash crossed his arms. "Are you going to reject my kindness, Rome?"

"Kindness?" Rome spat the word from his mouth as if it was poison. "Your kindness is my dishonor. I will not force this woman for your pleasure."

"Then do it for your own pleasure, Rome. Do it so that you can fulfill the promise you made to your father, do it so that your people's bloodline will not die with you. After all, she is your mate. The only woman you can have children with. The only way to fulfill your promise." Ash's words slammed into him with the power of a hypersonic missile.

Rome spun, his arm snapping out in a vicious strike. His fingers curled around Ash's throat and a terrifying growl issued from his chest. "You whoreson! If you were so concerned with me fulfilling my promise, why did you give her to Relic? You knew. You knew who she was to me. You saw it the moment I set eyes on her."

Ash lifted his hand, his power slamming Rome back into the stone wall. "Of course, I saw. I'm the master of this dimension, I know everything that goes on in it. I know every thought. I know every plot. I know every move on this chessboard. I found it amusing to bargain with your father. The fool. It never even occurred to him that I was responsible for your species extinction."

Rome gritted his teeth against the power crushing him, holding him in place. "He knew. He warned me. You are no Creator, Ash Morana. You are not omnipotent, nor are you omniscient. You are limited by the scope of what you are. Eventually, someone will find a way to destroy you."

Ash laughed. "But not you, Rome. Not this day." His eyes moved over the woman pressing herself back against the wall as if she could make herself invisible. "Lavender. Happy with the man I gave you, and yet so unaware of the great love that could have been yours. You were never meant for a place such as this. I wonder if you can live with the choices that are before you. I shall gain great pleasure from observing the results."

Lavender looked from Rome pinned to the wall by Ash's invisible power, and back to the Fallen Angel that she'd never believed the stories about. She'd thought him misunderstood. How could she have been so foolish?

Ash shrugged and sent her a boyish smile. "It's called deception, my dear, and I excel at it."

Lavender swallowed, her hands pressing against the cold stone wall.

"As much as I'm enjoying myself, I have work to do. What I have asked of you both is not much in the grand scheme of things. A few hours of pleasure to inspire my work. Relic would have grown bored with you in a few more weeks, anyways. A man like him is always looking for greener pastures."

Lavender stared down at the floor, the cruelty of his words slicing into her, leaving her heart bleeding.

"Before I killed Rome's father, I promised him that I would release Rome from my service, if he found his mate. You were an unexpected gift from that slave trader. I knew the moment I saw you, that you were Rome's one opportunity to have children, to preserve his people's bloodlines. It's a tedious affair." Ash waved his hand in the air. "I'm not pleased that you're both interfering with my promise to a dead man. After all that I have given you both, you dare to blacken my honor?"

Lavender blinked away tears as she stared at her feet.

Rome's growl echoed through the room. "Stop your games, Morana!"

Ash glanced over at Rome in irritation. "I'm trying to save your life, you ungrateful wretch." He turned back to the woman. "Look at me."

Lavender lifted her eyes to Ash's, terrified by what she saw in them. Death. Power—immense power. She swallowed against the sudden dryness of her throat.

"Your choices are simple, Lavender. You can give a few hours of your time today, allow this man to fornicate with you, and hopefully impregnate you or you can watch him die. Slowly. Painfully."

"Relic?" She whispered, her heart aching, knowing the answer wouldn't be anything good."

"Relic is no longer your concern. I have another match in mind for him. Someone much more suited."

"No!" Rome gritted out, fighting against the boundless force crushing him against the unmovable stone wall. "Do. Not. Trust. His. Words. The price is too great." He groaned as his ribs creaked.

Ash observed Lavender, a cold smile playing across his lips. "The choice is yours."

Creators help me! She screamed silently as a trickle of blood ran from Rome's nose. *Please, Creators! Help me!* Anguish colored her prayer, twisted her features. "P—Please." Lavender's voice was washed in tears. "I—I will do what you ask, Ash. Don't kill him."

"No!" Rome's voice was a harsh exclamation. "I won't be the pawn he uses to destroy you!"

Lavender's eyes rose to meet his. "He has already destroyed me."

"Such melodrama." Ash released Rome and watched him drop to the floor. Watched him as he slowly rose to his feet, using the wall to steady himself. "Rome." He waited for his greatest warrior, and ofttimes the man who executed his enemies with a cold brutality, to meet his eyes. "I will kill her if you fail to mate her."

"Why are you doing this?" The snarl was terrifying, and Ash smiled.

"Honor has no place here, Rome. When you finally break, when you have lost everything, when no hope remains, I will remake you into my weapon. You will be the hammer I wield against the masses that believe The Creators will save them.

"Like Lavender. She called out to 'The Creators' begging them to save her, to save you. Didn't you, my dear?" Ash smiled that charming boyish smile again. "While I might be Fallen, I'm still an Angel, and I can hear the prayers of the desperate. Yet here we are. No one's coming to save you."

Chapter Eighty-Three

THE IN-BETWEEN

RUNE AND ELIANA APPEARED in The In-Between in the exact same moment. The words of the desperate prayer echoing over and over around them.

"Who is that?" Rune flung up a screen with a complex map of the multiverse. Multicolored dots moved across the screen. Angels completing missions.

"It's coming from a planet named Nephara in dimension nine million, seven hundred thousand, two hundred forty-one." Eliana said as with a wave of her hand she zoomed into the coordinates. "Where are the Angels?"

"Not there." Rune glared at the screen.

"How is that possible? There is supposed to be a full host of Angels in every dimension."

Rune pulled up another screen and looked at the hosts of Angels and their assignments. "We are missing the Ethereal Light Warriors Host!"

"Wait." Eliana tapped the screen.

"Inverse mode activated." A male computer voice spoke. Everything that was darkness instantaneously revealed by the light shining through the screen.

"Rune." Eliana's voice was a horrified whisper. The screen was filled with thousands of moving black dots.

"They haven't all fallen. Look, there are three still holding on to the light."

"They are so faded." Eliana's voice broke.

"Faded is not fallen." Rune looked Eliana in the eye. "We will save them. Illuminated Warriors! Darkness Destroyer! Come forth." Two brilliant flashes of light filled The In-Between and two groups of Angels appeared, twelve in each of the specialized Hosts.

"We need immediate eyes on the planet Nephara in dimension nine million, seven hundred thousand, two hundred forty-one. The Ethereal Light Warriors Host has gone dark. Three remain in the light but they are fading. To lose this many means that Ash is heavily involved."

A tall Angel with red hair vanished.

Rune's eyes met the gaze of an Angel with black hair. "Lock on to the prayer echo. Get us the information."

The Angel disappeared and Rune turned to the others. The rest of you, we need to plan these rescues.

Seconds later both Angels returned. "Rune, there are an incredible number of Fallen Angels moving through that dimension. It's become a stronghold." The red-haired Angel spoke. "We are going to need an army to take that dimension back. The three remaining Angels of the Ethereal Light Warriors are being held in a lab and experimented on. They are in excruciating pain. I believe Ash is directly involved."

"Ash is involved." The black-haired Angel spoke up. "The prayer is coming from a Sheline named Lavender Wildstone. Ash has destroyed her marriage and now forces her to mate his high Warrior, a Zallaphan named Rome Amberfire."

Rune looked at Eliana. "Every scenario I see results in the liberation of that dimension if Rome Amberfire mates Lavender Wildstone."

"And fails if they do not mate." Eliana said quietly. "Ash's games are about to backfire on him."

"Love. Ash has always discounted the true power of love."

"I believe, from what I saw," the Dark-haired Angel spoke again. "That Ash is attempting to manipulate love. He is attempting to poison it. To change it to hate and bitterness, and possibly a thirst for revenge."

Rune nodded. "You are correct, Keir. If Ash had left Lavender with Relic, the man she was infatuated with, his plan would have succeeded. Rome would have become a monster. He would have been filled with hatred and bitterness and Ash could have used him to destroy any rebellion. Instead, Ash has instigated the loss of this stronghold."

"Stand ready, Warriors of light." Eliana said quietly as she lifted her hand, and the situation on planet Nephara in a far distant dimension began to play out along the blackness of The In-Between. The prayer echoing throughout the cosmos growing in power as time ticked by. "The timing must be perfect. Wait. Wait..."

All eyes turned to the scene, every zeptosecond feeling as if it was lasting an eternity. Rune clenched his fists, struggling with compassion and the truth of what must happen. Salvation for the three remaining Angels, Rome and Lavender, and the other beings of this dimension could only happen if they acted at the right moment. He saw Eliana wipe a tear from her eyes at the horrors playing out before them. "There! Did you see it? Ash has left the dimension. Go in... five, four, three, two, one. Now!"

The two Angelic hosts disappeared. Within seconds the Illuminated Warriors were back, carrying the three broken Angels. "I've got them!" Eliana shouted and vanished with the three.

"Army of Light!" Rune shouted and instantly The In-Between flooded with massive amounts of light as an army of Angels numbering in the hundreds of thousands appeared. "Recover Dimension nine million, seven hundred thousand, two hundred forty-one." The army was gone in another flash of light and the computerized voice spoke. "Light is returning to the targeted dimension. Inversion mode ended." The screen lit up with a multitude of glowing dots.

"Lavender and Rome?" Eliana asked as she returned.

"Safe. Rome has taken command of the Fortress." Rune replied as he stood arms crossed staring at the screen. "We need two Angels to guard Rome and Lavender. A mated pair."

"Why mated?"

"The most powerful force in the multiverse is love. They will understand as few others do, how important love is in the equation of Rome and Lavender."

Eliana nodded. "Zerachiel and Rabia. They have been mates since just after time began." A flash of light and two angels stood before them. Zerachiel a heavily muscled angelic warrior, and Rabia a slender gentle angel of light, who was deadly with the Angelfire sword she carried.

"We have a mission for you." Eliana spoke to the pair, showing them the information, they had on Lavender and Rome.

The two Angels looked at each other and nodded. They turned to Eliana and Rune. "We accept." They were gone the next instant.

"Ash is getting better at avoiding detection." Eliana glanced at her brother.

Rune nodded. "Things are changing Eliana, we need to be ready because Ash will not take this lying down. The Army of light has a fierce battle ahead of them."

Chapter Eighty-Four

EARTH DIMENSION TWO
  Caerleon, South Wales
  Fifth Century

ASH RETURNED TO EARTH dimension two invigorated and ready to execute his plan. He wore his best nobleman's clothes and went directly to Marrok's fortress. Where he was introduced as Lord Ash Morana. Lady Aalis greeted him prettily and invited him in. Within a day he was fornicating with the good Lady Aalis and seducing her mind with the promise of riches. On the third day, he knew it was time to move his plan forward.

Day One

Lady Aalis lay in her bed, her wrists tied to the headboard, and he'd toyed with her for hours. "Aalis, I need you to put a drop of this elixir into Marrok's drink everyday for a week. On the seventh day, there will be a full moon, make sure you put seven drops in his drink that night."

"Why?" she gasped, arching as he plucked at her sensitized nipple.

"Because I said so." Ash replied and stopped.

"Please, Ash!"

"Lord Morana." He kept his tone cool, his voice hard.

"Lord Morana." She squirmed on the bed.

"If you want me, you must obey me. If you want my riches, you must obey without question."

"Yes, Lord Morana. I will put the drops in his wine."

Ash Morana grinned.

Day Seven

Lady Aalis stared down at her husband's violently convulsing body before looking up at Lord Morana's face. "Will he die?"

Ash smiled. "Eventually. Come here. I have an urge to fuck you."

Lady Aalis stared at the man with the face of a fallen angel. She licked her lip nervously. "Now? Here?" She glanced at her dying husband and back to Ash.

"Now. Come here Aalis"

Day Ten

Lady Aalis lay naked on the floor of the beautiful home that she could not stop complaining about, in a pool of blood. Her throat had been ripped out, her lovely body torn as if by great claws. Ash allowed his body to shift from that of a werewolf back to the Fallen Angel that he was. It was convenient that an angel could take the form of any living being. He wiped her blood from his face and took a few moments to clean up. When he was presentable, he went to the cage he'd brought back with him from his lab and crouched down to peer into it. "You are quite a monster, Marrok." He said to the creature within, and he opened the door. A massive hulking beast leapt out, growls tearing from his throat. Ash vanished with the cage.

The beast, his amber eyes glowing in the darkened room, went berserk as the scent of blood filled his nostrils.

Chapter Eighty-Five

EARTH DIMENSION TWO – Fifth century
  Caerleon, South Wales
  Earth Dimension Three - Present time
  Mystic Haven, B.C., Canada

SARIEL WAS ON HIS WAY back from his counseling session with Eliana and Rune. He understood why he had to have these sessions, after all, he had attended a human cosplay convention without his glamour up. He did wonder though if they understood that he was a geek at heart. He'd been born an angel when he should have been born a human. He loved humans. They were so creative, and they loved so passionately, and they would make these delightful books and movies and games to live out their fantasies. He hadn't meant to cause a stir at the convention, honestly, he'd just wanted to mingle with the humans and be fully himself while he was doing it. He sure hadn't expected the human women to get so—excited. He knew at that point he should have left, but they were so cute, and they were wearing costumes! One thing had kind of led to another. He winced. It still might have been fine. After all there was nothing wrong with intimacy, but one of those ladies had gotten possessive. The next thing, he knew, they were in an all-out brawl. He'd been so taken aback that he'd just stood there in all his naked glory staring at the ruckus going on around him.

Put him on a battlefield in the middle of a war, and he would slaughter the enemy all day long. But a hotel with naked fighting human women? They were fragile. He might have hurt them if he treated the situation like a battle... even though it was—Sort of. He did wish he knew who had knocked over the candle though.

Police and firemen converged on the hotel. At least at that point, he'd had the good sense to glamour up. The hotel burned to the ground, and he'd been arrested along with the human women. He'd wanted to disappear so badly. In fact, as soon as they left him alone in an interview room, he planned to do just that. Unfortunately, Levi and Eliana had walked into the interview room, and they'd all had a nice long chat. The end result was counseling, and he was permanently assigned to Levi's host.

Now, he spent his days flying messages back and forth between the deities, until he was too tired to even think about the cute humans and their creative ways.

After his counseling session today, Eliana asked him to do a flyby of fifth century Earth in the second dimension, which was why he was hovering in space staring at the blue globe and debating if he should at least fly down into the atmosphere. If he was going to give her a thorough report, he should get closer. But would that be violating his no human contact order? If he didn't talk to anyone or appear to them in Angelic form, he should be fine, he decided. Swooping low over the medieval world, he noticed the unmistakable signature of an Angelic vortex leaving the world. That was odd. Eliana had said nothing about any angelic missions in this timeline. Neither had Levi. He was about to reach out to Levi when he noticed a disturbance in the energy. He swooped lower and gasped. King Arthur and his knights were chasing a—*A Werewolf!* He reeled back and started to fall. Frantically flapping his wings, he regained control. Oh, no. This could not happen. Not on his watch. He would be in counseling forever!

He quickly double checked that he was indeed in dimension two. Yes, he was. Okay, so he had to intervene. There were no superhumans on Earth in dimension two! None. This could not be good for the timeline. How in the Creator's name had a superhuman ended up here? He had no time for questions. He had to fix this. Flying low, he held to his invisible energy form and soared past the armored horsemen. His great wings beat at the air increasing his speed. He had to get to that werewolf before it was too late! Suddenly, the beast stopped and turned, and Sariel realized the Werewolf was going to take his stand here. *No. No. No.* This was not going to happen!

Turning in midair he flew in behind the beast and wrapping his arms around the creature's midsection he shot up into the air, ripping open a vortex as he went. The Werewolf struggled, his growls terrifying, and his teeth closed over Sariel's arm. "Stop that!" Sariel commanded. "I'm trying to help, you great big hairy monster!" They entered the vortex as Sariel struggled to maintain his hold, the beast growling and biting over and over again. "Who peed in your breakfast!" Sariel snapped. "The king wouldn't have been trying to kill you if you had remained in your own dimension!"

Seeing dimension three, Sariel let go of the vortex and with a mighty thrust of his wings soared down to Mystic Haven. The werewolf's struggling sent them into a spin. Sariel cursed, then gasped as one of his feathers turned black, cursed again, and tried to compensate. They slammed into a meadow tumbling head over heels until they crashed into a large tree. Groaning, Sariel managed to sit up. The Werewolf was sprawled out on the ground in front of him. "Oh no! Come on you wee beastie. It was a little fall. You can't be dead!"

Sariel crawled over to the creature, his wing dragging. The massive werewolf's form shimmered and became a man. Sariel touched the man's throat, finding a pulse he sighed in relief. Carefully, he picked up the unconscious being and with his wing dragging, limping, blood flowing from the savage bites on his arm, made his way slowly across the field. He had to get the Werewolf help. Mere moments later, Levi and some of his host landed. "Sariel! Are you alright! We saw you fall."

Sariel shook his head. "I am not okay. I need chocolate, and a Star Wars movie. I found this werewolf in the fifth century in Dimension Two. King Arthur was going to kill him. I don't know how he got there." Sariel swayed and Levi grabbed him. Another Angel took the man.

"Sariel, we are taking you and the werewolf to the hospital. I think your wing is broken and your arm is..." Levi hesitated. "Well, it's mangled. You did a good job bringing this man here. Do you know who he is?"

Sariel shook his head. "I didn't have time to ask questions. I grabbed him and got out of there."

Levi nodded and flew up into the sky with Sariel, "I'll talk to Caden, and hopefully, we can figure out who he is."

Chapter Eighty-Six

EARTH DIMENSION THREE
Mystic Haven, B.C., Canada

DR. DANIEL BRODY, A white tiger shifter, stepped out of his patient's room to find his son, Caden, waiting in the hall.

"Hi, Da, can I see the patient for a few minutes?"

"We have to talk first, Caden. Let's go to my office."

Once in his office with the door closed, Daniel poured them each a coffee. Handing one to his son, he took the seat behind his desk. "Caden, do you know who this man is?"

Caden shook his head. "Levi called and told me he was here along with an Angel named Sariel. Levi didn't know his name. He only told me that Sariel saved a werewolf who needed sanctuary."

Daniel sighed and took a drink of his coffee. "He's not a werewolf."

Caden frowned. "Levi seemed sure he was a werewolf."

"It's complicated, Caden. This man is a human, but—" Daniel shook his head. "Something has happened to his DNA."

"What do you mean?"

Daniel rubbed his neck. "Hell, I don't know what this is. It's like someone added werewolf DNA. The sequencing is not the same as a naturally born werewolf."

"You think someone deliberately changed this man into a werewolf? You're talking about genetic manipulation. Are humans advanced enough to successfully use superhuman DNA in that way? How would they even get their hands on Superhuman DNA? We have strict laws about revealing superhumans to humans."

Daniel nodded, his face grave. "It's more complicated than that, Caden. This man is not from our time. He's not even from our dimension."

Caden stilled. He opened his mouth to speak and closed it without saying a word. "Hmm." He picked up his coffee and took a sip as he gathered his thoughts. "How can you tell this?'

"We first learned about dimensional markers from the Angels. Angels can move through time and space and dimensions. They definitely don't originate from our dimension.

"Thankfully, they have shared their medical knowledge with us so we can treat them if they are injured and can't get to an Angelic Healer. One of their healers delivered that information and had a meeting with the doctors here. What was included in that briefing was the information that all species from every dimension have a dimensional marker in their blood. We never knew because everyone from our dimension has the same marker. It's only seen as a component of our blood."

Caden nodded. "Do you know what dimension this man is from?"

Daniel shook his head. "You could ask Levi or Sariel, but I've found the Angels are closed-mouthed about other dimensions. I can tell you that he is human and that means he is from Earth. Specifically, sometime during the Middle Ages."

Tilting his coffee cup, Caden peered down at the dark liquid. "Did you put something in here?"

Daniel laughed and shook his head. "I believe drugging an officer of the law, even if he is my son, would mean an arrest, and I'm pretty sure your mother would kill me." He grew serious. "I know this sounds outlandish, but it's true."

"Was that part of the Angelic briefing? Is there a marker for being from a different time?"

"Yes. Some physical characteristics too. Honestly, I never thought we would need to treat anyone from the past."

Caden shook his head. "This is a helluva situation. How are we going to help this man adapt? I can't even imagine the trauma we are talking about here. He was obviously experimented on by a being he had no way of understanding, and now he has been taken from his dimension, his time, his people. He can shift into something that he would most likely consider to be a monster. Wait. Can he shift back into a Werewolf?"

"Yes. He is human but his altered DNA has changed him into a Werewolf. He should be able to shift and have all the abilities of a Werewolf. But I seriously doubt he has any understanding of what those entail. It's an incredibly dangerous situation."

"Da, you need to call Dr. Esteban. This man is going to need help to adapt. I will contact a Werewolf counsel member, and maybe Stone would be helpful as well. As the Alpha for our wolf shifters, he might have some insight. Gods this is a messed-up situation."

"I have to agree with you there, son. Right now, we have him in a medically induced coma. I didn't want to risk him shifting before his brain could heal from the concussion he sustained when Sariel crashed."

"How long before he will be conscious?"

"If he survives, we will bring him out of it within two weeks. The best-case scenario would be a week, but he has a severe traumatic brain injury." Daniel shrugged and shook his head. We'll see, Caden."

Part Twelve

'Though my soul may set in darkness,
it will rise in perfect light,
I have loved the stars too fondly,
to be fearful of the night'
Sarah Williams 1837–1868

Chapter Eighty-Seven

EARTH DIMENSION THREE
Mystic Haven, B.C., Canada

BAYLEN TOSSED IN HIS bed, his head moving back and forth as, in his dreams, he heard her voice.

It came to him as a whisper in the wind. A terrible wind that tore at the great stone castle that he lived in. The mighty fortress that protected his children. The refuge that all Fae could flee too for safety.

The weight of his guilt pressed down on him, a boulder he could not lift, a mountain he could not crawl out from under.

Her name whispered in his ear. Wisteria. The memories came rushing back. Her beauty, the sheer sensuality that clung to her like the finest of silk, disguising the purity of her evil.

The dreamscape changed, and he stood in the sunlight burning as the light rejected the blackness he had been infected with. His screams echoed as The Ones Who Had Gone Before stood in front of him. Their voices rose in accusation against him. Crying out that her people had fed on them. Her people had devoured them.

And he had lain with her. He had embraced her. He had allowed her to feed off him. The memories rose before him—millions of memories not his own. Memories of such agony and horror that he wanted to tear his brain apart.

With a guttural howl of anguish Baylen's eyes snapped open. "Oh, Gods." His breath rasped from his throat. He was icy cold from the sweat that covered his body. He swallowed and stared wildly around his room searching for danger. Slowly, he rose, his whole body trembling. "Fuck." He sat on the edge of the bed, his face buried in his hands as he fought back the darkness. Through his window shimmered silver moonlight. He stood up and walked over to look out into the night, his senses spread wide. Nothing was out there. Shoving a hand through his hair, he turned and walked into the bathroom. After showering, he dressed silently. Black jeans, black shirt. Hiking boots.

He walked down the hall to his children's bedrooms and checked on each of them. He adjusted blankets and tucked fallen stuffed animals back into their little arms. He smoothed their dark hair and finally drew on pure Fae energy and shone it down on each one of them. Checking. Always checking for any sign of the darkness that was part of him. There was none. There was never any, but he knew in the morning he would call Shirina and ask her to come and check too.

The scar on his chest ached and he pressed on it absent-mindedly as he turned away from their rooms. Their bodyguards and nanny would watch over them for the rest of the night.

Striding through the castle to his office, he walked through and out onto the balcony. Soaring up into the night sky, he flew around the island, pausing every now and then to check in with the night watch that Caden had implemented when he became the leader of Mystic Haven. When he'd made a complete circle around the island that was his home, he turned and headed to the mainland. He needed to purge the memories. He needed to force all thought from his mind. He let his darkness rise to the surface and began to hunt. Yet, he could not wipe away the knowledge that she lived. That she would be back.

Chapter Eighty-Eight

EARTH DIMENSION THREE
Mystic Haven, B.C., Canada

"DADDY. DADDY! THERE'S Pandora! Can we go see her?" Aurora, Jewel, and Falcon were practically dancing with glee, and a smile curved Baylen's lips. He set their gifts on the gift table and nodded his head. "Don't forget to say Happy Birthday to her. Be good." The three miniature hoodlums ran off to join their friends. Children's birthday parties were not his normal idea of entertainment, but as a single parent, he'd learned to deal. He crossed his arms over his chest and watched, thinking he better keep a close eye on his kids. They were a handful. A moment later golden sparkles filled the air.

The kids all began to shout. "Ali! Ali! Ali!"

He took a step forward as a woman began to materialize out of thin air. *What the fuck?* He took another step forward intending to protect his kids from this unknown bit of magic when Caden Brody stepped up beside him. "Wait. Watch."

The woman wasn't tall, but she was all curves. Her multihued dark copper hair curled down her back, but it was her soft pink medieval dress that made him pause.

231

Oh hell no. He knew who it was. That pretty little wench who'd spilled her iced coffee all over him. The woman who had instantly triggered his Fae mating signs. *Fuck.* "Who is that?"

Caden grinned. "That is Aliora Aurelius. Mystic Haven's children's party entertainer."

Baylen stared at Caden. "We have a party entertainer?"

Caden nodded, looking pleased with himself. "She's been here for about three years, Baylen."

Baylen eyed Caden. *Shit.* He looked at the woman again. *Fuck.* "She bumped into me a few weeks ago. At the Chicco di Caffe. Literally. I ended up wearing her sticky coffee."

Caden chuckled. "Yeah, that doesn't surprise me at all. Ali is a handful."

"What is she?"

"You can't tell?"

Baylen looked at the woman again. She was hovering about three inches off the ground and talking excitedly to the children. She waved a hand and golden sparks flowed from her fingertips and flowers began to bloom all over the lawn. The kids cheered. Baylen raised an eyebrow. "No wand so she can't be a Wizard. The fact that she is floating makes me think she is part Sprite or Fae. Though I have no fucking idea how she's hiding her wings."

At that moment all the children's clothes changed into the clothing of a medieval court. Long princess dresses in a rainbow of colors, multicolored capes and tunics with leggings, and crowns. So many crowns. The children squealed in delight. Baylen stared with his mouth wide open. "What the fuck?"

Caden laughed. "I'll introduce you when the party's over. I think you should meet her."

Baylen frowned, "No sticky iced coffee." but he nodded, before turning back to watch the woman. She clearly loved the children she was patiently entertaining. She leaned forward and cuddled a little girl who'd tumbled over, distracting her by producing a bird out of thin air. She released it and a little boy asked if she could show him a butterfly. She smiled and with more golden sparkles from her fingers the air filled with butterflies of every size and color.

Baylen kept a tight leash on his glamour, as he realized the woman was light, her gentleness a powerful force all on its own. His jaw began to ache, and he forced a bored smile to his lips before he turned and went in search of coffee. Though he fucking wanted a whisky. *Why? Why the hell, were the Ancients fucking with him. Hadn't he been punished enough?* He poured himself a coffee at the table set up with refreshments intended for the parents and took a long sip before turning to watch his children and that woman.

He saw how kind she was to his children, to all the children and crossed his arms over the strange ache in his chest. Instinct told him that she had no concept of darkness. No understanding of the danger he represented. The darkness, all that remained of the man who he'd once been, would swallow her whole. Suffocate the light that she was.

Grimly, he wrestled his glamour into control, no one would ever know. He refused to submit to the interference of the Ancient Ones yet again. His heart was long dead, it had been fucking torn from his chest and burned to ash before his eyes.

He knew that evil stalked him, and he refused to have any part in the death of another woman.

What tiny spark of flickering light that remained in him was for his children and his people. He would do anything to protect them. Anything—And may the gods have mercy on anyone foolish enough to try to harm them. Because he would not.

Chapter Eighty-Nine

EARTH DIMENSION THREE
Mystic Haven, B.C., Canada

ALIORA SMILED AS SHE walked over to the refreshment table. The last of the children had left with their parents and Caden wanted her to meet someone. But first, she was going to have a coffee. While the children had been wonderful and the party fun, it did not mean that she wasn't exhausted and needing a moment of quiet.

Caden found her a few minutes later. "Ali. Come on into my study. I want you to meet the Fae king."

Aliora paused mid-sip and stared at Caden before swallowing. "The Fae king?"

The Cop grinned. "He doesn't bite... much."

Aliora stared. "Much? That's not reassuring, Caden." She set down her coffee and glanced down at herself. Yeah, that was not going to do. She had children's sticky handprints on her skirt, and a large purple area over her chest where a child had spilled their grape soda. She waved her hand, golden magic filling the air, and her dress changed into a lovely medieval gown of teal blue with a small train, and velvet off-the-shoulder neckline. A golden girdle hung around her hips, the long chain falling gracefully down to her ankles. She produced a small hand mirror and frowned at her face, before magically applying clear lip gloss and a dash of pale peach eyeshadow. Another wave and her hair became a braided rope down her back with a few curls escaping around her face. There, that would do. At least she was presentable now. The mirror vanished and she looked over at Caden. *Oh!* She'd almost forgotten. A snap of her fingers and her favorite tiara perched perfectly on top of her head.

Caden's eyes widened. "You should not exist, Ali. I don't have any clue how you do that."

Aliora laughed and shrugged. "Neither do I, but it's all very handy when you are about to be unexpectedly introduced to royalty."

"Ali, Baylen is the most unroyal person you are ever likely to meet."

Aliora paused and tilted her head a little bit. "It's the tiara, right? It's too much?"

Caden gave her a wink. She sighed dramatically and wrinkled her nose. The tiara disappeared.

Following Caden into his house, she smiled as she heard the kids quietly playing in the living room. Caden opened a door and they stepped into his study. Aliora stopped as soon as her eyes lit upon the primal Fae leaning against the wall staring out the window. *Oh, no.* The man turned. One eyebrow raised. "So, we meet again."

"Oh, dear." The man from the coffee shop. The man she had entertained far too many illicit dreams about. Her eyes met his, and she could feel her cheeks heating up. *Well, this was fun. Not.*

"Baylen, this is Aliora Aurelius. Ali, this is Baylen Knight. King of the Fae. Since you are part Fae, he is your king too."

The man nodded to her, his long black hair sliding over his shoulder.

Oh my gosh! What did you call a Fae king? Wait. Her king? Hmm. But she could be polite. "Uhm... hello, uh... Your Majesty?"

Caden coughed, and Baylen glared. "Baylen. I'm Baylen. No fucking titles needed. Ever." He drained the whisky in his glass and set it down on the desk.

Aliora swallowed and frowned. He was swearing again.

"Welcome to Mystic Haven, Ms. Aurelius."

"Thank you?" *Didn't he know that she had been here for three years already?* "It's nice to meet you."

"Baylen," Caden put his hand on Aliora's back and urged her over to a big comfy chair. "Aliora is a favorite with the children in Mystic Haven, and their parents."

A favorite with children and their parents. Baylen scowled. All that meant was that she was kind and gentle. He already fucking knew that. He'd seen her with the kids today, and he'd had her investigated. Not because she'd spilled coffee on him. No, it was the fact that he did not understand what she was. Normally, with the sheer amount of Fae powers he wielded he could identify every species on this planet including the few aliens that made Earth home. Not her though. Those moments in the coffee shop had left him damned suspicious. *I mean her Fae energy was fucking golden sparkles.* Of course, his reaction to her had not helped either. But there was no way in hell, she could handle what he was. "Where are you originally from?"

Aliora smiled. "Calgary."

Baylen tilted his head and watched her, with an intensity that was unnerving.

Well, that was uncomfortable. She rubbed the tip of her ear with her left hand. Perhaps she should—

Caden cleared his throat and shook his head at her. Aliora huffed and crossed her arms, settling back into her chair.

"Fangs Aliora?" Baylen grinned.

Her eyes widened and she reached up to discover fangs barely peeking between her lips. She took a deep calming breath and they retreated.

"You're a Sprite Fae halfling."

"No."

Baylen gave her a hard smile. "I can see the Fae in you. From the de Fae lineage. It's part of the perks of being your king."

Aliora rose to her feet. "I would never deny my Fae blood. My Grandfather is Edge de Fae." She started across the room. Pausing, she turned back to face The Fae king, Baylen Knight. "Just one more thing. You are not my king."

Aliora Aurelius walked out the door.

Chapter Ninety

EARTH DIMENSION THREE
Mystic Haven, B.C., Canada

BAYLEN STARED AFTER Aliora. "Did she say," He swallowed. "Her grandfather is *Edge* de Fae". His voice had grown fainter with each word. Caden nodded, looking as shocked as Baylen. "Couldn't it have been any other de Fae?" They both groaned.

"Edge is an Ancient."

They both groaned again.

Chapter Ninety-One

THE IN-BETWEEN

RUNE EXAMINED THE STARDUST Chalice. His mind busy shifting through the many pieces of information that made up the complex puzzle of this mysterious relic.

Eliana stepped into the room and walked over to her brother. "Rune there is something going on with the Sol Star System."

"Again? Why is Earth always a trouble spot?"

Eliana laughed. "I guess there must be one trouble spot in every Multiverse."

"You have created more Multiverses?"

"Heavens no! We have enough problems with one."

Chuckling, Rune looked at his sister fondly and sent the chalice back to its protected container. "What's going on with Earth this time?"

Eliana frowned. "Come to think of it. There is a slight issue with Earth Dimension Two, but I think I can resolve that on my own. I have not been able to find a friend of mine for some weeks now." She thought about that for a moment. "Never mind about that. Dimension Three. There was some kind of attack. I spoke with Levi Hariel. It sounds like Ash was there with a bunch of his followers. I don't know how, but that small island in the northern and western hemisphere, Mystic Haven, managed to fight them off."

Rune grinned. "Ha. That's the Fae Guardian and that wild Fae king! Ash has no idea what he is up against with that bunch."

Eliana shook her head. "Levi said they were heading to investigate another sanctuary city that has gone silent. Cordelia, I believe he called it."

"Cordelia?" Rune paused and swore. "That's a Mer city. They've just recovered enough to begin to spread back through the oceans. How the hell would Ash know about it?"

"I don't know, Rune, but we better find out."

Chapter Ninety-Two

EARTH DIMENSION THREE
Mystic Haven, B.C., Canada

TODAY HAD BEEN A DISASTER from the moment Amara had woken up. She'd managed to spill toothpaste on her nightgown, she'd forgotten her coffee until it was barely lukewarm, she went to get a dress out of the closet and discovered that it had fallen to the floor and was now a wrinkled unwearable mess, and she'd burned her toast for breakfast.

She was reaching for her jeans and a hoodie when the urgent call from her new Angelic host came in. Dressing quickly in her leathers, she strapped on her swords and opened a vortex that took her right into the midst of a bloody war.

Levi was waiting for her and the rest of the host to arrive. Their orders were to stand with the few survivors of this world. The fight was violently brutal, the survivors of the initial attack, had fallen one after the other, even though the Angels fought with valiant determination.

In the end, the lone survivor of that civilization was a baby born during the battle, a baby that they were told to protect at all costs. With hard eyes, every Angel created an identical illusion of the newborn and they scattered across the multiverse.

As Amara held her illusion and began to open the vortex that would take her a million dimensions from this one and a million more from her home, her warrior's instinct went off and she whirled around her sword rising, but it was too late. The being who confronted her, slammed his sword deep, the blade entering just under her collar bone and exiting out the other side before he yanked it back and brought it swinging down. It would have been a killing blow, but she managed to get her sword up. The impact of the powerful strike slamming into her steel shattered both blades and sent agony streaking through her arm. She scrambled back from her assailant, clutching the fake baby to her, knowing that her sword arm had broken with that blow. She kicked out and managed to knock the male back, knowing her next move would involve letting go of the illusion of the baby so she could reach for the other sword strapped to her back. It was a good thing that she fought with both hands. But even she knew her chances of survival were small, the wound to her chest was going to hamper her abilities. Cursing silently, because revealing the illusion would mean this enemy would set out after the others, she prepared to reach for the sword. Without warning a vortex opened behind her and a hard hand on her shoulder yanked her backwards into the turbulent time storm.

Chapter Ninety-Three

EARTH DIMENSION THREE
Mystic Haven, B.C., Canada

CADEN WAS ON THE LAST leg of his morning run. One mile to go till home. and he was looking forward to a hot shower before he got ready for work. Ahead he could see clouds building in a dark mass and frowned as he considered how fast that thunderhead was developing. The deafening roar of thunder shook the ground, even as the sky lit up with the color of flames. What the hell was happening?

Another massive boom as more and more clouds roiled across the sky. A heated wave of air that sent leaves, and debris flying, blasted across the forest path. He lifted his hand to shield his eyes and reached for his phone.

"Caden Brody"

His name filled the air as the space in front of him twisted and turned, churning wildly as the turbulence became more and more violent. He took a step back as a rupture appeared, sparks and flames rushed out of the jagged tear. The aperture grew larger and through the sparks, smoke, and flames, he saw a figure come striding towards him. "We do not have much time."

The figure stepped out of the vortex, his shimmering white wings spread as if to protect what he carried. As the smoke cleared, Caden suddenly recognized the man. "Levi!" The Angel was grim faced, his sword bloody and in his arms, he carried a baby wrapped in a pink blanket.

"We don't have much time." Levi placed the baby in Caden's arms. "Listen carefully. Her name is Safire. She was born mere hours ago. She's yours. You must be the one to raise her."

"What? Hold it!" Caden cut in.

"We do not have time, Caden! Listen. Safire is a Changeling Fae. Look at her eyes. Do you see?"

Caden stared at the powerful Angel before looking down at the tiny baby in his arms. She blinked up at him. Her eyes were filled with—*sparks of color glowing hotly against a deep purple background.* "Opals. Her eyes are like opals." He breathed. *Changeling Fae were a myth, a legend told by his people.* He looked back up at Levi. "How is this possible? Where did she come from? Why did you bring her to me?"

"The how, where, and why doesn't matter. She is a Changeling Fae. The full extent of her abilities won't surface until she is an adult." Levi paused, staring into Caden's eyes. "Safire is from another world, another dimension, another time. Her people are no more. Look at her eye's, Caden! They mark her as having an ancestor who was thought only to be legend. She will have immense powers someday. You must teach her to use her powers for good. Only for good."

Levi stroked a gentle hand over the tiny baby's head before looking at Caden again. "She must survive. Her destiny is important for the Universe, for Earth and for many other worlds. She is being hunted by an ancient evil. He must not find her. One day the mystery will be revealed to you, but for this time, the important thing is that she must be protected at all costs. Promise me, Caden Brody. Promise that you will protect her."

Caden nodded slowly. "I'll protect her, Levi. You have my word."

The Angel stepped back and instantly an illusion formed of a tiny baby in his arms. He looked at Caden again. "All of my host have created an illusion of the child, and we have all gone to different dimensions and times. The battle is not over." He paused and tilted his head as if listening to something. "Amara has been injured." Levi's eyes betrayed his fury. "I must go." With a final glance at the baby, Levi stepped back into the tear in time and space and sealed it. Vanishing from Caden's sight.

If not for the light weight of the baby in his arms, he would never have known that something out of the normal had occurred. Caden looked down at the baby, she was such a tiny being with huge eyes and little pointed ears. He could see the faint glow of her energy wings against the blanket. A distinctly newborn cry filled the air. "Hello, Safire. I'm your new Da. I bet you're hungry." He gently gathered her up against his shoulder, and dropping his glamour, he shot up into the air. First things first. His new daughter needed to be fed and seen by a doctor, and he knew just the doctor. "Let's go meet your grandfather."

Chapter Ninety-Four

EARTH DIMENSION THREE
Mystic Haven, B.C., Canada

MICAH STOOD ON THE street staring at the Angel sitting on the black iron steps that led up to the back entrance of her apartment over the bookstore. It was the fact that she was unconscious and bleeding that triggered the memory of when he'd first seen her. He'd been the one to carry her from that dirty little shack, when he'd helped Caden's team take down a bunch of human traffickers. His reaction had been the same then as it was now. He looked at his glowing hands. Shit. He lifted her slight weight into his arms and shot up into the sky, heading for the hospital.

Chapter Ninety-Five

EARTH DIMENSION TWO
Realm of The Forsaken Dimension Five

RUNE STOOD BESIDE SARIEL in Dimension Two. "I have a message for you to deliver. The timing had to be perfect for this one, I've been holding it in statis waiting for this moment." He handed Sariel a sphere that glowed an unearthly blue, contained within were the urgent words of a coded message. "Release this in Dimension Five." Sariel nodded once and opened a vortex.

Chapter Ninety-Six

EARTH DIMENSION THREE
Mystic Haven, B.C., Canada

MOONLIGHT SILENTLY crept through the window as if drawn to the gently glowing woman sleeping in her bed. The loud roar of a motorcycle filled the night air, and Aliora opened her eyes.

"Why don't some people have any respect for the sanctity of sleep?" She punched her pillow and turned over. The motorbike grew louder the closer it got to her house. Glaring at the wall, she contemplated using her telekinesis to float that jerk and his loud motorcycle right into the ocean. Her eyes widened as the motorbike abruptly went silent—Outside her house. She grabbed her phone from the charger and saw that it was midnight. Who was out there?

Climbing from her bed, she walked into the living room and cautiously peered out her curtain. She lived too remotely for random people to stop by in the middle of the night. Why were her security Wards silent? She bit her lip and eased her front door open a bare inch. Peeking outside, she could see a tall man in dark leathers and a dark helmet getting off the bike. Heart racing, she tapped her phone app. Better safe than sorry right? She brought the keypad up and glanced back at the man, finger hovering over the nine. He reached up and took his helmet off, his long dark hair tumbling down his back. *Baylen Knight? Oh, for heaven's sake!* What did the Fae king want? Her eyes narrowed and she stepped outside, her arms crossed over her chest. "What are you doing here? It's the middle of the night!"

Baylen looked up and paused. She was fucking glowing. He growled. "I doubt you were sleeping."

Aliora shook her head. "What? It's the middle of the night! What the heck else would I be doing? Wait. Maybe this is some kind of weird dream."

Baylen smirked. "Nope, not a dream. But—have you been dreaming?"

Ali huffed. "For your information, I was sleeping—Soundly."

Baylen narrowed his eyes. "You were sleeping? Not dreaming?"

Ali blinked. "I need coffee to deal with this." Turning she walked into her house leaving the door open for him to follow if he wished to continue the insane conversation he appeared bent on having with her. Why? She had no idea. Maybe it was a regular habit of the Fae king? Was he a crazy Fae king? She blinked. *That would explain so much!*

"Cute." He closed the door behind himself.

She glared over her shoulder. "You better be speaking about my pajamas."

He smirked and let his eyes drift over her turquoise PJ bottoms with mermaids and seashells scattered over them. Taking note of her fuzzy pink slippers and white tank top "Of course." *Fuck. Her ass.* Hell, he'd been floored by the front view, and then she turned. He was in deep water here. *Say something. Something logical.* "So, I'm not your king?"

Ali paused. *Again, with this?* "Coffee first." She muttered and walked into the kitchen. A small wave of her hand, and golden magic streamed across the room to the coffee maker. It turned on and began to brew. She walked over to her cupboard, got out two mugs, and set them on the island.

What the fuck? That was not logical! Baylen glanced around, thankful that no one was here, before following her. He did not need anyone to know about his brilliant comment.

Walking over to the island, he picked up the two cups and read them out loud. "Life is so much funnier when you have a dirty mind." He looked at Ali, his eyebrow raised, and read the second one. "Give me some sugar."

"Ugh." Aliora muttered as she got out the sugar. "My grandfather gave me those. He thinks he's funny. Every birthday, he gets me another coffee cup with another saying on it. If you knew my family..." She glared at the man disturbing her sleep. "...You would understand."

She pointed a finger at the coffee pot, and it floated up into the air. She looked at Baylen and raised her eyebrow. He set the cups down, and the coffee pot floated over and poured coffee into both cups without spilling a drop.

That was some incredible telekinesis skill he thought as he picked up the dirty mind cup. "So, I'm not your king?"

Aliora held up her finger and took a long sip of her coffee. *What is with this guy?* "You seem to be stuck on that."

"Just making sure I understand. So, you don't see me as an authority figure?"

Ali stared at him thinking he smelled good. Really good. She saw his eyebrow go up as he waited for her to answer and gave herself a mental shake. "Which part of you're not my king, didn't you understand?"

"You're pretty sassy for a woman who is only what? Five foot four inches and maybe all of 155 pounds soaking wet."

"154!" Ali gasped. "What the heck does my physical build have to do with this?"

She was gorgeous, and she smelled delicious. Her nipples were hard little nubs pressing against her thin top. "This." Baylen reached out, captured her chin, and leaned down to kiss her.

A wave of magic rose between them, and he was shoved backwards a step. *What the hell?* His eyes met hers, and he realized what he'd done. *Shit.* "Uh." He cleared his throat. "I'm sorry. That was out of line." *What the ever-loving fuck?*

"Yes, it was, Mr. Not My King." She lifted her chin and crossed her arms over her chest, trying to hide the evidence that she'd been tempted. "Why are you here?"

That was a good question. Why was he there? Just because he'd woken up from yet another sexy dream starring Aliora Aurelius, just because he'd been having x-rated dreams of her since she spilled her coffee on him, didn't mean that she shared those dreams with him. Or that she would even be receptive to—" He frowned. She'd been glowing when he saw her on the front step. "Why were you glowing?"

"Glowing?" She gave him a blank look. "Oh. That's a Sprite thing. Why?"

Baylen nodded and took a sip of his coffee. "You lied to me."

Her fangs popped out, she rubbed her ear with her left hand, growling. "I did not lie. I'm not a halfling."

"You admitted to being Sprite, and even if you hadn't admitted that your grandfather was a Fae, I would know it with those." He waved his hand at her.

Those? Her eyes got larger. She glanced down, her nipples were hard, and her cheeks heated before she realized he'd been waving at her back. She glanced over her shoulder at her colorful energy wings. *Wow.* Normally her glamour was fool proof. It was his fault. Him and his intoxicating scent. *Damn it.* "I'm still not a halfling, Mr. Knight, and I see no reason to discuss this with you in the middle of the night or any other time."

Baylen nodded. "Perhaps you're right." He needed to get out of there. What had he been thinking? "Even though you don't recognize me as your king, if you ever need anything, I'm happy to help."

Ali stared at him. He set down his coffee, turned and walked out the door. His motorcycle started and a few seconds later it roared off down the road. Ali stood there staring at the door. *Maybe it had been a dream?* She'd been having way too many sexy dreams about the Fae king. Though this one certainly wasn't sexy. *Okay. No more pizza before bed.*

Chapter Ninety-Seven

EARTH DIMENSION THREE
Mystic Haven, B.C., Canada

LEVI LANDED ON THE island and immediately raised his glamour to hide his wings. His long blond hair was tied back by a strip of leather, he wore dark jeans, hiking boots, a black t-shirt, and a black hoodie. The alley he'd chosen for his landing was situated behind the bookstore that Amara owned. The walk to the Police Station only took a few minutes and Levi enjoyed seeing the people hurrying about their business. He decided he wanted to stop at the coffee shop with the delicious aromas coming from the open doorway, on his way back to Amara's bookstore. He did not often get to spend time on any one planet, but that was about to change. He had new orders.

Opening the door to the Police Station, he walked in taking note of the big counter for people to make their initial requests and that it also served to prevent entry. There were multiple desks behind it and an open doorway that led to what he assumed to be cubicles and offices.

He stepped up to the counter and asked to speak to Caden Brody. Moments later he was ushered down a hall to an office with the name plate reading Caden Brody, Chief of Police. The door was open, so he walked in.

"Hello, Levi. I was surprised when they told me you wanted to see me.

"Chief Brody."

Caden waved away his words. "Caden. Call me Caden."

"Alright. Caden, I have some important information we need to discuss." Levi took the seat in front of the cop's desk as Caden walked over and closed the door.

"I think the first thing is to tell you that my host and I have been assigned to Earth on a permanent basis and that Mystic Haven will be our base of operation. Do you have any objections?"

Caden leaned back in his chair and considered the Angel before him. "Doesn't a host of Angels usually number as many as there are stars in the sky? Mystic Haven is a bit small for that many Angels."

Levi laughed. "There are different types of hosts. My host is small by comparison and..." He shrugged. "...Unique." We are a covert team sent in to protect and, in some cases, work with the local leadership to prevent an undesirable element from gaining a foothold.

Caden crossed his arms, a faint smile curving his lips. "Nice double talk. How many is a 'small' host, and who the hell is the undesirable element you are trying to prevent from gaining a foothold on my island?"

"Twelve including me."

"Amara is part of that number?"

"She is now." Levi nodded.

"How badly was she injured?"

"Broken arm, a stab wound through her shoulder. Your man, Micah, found her before I arrived and got her to the hospital. She's home now."

"How's she handling things? She was in bad shape when we rescued her from those traffickers."

"She's done well so far, but she keeps to herself."

Caden nodded. "Has she talked about how she was captured?"

Levi shook his head.

"Who is this undesirable element?"

"Ash Morana."

Caden paused, straightening. "We showed that bastard that he wasn't getting into Mystic Haven."

"You did. But from my intel, that was just a test. He wanted to know how strong your defenses were."

"Why?" Caden's voice was grim.

"Ash has been building his forces on Earth for a while now. We have reports of incursions starting on Earth Dimension Two back in 437 AD. He appears to have abandoned that dimension and settled in this one. He has been here since 437 AD as well. That is well before the Fae arrived in 932 AD. At first, we thought he was searching for someone, but when we go back to that time period, we haven't found any person that would be of interest to him. The biggest difference between dimension two and dimension three of earth is the superhumans. Dimension two has no superhumans. It never has, though it has a rich mythology surrounding legendary super beings."

"Okay." Caden took a sip of his coffee, considering what Levi had told him. "You think superhumans are why he decided to stay in dimension three?"

"It is our current theory. He could move more freely here. His men could survive better."

"My intel says that he has the biggest superhuman crime syndicate on Earth. When I fought him, he claimed to have a 'slaveling' here in Mystic Haven. Levi, that was true. Asterine Skyfire was his prisoner from shortly after the Fae arrival for several years until she was rescued by the Deity, Adler Llywelyn. Adler is a mystery. We have no information on why he was associated with Ash."

Levi frowned. "I will speak to Adler. I would also like to speak to Asterine. Perhaps she has information that could help us."

"You know, Levi, there is something I'd like to understand about Angels and Deities. I know that Angels are beings with incredible powers, and the mandate to use those powers to protect all life that the Creators created in the multiverse. Is this mandate the same for Deities?"

Levi nodded. "Yes, but the Angel mandate is more complex. Angels are the watchers. We have the power to intervene if a Deity should choose to harm instead of protect. We also report directly to Rune and Eliana, though we can also be assigned to certain Deities at Rune or Eliana's discretion."

Caden nodded. "Thanks for helping me to understand."

"No problem. There is one more thing that is important concerning the situation with Ash. We know that the Mer have taken sanctuary in the waters of Mystic Haven."

Caden nodded. "Their cities were attacked by an unknown enemy several years ago. The reports say descriptions were consistently of some kind of monstrous Mer beings. Riley Muirgheal and her second saved Baylen Knight when his helicopter crashed. I invited the Mer to Mystic Haven. They've done well. In fact, they recently began to build their own sanctuary cities."

"Cordelia has gone silent. I investigated. Caden, Cordelia has been captured."

"Captured! By whom? Why haven't the Mer let me know!"

"It looks like Ash took the city. We saw some of his men there, and we saw those monstrous beings. We think they are some kind of hybrid offspring of a Demonic union with a Mer. Is it possible that the Mer were doing experiments and that is how their cities were destroyed?"

Caden shook his head and stood up. "I don't know, but I intend to find out. They have been loyal to Mystic Haven and have contributed to our defenses. I know the Mer are a dangerous race, but they are also honorable. They would not stand by while their cities were attacked. Whatever has happened I intend to offer our aid."

"Caden. I'll go with you to the Mer. We will find out what's happened together. I need you to understand that my orders are to protect Mystic Haven and help you to defend the other sanctuary cities of Earth."

Pausing, Caden looked at Levi. "Why does this sound like war?"

Levi's eyes met his. "We do not yet have enough intel to determine that. Let's go see the Mer."

Chapter Ninety-Eight

EARTH DIMENSION THREE
Mystic Haven, B.C., Canada

CADEN EMERGED FROM his SUV and heard his name. He looked over at the man walking toward them. "Hello, Finn."

Finn nodded. "I was coming to see you. This is much simpler. We've had one of our new cities, Cordelia, go silent. At first, we thought it was the tech. We started the investigation here, but also sent a team of our special forces to the city. They just got back. We need to talk."

"I found out there was a problem with Cordelia. I was coming to find out what happened. This is Levi. He's the leader of the Angelic Host that's been assigned to Mystic Haven."

Finn shook hands with the scarred Angel. "Welcome, Levi. Riley's in our security center. Let's head in there."

Riley stood in front of a clear screen looking at video feed and shaking her head. "Who the hell are those people in my city?" She turned as they approached. "Caden. Some outside force has taken over Cordelia. I saw a bloody dragon in my underwater city!"

"Levi came to me earlier and told me the city had gone silent and there's concern that it's Ash Morana's doing."

Riley looked at the man who'd entered with Finn and Caden. She held out her hand. "Riley Muirgheal. I lead the Mer. How did you find out that Cordelia was under attack?"

Levi's hand closed over hers. "The Sol System and its dimensions are part of our assignment. In fact, as of this morning they're our only assignment.

"We think Ash attacked it at the same time that Mystic Haven was under attack. That's only a theory. We scouted the city a few days ago. There are some beings there that resemble those you spoke of in the original attacks. Were you performing genetic experiments at that time?"

Riley stared at the Angel. "What kind of question is that? Of course, we weren't. Why the hell would we want to mutate our own people?"

Levi watched the blonde for a minute before answering. "It was a theory. My job is to investigate all theories. As I said, we believe the two attacks were connected. Perhaps the attack on Mystic Haven was a distraction. My host is ready to assist if you need us."

Caden winced as he listened. That had not gone over well. "Riley, we will sort this out. We'll get your city back. Tell me what you know."

Chapter Ninety-Nine

EARTH DIMENSION THREE
Mystic Haven, B.C., Canada

ALI RELUCTANTLY UNCURLED herself from the couch when she heard the knocking on her door. She hadn't realized how long she'd been lost in her book. She tucked in her favorite Aquaman bookmarker to save her place, and as she was walking to the door, she was struck by how much Jett Sidhe, the Royal Protector, looked like Jason Momoa. Frowning, she opened the door to find Shirina waiting impatiently. "Ali! Quickly get changed. We're going out."

Ali stared at Shirina blankly, not noticing the short sexy deep purple dress that Shirina had poured herself into. "Shirina, have you ever noticed how much Jett looks like Jason Momoa?"

Shirina paused and started laughing. "You're just noticing that now? That man is fine. Now, go change."

"Where are we going?"

"The Mystic Brew. It's ladies' night."

Ali hesitated and looked down at herself. "Won't this dress do?"

Shirina tsked and looped her arm through Ali's. "We're not going to a children's princess party, Ali. Think sexy. Which way is your room?"

Ali blinked and pointed. "Shirina, this is how I normally dress. I don't even own jeans."

Shirina opened the large walk-in closet and flipped on the light, gasping as she saw the huge closet filled with princess dresses in every color. "Wow."

Ali beamed. "It's amazing right? You know I was teased a lot in school because I'm different and not exactly slim. I tried so hard to fit it. I wore the latest fashions and tried every single diet. But one day I realized that no matter what I did, I was never going to fit their standards. So, I asked myself what would make *me* happy. The answer was amazingly simple. I needed to be who I truly am. This is me. Short, a little plump and in love with medieval dresses. But sexy? Uh, I don't have sexy in my closet. It wouldn't be appropriate for my job. Besides, after work I come home and read mostly."

The blonde healer smiled. "I firmly believe that we should be ourselves and owning something that makes you feel sexy is perfectly normal if you wish to. We are going to get you out more. There are some seriously hot men on this island."

Ali rolled her eyes. "Who would not be interested in me, but alright, Shirina, I'll go with you." She looked at her dresses and finally walked over and picked out a forest green lace princess dress. "I can modify this one." She snapped her fingers and was instantly wearing the dress.

Turning to face Shirina, she asked. "What do you think? What should I change?"

Shirina walked around Ali, making hmming noises. When she faced Aliora again she nodded. "I know what to do. Make it lower cut, and tighter." Ali looked in the full-length mirror and golden sparks began to flow from her fingers. By the time they were done, Ali had a sexy corset style dress that gave her spectacular cleavage. The silk underlining had been shortened to barely decent and the lace skirt, while it came down to the floor, revealed everything up to the lining, and shaped itself lovingly over every curve. Ali stared at herself in the mirror and glanced at Shirina. Her friend wolf whistled, and they both dissolved into laughter.

They were still laughing when they got to the pub. Shirina found them a large table and soon more ladies joined them. Janie Valeska, and four of the Brody sisters. Two women walked into the pub and Shirina stood up and waved them over. Asterine Skyfire and Nerys Daenala. All kinds of appetizers were delivered, and they gave their drink orders to the cute male waiter.

Ali noticed that a lot of men were there, and she looked at Shirina. Shirina grinned. "Dance partners." Some of the other ladies chimed in what else the men were good for, and the youngest Brody sister, Catelyn, stood up. "I've been inspired." Everyone started to hoot and holler as she walked over to a man and took his hand, walking to the dance floor.

Within a couple minutes, all the ladies were dancing, some with each other and some with the guys who'd clearly come out tonight to meet the ladies.

Ali had just sat back down and taken a sip of her drink when Jett Sidhe approached. "Dance with me."

Her eyes widened and she nodded. As he tugged her into his arms on the dance floor, Shirina gave her a thumbs up over the shoulder of her dance partner, Striker Barron.

When a faster song came on, the four of them danced together, switching partners, and laughing at each other's dance moves. After several numbers they went back to the table and collapsed into their seats with Jett and Striker dragging over a couple chairs so they could join them.

Ali listened to the blatant flirting going on between the women and men, when a shiver worked down her spine. She looked up and Baylen was leaning against the wall watching her. His eyes met hers, and she didn't look away. The Fae king was one gorgeous sexy man. Not pretty, he was far too real, far too masculine for that, far too arrogant. He straightened and walked over to her, his eyes never leaving hers. She swallowed. Her nipples hardened and a rush of heat arrowed to her intimate places.

"Aliora, you look stunning." He held out his hand, and the look in his eyes dared her to run. Maybe it was the drinks, maybe it was the butterflies that launched in her stomach when he smiled slowly. She placed her hand in his and rose to her feet.

Being in Baylen Knight's arms was not something she'd expected. Why the Fae king was at the Mystic Brew on Ladies Night was a mystery to her. The fact that he'd asked her to dance was even more mystifying. His hand felt warm on her back, and that simple touch was doing things to her. Wicked, wicked things.

"Aliora." His voice was a dark whisper.

She met his eyes, and swallowed, her breath increasing, arousal a simmering effervescence in her blood. This man should come with a warning label.

Baylen gave Ali a lazy smile and fuck if he didn't want to haul her out of here and take her somewhere private. Her body moved against his, all lush curves and softness. He could feel his cock hardening. Somewhere he could look his fill of her, breathe in her intoxicating scent, and fuck her until he worked this insanity of his system.

His hand drifted a little lower on her back, a dark sexuality simmering in his eyes. She wondered what he was like as a lover. As fast as that thought occurred, she knew that he would be very demanding. Expecting things, she had no experience with. She bit her lip and he groaned roughly, his eyes darkening with wild lust.

Aliora stepped back. Moving out of his arms, she turned and walked back to the table full of single ladies. She could feel the heat of his gaze the whole way, but playing with fire was never a wise idea. Her cheeks flushed, she snatched up her drink, drank the whole thing, and ordered another.

Chapter One Hundred

EARTH DIMENSION THREE
Mystic Haven, B.C., Canada

BAYLEN HELPED JEWEL onto the stool in the kitchen, a brush in his hand. Her long black hair was a mass of curls and knots from sleeping without a braid. He'd warned her, but his little princess was one determined child. Aurora stood on a stool at the island putting healthy snacks into their lunch bags. Falcon, who sat at the table eating his cereal, paused and pointed his spoon at Jewel. "Daddy told you, Jewel."

Jewel stuck out her tongue at her brother and handed Baylen a pretty green hair clip. "This one please. It matches my dress."

Baylen set the clip on the table and sprayed Jewel's hair with a detangler that he'd gotten from a salon. "Aurora, how many granola bars did you put in your lunch? One each, and two fruits each. I'll make your sandwiches when I'm done with Jewel's hair."

"I can make the sandwiches, Daddy." Aurora hopped off the stool and ran to the pantry.

"Hold it, Aurora. You need to eat some cereal, get dressed, and put your homework in your backpack."

Falcon carried his bowl and spoon to the dishwasher, put them in, and raced from the room shouting that he was going to dress and find something for show and tell.

"Don't forget to put your homework in your backpack, Ace, and brush your teeth!"

His morning routine was chaos. He shook his head and put the clip into Jewel's hair. "Have your cereal, Warrior Princess." There was nothing on the face of Earth that could have prepared him for being a single parent of triplets. Nothing. But he wouldn't trade it for anything. Being the Fae king only added to the importance of spending time with his kids. Mornings were family time. His staff didn't start until after he left to take his little mischief makers to school. There were just some things he refused to sacrifice. Was he super dad? Fuck no. He was simply a dad who loved his kids and was doing the best he could under the circumstances.

"Can we fly to school today, Daddy?" Jewel asked and gave him a sweet smile.

He looked at her hair that had taken him 15 minutes to detangle and shook his head. "Nope. Today, I'm driving you guys to school in the Hummer."

"Can we stop for a coffee at Arianna's shop?" Aurora piped up.

Baylen paused. He needed a coffee after last night's misadventure. "Not this morning, Ladybug." Truth was, he fully intended to have that coffee, but a man needed to have his coffee in peace sometimes. "Grab your coats and your backpacks. Let's go."

Half an hour later, Baylen entered the Chicco di Caffe. He ordered his coffee from Arianna and laughed when she hassled him about escaping his kids. Taking his coffee, he headed to the back corner of the little coffee shop and sat down to have a few minutes of peace and quiet before he went back to the castle and began the day's business. He took a sip savoring the dark flavor. A moment later Shirina plopped down in the chair across from him. "Hi, Baylen."

"Shirina." *Why was the Ward expert sitting across from him?*

"Didn't Aliora look amazing last night?"

His brow rose. *The fuck?* "The kids would have been traumatized if they saw her dressed like that."

Shirina laughed. "I'm pretty sure you were the one with trauma going on."

The little wench had the audacity to wink at him.

He took another sip of his coffee, relishing the bitterness. "Yep. I wanted to haul her back to my castle and fuck her."

Shirina blinked. "But you didn't."

"Nope. Just because I have a craving doesn't mean I'm going to indulge it."

"Why not?"

"Aliora is not the kind of woman you fuck once and forget about. I'm not walking down that road."

Shirina leaned forward. "Baylen, you had a glow-on last night. I know you quickly hid it, but you know what that means."

"It means the Ones Who've Gone Before and The Ancients are fucking with me. I've been fucked with enough, Shirina." He stood up. "I'll see you around."

Chapter One Hundred One

EARTH DIMENSION THREE
Mystic Haven, B.C., Canada

CADEN WALKED ALONG the beach and considered the phone call he'd received from Ciara Walker a few minutes ago. She'd sounded scared. That concerned him. Ciara had been through way too much. But in the last few years, since her daughter had been born, she'd seemed to finally be getting past the trauma. He saw her just ahead, sitting on the sand, looking out over the ocean. Walking over, he sat down beside her. She turned to look at him, her long dark curls blowing in the breeze.

"Hello, Ciara."

"Hi, Caden."

"Are you alright?"

She nodded. "I dreamed of being back in that basement last night."

He took note of her strained voice. "Do you have nightmares often?"

She shook her head. "Last night was the first time in years."

He could see her fingers tremble as she tucked a wind-blown strand behind a delicately pointed ear. She was obviously shaken enough that she was struggling to maintain her glamour. "Have you talked to Dr. Esteban about it?"

She drew up her knees and wrapped her fingers around them. Turning her head, she looked at him. "Caden, it was different. I could hear Wisteria calling me. She said she wasn't done with me yet."

"That's a damned scary dream."

Ciara was shaking her head. "I— I don't think that part was a dream."

Caden looked at her sharply. He wanted to reassure her that of course it was a dream, but he'd seen what that creature had done to her, and to Baylen—and to Baylen's second mate, Charli.

They'd never been able to capture Wisteria.

"Alright, Ciara. I believe you. Tell me everything."

Chapter One Hundred Two

EARTH DIMENSION THREE
Mystic Haven, B.C., Canada

CADEN RAN THROUGH THE forest as the sun rose, his feet pounding out a hard rhythm as Queen blared 'We Will Rock You' in his earbuds.

It's been a hell of a long time since I've had sex.

A rueful grin curved his lips. *Hell.* It really had been a long time if he was thinking about it when he was out for his run. He needed to make a list of things he needed to get done, and sex could go on the top of that list. Maybe he'd even put a star beside it and bold it. Hell, he'd underline it. Twice.

Obviously, the stress was getting to him. He shook his head. His life had a bad habit of getting in the way of the things he needed to do for himself, the things he enjoyed. Lately, he found himself going home after work and avoiding everyone but his kids. He hadn't gotten a haircut in forever. The stack of reports on his desk was piled high and getting higher every day, and he swore that people had forgotten how to drive. Last week he'd handed out thirty tickets, one of them to Micah Thallan who'd forgotten to signal three turns in a row.

He'd followed the tattoo artist, his lights flashing, right into the tattoo shop parking lot, got out of his vehicle, and walked up to Micah as he swung off his motorcycle. Micah looked surprised to see him.

"Hell, Micah. I should ticket you for distracted driving. I've been following you for several blocks with my lights on, and you never even noticed. You realize that you forgot to signal for the last three turns, and you ran a red?" He flipped open his ticket book and looked at Micah, who swore. "License and registration, please."

The big, tattooed Fae started patting his pockets and his eyes got wide. "Shit. I don't seem to have my wallet with me."

Growling, he'd glared at Micah. "Distracted driving, three missed turn signals, running a red light, and no license or registration? Micah, I was on my way to get my Tim's when you cut in front of me. This is not how I wanted to start my day." Growling again, he scribbled out a ticket for one missed turn signal, handed it to the sweating tattoo artist and stomped back to his car. He never did get his coffee that day.

There was a haze in the air today, and his tiger was irritated by the faint smell of smoke. He ignored the cat's pissed off growls and kept running. Hell, they had four fires burning on the island right now. Four damn fires. Bashaya, his sister, and the Fire Chief had shown up in his office for a few minutes yesterday and told him they were concerned arson was a factor. *Arson. The hell?* Forest fires were a dangerous thing, to think that someone might have set them deliberately was mind blowing. He'd had Kai head out to the start points of each fire to see what he could find, and that was another thing. He was worried about his sister. She was second in command at the fire station and that meant she was out at every one of those fires. Yesterday there had been a 911 call for an ambulance to be sent to the fire burning along the Woss Lake Provincial Park border. He'd known that Bashaya was up there. Thank the ancients, she'd called him mere minutes later to let him know it wasn't her.

Breathing hard, he rounded a bend in the trail, and realized that he'd run a hell of a lot further than he'd intended. He was close to Englishman River Falls. He decided to run to the falls then head home. As he approached the falls, he saw the glow at the top, the beauty of the scenery was instantly forgotten as his heart slammed hard in his chest and his mind filled with thoughts of a fire. Pulling out his phone, he dropped his glamour, and shot up into the air, flying hard and fast toward the glow. At the top of the falls, he hovered and stared around in relief. No fire. It was The Ward. Torn between laughing and swearing he landed and walked over to the island Protector. It swirled around him in shimmering golden colors, and he smiled, albeit a bit grimly.

"Caden. Guardian." The Ward began to pour a tumble of images through his mind as it expressed its delight in seeing him.

"Why are you here?" He pathed the mind link to The Ward.

"Remembering." Images of the last time he'd joined his friends and family playing in the falls tumbled through his mind, and he understood. The Ward was lonely. More images filled his mind. Images of his kids and family and he

paused as he realized how lonely he was too. How much he missed the laughter and the love of his family. He turned and made a decision. A couple phone calls later, he'd taken the day off work, called his kids and his parents who were calling his sisters. They would pick up his kids and all head up here. He put his phone away and walked over to sit on a fallen log. He hadn't had a conversation with The Ward in a long time.

Chapter One Hundred Three

EARTH DIMENSION THREE
Mystic Haven, B.C., Canada

THE KNOCK AT THE DOOR early in the morning had Aliora skipping across the room. Her delivery was here! She opened the door and was surprised to see the delivery woman had two packages. "Sign here please."

Ali signed and watched the delivery person walk away before using her telekinesis to move the two packages inside. The first was her new Star Wars Princess Leia gowns. She'd gotten them all! How could she resist? She tore off the strip on the box and opened the flaps. *Oh, My Gosh! They were perfect!* After making sure they fit, she sent them to her washing machine and looked through the accompanying accessories, most excited about the lightsaber. She paid a pretty penny for that. She turned it on and whoosh, it lit up. Purple light glowed and she squealed as she stood up and swooshed the lightsaber through the air. *The kids are going to love this!* Smiling, she sent the lightsaber and other accessories floating off to her closet.

Taking a deep breath, still smiling, she picked up the other box and brought it into the kitchen. Setting it on the island, she opened it and gasped. Oh, her family had sent her a care package! Eagerly she began to go through the goodies. A Tupperware container was filled with her favorite cookies from her mom. Her dad had sent bear spray—She blinked. *Bear spray?* Shaking her head and laughing she picked up the carefully wrapped plant that was tucked in beside a new mug. It was a seedling from her Grandma Ciska's lavender plant. She smiled and set the plant on a table in a bright patch of sunlight. Carefully, she removed the packing and watered it. It was like her grandmother had reached across the miles that separated them and given her a hug. She set the mug to the side for the moment and picked up the four hand-painted pictures from the bottom of the box. Her human adopted and foster siblings had painted pictures of her at the beach. She laughed, delighted with the bright colors, and exaggerated stick figures, knowing that they were excited to come for the visit they'd been promised next summer. She set them on her island countertop. She would need to purchase frames for them. Finally, she picked up the mug her grandfather, Edge, had sent her and read the paper he had taped over the mug.

This mug is not from me! It's from your grandmother. I just thought the birds were cute, and I couldn't stop laughing. Okay. It's totally inappropriate. That's why it's from your grandmother.

She unwrapped the paper and burst into laughter at the words. *'Nice Tits!'* and all over the mug were pictures of birds with their names written under them. 'Blue tit, Crested tit, Willow tit, Marsh tit, Coal tit.' She was still laughing when she opened her laptop and initiated a video call. Her grandfather, Edge, answered, and she lifted her freshly washed mug, filled with steaming coffee. "I'm telling Grandma Ciska on you Grandpa."

His laughter filled the room and his eyes sparkled with mischief. "You needed a birdwatcher's cup, Ali. I'm sure that your island has a lot of birds."

"Uh uh." She shook her head. "We call them 'Chickadees' in Canada, Grandpa!"

"Edge, what did you do?" That was her Grandma Ciska's voice and a moment later she sat down beside her husband.

Ali lifted her mug of coffee and her Elven grandmother laughed and looked at her husband. "Edge! You are such a rascal." Her voice was affectionate though. The rest of her family drifted into the room, and the conversation that followed was full of laughter and love. Eventually, everyone but her Grandma Ciska drifted off to do their normal things. "What's on your mind, Ali?"

Aliora smiled. Her Grandmother knew her so well. "I wanted to ask about mating signs."

"Have you met someone?"

Ali bit her lip and shrugged. "I'm not sure that anything will come of it. I just found myself wanting to know. I mean, I'm not exactly normal."

Ciska smiled. "You're normal for you. You don't need to be 'normal' for anyone else my darling. Grab a pen, you might need to write all this down. You are a unique being created through love. Your family is made up of different species. The mating signs that you have will be diverse, and I believe, an unexpected mix, just as you are."

By the end of the conversation Ali's head was spinning, and she knew that those sexy dreams of a certain Fae king were a definite mating sign for the Fae. She also suspected that the moment when she lost control of her magic in the coffee incident was a mating sign, and the intensifying color of her energy wings, and if she was honest, the fact that Baylen Knight smelled so good to her. She pondered this unexpected development for a few minutes. Getting up she went to the fridge and opened the freezer. She contemplated her choices and finally picked the tub of 'Death by Chocolate' ice cream. Carrying the small tub, she got a spoon out of the drawer, walked out onto her back deck and curled up on her porch swing.

This was an unmitigated disaster. How could she be the mate to the Fae king? *How?* Had the Creators lost their ever-loving minds? She scooped a bite of ice cream into her mouth pausing to savor the rich chocolate flavors. Mmm.

The sheer amount of power that the Fae king contained made her shiver. The intensity of his dark gaze whenever he looked at her sent her into a spiral of lust. But she also knew the stories. He'd lost two mates, and now, had at least a local reputation for having a different woman on his arm to every event he attended. Nope, nope, nope, this was not a man she could get involved with. A thought popped into her mind, and she brightened. There were no mating marks. She relaxed back into the swing and had another bite of ice cream. She'd been worrying about nothing.

"Looks like you're enjoying that."

Ali screamed and jerked up straight. The bite of ice cream she'd been about to eat flew off her spoon and landed on the t-shirt of the very man she'd been thinking about.

"Whoa." Baylen laughed. "It's just me. You know, the king who is not your king."

Ali stared at him, her eyes wide. "How did you get here?"

"I flew. It's a perk of being a Fae."

"I—" her eyes followed the glob of chocolate ice cream sliding down his shirt. "Oh, dear. I'm sorry." She lifted her hand, golden magic spilling from her fingers. The instant her magic touched him the ice cream vanished, and he hissed in a breath. His dark eyes met hers and she swallowed. "Sorry. I should have asked first."

He shrugged, trying to appear nonchalant. Which was fucking near impossible with the instant hard on that had risen the second her magic had touched him. "I wanted to ask you about something."

Ali rose to her feet, her long skirts swishing around her ankles. Her bare toes with their painted purple nails peeking out from under the hem. "Come in, I have coffee on." She led him into her kitchen, stashed her ice cream back in the freezer, and reached into a cupboard to grab him a mug. She poured him a coffee and brought it over to the table, where he was standing holding her new mug. He looked at her and lifted his eyebrow, before glancing down at her chest. He looked back up and winked. "Agreed." He handed her the cup.

She rubbed her left ear and set his coffee down. Picking up the mug he read out loud. "Good morning, I see the assassins have failed." He chuckled. "Guess I deserve that."

Willing her fangs to retreat she picked up her notebook, closed it, hoping like hell that he hadn't read her notes, and set her laptop on it. "Have a seat. What can I do for you, Baylen?"

"You're part Sprite, correct?"

Ali nodded. There was no point in denying it when she kept having fang issues, and he'd seen her nightglow."

"By the way, your fangs are showing."

She forced back a growl. "Sprites bite when they get angry. Just a warning."

He smirked. "I bite back. Just a warning."

She shook her head and turned to the Mediterranean blue cabinet by the table and pulled out a bottle of Irish whiskey. She poured a generous amount into her coffee and held up the bottle offering him some.

"Sure. Why the hell not. Even though it's only," He glanced through the glass doors to the sun. "Eleven in the morning."

"Don't judge," she snapped and set the bottle down on the table with a thump.

Laughing, Baylen picked up the bottle and added the whiskey to his coffee. "Trust me, Aliora, I would be the last person to judge you. I've got more sins than you can count."

Exasperated, Ali took a drink of her coffee. "What do you want to know about Sprites?"

"The mating signs."

Ali choked on her coffee, swallowed hard, and started coughing.

Baylen was up and pounding on her back in an instant.

She lifted her hand and managed to gasp out. "I'm" —cough, cough— "fine. Just swallowed wrong." She took a small careful sip and managed to clear her throat. Creators, she was so embarrassed. She could feel her cheeks heating. "Why do you want to know about Sprite mating signs?"

"Are they a closely guarded secret?"

Ali shook her head.

Baylen studied her face. "I'm curious. Indulge me."

"Uh." She eyed the man sitting across from her. *Why was her life so freaking messed up lately?* "Sprites, uh, have this pheromone, and their wings get brighter, and there's a mating mark."

Baylen took a drink of his coffee and watched her. "Your wings are pretty bright."

Ali blinked. "My—?" She shook her head. "I have Fae wings."

"Why does that matter?"

"Sprite wings are like a butterfly's wings. They're physical wings made of a similar material to butterfly wings, and they are usually softer colors until they mate when they become vivid. My wings are made of energy like yours. Your wings are pretty brightly colored from what I remember. I only saw them once. You know, during the coffee incident."

Baylen nodded and stood up, letting go of his glamour. That was the thing with Baylen Knight, she realized. Letting go of his glamour only changed the fact that you could see his wings. Not like most Fae who looked fully human with their glamour. She fought against the insane urge to stroke them, tucking her hands behind her back. *Bad Aliora. Bad.* "Your wings are amazing."

He had the audacity to wink at her. "Go ahead, touch them."

She gasped.

"You were projecting. I'm a Fae. I catch those thoughts."

She groaned and shook her head. "Stop tempting me. We both know that's not a good idea."

Baylen grinned. "Are you ever bad, Ali?"

She swallowed remembering how she had walked away from him the other night.

"Show me you. Let go of your glamour."

She stared at Baylen, her eyes huge. This was an intimacy that she rarely allowed. Only her family saw her without her glamour.

"Come on little halfling, I'm not asking you to get naked. I want to see you without your glamour. The real you. Like you're seeing me."

Aliora bit her lip and nodded hesitantly. She could show him some. Moving around the table, she stood in front of him and took a deep breath, allowing the first layer of her glamour to slip away. Her long curly hair brightened, all the color of the sunset streaking through it. The unusual dual color of her eyes intensified, earth and water, an impossible combination. Her ears developed delicate points. —and finally, energy wings that shimmered with brilliant colors.

Baylen stared in amazement. "Beautiful." He stepped closer. "You're not like any halfling I've ever known, Aliora."

She shrugged. "I told you, I'm not a halfling."

"You did, didn't you." She was the most stunning being he'd ever seen.

"May I? He lifted his hand towards her wing. Her eyes met his, she bit her lip, and finally she nodded, her hand reaching out. He groaned silently and stepped closer so she could reach his wings. Gently, he ran his fingers over her wing hissing at the instant electric reaction. She inhaled sharply. Her fingers grazed his wing. *Fuck.* His eyes met hers. The exquisite pleasure had turned his cock to stone. He watched her nipples harden under her dress and it was all he could do not to tear it from her body. She swallowed, and he fucking had to step back. The primal part of his Fae nature demanding that he take her. He took another step back.

"You're fucking beautiful." Tearing his gaze from her, he launched into the air, his massive energy wings easily carrying him up into the stratosphere. Fire. He'd fucking played with fire, and he knew why. He'd never expected to ever have another mate, and fuck if he didn't miss that intensity that only came with that bond.

Banking, he headed toward the Castle. He needed a shower, a fucking ice-cold shower, and he needed to remember that two women had died because he had failed to protect them. He needed to remember his fucking enemies. He needed to remember that he was darkness, and that he destroyed.

Chapter One Hundred Four

EARTH DIMENSION THREE
Mystic Haven, B.C., Canada

SHIRINA DROVE ROSIE through a mountain pass deep in the interior of the island. The road wound through the mountain passes, sheer rock faces rising thousands of feet into the air, the ditches showing evidence of the falling rocks that the road signs warned about. Small waterfalls cascaded down the mountainside, a light mist rising in the morning air. Lush growths of ferns, shrubs, trees, and flowers grew up everywhere they'd found a foothold. The sight caused a deep peace to settle into her heart. Truly this planet was a beautiful haven.

A quiet beep sounded from Luna, and her windshield took on a blue glow as information began to scroll. Shirina frowned. "Luna, take over while I study these alerts."

The computer instantly went into autopilot mode. She quickly turned her seat and moved into the passenger side of the van, touching a hidden control that brought up another holo-screen. The Ward that inhabited this mountain range was behaving strangely. Very strangely. Concerned, she began to bring up information on all the Wards. An anomaly was the last thing they needed. Especially with that bastard, Ash Morana, in the area.

The remaining Wards appeared, each one a shimmering ever-changing iridescent dot with information particular to that Ward updating continuously. She studied each Ward and the readings that were being relayed and was relieved to see that all the other Wards were fine. "Close down all the Ward readings except the one we have the alert on." The dots marking the Wards winked out. "Enlarge the readings for the Ward with the anomaly. How far are we from that Ward, Luna?"

"The anomalous Ward is fifteen point eight nine kilometers southwest of our position."

Shirina studied the readings again.

"Proceed to the Ward, Luna." She began to pull up the history of this Ward. She grew more concerned the deeper she dug into this one's history. This Ward was remote, and that meant it was not visited often by the Fae. She sighed and leaned back against her seat, considering the problem. Wards gained strength from the goodness of the people that came and spent time with them. The simplest solution would be to hold a Fae Gathering at that Ward. In fact, it was imperative. She would also have to hold another series of educational meetings for the Fae about the Wards. She shook her head. No. Not just the Fae. The whole island's population needed to be educated. There should never be a time when any Ward was not receiving frequent and regular visits from the people of this island.

Parking Rosie, Shirina climbed out of the van and walked over to the cliff, astonished by the brightness of the Ward that was hovering over a large waterfall. *What on earth was it doing?*

Dropping her glamour, she flew over the waterfall, then down the cliff, skimming close along the Ward, her wings brushing against the water that tumbled over the cliff. The Ward glowed a brilliant gold, almost blinding in its radiance. She swooped into the light and the desperate loneliness of the Ward flowed into her. Gently she opened her mind to the sentient being.

A tumble of images filled her mind as the Ward surrounded her, images of its sorrow and grief, and its unbearable aloneness.

This could not continue. With a push of powerful Fae energy, she sent out a call to the Fae. *"All available Fae, come to the Ward!"*

It was not a call that could be ignored. She was an ancient being of power, her station as The Ward Expert, a Royal appointment.

Baylen, Jett, and Striker were in the middle of a poker game with Micah, and Rhys when the urgent Fae call from Shirina blasted across the common Fae mind link. They didn't even hesitate. If Shirina said to come, they needed to come. Dropping their cards, they stood up and Rhys scowled at them. "Just when I was winning, you get called to a Fae party. It's no fun being the one to miss out on the shenanigan's boys. Go. I'll clean up here and head home. You guys owe me."

Baylen laughed and shook his head. "I'll bring steaks and beer on the weekend, and we can have a barbeque at your place."

"Bring the kids. I miss the little hooligans."

Baylen nodded and stepped out onto the balcony with his Trium and Micah. They soared up into the sky, even as he sent Fae energy sweeping outward in a powerful wave, seeking out the emergency.

"*The Mountain Ward.*" Shirina's mind touched his, her data flowing over the mind link.

He swore harshly and added his voice to the common Fae mind link. "*We have a situation. Haul ass to the coordinates that Shirina is providing!*"

The power of the ancient Fae as they lifted off was unmistakable. Maxen and Blade, the former Trium, spoke over a mind link to him. "*Do you know what's happened, Baylen?*"

"We have a Ward in crisis. From what Shirina has sent to me, the Ward has activated its reserve energy stores." He heard Maxen's sharp intake of breath.

"*Baylen, that hasn't happened since the war on Erendrial.*"

Blade cut off Maxen "*Are you sure that there hasn't been an attack?*"

"*Shirina confirms there is no attack. She says the Ward hasn't been visited by the Fae in well over a year.*" He heard some of the other Ancient Fae over the mind link. —Ryder's muttered a curse, along with Sam Walkers. The feminine voices of Asterine and Nerys. They were angry. Furious might be more accurate. Not at the Fae community, at themselves—at their own failure in doing their part to keep the Wards healthy. That was the true way of the Fae. To look first at what you could do and then do it, and to also gather as a community to help each other, to have communion and fellowship. To gather in the face of life.

They would handle this crisis as a gathering, and as Fae, they would decide together how to prevent such a problem from ever happening again.

As he flew up to the Ward he was met with the most astonishing sight. The Ward was glowing gold, orange and red as it hovered over a beautiful waterfall and in the midst of the Ward was Shirina. Fully Fae, her glamor burned away as she drew and poured massive amounts of Fae energy into the Ward. Her silvery blonde hair floating around her shoulders, her purple eyes glowing as she communed with the Ward on a level that no other Fae had ever been able to achieve.

She smiled when she saw him and, through a mind link, invited him to join her. Baylen flew into the Ward, and instantly felt the desperate aloneness of this sentient being. With a single word over the Fae common mind link, he released the gathering Fae to come forward into the Ward.

Shirina smiled and touched his arm gently, then pointed to the sky. To his shock, he saw not only Fae, but Wards from all over the island. The Wards created on Earth had been given the ability to learn and to grow and today they demonstrated how much they had learned. He reached out and invited them to gather with the Fae as they sought to bring healing to one of their own.

Noticing Micah sitting on a large boulder, Baylen landed and walked over to see what he was doing. Micah was deeply immersed in drawing the gathering. Baylen knew it would be an important historical piece in the future.

As the sun set that night, Fae glow orbs began to appear. Fires were lit and food prepared. The Fae Community had decided to stay until this Ward was fully restored.

He turned and looked again at the Ward and was relieved to see that it was shimmering and starting to show its normal iridescent coloring. The Fae had lived with these powerful sentient beings for thousands upon thousands of centuries. They were created from the essence of the Fae, the best parts of them. To lose even one would be a devastating loss.

Chapter One Hundred Five

SWIMMING IN THE EARLY morning had become a habit she supposed. But it was a practical one. Greeting the sun while swimming seemed to fill all the needs of her mixed genetics. She was wading out of the ocean a step or two from her private beach when the Fae king landed in front of her. His long black hair was tied back, revealing his pointed ears. Black t-shirt, black jeans and his wings shimmering vividly in the sunlight. *Creators, he was beautiful.*

Baylen's eyes widened as they met hers, and a half smile tilted up the corner of his mouth. *Fuck, she was beautiful.* She obviously hadn't expected company. He let his gaze drift down her body. Her naked body. *Does she skinny dip every morning?*

Ali gasped as she remembered she was naked. Her cheeks flamed red. *How could she have forgotten?* She blamed him and his pretty Fae looks. *Damn it!* She opened her hand, golden magic sparkling in the air and the waves along the shoreline rose to wrap around her in a dress of seafoam and turquoise water.

"That's a shame. I could look at you all day, rising from the sea, the sun highlighting your body."

Ali stepped onto the beach, the ocean trailing behind her. "What are you doing here?" Yes, her voice was sharp, but damn it, he had caught her skinny dipping!

"I have some more questions."

"More?" She stared at him and gave a strangled sounding laugh. "I—I need coffee."

"Coffee sounds good."

"Damn it." She muttered under her breath, as she glanced down at her ocean dress. She couldn't wear this into the house. She glanced at Baylen, and he watched her.

"I'm curious. What are you going to do now? I'm pretty sure you don't want to bring the ocean into your house."

She growled and between one second and the next vanished and reappeared. Baylen jerked back as she came dangerously close to biting him, his hand closing over the back of her neck. "Fuck. Aliora!" His free hand came up to wipe a drop of blood from his neck. Her fangs had grazed him.

She growled again and struggled against his hold. "Hellcat!"

"Sprite." she replied. "Let go."

"So you can bite me? I don't think so."

She took a deep breath and lifted her hand, golden magic spinning around the seafoam and water dress she'd created. The dress began to change, liquid becoming silk, the water and seafoam sliding back into the ocean. "You can let go now. I won't bite you."

Baylen observed the whole process with surprise. He could feel the draw of Fae energy she used but there were other magics and energies involved as well. His eyes narrowed at her words. "That's a shame, I was looking forward to biting you back. That's a skillful blending of magic." He released his hold on her neck.

Aliora shook her head and walked up the steps to her deck. Opening the patio door, she stepped inside, and with a sparkle of magic, the coffee began to make itself. She opened the refrigerator and took out the ingredients to make omelets. She heard Baylen's footsteps as he came in behind her and shut the patio door. "Are you hungry?"

"Yes, all that fresh sea air and a wild sprite halfling left me with an appetite."

She glanced over at him, and he grinned at her. "I'll chop while you grate the cheese."

Aliora sighed. Looked like she was not going to be rid of the Fae king that easily. "What are your questions?"

"Tell me about this pheromone."

Ugh! "Why is this important?"

"I'm a curious man, and it's important for a king to understand any mating situations that might arise for his people."

"Hmm." Ali finished grating the cheese and broke some eggs into a bowl, adding a small amount of cream and seasonings before she began to whisk the eggs. "Sprites have a pheromone they release which makes them irresistible to their mates. Please be aware though, that while there might be wild sex going on, that's not enough to complete the mating. Love is critical for a successful mating."

Baylen watched as she poured the eggs into pans. When she was done, he picked up the cutting board and added the mushrooms, peppers, and onions that he'd chopped. Ali put the lids on the pans and walked over to the coffee maker that had finished while they were getting the omelets ready to cook. She poured them both a cup and motioned to the stools along the island. She waited until he sat down before taking a seat. He reached over to her stool and dragged it next to his.

"What do you know about Fae mating?" He asked after taking a sip of his coffee.

Ali shrugged. "Fae glow when they find their mates, and they share dreams."

"Sexy dreams." Baylen looked at her.

She nodded. "Is that all it takes to mate a Fae? Sounds to me like there is room for error in that process."

Baylen laughed. "When Fae mates have sex in their natural form, the male Fae creates a soul bond between them."

Aliora's eyebrow rose. "They don't create it together?"

Baylen shook his head. "The Fae were a primitive species when they first evolved. We have no idea why that part of the mating has not changed in all this time. But I can tell you that our women have risen to the challenge. They do not ever have sex in their true Fae form unless they are certain the man is their mate."

"Hmm." Aliora shook her head and took a sip of her coffee.

"I imagine that mating is much more complex for a halfling."

Aliora shrugged. "It might be"

"How would you know if it happened?"

Scrunching her nose, Aliora put her hand behind her back and crossed her fingers. "Well... I assume there would be pheromones and dreams." She frowned. "But maybe the Sprite and Fae signs would cancel each other out, and I'll never find a mate."

"I hope that you find your mate, Ali."

Her eyes met his and she tilted her head as if trying to figure him out. She lifted her hand and touched his face. "What about you, Baylen? Do you wish to find your mate? Do you wish to fall in love?"

He shook his head. "I've had two mates. My quota is used up."

She shook her head, feeling his sadness through the connection physical touch created for her. He reached up and took her hand, easing it away from his face. "I do, however, still enjoy sex." He winked at her and she laughed. Getting up, she served the omelets and poured them more coffee, glad the subject was closed.

Chapter One Hundred Six

EARTH DIMENSION THREE
Mystic Haven, B.C., Canada

BAYLEN BLINKED AWAKE. His dream had offered a tantalizing glimpse into his people. Thankfully not a horrific one, tonight. in fact, he hadn't had a nightmare in a few weeks. He wasn't sure why exactly, but he'd fucking take the sexy dreams he'd been having of a certain halfling without complaint if it meant the nightmares stopped.

His mind moved back to the rich imagery of his dream. Since that terrible day, so many years ago, when desperation had forced him to tap into the essence of all the Fae that had gone before, from the smallest Fae to the greatest warriors and kings, his dreams had changed. So many dreams, so many memories that were not his own.

He stood up and shoved a hand through his hair. Tonight, he'd dreamed of an ancient named Arion Aossi. The man had been an incredible warrior. A Fae of integrity and honor. The dream had shown Arion warning his king of a traitor, and a dangerous plan. Baylen grinned. The man had balls. He suspected he would have enjoyed knowing this man. Perhaps he would ask Ryder about him. Ryder should know who the king was, that Arion warned. He wondered how many eons before Ryder this mystery king had reigned. Much of their history had been lost in that terrible war that sent the Fae fleeing for their lives. He padded barefoot through the castle halls, checked his kids, went to the kitchen, and got a coffee. Sipping his coffee, he made his way to security and spoke with the Fae warriors who stood watch, then stopped by the cyber security division. He had some of the best minds in the world hunting down threats and mining the dark web. He walked over to his best threat hunter, and they spoke for a few minutes before he went to his office and opened his computer. It was important that he record every memory, every dream that was not his. His people's history deserved to be preserved.

Chapter One Hundred Seven

EARTH DIMENSION THREE
Mystic Haven, B.C., Canada

ALIORA PERCHED CAREFULLY on the red leather sofa at the front of the tattoo parlor as she turned the page of the tattoo sample book. She admitted this was an impulse, but she had always wanted a tattoo. Something small and fun. She was considering a small tattoo of the Sol star system. Or maybe she should do a dragon? A small one on her ankle. Or maybe she would be more daring. A smile curved her lips. She knew what she wanted.

The tattooed dangerous-looking Fae who owned the shop came back into the front. "Have you decided, Sweetheart?"

She nodded. "I'd like a black heart and protected inside it a bright star. The glow in the dark kind of tattoo please.

The man nodded. "Sit with me, while I draw this. I want you to tell me if I'm getting it right." He got out a drawing pad. "By the way, I'm Micah Thallan." He noticed the bar stool was a little high, and he was nothing but chivalrous. Lifting her gently, he sat her atop the stool.

Ali gasped, blushing. This man, whose whole being shouted danger, was also beautiful, even if he was covered in his art, and she was not used to dangerous beautiful men handling her. "I'm Aliora Aurelius. I could have just flown up." She adjusted the long skirts of her crimson gown. *Why were men always lifting her up?* It was annoying but she gave them all their one lift. After that she got growly.

Micah was a skilled artist, and she was delighted as she watched the swirling lines he drew lead to a heart and the beautiful multi-faceted star. The top and bottom rays of the star stretched out to become the heart. The star nestled safely inside, its glow pushing back the darkness. "I love it!"

Micah smiled. "Where do you want it?"

Ali bit her lip and touched her chest between her breasts.

Micah lifted a brow. He hadn't expected that. Apparently, the little super was more than he'd pegged her for. A slow smile curved his lips.

The door opened, and Baylen strode in.

Micah grinned. "Give me a couple minutes, Aliora. I need to talk to my friend."

Aliora's eyes widened. The Fae king was friends with this man? How interesting. She flipped over Micah's drawing tablet and smiled at Baylen.

Baylen's eyes narrowed as he saw Aliora sitting beside Micah. *What the fuck?* "Hi, Micah. Are we still on for that barbecue?"

"Yep. I've picked up some craft beer for us to try. It's in the back waiting."

Baylen nodded, his eyes drifting to Aliora again. Why was she sitting beside Micah? He frowned. "I can take the beer now, Micah. That way it will be cold when you get to the castle."

Micah nodded and walked into the back.

As soon as they were alone, Baylen spoke. "What are you doing here?"

"I have an appointment. I want to get a tattoo."

"You? You want a tattoo?" What the ever-loving fuck was going on? Baylen stared at the small curvy woman perched on the stool behind the tattoo shop counter. "How did you meet, Micah?"

"I walked into this tattoo parlour."

"You know, he's quite a ladies' man."

"Is he? He's rather delicious with that air of danger that always—" She stopped, fighting the blush that threatened to color her cheeks. Clearing her throat, she decided it was wiser to change the subject. Especially since Baylen was growling. "How do you know Micah?"

"You don't need a tattoo."

"Not your business."

Baylen growled again.

Micah noticed the change in the atmosphere as soon as Baylen walked into the shop. Standing behind the door he heard bits and pieces of the conversation. *Him, a ladies' man? Please. Baylen was just as much a ladies' man as he was.* Shaking his head, he chuckled. There was something going on there.

He grabbed the beer and headed back to the front, eyes watchful. "I'll be there at 5:30. Can I bring a date? Or is it a guy's night?"

"Guy's night." Baylen took the beer. He watched Ali for a brief moment and walked out the door.

Micah turned to Aliora with a frown. Baylen was acting weird. He was going to have to ask him about that when he got to the castle. "Come on to the back, Aliora. I've got a private room. You're going to have to take off that dress."

Aliora nodded and shook her head when he reached for her. "I've been getting off chairs and stools by myself since I was three. I'm good."

Micah laughed and opened the door for her. "Hey, Shade, watch the front. I have a client."

He ushered Aliora into the small room that he did his tattoo's in. You're either going to have to take off the whole dress or drop it to your waist. It's your choice." Micah said as he began to assemble his inks. "There is a sheet to cover up with." He glanced over at her and paused. "Sorry, the bra is going to have to go too."

Ali closed her eyes for a moment. *Damn.* She maybe should have thought this through more. *Brave. She was brave and confident. This was nothing but a thing.* She turned her back, undressed, and took the sheet that Micah handed her.

"We can arrange this to cover you up and allow me to work. Hop up on the table. Do you want a numbing agent?"

She flew up and onto the table and tucked the sheet around herself. Micah helped her to adjust the sheet so he could work without revealing too much.

"Numbing agent?"

Aliora shook her head. "It's just a small one. I'll be fine."

"Okay. Relax, this will not take too long." As he worked, he began to ask her questions.

"How long have you been here, in Mystic Haven?"

"Three years."

"Three years? How have we not met before this?"

Ali laughed. "I guess I hang out with a younger crowd."

He looked up at her statement. "Younger crowd? How old do you think I am, sweetheart?" He grinned at the look of dismay on her face. "Relax, I'm a whopping thirty-six. In Fae circles that's considered young. You do know the Fae live close to twenty millennia."

Ali laughed. "I do know that. I'm thirty-two. Years not millennia. You seem to know the Fae king really well."

"Baylen and I have known each other since we were kids. We grew up together and have been best friends ever since. We were in the same grade, and we joined the Fae military together."

"So, the Fae king is an old geezer like you."

Micah looked at her with a stare. His lips twitching in amusement. "Old geezer? Let me say, these old geezers can run circles around this younger generation. Not to mention we have more experience and stamina. Now, if you wanna see *real* old geezers, you should meet some of the ancient Fae on this island.

"Ha. I doubt either of you have more stamina than me. I'm a children's party entertainer."

He laughed. "When you get with someone you are really into, you would be surprised at the stamina you will have. It's like automatic energizer bunny time. You keep going and going..."

Ali rolled her eyes. "You're talking about tricks. Magic tricks."

"Sweetheart, nothing I do is magic tricks." He smirked. "You ever been with a Fae male?" He grinned at her blush. "Lemme just say that there is a difference between all the Supes in this community. When I use my "magic" it's for the sole purpose of pleasure." He waited to see her reaction.

Aliora shook her head and groaned. "Please. Do you know how many times I've heard superhuman males say that? Now, on the other hand, I really do magic tricks."

Micah looked at her with a raised eyebrow. "Tricks?"

"Well, not tricks. I'm good with telekinesis and glamours and a few other things. The kids love it."

"Hmm, I might like to see you in action."

Ali winked and a tiara appeared on her head. She scrunched her nose, and a sword leaned up against Micah's workstation.

He blinked at the sword, momentarily at a loss for words.

Ali grinned. *That's how you finish a conversation with a male about their 'magic.'*

Micah handed her a small mirror to look at the tattoo. *Damned if he wasn't still smirking.* Aliora was a handful.

"I like it. The star shows up well against the black heart."

This tattoo, he thought as he stood up. *Just might have made it to his favorite's list.* "I'll turn out the light and you can see it glow." He suited actions to words, and the light blinked out. He paused, surprised by the way her skin glowed a soft neon blue in the dark. Aliora had some sprite in her. But she also was Fae. That golden glow edging the neon blue was purely Fae—and since he was not glowing along with her, it meant that she was not his. She had to have recently come into contact with her mate. *Huh.* He thought of Baylen's reactions earlier. *Shit.* Baylen Effing Knight, King of the Fae, was this little sweetheart's mate.

"It's beautiful." She whispered, amazed by how the star glowed iridescent white and blue, lighting up the heart. It was so much better than she'd imagined. The way the lines of starlight flowed over her skin and framed her breasts surprised and delighted her. It was her secret. No one would know unless she was wearing a bikini, or naked.

Micah covered the tattoo with cling wrap and gave her care instructions and a small metal container of ointment. After that he went out to the front, giving her privacy to get dressed. She looked at her bra and frowned. Ugh, that was not going back on until she healed. She stuffed it into her backpack and finished dressing. Walking out into the front, she paid Micah, giving him a generous tip.

"Now that's done." Micah walked around the counter and over to her. He handed her a business card. "My private number is on here." He gave her a slow grin. "Can I have your number?"

"You want my number?" Ali smiled. She'd never been asked for her number before.

"It's much easier to ask you to lunch that way." He winked.

Chapter One Hundred Eight

EARTH DIMENSION THREE
Mystic Haven, B.C., Canada

"ARE YOU FOLLOWING ME?" Ali said, as Baylen walked up to her.

"Following you? I've been here since this morning. What are you doing here?"

Ali raised her eyebrows and shrugged, wondering why the Fae king would be hanging out at the wharf all day. There were lots of shops and restaurants, of course, but it seemed odd to her. "Ice cream."

"Ice cream? What kind?"

"Chocolate with salted caramel."

"Sounds good." He said watching her with an intensity that made her stomach get that fluttery feeling.

"Show me."

"Show you what?"

"Your tattoo." Baylen's eyes met hers and she swallowed.

"I can't show you that here!" She laughed. *Ice cream. She really needed her ice cream.* She glanced over at the ice cream shop. A low growl had her snapping her head back around to stare at Baylen. The next moment he grabbed her arm and hustled her down the steps that led to the beach.

"Wait. What are you doing?"

He steered her over the sand to the brightly colored cabanas spaced out along the beach, and the look on his face was doing strange things to her.

"Baylen! What are you doing?"

He stopped at a large turquoise one and with a slight movement of his hand sent Fae energy into the high-tech security pad. The locks all snapped open, and he ushered her into the small building, shutting the door behind them. Fae glow orbs began to materialize until they were both cast in soft light. "Show me."

She laughed, shook her head, and started to shrug out of the top of her dress. Baylen put his hand on her arm. She paused and looked up at him.

His face was a study in bemusement. "Am I going to have to kill Micah?" That low growl in his voice sent shivers down her spine. She couldn't stop her laughter as she shrugged out of the top of her dress, revealing a black swimsuit with a deep V-neckline. "I'm going to swim after my ice cream. Don't kill my tattoo artist."

He was silent for so long that she looked at him. The heat in his eyes made her swallow. He lifted his hand and traced the dark tattoo and elegant curving lines between her breasts with his finger. Her nipples pebbled and she swallowed again.

"It glows in the dark." she said to break the silence.

Instantly the glow orbs snapped out of existence. His finger gently retraced the luminous lines that framed her breasts, before moving over the shimmering star that pushed the darkness back from the heart. He looked up at her and a single orb appeared barely lighting their faces. The next moment, his hand curved around her neck, and he lowered his mouth to hers. Her hand rose to clutch at his shoulder as he plundered her mouth. *Oh, gods! He was so good at that.*

Fuck. What was he doing? He tore his mouth from hers and stepped back. *What the fuck was he doing?* Stepping back further, shaking his head, he saw her tug her top back up. He took another step back. The door swung open, and he launched into the air.

Ali stared after him, her fingers pressed to her lips. *What on earth had just happened?* She looked out the door and stepped out of the building, carefully closing the door behind her. *The Fae king had kissed her.* Okay, she needed that ice cream. Now.

Chapter One Hundred Nine

EARTH DIMENSION THREE
Mystic Haven, B.C., Canada

ALIORA OPENED THE DOOR to find the king of the Fae leaning against her door frame.

He gave her a slow up-to-no-good grin.

Her eyebrow rose. "Would you like to come in"

"Yes, Majesty"

She snorted and turned heading back to the comfy nest she'd made on the couch." Coffee's in the kitchen or there's beer in the fridge, Mr. Not My King."

Baylen sauntered into her kitchen, and she picked up her romance novel and got comfy on the couch. A couple minutes later, Baylen sprawled on the couch beside her, beer in hand. "You know, that's something I really like about you, Aliora."

She set down her book curiosity getting the best of her. She was probably going to regret this but... "What's that?"

"You don't get all worked up about the damn title."

She laughed. "Oh, come on, Baylen. There must be somethings you like about being king."

"Nope. It's just a fucking job."

She gave him a look of patent disbelief.

"Okay, I like the castle." He paused "And working with Jett and Striker. You should see us when there's danger, and we need to fight as team. That's the fucking coolest shit ever. Never seen anything like it."

"And?"

He took a sip of his beer and seemed to be thinking. "That's it."

Chapter One Hundred Ten

EARTH DIMENSION THREE
Mystic Haven, B.C., Canada

SITTING WITH MICAH in the popular little diner, Aliora laughed at the story he'd told her about his friends, Helio, Shade, and Reef.

"Micah. Aliora."

She blinked and looked up, shocked to see Baylen standing beside their table. "What are you guys doing?"

Ali glanced down at her sandwich and back up at Baylen. *Wasn't it obvious?* "Lunch."

Micah grinned. "I'm trying to convince Ali to get another tattoo—Or maybe a piercing." He winked at Aliora.

"Uh uh. I'm not doing that." She laughed and shook her head. "Some places are not meant to be pierced."

Baylen scowled. "What? What places?" He glared at Micah.

"That's Ali's business," Micah replied, his eyes narrowing.

"You guys don't mind if I join you, right?" Baylen sat down in the booth beside Ali and signaled the waitress.

"Uhm."

Micah crossed his arms and gave Baylen a hard look. "Buddy, I'm trying to have a nice lunch with Aliora."

Baylen nodded. "Lunch with Aliora sounds like a good idea to me. I enjoyed breakfast with her the other day." He slid his arm along the back of the booth.

Ali gasped, her eyes wide. "Baylen!" She looked apologetically at Micah. "It wasn't like that. Baylen came over as I was finishing my morning swim." She could feel a soft heat in her cheeks. "I hadn't had breakfast, so I offered him an omelet too."

Micah looked at Baylen quizzically. "Sounds innocent enough to me." He looked at Ali and winked. "Plus, you don't owe me an explanation. Though I would not turn down breakfast." There was a whole lot of innuendo in the last part of that comment.

Ali blinked, glancing between the two men. Clearing her throat, she picked up her glass and took a drink. Time to change the subject. "I have a private beach if you ever want to go for a swim, Micah."

Baylen growled.

She turned to stare at him. "What on earth, Baylen?"

"Micah doesn't need to go swimming with you, Aliora. I saw what you swim in."

Aliora sat up straight. "You need to go, Baylen. Right now!"

Micah smirked and looked at Baylen as he stood up. "You might want to go for a swim yourself, Baylen. Somewhere nice and cold."

Growling, Baylen walked out of the restaurant.

Chapter One Hundred Eleven

EARTH DIMENSION THREE
Mystic Haven, B.C., Canada

THE SUN HAD STARTED to set when Micah pulled up in front of her house. She climbed off the motorbike and removed her helmet, handing it to Micah who'd already taken his off. He fastened it to his bike as Ali ran a hand through her hair. "I had a lot of fun, Micah." She caught a movement out of the corner of her eye and started to turn but Micah hooked a muscular arm around her waist and pulled her closer.

"Go along with me. Baylen is on your porch."

Before she could reply he set his hands on her hips and tugged her between his parted legs. "Micah," She whispered. "What are you doing?"

He ducked his head down and spoke in her ear. "Giving Baylen something to think about."

"Why?"

"Baylen's my friend and he's been through some dark shit. Whether he admits it or not, you're his mate, and he needs you."

Ali's eyes widened but she didn't have time to refute Micah's mistaken conclusion before she heard footsteps and glanced behind her, Baylen was close to them, and he did not look so happy. Ali swallowed. She looked back at Micah, her eyes wide. "Do you have tattoos everywhere?" *Oh my gosh, why did I ask him that?*

"Uh huh. Everywhere. I'll show them to you, sometime, if you want." He smirked at her and winked.

Ali nibbled on her lip. She nodded. "Uhm, yeah that would be cool." She was sure that Baylen was close enough to have heard.

"Listen, whatever you do, give him hell." Micah's voice was so quiet that she barely heard him. "He was being an asshole. No sweet, nice Ali. Set your boundaries." He glanced over her shoulder. "Time for me to go, sweetheart." Micah said out loud, he dropped a quick kiss on her lips and gently set her away from him as he initiated a mind link with her. *I won't be far. If you need me, holler over the mind link.*

His motorcycle roared to life as Baylen's hand came down on her shoulder. Micah glanced at her, winked, and gunned his engine, roaring off down the road.

Baylen's voice was suddenly in her ear, his breath warm against her. "You don't want me to kill one of my best friends do you?"

Ali turned. "Why are you here, Baylen?"

"You've been gone for hours."

Ali narrowed her eyes. "That's not your business."

"I'm making it my business."

Ali pressed her lips together and crossed her arms. "No."

"No? No, what?"

"No, you don't get to make my business your business, especially when you were being an ass."

Baylen rubbed the back of his neck, watching Ali through hooded eyes. "Fuck this shit."

The next thing she knew he'd tossed her over his shoulder and was striding toward her house.

"Put me down!"

"Nope."

"I swear, I'm going to bite you so hard!"

"Good. I've been wanting to bite you too."

She gasped and drew a bunch of Fae energy.

"You zap me, Aliora and I'm going to paddle your ass."

She slapped her hand against his back and sent all the Fae energy she'd absorbed zapping into him."

"Fuck! Aliora!" His hand smacked her ass hard enough to make her shriek. "I warned you." He put his hand on her doorknob and with a little burst of Fae energy, disengaged her locks. Opening the door, he strode inside, slamming the door behind him. He tossed her onto the sofa and stood glaring down at her. "I catch Micah touching you again, and I'll fucking beat the shit out of him."

"What is wrong with you?" She shouted, standing up.

"You don't belong with Micah."

She reached back and grabbed one of the many fluffy soft pillows piled on the couch and whacked him with it. "I belong with whomever I choose!"

"You belong with—" His voice was a low growl of fury.

She whacked him again with the pillow. "Whomever. I. Choose." She punctuated her words with whacks of the pillow.

Baylen growled again and his glamour dropped away. He tore the pillow from her hand, wrapped a muscular arm around her and took her down onto the couch, his body heavy against hers. "What are you—" The rest of her words were lost as his mouth slammed into hers. His tongue invaded her mouth, and electricity coursed through her body in a rush of lust that blazed so hot she lost her inhibitions. Her hand closed in his hair, and she kissed him back, fury and lust converging in the perfect storm. She hissed as he broke the kiss and lifted her eyes to his face. His cheeks were flushed, his eyes dark and she could feel the hardness of his dick against her.

Between one second and the next Aliora vanished and reappeared, standing in front of the couch. She glared at the Fae king, who'd landed face first in her pile of pillows when she disappeared. "Get out!"

Baylen turned and sat up slowly. He looked at her from beneath hooded eyes as he rose from the sofa. Crossing his arms, he planted his feet wide. "Stay away fro—"

"Oh, no! You do not get to come into my home and tell me what to do!"

"I'm the Fae—"

"You are not my king!" Aliora shouted. "Even if you were, you have no right to even for one second think I will ever be your play toy! Get out!" She used her telekinesis to slam open her front door.

"I don't think—"

"You're right! You didn't think! How dare you treat me with such disrespect, and don't you ever think you have any right to tell me who I can see and who I can't see! Get out." This time she used her telekinesis to shove him back.

The shock of her telekinetic shove had him stepping back. He stared at her for a minute, a sick feeling rising as he realized what he'd done. What the fuck had he been thinking? *Fuck! Fuck! Fuck!* He knew that it was a good thing that she'd stopped him. Gods. He'd lost control of his darkness. That primal side that could have forced a Fae mating. Fucking Ancients, the risks to her if they ever mated— Images of the broken bodies of his lost mates filled his mind. He swallowed the bile that rose in his throat and choked off the howls that wanted to tear out of him. *No. No.*

He turned and walked to the door. Pausing, his hand on the doorframe he turned back to look at her. She was glorious in her anger, but he could also see the hurt in her eyes. He'd fucked up royally. "I'm sorry, Aliora. You are correct. What I did was inexcusable." He turned and walked away.

Chapter One Hundred Twelve

EARTH DIMENSION THREE
Mystic Haven, B.C., Canada

THE DOOR OPENED A COUPLE minutes later, and Micah stepped inside and turned to close the door. "You didn't really think I would leave you here by yourself with an angry Fae king, did you? I waited around back. I just saw Baylen take off like a bat out of hell. Is everything okay? He turned around and froze at the look on Aliora's face, the tears in her eyes, her red swollen lips. Her clothes looked disheveled. "What did Baylen do?" His voice was dangerously quiet.

"Nothing terrible. He was angry. He ordered me to not see you anymore, made some stupid threats, and he kissed me. But I dealt with him."

Micah nodded and walked over to her, a wry look on his face and pulled her into his arms for a gentle hug. "I'll talk to King Idiot. Did you give him hell?"

Ali leaned into Micah's hug. Why couldn't she have been a mate to someone like Micah. For all the tattoos that covered him, for all his fierce appearance, Micah was incredibly sexy and a really nice guy. Instead, it was Baylen Knight who invaded her dreams on a nightly basis. Baylen

Knight who didn't want another mate. "I set him straight and told him to get out."

"Good. Baylen has too many people who jump at his every command." Micah stepped back from the hug and slung an arm over her shoulders. "Do you have coffee? I could use a cup."

Ali nodded and set the coffee to brewing as they walked into her kitchen. They sat at her kitchen table drinking coffee, and she began to relax.

"Aliora." Micah waited until she looked at him. "I saw you glowing when I gave you that tattoo."

"That's a sprite thing."

"Not the blue glow. I once dated a sprite, so I know all about that glow in the dark thing. It's damn sexy but that isn't just what I saw. I saw the golden glow of your Fae, and since I wasn't glowing and having uncontrollable lust for you, I knew you were not glowing for me. However, Baylen had just left. He's your mate, isn't he?"

She shook her head. "It's not that simple. He is potentially my mate."

"Do you have crazy sex dreams about him?"

Ali's eyes got big, and she could feel her cheeks heating. "Micah!"

"I'd say that's a yes." He grinned.

"I'd say that is none of your business." Ali took a sip of her coffee.

"Look Ali, mating is intense for a Fae. They act out of character. They get jealous and want sex all the time. The whole purpose of those dreams is to leave you needing. To drive you into your mates' arms. The dreams will keep escalating for both of you."

"That justifies his behavior?" She lifted her chin.

"Hell no. He was being a dick, and you need to make sure that you don't let him off easy. He needs to be held accountable for his actions, just like you would hold anyone else accountable. Sweetheart, no one has the right to treat you like shit. Mate or not." He set his coffee down. "I can tell you straight up that neither Jadeah nor Charli would have tolerated any bullshit from Baylen either."

"The mates he lost?"

Micah nodded.

"Micah, Baylen doesn't want another mate. He straight up told me that."

"Do you see Baylen often?"

"Several times a week."

"You run into each other at the coffee shop, and he stops to chat?"

"He shows up here every day, and if he sees me uptown, he comes over to me."

Micah laughed and shook his head. "That's gotta be that mating urge and I suspect it's driven by Sprite pheromones."

Aliora shook her head. "You're not listening to me, Micah. He doesn't want another mate."

"I know he doesn't. But he needs one, he's too dark. What do you want, Aliora?"

"It's different for me. I'm not fully Fae and I'm not a halfling. My genetics are a mixed bag of crazy. I won't mate with anyone unless I'm in love with them."

Micah sat back in his seat and gave her the most satisfied grin she'd ever seen. "I'm going to enjoy watching this. Baylen has met his match in you."

Chapter One Hundred Thirteen

EARTH DIMENSION THREE
Mystic Haven, B.C., Canada

BAYLEN HADN'T SLEPT much last night. It had little to do with the dreams he shared with Aliora and everything to do with his actions the day before. The actions that still haunted him. He took a sip of his coffee as his laptop started. He had some reparations to make. Of course, what he was about to do wouldn't make up for his being a total asshole, but it would be a start. He got out a notebook from his desk and began to list everything he knew about Aliora. After he was done, he began to search the internet.

Chapter One Hundred Fourteen

EARTH DIMENSION THREE
Mystic Haven, B.C., Canada

ALIORA HAD CURLED UP on her porch swing, reading a book and drinking a hot chocolate when the doorbell rang. She sighed before rising and walking through the house to her front door. When she answered, a delivery man was setting down the last of a dozen parcels. She blinked. "I didn't order anything."

"Sign here Miss."

"But..."

"The invoice says they are from a Baylen Knight."

Aliora's eyebrow rose. "Thank you." She signed looking at all the packages and began to set them inside her house. As she finished, another delivery van drove up. Across the side in a fancy scroll were the words. 'Books from Another Dimension.' The large red-haired shifter who'd been driving opened the back of the van and lifted out a large box. "You'd best let me set this in your home, lassie. This box is heavy." He winked at her as she stepped back to let him enter. "I'm Helio MacConaill. I normally work over at the Mystic Ink with Micah, but the wee Angel, Amara, needed some muscle to make her delivery."

Ali laughed. "An angel needed muscle? I think she hoodwinked you."

Helio laughed and set the box on her coffee table. "Aye. But now she owes me dinner."

"Any idea what's in the box?"

"Torrid romance books, lass. If you get bored, give me a call, I can surely give you a better fantasy than what's in a book. Also, I'm verra good at cuddling." He winked at her.

A knock on the open door behind her, and Ali turned to see the teen who worked at her favorite ice cream shop 'What's The Scoop." with a large box. "Hi Ms. Ali. I was told to deliver this box of chocolate, salted caramel ice cream. There are ten tubs here. Where's your freezer?"

She pointed the way to the freezer and escorted Helio out, shaking her head at his flirting, only to see a flower delivery van, and the owner of the local jewelry store parking their vehicles, and coming down the road, the van from a local winery.

Aliora sent a mind link. *'What are you doing Baylen!'*

'Saying I'm sorry.'

"My living room looks like a parcel factory exploded in it!"

She could almost hear his grin. *"Need help?"*

"I'm not done being angry yet."

Baylen sighed. *"Fair enough."*

By the end of the day, a gourmet dinner had been delivered by five-star chef Stone Zeyev, the wolf shifter alpha. An assortment of goodies from the local bakery, a giant bag of candies from the local candy shop, eight dresses in jewel tones by a top cosplay designer, a tiara from the jeweler, five vases of flowers, and a whole case of expensive wine, oh, and Arianna, owner of her favorite coffee shop, had driven out to personally deliver a large iced caramel macchiato.

She was deep into one of the most shockingly erotic books she'd ever read, a glass of wine beside her when there was a knock at her door. Fanning her face, she set down the book, wondering who on earth was at her door at this time of night. She really should have expected Baylen to be standing there.

"Are you done being angry?"

She cleared her throat. "Partially."

"May I come in?"

She nodded, because frankly she was trying to wrestle her thoughts into submission. That book had left her tongue tied. "Would you like some coffee? Or—uhm—wine." She glanced at her own glass sitting on the coffee table beside her book. A book he had sent her.

Baylen stood in the entrance way and studied Aliora. She looked a little flustered and there was a faint pink glow to her cheeks. "I'll have whatever you're drinking."

She nodded and invited him into the living room as a wine glass and a bottle of wine floated in from the kitchen. Curling up on the couch, she watched as he sat down in the big comfy armchair.

"Look, Ali, I was out of line last night. I have no excuses. I'm sorry, and I know that buying you all this stuff, doesn't mean jack. I guess it was my way of saying that you deserve to be treated like a queen. Thank you for standing up to me and calling me on my shit."

Ali took a drink of her wine before answering. "Thank you." She glanced down at her hands before looking back up. "What made you so upset?"

Baylen rubbed the back of his neck, before leaning forward, his hands between his knees. "I'm going to be honest with you, Aliora. I'm attracted to you. I think you know that. I was jealous of Micah. Which was bullshit. You have the right to see whoever you want. The fact is that I have strict rules around who I get involved with. I'm not looking for a mate, Ali."

Ali stared at him for a moment. *Wasn't that interesting?* She swallowed. Well, she wasn't about to go where she wasn't wanted. "I honestly don't recall ever saying anything to lead you to think I saw you as a potential mate or a potential lover."

Baylen watched her silently for a moment. "You didn't."

Ali stood up and walked over to the side table where the big bag of candy sat. She reached in, her hands trembling, and pulled out a box of Pink Himalayan Salted Caramels. Setting the box on the coffee table between them, she lifted the lid, took a chocolate out of the box, and curled back up on the couch. "Help yourself." Picking up her wine glass she took a big sip, swallowing past the lump in her throat and popped the chocolate into her mouth.

Baylen watched her silently, then took a chocolate. "How's the book?"

Ali swallowed the salty sweet treat and took another sip of wine before she answered him. "The book is good. Inspiring."

Baylen gave her another look. *Inspiring?* His eyes narrowed. She forced herself to meet his eyes. "So, we've cleared up this misunderstanding?"

He nodded, watching her.

"Okay, if I see Micah or anyone else you are not going to freak out again on me?" She took a sip of wine, hoping he wouldn't notice the stiffness of her smile.

"No more freaking out."

She glanced around the room before forcing her eyes back to his. "Good to know. Well..." She stood up. "Thanks for stopping by and the..." she waved her hand. "Stuff." The wine is great. I'm going to have reading material for a long time, and enough chocolate that I'll need to take up some form of exercise." She needed him out of her home. Now. Before the tears burning her eyes fell.

Baylen rose to his feet. "Aliora..." She looked at him and he was struck by her quiet dignity. "I'm sure we'll see each other around." He opened the door and stepped outside, closing the door softly behind himself. *Fuck.* He launched into the air.

Chapter One Hundred Fifteen

EARTH DIMENSION THREE
New York City, NY, USA

ASH FLOATED IN SPACE, contemplating the blue planet in the Sol Star system. It was interesting that Rune and Eliana had an interest in dimension two of this planet and had visited it often. Well, he modified his thought. They visited the fifth century.

But every other dimension of earth? They had assigned a couple deities to keep an eye on things. There hadn't even been an Angelic Host assigned to this star system until recently, and it was a small one at that.

Maybe they were trying to hide the fact that the Fae remnant had found their way here? They'd failed in that of course. He was well aware of their presence in this world.

He looked back through time and dimensions and studied the Creators' patterns in regard to this place in the multiverse. The facts spoke for themselves. This was an inconsequential planet, and that made it perfect for his plans. He'd already established crime syndicates in several dimensions as a test. There had been no notice taken by the Creators' or their Angelic Warriors. He'd moved on to a second test in dimension three. The capture of the newly established Mer city, Cordelia, showed that he had enough resources to do more, and he'd learned from his failure with Mystic Haven, and again, there had been no retaliation from the Creators' forces.

With a small smile he opened a vortex and stepped into it. A few seconds later he stepped out in the third dimension of planet Earth, in the City of New York. His shoulder length blond hair was tied back neatly, he wore a dark grey suit with a burgundy tie, and he carried a briefcase. He entered a building and showed his credentials. After being scanned for a weapon, he was allowed to enter the secret meeting that was being held to discuss the global security risks associated with the discovery of a powerful unknown people group that identified themselves as Elves.

He listened carefully and made notes.

"We will now hear from Dr. Morana. His team made the initial discovery, and he has first-hand knowledge of their strengths."

Ash stood up and took the podium. He looked out over the scientists and world leaders gathered there and knew his moment had come. "Good afternoon. I'm Dr. Ash Morana, Head of the Genetic Experimentation Non-Human Evolutionary Testing Counsel of Scientists (G.E.N.E.T.I.C.S)" He nodded his head courteously. "Our discovery of a people group so powerful was, of course, a shock. The fact that they are genetic cousins to humans was staggering. The Elven people are clearly far more advanced than the average human. They have abilities that we did not even know existed. Indeed, we would never have known if they had not engaged in a civil war. A civil war that killed many humans.

"From our interviews with the few we managed to capture, they have no regard for human life. Their powers make them superior to us in every way.

"After a thorough evaluation of the ones we captured, we know it is possible for us to add their genetic advantages to our military personnel. Creating an even playing field.

"Is this a necessary step? We believe it is. With their abilities, they could take over the world. Their civil war and complete disregard for humanity leads us to conclude that we need to take steps to protect ourselves.

Ash turned and waited as a tall dark-haired male made his way to his side. "Please allow me to introduce Major Arrow GenOne. Major GenOne is a decorated officer in the American military. He volunteered to be the first genetically enhanced military personnel. His enhancements began five years ago and are documented in the file that has been uploaded to your stations. You can see that he now has superior strength, speed, hearing, and eyesight. There have been no side-effects from the serum we created. We will now begin a trial group of a thousand soldiers, worldwide. Information is now being uploaded to your stations about how to apply for your military to be part of the trials. Thank you."

Chapter One Hundred Sixteen

EARTH DIMENSION THREE
Canada

ASH STRODE INTO HIS next meeting, his hair lighter blond, his eyes brown instead of blue, and wearing a black suit with an orange tie. "Hello, gentlemen."

His eyes traveled over the men who were the generals of his crime syndicate. They were all handpicked and loyal even in death. They represented the darkest elements of the Superhuman society. "I've asked you all to meet with me to begin planning for our next incursion, and to inform you that I have decided to set up my base of operations here. Earth dimension three is going to become my stronghold." This time, Rune and Eliana wouldn't find out about it until it was much too late.

Chapter One Hundred Seventeen

EARTH DIMENSION THREE
Mystic Haven, B.C., Canada

SINCE IT LOOKED LIKE she wasn't going to have a mate or a lover, Ali decided that she needed to invest in the mechanical type of boyfriend. Her dreams starring the unavailable Baylen Knight hadn't stopped. In fact, if anything, they'd worsened. A girl could only take so much torment. After a discussion with Shirina, she decided to check out the small store called Kink. But it took two more weeks before she found the nerve to go to the store. The whole way there, she argued with herself. She should have just gone to an online store. She sighed and glanced wistfully at the coffee shop. Nope, that was her treat for going in person to the adult store. Two weeks of brooding was more than enough. *She needed to people.* Pulling her list out of her backpack, she read through it.

1. *Check the mail.*
2. *Stop at the drugstore.*
3. *Go to Kink.*
4. *Get a mocha from Arianna's.*
5. *Go to the Wharf and get fish and chips from the food truck.*

> *6. Eat at one of the picnic tables along the wharf and
> watch the sunset.*

Everything on her list was something she normally enjoyed. Well, with the exception of Kink. She'd never set foot in that store before, though she had been curious. Today it was all a chore.

Walking down the sidewalk, her silver skirts swirling around her feet, she focused on her destination. Opening the door, she peeked inside. Nice clean aisles, cheerful pop music playing, and a kindly grandmotherly looking woman sat behind the counter. Aliora blinked. Not what she'd expected at all.

She walked in and began to browse through the shelves. My goodness there were a lot of fake penises. Every color under the rainbow, every size and some were decked out with bumps and moving parts. Were they supposed to represent alien dicks?

She looked through the collection of erotica on a bookshelf and considered the selection of movies intended for a female audience. She was sure her eyes were wider than they'd ever been in her life. In the end, she made a single purchase and hurried out of the store, her package clutched tightly in her hands. She hadn't counted on barrelling into the man walking by. One moment she was contemplating the mocha she was going to get, and the next she was laying on the sidewalk blinking up at the sky. Her hip hurt so bad that she dreaded standing up, and her package? It was in the hands of the Fae king as he stared down at her in bemusement before looking up to see what store she'd rushed out of. His eyebrow rose, and he looked at the package in his hands. By the time he reached for her hand to help her up a wicked light had entered his eyes. *Just kill me now.* She thought. "Thank you." Is what she said. "I, uhm, I'm sorry I didn't see you."

Baylen nodded, trying not to smirk. "Are you okay?"

She nodded and took a step and groaned at the sharp pain shooting down her leg. "Y-yes."

"Liar." Baylen frowned. "Where are you hurt?"

"It's nothing. I just need to walk it off. Uhm," she held out her hand. "I'll put that in my backpack." She reached for the package.

"Uh Uh." Baylen shook his head. "What were you shopping for?"

Aliora's eyes widened. "Uh, just stuff. You know... stuff. Nothing important or interesting." Oh, heavens, she was babbling.

"I like stuff." He started to open the bag. Ali snatched it out of his hands.

"Not that stuff. You wouldn't like that stuff. It's uh lady's stuff. You know?"

"Ladies stuff, huh? Why don't I put that in your backpack for you?" He took the package back and picked up her backpack from where it lay forgotten on the ground.

Ali took a step toward him, alarm written all over her face, and her breath hissed out of her as pain streaked down her leg. Instantly, Baylen scooped her into his arms. "I think you need to see a doctor."

She started to shake her head, but he was already flying up into the air. At least he'd set the package and her backpack on her stomach. She quickly tucked the package into the backpack before looping an arm around his neck to hang on for dear life. "You're flying a little fast!"

"You're a little hurt."

Within a couple of minutes, he'd landed and walked into the hospital with her still in his arms.

"Put me down, Baylen!" She hissed and glanced around, her face heating. "It's just a bruise."

A nurse ushered them back to the emergency room, and Baylen laid her on the gurney the nurse indicated.

"It's a bruise." she said again,

but no one was listening to her.

An hour later, Baylen carried her into her living room and set her down on the couch. "I'll get a bath running for you. Where do you keep your Epsom salts?"

Aliora wanted to scream. "Baylen, I can manage. It's just a bruised hip."

"The doctor said it's deeply bruised, and you are lucky it wasn't a fracture. He said you are to stay off your feet for a few days."

"I'm generously padded, Baylen. In case you haven't noticed!"

"I notice everything about you. Epsom salts."

She counted slowly to ten. "In my master bath, under the sink. But I can—"

"Look, Ali, I'm not going to leave you like this. Stop arguing," Baylen growled, before stomping off into her bedroom. Seconds later, she heard water running in her bathtub. *Creators, she needed a coffee. Screw that. She needed alcohol.* He was back moments later, lifting her up and carrying her into the bathroom. He set her on the toilet and reached down to gather her skirt into his hands and started lifting. "Whoa there big guy! What are you doing?"

"Helping you to get into the bath." He pulled her dress off over her head. She glared at him and pointed her finger at the door. "Out! I am a fully functioning superhuman with skills you can't even perceive. I can and will get myself into the bath. Now, out before I zap you so hard, you will have burns!"

Baylen paused and blinked down at her, and that was when he saw the sexy lingerie she was wearing and the part of him that had gotten him into so much trouble a couple weeks ago shot to attention, nearly scarring itself against the zipper of his jeans. "Uhm. Yeah. I'll, uh, get you a glass of wine." He turned around and walked out of the bathroom.

He could hear her moving around in the bathroom, almost feel every single wince. *Fucking mating shit.* He went to grab the wine out of the fridge and remembered the Irish whiskey she had stored in the fancy cabinet by her table. He shut the fridge and got out the whiskey. After a hunt through her cupboards, he found a couple of glasses and set them on the island. He poured the whisky and turned around to lean against the island, his arms crossed over his chest. Fuck, his hard on still hadn't gone down. He downed the whiskey and poured himself another. By the ancients, his fucking dreams had been intense the last couple of weeks, and now he was here. In her house, and she was naked just a few feet from where he stood. He'd never fucking expected her to be coming out of Kink —with a fucking package in her hands. If his creatorsdamned brain hadn't been so wrapped up in his last cursed dream, he would have seen her coming. He rubbed his neck. He was hurting her no matter what he did. Straightening, he walked into the living room and noticed her backpack sitting on the floor. He picked it up, intending to put it on the couch and paused. *What had she bought at Kink?* He stood looking at the pack in his hands. *Put it down, Baylen. Don't look. Put it down and walk away.* He opened the canvas bag and pulled out the package. "How are you doing in there?" He called out to Ali.

"I'm fine, Baylen."

"Ready for a glass of wine?"

"Not yet."

"Ok. Holler if you need anything."

"Or I could just mind link you. Why are you yelling when you can talk to me this way?"

Baylen glanced over his shoulder toward her bedroom. *"I don't know."* He knew. He fucking knew. She was talking to him on the mating link that connected the two of them from the instant he'd first seen her. He also knew she didn't realize that this mind link was different from the common pathways that most superhumans used. His advantage was that he'd had two mates and he knew exactly how a Fae mating worked. The mating mind link was an intimacy he'd been trying to avoid.

He looked at the package in his hand and turned it over and over before opening the bag. He set the bag on the coffee table and considered the green alien looking dildo in his hands. A half smirk half smile turned up the corner of his lips. It was just so typically Aliora. She might dress like a medieval princess but the backpack, the flat soled leather boots, and sci-fi novels he'd seen around her house pointed toward another fandom. Hell, last week he'd seen her coming out of Chicco di Caffe, wearing a Princess Leia dress. He'd been so fucked. For the next three nights, he'd dreamed of making love to her in that dress, stripping her out of that dress, abducting her at lightsaber point and taking her on a trip across the galaxy, where he fucked her in a million different ways. Hell, he wasn't even a big Star Wars fan, but for Aliora, he'd fucking learn to be. He closed his eyes. *No. He couldn't do that to his Ali. He couldn't risk her that way. No mating.*

He took a deep breath and started to return the dildo to the bag, and an insidious thought slid into his mind. What if he didn't mate her? Just because they fucked didn't mean they had to mate. In fact, he could only mate her if they were both in their true form. Maybe the dreams would end for them both. Maybe they could relieve this infernal arousal that never left them. *And he fucking knew that she shared those dreams.* That's how a mating worked. He glanced toward the bedroom. An experiment was in order.

Chapter One Hundred Eighteen

EARTH DIMENSION THREE
Mystic Haven, B.C., Canada

ALI RELAXED IN THE warm water, bubbles up to her neck, her eyes closed, when she heard the bathroom door open. "I didn't ask for wine yet."

"I know."

She reluctantly opened her eyes. Yep, the Fae king in all his masculine glory stood in her bathroom. She looked at the glasses in his hand and arched her eyebrow. "That's not wine."

"Nope. I found your whiskey."

"You trying to get me drunk, Bay?"

He laughed, his teeth flashing white. "Can you even get drunk? The Fae sure can't with any normal alcohol. Our metabolism neutralizes the effects."

Aliora sighed and held out her hand for the glass of whiskey.

He handed her the glass and held up his. "Slàinte mhath"

"Good health." She replied and shook her head before taking a sip. "Irony, eh. You have a strange sense of humor, Bay."

"You've decided to shorten my name."

She shrugged, bubbles sliding down her shoulders. "You call me Ali, so fair is fair. Do you mind?"

"Naw. My friends call me Bay."

"Guess this means we're friends?"

He watched her silently for a moment before nodding. "I'll always be your friend, Ali."

She narrowed her eyes and lifted a hand to flick water at him.

He stepped back. "Careful, Ali. Today is not the day to start a water fight with me."

She sighed dramatically. "It's just a bruise!"

He smirked. "You know I could apply a little Fae healing."

Aliora shook her head and laughed. "Oh, you'd like that."

"Yeah. I would." The look in his eyes was intense.

She eyed him silently. "I'll spend time in the sun tomorrow morning. That should help a lot. Now, out. I need to get out of here."

He nodded and stepped back out the door, closing it softly behind him.

Even though she felt drained, she used her magic to disappear from the bathtub and materialize standing on the bathmat. Taking a towel from the cupboard, she dried herself and wrapped the towel around her. Pausing to examine the bruise that traveled down her hip and over her bottom, in the mirror. Glancing at the door, she sent a little magic to lock it, before looking in the mirror once more. She had never been great at healing, but her Elf blood should be enough to help at least some. Dr. Brody had told her this kind of injury would only take a couple of days to heal. She was a superhuman after all. He told her to spend time in the morning sun and open her curtains to the moon at night. Mixed genetics meant that she needed both. He'd also told her not to waste too much of her energy on trying to use her healing abilities, and he would be happy to call an Elf healer or a Fae healer if she wanted. She had declined, already embarrassed to have been brought to the hospital over a bruise. She smoothed her hand gently over the bruise, golden and green sparkles flowing from her fingers. She wrinkled her nose when the sparkles died out after only a few seconds. Yeah, Doc Brody had been right. She needed to recharge her energy.

She walked into her bedroom and over to her dresser and took out a white tank top and red pajama bottoms decorated with sparkly silver images of books and wine glasses. She had just finished dressing when a knock sounded on her door.

"Come in, Baylen."

He walked into the room with his hands full. "Into bed, Ali."

She narrowed her eyes and shook her head slowly. "Dude. You are not my parent."

"Hell, no. No chance I have any parental feelings toward you. You still need to rest. Do you need help?"

She glared at him and limped over to her bed. A little telekinesis pulled back the blankets, and she floated herself into bed.

Baylen watched and tried to hide his smile. Independent little wench. He walked over and set three books on her nightstand, making sure the one she had book marked was on the top. He set down the box of chocolates he'd taken from the bag of candy she still had on her living room side table and made sure it was within easy reach. He added a couple bottles of water that he'd wrapped Fae energy around to keep them cold. When he was done, he turned and looked at Ali. She was struggling to pile her pillows behind her back. He shook his head. "Let me." He adjusted the pillows and added a couple more. Why did this woman have so many pillows on her bed? When he was finally satisfied, he looked at her. "How's that?"

Ali wiggled around. Carefully. Before nodding. "Thanks, Bay."

He nodded, watching her for a minute. Finally, he sat on the bed beside her, and he handed her the dildo that had been in her backpack.

Aliora's mouth dropped open, heat rushing up her body, and coloring her cheeks. "Baylen Knight!"

He smirked. He couldn't help it. It was exactly the tone he imagined she would use if she was his mate, and he'd done something to piss her off. "Do you have a collection of those?"

She gasped. "What? No! Oh, my gosh. That is so not your business!"

He shrugged. "I'm curious. Indulge me."

She started to tuck the toy under the covers, but his hand came down over hers. "We're both adults, Ali. Having a sex toy to meet your needs is nothing to be ashamed of."

She glared at him, her cheeks red and he could only think that she looked adorable. But he was wise enough not to mention that. He'd learned that lesson the hard way with his first mate.

"You delight in shocking me."

He grinned. "I admit it. It's a guy thing. Your past lovers probably were the same."

She bit her lip. "I haven't had a lot of experience with guys."

"Define not a lot of experience."

"Uhm." She shrugged uncomfortably. "A few years ago, I had a boyfriend and we had sex a couple times."

"A couple times? As in two times?

She fiddled with the sheet. "Yeah. He found someone else after that."

"Idiot." Baylen shook his head. "So, you look after your own needs now." It was a statement not a question, as if to him that was perfectly normal.

She nodded. "I've just never used a... uhm...." She half lifted the hand with the dildo in it. The hand he still held.

"Never?" He let go of her hand. "Move over." He propped himself up on the pillows beside her, his legs stretched out in front of him, crossed at the ankles.

What? Her brain blanked for a few seconds, but she gingerly eased over.

"What do you use?"

She blinked. "Why are we having this conversation?"

He looked at her, his eyes drifting down over her body before he looked at her face again. "You already know I'm attracted to you, Ali."

"Didn't we establish that we're friends?"

"Yes. We should be able to talk about anything, and frankly, everything is so much better with friendship. Including sex."

Ali paused. "What?" Her voice squeaked.

He laughed. "Come on, Aliora. Talk to me. What do you use to get yourself off?"

Wow. She shook her head. "My fingers. Now, can we change the subject."

"Uh uh. Why'd you buy an alien dick?"

She blushed. "Baylen! I was curious, okay?"

He nodded, still grinning. "I admit, I'm curious too."

Her mouth fell open. "You're curious about an alien dick?" She stared at him incredulously.

"I'm curious about how much you would like it. I'm curious about how powerful your orgasm would be. Can I watch? Or better yet. Can I help?"

Her nipples hardened, and arousal heated the tender flesh between her legs. Biting her lip, she glanced at him from under her lashes. He was watching her, and she swallowed. "Uhm"

He lifted his hand cupping her jaw, his thumb stroking across her cheek. "Bad timing, right?"

She shook her head, her eyes meeting his. "Uhm, no. I—I've never done anything like this before." Gods, that slow smile of his. Her lips parted.

"Ali. I'm going to kiss you." His voice was a low rough growl, and she heard the warning, knew if she said no, he'd stop. His lips brushed over hers. Gentle, warm and inside her the feeling of tumbling. She lifted a hand the heat of his skin, a warm and wonderful thing as her fingers curled along the back of his neck. His lips moved over hers, urgency blazing through them both, an urgency that he was fiercely controlling. The hunger that he was banking. A shiver worked over her body, and she pressed closer to him. He smiled against her lips. "More?"

She smiled back. "Yes."

He nipped her bottom lip, licked the sting away and settled his lips back on hers. This time a little harder, a little rougher. Passion building but still controlled. A slow sizzle that turned into fire with each lazy open-mouthed kiss. She moaned softly and he took the kiss deeper, allowing more of his hunger to feed hers. When he lifted his head, they were both breathing heavily. His eyes glittered and she licked her lips, unconsciously. He groaned. "Yes." she whispered.

"Yes?" His voice was lazy with a roughness that seemed to slide over her whole body.

"The—the toy." she swallowed.

"Your hip."

"I'll tell you if it's too much."

His eyes met hers. "Promise?"

She nodded. "I promise."

He sat up and nodded toward the bathroom. "I need to—" He lifted the dildo still in its packaging. She nodded and watched as he walked into the bathroom and tore the packaging off the toy, before carefully washing it and rinsing it. Why did that feel so intimate? So caring? Biting her lip, she tugged her tank top off. She looked back to the bathroom, to find him crossing the room toward her. His gaze moved over her body. "You're fucking beautiful." He set the toy on the pillow by her head and pulled off his shirt.

She could feel her nipples tightening more as his muscles flexed and she bit her lip at the sight of all that sculpted perfection. He knelt on the bed beside her, and his hand closed over her breast, gently squeezing. She inhaled. He kissed her and spoke against her lips. "What do you do when you want to come?"

"I, uh, usually just go straight to my clit."

He pulled back and looked down into her face. "Why no build up?"

She shrugged. "I—I don't know."

"Do you like this?" His dark brown eyes watched her as he tugged on her nipple.

She gasped as pleasure zinged through her. "Y—yes."

"How about this?" He rolled the hard tip between his fingers.

"Yes!"

"I can play?"

She nodded, her breasts rising and falling with her breaths. "Yes."

He gave her a crooked grin. "Good. I like to play. His hands moved to her hips, his touch gentle. "Can I take these off?"

She nodded, her tongue slicking over her lips. His fingers moved beneath the drawstring waist, and she inhaled sharply, her stomach clenching. He winked at her and gently eased her pajama bottoms off. "You are so fucking beautiful."

His voice was a low growl as his eyes moved over her, and it was as if he'd touched her.

"Gods, the things I want to do to you. With you." He lifted her legs and moved between them, still on his knees. "Tell me if you need me to stop. At any point. Understand?"

Ali nodded. His hands smoothed over her body, slid up to cup her breasts and toy with her nipples, until she was gasping, her head moving restlessly against the pillows, her hips shifting, as he watched her. The intensity of his gaze left her with no doubt that he was learning what pleased her. One of his hands moved down, caressing her stomach, sliding over her waist, down her hip with gentle care, his fingers traced the crease where her leg joined her body before he cupped her pussy. His fingers eased between her folds, and he parted her. His eyes were so heated that she caught her breath. He looked up at her. "Watch me, Ali. Watch what I do to you." She swallowed. "Give me the toy, Ali."

Her eyes widened but she picked up the toy and handed it to him. Gods that feeling swooping through her stomach. He set the toy beside his knee and stroked his finger through her parted folds. Circled her clit and smiled up at her at her choked cry. "Too much?"

She shook her head. "More. Please."

"Your wish is my command." He focused his attention on her pretty pussy, his tongue peeking through his lips as he learned what his touch did to her. What sent her higher, what slowed down her gasping breaths. "You're so wet." He toyed with her clit, rubbing, circling, a gentle tug, a careful pinch. She cried out, her hips tilting up. He eased a finger inside of her, and after a moment a second finger. She moaned, her hips working to impale herself farther on his fingers. He reached up and tugged on her nipple. She cried out and he felt the smallest of contractions in her pussy. "Easy baby. I want that toy in you before you come." He slid his fingers free and sucked them clean as she watched. His lips curved in a smile. "Delicious." He plunged them back into her and she gasped. One thrust, two and he stopped. Easing them from her again. But this time he brought them to her mouth. "Taste"

Hesitantly, her eyes wide, she licked his finger. Oh. Her taste washed over her, and she met his eyes as she licked again. Gods, the heat in his eyes. He rubbed his fingers over her lips spreading her flavor over them, then he took her mouth in a rough wild kiss that left her shaking. When he pulled back, he looked into her eyes. "I'm going to use that toy on you now."

"O—kay." She whispered.

He smiled and picked up the green toy. He flicked the little switch and watched as bumps rose along the surface, some rising and falling, some rotating. He looked at her and winked, then eased the toy against her entrance. She inhaled, but he slid it up through her folds and circled her swollen clit, rubbed over it. She bucked and he moved the toy back to her entrance, slowly easing it inside her.

"Oh, gods!" Her voice rose as she arched. He pushed it in further and silently told his own dick to settle the fuck down. "Oh! Baylen!" She gasped.

"Too much?"

Her head tossed against the pillows. "No. no."

This is why we have safe words, he muttered silently to his lust addled brain. Rising up on his knees, he leaned over her, placing a hand beside her head on the pillow. "Aliora. Do you want me to stop?"

"Don't—stop." She was close to whimpering.

"Look at me."

She blinked her eyes open.

"If you need me to stop, say red. Understand?"

Aliora nodded.

"What do you say if you want me to stop?"

"Red. But I don't want you to stop. I want more. I need more, Baylen. Please."

He pressed a hard kiss to her lips. "More coming right up. Creators, you're sexy, Baby." He eased back and began to work the toy in and out of her tight clasping pussy. His other hand working her clit. Circling, rubbing, gentle pinches that made her arch. "Play with your nipples, Baby."

Pleasure swamped her, but she lifted her hands to play with her nipples. Her eyes met his and she could see his lust in their glittering depths. He moved the toy in and out of her and she panted at the sensations. Creators she needed too... She needed... a cry left her mouth, and she pinched her nipples as the toy drove deep and he tugged on her clit. Her whole body stiffened, and she bowed up.

"Look at you. So beautiful. Come for me Aliora. Fuck, that's sexy!"

Her body tightened impossibly further and as he circled her clit, she cried out her body convulsing over and over again until she collapsed limply to the bed. The toy shut off and eased from her pussy, and Baylen came down beside her, pulling her into his arms. "That's the fucking sexiest thing I've ever seen." He kissed her forehead, then pressed a gentle kiss to her lips before snuggling her up against him, his arms holding her close. Within seconds she was sound asleep.

He waited until she was deeply asleep before he eased from the bed, ignoring his raging hard on. Fuck. His mind was blown. Tonight, had been a whole new level of sexual satisfaction for him and it hadn't even involved him coming. Creators, he was about as far from a virgin as a man could get. He'd fucked often and he'd played hard. He wouldn't have believed there were any new experiences for him, that there were any new levels of pleasure and yet here he was. Totally blown away by Aliora's trust and the pleasure she'd let him wring from her. He padded into the bathroom and washed her toy carefully, before storing it in her bedside table. He struggled with the urge to take it home with him so no one else could ever use it on her but him. Gods. He forced himself to leave her room, making sure her doors were all locked. He stepped outside and double checked the locks and her personal protection Wards. Soaring up into the air he knew he was going to try his damnedest to convince her to let him do that to her again. For tonight though, he was heading directly to his shower to jerk off.

Chapter One Hundred Nineteen

EARTH DIMENSION THREE
Mystic Haven, B.C., Canada

IN THE MORNING, BAYLEN knew he had fucked up again. Why the hell was he having such a hard time staying the fuck away from Aliora? Could it be that Sprite pheromone? No. That couldn't be it. Hell, she'd told him that she wasn't having any mating signs. That ruled out pheromones. Besides, as a pure Fae, with immense powers, surely, he could resist the pheromone she'd talked about? Lust. This was simply good old-fashioned lust on her part, and yeah, he had more to deal with than her with those fucking dreams. He paused in his thoughts a frown curving his lips. *The fuck she wasn't sharing those dreams.*

He turned on his computer and pulled up the files he needed for today. But his thoughts spun out of control again and he cursed. Leaning back in his chair he turned it to stare out the window that overlooked the mountains to the south of the castle. It occurred to him that he hadn't dreamed last night. He considered that. Maybe his experiment had been a good idea after all. They'd both enjoyed the encounter. Maybe friends with benefits was a doable option. Nothing exclusive of course, it would be good for Aliora to go on some dates, maybe meet her mate. Honestly, if she met her mate, that would be a good thing. A very good thing.

Baylen frowned, not liking the feeling that idea generated. But fuck it. His feelings did not count. He was fucking saving her life by refusing to act on his mating urges. He began to consider who her mate might be, and his thoughts came to an abrupt halt when he realized that it was entirely possible it was Micah.

Wait. Could that happen? Could he show mating signs for a woman that Micah was the legitimate mate for? Fae mating was only a possibility, right? There was no law that anyone had to accept a mating. He frowned. Maybe he should encourage her to go out with Micah?

The thought left him feeling unsettled. He got up and walked over to look out the window. Maybe he should tempt her into a threesome with Micah and him? He was certain that it would resolve this whole mating situation instantly. His mating signs would naturally dissipate, and Micah would probably mate her on the spot. *This. This was a good plan.* He turned and grabbed his leather jacket, shrugging into it. He needed a coffee and maybe he would stop by and check on Aliora. Make sure she was getting around okay with that bruised hip. That's what friends did. Right?

Chapter One Hundred Twenty

EARTH DIMENSION THREE
Mystic Haven, B.C., Canada

BAYLEN KNOCKED ON ALIORA'S door, two coffees balanced precariously in his other hand. He frowned when there was no answer. As he lifted his hand to knock again, he received a mind link from Aliora. *"Baylen, is that you?"*

"Yeah, it's me. I have coffee. Let me in."

"Could you come around to the back? I don't want to move."

"Hip?"

"Yeah. I guess I should have listened to you last night when you thought it might be too much."

Releasing his glamour, he flew up and over her house, landing in her backyard. He strode up steps onto the deck, and over to the porch swing that Aliora was currently cuddled up on, a soft blanket wrapped around her. Crouching down in front of her he handed her the coffee that Arianna had assured him was Aliora's favorite. He'd taken the time to get Arianna to tell him all the drinks that Aliora ordered and make note of them in his phone. If he was going to bring her coffee, the least he could do was make sure he got it right.

"How bad is it?"

Aliora frowned and scrunched her nose. "Dr. Brody was right. It hurts more today. I should have let him call the healer."

Baylen nodded. "I can help with the healing." He wiggled his eyebrows. "I've got special Fae king skills."

Aliora laughed. "I'd be happy with a heating pad."

He grinned and stood up, scooping her into his arms. "I prescribe another hot bath and a little Fae healing."

Ali squeaked as he lifted her up. "We already had the bath discussion! I can handle it on my own."

Baylen winked at her. "After last night, I think we have removed the shyness obstacle."

She rubbed her ear and he laughed. "Ali, I will run you a bath and you can get in on your own. I want to talk with you about something so don't freak out when I come in."

When Ali had settled in the tub with bubbles up to her ears, Baylen came in and sat down on the floor beside the tub. "How are you feeling about last night?"

She looked at him for a moment trying to will away the heat she could feel in her cheeks. "Uhm. You have skills."

He laughed. "I do have skills. All kinds of skills, but my favorite has to be coaxing an orgasm out of a princess with an alien cock fetish."

Ali blushed and dumped a handful of bubbles on his head. "Would you teach me?"

Baylen raised an eyebrow. "Teach you to coax orgasms out of princesses?"

Ali shook her head, her bright laughter filling the bathroom. "No! How to coax orgasms out of a certain Fae king."

He smirked. "I will indeed aid you in your quest."

"So—" She bit her lip. "What is this?" She gestured between the two of them.

Baylen gave her a half smile, his head resting against the wall. "Since you're not having any mating signs, and I'm not looking for a mate. I would say this is us being friends."

She nodded and tilted her head, her eyes serious. "Do you share orgasms with all your friends?"

He choked. "Fuck no!" *Gah, he needed mind bleach.* "Micah would like to of course, but you know, I have some standards. No males, and most of my female friends are mated."

Ali laughed. "I suspect that if Micah heard you say that he would swear at you."

Baylen grinned. "That he would. He might even punch me. To be honest with you, Ali, I've had a few relationships with women who knew the score. I'm not involved with anyone right now. Though in the name of fairness, Micah and I have shared women before. Since you are a woman and we're all friends, if you wanted to consider such an arrangement, I'm sure I could convince Micah."

Ali blinked. "Uhm. Okay this conversation has gone down enough rabbit holes now."

Baylen smirked. "You blush so pretty, Ali."

"Ugh!"

"Want to look at an online sex store with me?"

She stared at Baylen, wide eyed. How did this man continue to surprise her? "Why?"

"We could find more alien cocks for you to try out. Did I mention that us Fae are aliens?"

Laughing, she shook her head. "I already knew that. How far are we taking this friends-with-benefits thing?"

Baylen gave a lazy shrug. "As far as we want."

She nodded, and that was the thing. How far did she want to take this? He didn't want a mate. Could she be satisfied with simply accepting a lover? At this point, her feelings for Baylen were complicated and confusing. Love had to be part of a mating for her. He certainly did not love her. Though he seemed to like her. Heck, maybe he just wanted to have sex, and she was convenient. She looked at him, sitting against the wall watching her and she knew that she wanted to have sex with him. "Fine. My tablet is on the coffee table. Show me this online sex store."

Baylen grinned and rose to his feet. "Should I call Micah, too?"

"Only if you want to die today."

Chapter One Hundred Twenty-One

ALIORA SAT ON HER PORCH swing, watching the ocean, and contemplating what had happened with Baylen last night. Baylen had made it clear this was an affair. But from the moment she had awakened she'd wanted nothing more than to be in his arms again. She sighed and curled her legs up on the swing. What was she doing? She could not think like this. She had to be realistic. She groaned and shook her head.

A knock sounded on her front door. She glanced toward the house and sighed. Maybe it was the delivery of the tiara's that she'd ordered. Rising, she walked through the open patio doors and headed through the house.

Opening the door, she found two huge Fae waiting. She swallowed. Baylen's Trium. "Hello. Baylen isn't here."

"We know, that's why we're here," Jett said, his expression serious.

"Can we come in?" Striker asked.

Aliora bit her lip and nodded, stepping back. "Is he alright?"

"Yeah, he's fine. There is something we need to discuss with you though."

"This sounds like a coffee discussion. Come on in." She led them into her kitchen, and they abruptly stopped short. She looked at them puzzled. "Is something wrong?"

Jett stared at the coffee cups floating from the cupboard and the water filling the carafe all by itself. "How are you doing this?"

Ali turned, a frown on her face. Realizing what the problem was she laughed. "Mostly telekinesis."

"Mostly?" Striker raised his eyebrow. "That is the strongest telekinesis demonstration I've ever seen."

Ali shrugged. "Has Baylen told you anything about me?"

"Not a lot," Jett said, taking a seat at her table. "I have a feeling he should though."

"You're not pure Fae," Striker said as he sat down across from Jett.

The carafe, full of coffee, poured the steaming brew into three mugs and returned to the coffee machine to stay warm. The full cups floated over to the table while Ali grabbed the cream and sugar before taking a seat at the end of the table. "Nope. I'm a halfling, and honestly, I've had this discussion way too many times since I met your king. It's kinda rude."

Jett grinned. "It's our job to protect our king."

"I'm no threat to Baylen."

"You know, Aliora, I would normally agree that a gentle person such as yourself is no threat to the Fae king." He took a drink of his coffee. "But there is nothing normal about this situation."

Ali frowned and glanced over at Striker. He was watching her, too. "What is so abnormal about Baylen having an affair? The man's no saint. The rumors are rife with the women he's been seen with."

"Those women are not you, Aliora." Striker answered. "You're his mate."

"He hasn't—" She began, shaking her head.

"No." Jett interrupted. "We are aware that he has not mated you."

Ali rubbed her ear.

"Aliora, we want to ask you to proceed with caution," Striker said, his voice quiet.

"Why?"

Jett stared at her for a long moment. "Aliora, you would be his third mate. It's so rare that it scares the hell out of us. His first two mates were brutally murdered."

Ali swallowed. "Murdered? I knew they died but—How? Why?"

"You didn't assume it was Baylen."

Ali glared at Jett. "Of course not. I see Baylen. He's dark—and dangerous." She paused and shook her head. "But he would never have killed his mates. He's broken, not a murderer."

Striker nodded. "You're correct. He barely survived the loss of his first mate, Jadeah. Losing Charli too—" Striker shook his head. "I think the only thing that kept him in this world was his kids." The Healer leaned forward, his eyes holding hers. "You must understand, he's not the same man he used to be. Not after surviving that kind of trauma."

Ali's heart hurt. She blinked back tears. "Tell me you caught the people responsible."

Jett sighed and turned his coffee cup. "We tried. Baylen had his own secret investigation going. He got the information before we did. There was this cult of Wizards that called themselves 'The Untainted Earth' Wizards. They were purists. They wanted all aliens to leave Earth. That included the Fae. Baylen found their hideout, and he killed them all. It was one of the bloodiest battle scenes I've ever attended."

Aliora's eyes widened, and she covered her mouth with the palm of her hand. She looked away, fighting the tears that welled in her eyes. Forcing herself to look back at the two men she desperately tried to find the words she needed. "I— that's terrible." She swallowed against the ache in her throat. "I—don't know what I would do in such a horrific circumstance."

Jett nodded slowly, his eyes never leaving hers. "None of us do. I think most Fae would never sit back and wait for justice. As much as we are people of honor, we are also warriors. Baylen is the king of the Fae. The man our people look to for protection, for justice, for safety. Even if his heart was not involved, he couldn't let this go unanswered. He could not allow our enemies to ever think they could harm a Fae without deadly repercussions."

Striker leaned forward in his chair. "Charli's death was a different matter. She was killed by an ancient enemy of our people. A female who's obsessed with Baylen. She's convinced he's her consort."

"Did he kill her too?"

Jett shook his head. "No. Wisteria still lives."

Aliora studied them, a sick feeling in her stomach. "What aren't you telling me?"

"Baylen had a run in with Wisteria many years ago, before he ever met either of his mates. He barely survived the encounter. You need to get Baylen to talk to you about all of this."

She stared into her coffee. "Do you think she will come back?"

"Yes."

Striker reached out and put his hand on hers. "Aliora, if she comes back, there is a high chance you could be killed. Baylen will not survive the loss of another mate. I don't know how we could prevent the catastrophic harm he is capable of. Do you understand?"

She stilled. "Baylen would not hurt his people."

"Baylen is darker than you realize." Jett said quietly. "Far darker, Aliora. You're so pure and good, Aliora. Hell, I can see that he could heal with you. But the risks are immense if something were to happen to you."

Aliora stared at them. "I am neither pure nor good. I am simply a woman." She stood up and walked over to stare out the patio door at the ocean for a long moment before turning back to face the two men that knew Baylen on a level few others could. "What defeats the darkness?"

Both men watched her carefully.

"The light. It's simple physics. Wherever there is light, darkness must flee. I see Baylen. I see the darkness that tries to claim him—but no matter how deep the darkness, it is never able to extinguish the light. If this creature of evil, this Wisteria, comes for me, she will regret it. I am the light, and Baylen needs me."

Chapter One Hundred Twenty-Two

EARTH DIMENSION THREE
Mystic Haven, B.C., Canada

THE NIGHTMARE THAT drove him out of his home and into the night skies, was bathed in blood. He hadn't stopped shaking since he'd woken up. Images of Jadeah and Charli covered in blood, their bodies broken, their precious lives snuffed out, had driven him to his knees, had broken him. But the blood covered body of Ali had left him screaming. The monster that arose, in the darkness of his dream, had lost all honor, all sanity. That monster painted the world with blood.

He pushed the memory of the dream away and flew faster, as if he could outrun the nightmare. As if he could outrun fate. From the first moment he'd laid eyes on Ali, he'd known. He'd known she would be his destruction. As he would be hers. He couldn't let it happen.

His hunters were working to track down every threat. They had highly advanced spiders crawling the web, and even more advanced technology deeply monitoring the dark web, sifting through data, analyzing every possibility. He had satellites, advanced beyond human technology, monitoring the earth. Others were pointed into deep space not only receiving intel but transmitting an encrypted beacon in the unlikely event that there had been any Fae survivors from the attack on the Tuatha Star System. Still, he knew the threat remained. He'd memorized the information passed to him tonight. A possible hit arranged by the Ashes of Death crime syndicate.

He landed in the darkness of the huge city on the coast of the mainland, deep in the most crime ridden area. Shots rang out and he smiled coldly. He'd found his prey.

Chapter One Hundred Twenty-Three

EARTH DIMENSION THREE
Mystic Haven, B.C., Canada

"HAVE YOU THOUGHT ANYMORE about my suggestion?"

Ali paused with her chopsticks halfway to her mouth. "What suggestion?"

Baylen swallowed his bite before answering. "Micah."

"Micah?" Ali gave a slight head shake. "What about Micah?"

Baylen sent her a wicked grin. "You are friends with him."

Ali frowned and lifted her chopsticks to take the bite of fried rice. She chewed, trying to figure out what Baylen was talking about. She swallowed the bite. "So?"

"When was the last time you saw Micah?"

Shrugging, she wrinkled her nose as she thought about when she'd last seen the tattooed Fae. "Hmm, last weekend we bumped into each other on the wharf."

Baylen nodded. "And?"

Ali blinked. "And? And what?"

Baylen gave her an exasperated look. "Did you guys hang out?"

"Naw." Ali took another bite, chewed, and swallowed. "Why not?"

Ali shrugged. "I don't know. He was with his friends. Helio, Shade, and Reef. Did I ever tell you that Helio delivered all those sexy books you ordered? He's a big flirt!" She laughed. "He offered to give me a better fantasy than I would find in those books and told me he was verra good at cuddling." She imitated his Scottish brogue, laughter spilling from her lips. "What a rascal!"

Baylen paused and narrowed his eyes. *What the fuck? Helio?* He struggled not to growl as a thought struck him. *What if—No. She wasn't that stallion shifter's mate.* He paused, a frown tilting his lips down. "Did he ask you out?" His voice ultra casual.

Ali shook her head still giggling about the red-haired man. "Nope. But he did say I could call him anytime."

"You should."

Ali blinked at Baylen. "I should call, Helio?"

Baylen forced a grin. "Yeah, you know, go out. Have some fun."

"Fun?" She frowned. "I thought that was what we were doing."

"We are." Baylen gave her a wicked grin and a wink. "I fully intend to play some wicked games with you tonight. But we're friends. What if Helio is your mate? Shouldn't you at least go on one date with him just in case?"

Ali stuffed a sweet and sour chicken ball into her mouth. *What was going on here?* She chewed carefully before swallowing. "Is that why you were asking me about

Micah, too? You think I should go on a date with him as well?"

Baylen shrugged. "I was going to ask if we could invite him over."

Ali narrowed her eyes. "I'm pretty sure that Micah doesn't think of me like that."

"Bullshit."

Her eyebrow rose, and she rubbed her ear.

"Don't even think about it, Ali. I will bite you back." His voice was a hard, dark whisper that told her he meant exactly what he'd said. He tossed his phone to her. "Call Micah."

Ali rose to her feet. "No."

"Scared?"

She watched the man who'd managed to give her more orgasms in the last few weeks than she'd ever thought possible. The man who'd never actually made love to her. "Go home, Baylen."

Chapter One Hundred Twenty-Four

EARTH DIMENSION THREE
Mystic Haven, B.C., Canada

BAYLEN WOKE WITH A roar, fighting imaginary monsters and soaked in sweat that he was convinced was blood until he'd turned on the bathroom light. He stood shuddering as he stared in the mirror, and he wondered who the bigger monster was, the image in his nightmares or him—because he was going to hunt again.

Chapter One Hundred Twenty-Five

EARTH DIMENSION THREE
Mystic Haven, B.C., Canada

BAYLEN SMILED AT HIS kids as they industriously worked on making sandwiches for their lunch. "Don't forget to pack some fruit, Ace." He winked at his son.

Taking a sip of his coffee, he grimaced as the hot liquid almost sloshed over the edge of his cup. Fuck. He couldn't stop his hands from shaking. He hadn't slept in two nights, the nightmares pursuing him relentlessly if he so much as closed his eyes. Blood. So much blood. Jadeah's blood, Charli's blood. Aliora's blood. But never his blood. Never his death. Only the horror of surviving.

Chapter One Hundred Twenty-Six

BAYLEN STARED INTO the mirror, frowning at the image staring back at him. Dark shadows underlined his eyes, his beard untrimmed, and his eyes filled with feral shadows. He turned away and strode to his balcony. Jett had been right to suggest the kids spend a few days with his parents. He didn't want them to see him like this. His hunt tonight would finish it though. After tonight the nightmares wouldn't haunt him. Tonight, he became the nightmare.

Chapter One Hundred Twenty-Seven

Mystic Haven, B.C., Canada

BY THE TIME THE KNOCK sounded on the door, Caden was sipping a coffee and trying to temper his irritation at being woken in the middle of the night. He opened the door to the royal Trium minus the Fae king. "Jett. Striker. Come on in." He offered them a coffee, and they sat down around his table.

"Sorry to wake you up, Caden, but we have a situation we need your help to deal with." Jett spoke first.

"With Baylen?"

Striker nodded. "You know we've been trying to handle his darkness."

Caden nodded, well aware of the dangers Baylen Knight represented.

"The thing is, since he met Aliora, it's gotten worse."

Caden shook his head. "I was hoping she'd be a calming influence."

"I have absolutely no doubt that Aliora is exactly what Baylen needs, but he refuses to even consider a mating." Jett took a drink of his coffee before continuing. "Striker and I tried to talk to him about it."

"I can imagine how that went." The three men were silent for a long moment.

"He had another nightmare tonight. I don't think I've seen him that shaken in years. He headed out to the mainland. Caden, one of these days he's either going to get himself killed, or he's going to do something there's no coming back from." Jett pushed back from the table and strode over to look out the kitchen window. "I don't know what to do."

Caden watched The Royal Protector. Things were bad when the Trium came to him. It had to be eating them alive. Baylen was more than just their king, he was also their friend. Hell, they went beyond friendship. Being part of The Royal Trium meant that they were so tightly connected that, in battle, they operated as one. Even men who had fought together for years did not have the deadly symmetry of the Royal Trium. "My sister, Samara, is on her way over to watch my kids. It's time for us to confront him together."

Striker nodded. "I agree. For the record though, I think we are going to get our asses handed to us."

Caden said nothing. What was there to say? Striker was most likely right that it had a high probability of ending in a fight. It didn't change the fact that as the Guardian, it was his job to rein in a Fae king who was edging ever closer to the blackness that could destroy him—and many others.

Chapter One Hundred Twenty-Eight

EARTH DIMENSION THREE
Mystic Haven, B.C., Canada

HE'D NO SOONER STEPPED outside with the Royal Trium when his phone sounded an emergency call. He hit speaker. "Brody here."

"Caden. It's Josef. The Mer just contacted me, they're under attack."

"By whom?"

"Sounds like the enemy that attacked them a few years ago."

Caden met Jett and Striker's eyes, his mind running through possibilities. He knew damn well that the Trium coming to him meant things were bad with the Fae king. "Can you and Striker handle the Mer situation?"

Jett nodded. "I'll contact the former Trium. They have some 'top secret' vessels that have the potential to solve this problem once and for all."

With a nod, Caden launched into the sky. When he landed, he stood at Aliora's door. He was either going to make things better or much worse, but either way, Aliora had to know who the man she was tangling with really was. His best hope was that she would choose to save him.

He knocked. A minute later, Aliora opened the door. "Caden?"

"Get dressed, Ali. We need to go save Baylen."

Aliora regarded him with narrowed eyes. "An adventure for the children's party princess? Baylen won't be pleased."

Caden laughed. "Don't even go there. I know that Edge and your father probably taught you every move in the warrior's manual."

Aliora laughed. "Shhh. No telling my secrets."

"Your secrets are safe with me. As for Baylen—" He looked at Aliora. "Does he even deserve to be pleased at this point?"

"No. I'm only going to save him because you asked."

Caden tried not to laugh, watching as she snapped her fingers and her pajamas turned into skin-tight black leather. Not the fun kind. The kind you wore when you were going to kick serious ass. At her nod, they both shot up into the air.

Chapter One Hundred Twenty-Nine

EARTH DIMENSION THREE
Mystic Haven, B.C., Canada

BAYLEN'S STEPS ECHOED in the silence. Fae orbs floated along beside him casting long shadows in their wake. A dark smile edged his lips as he sensed movement nearby, he drew in Fae energy fully prepared to deal a death blow to this would be terrorist cell. This was the third one tonight, and still his anger raged. How dare they come into his territory and think they could target innocents.

Something slammed into him, throwing him across the alleyway. He crashed into a brick wall. Shaking his head, a growl echoing in the night, he rose to his feet, only to be picked up and thrown back into the wall. His head hit the brick wall with a sickening crunch. *What The Fuck! Shit!* He could barely think. He threw up an energy Shield and staggered to his feet. A roar filled his ears and he stared in stunned disbelief as a Fallen Angel slammed a sword into the shield he'd erected. He swiped at the blood that trickled down his chin. Fuck. He hammered his fist into the Fallen Angel's face and ducked a return punch. "What the fuck are you doing here?"

"You chose the wrong place and the wrong time to play vigilante, Fae. Go home to your protected island." Another powerful sword strike. Baylen pushed more Fae energy into the shield.

"Go fuck yourself."

The Fallen being gave him a slight smile, and burst through the energy shield, driving his fist into Baylen's jaw.

Reeling back, he slammed Fae energy into the Angel. The creature staggered but kept coming. "Back the fuck off, you son of a bitch!"

A second Fallen Angel stepped up beside the first.

Fuck!

A hard fist caught him in the side of his head, and he saw stars for a moment, but he was already moving. He grabbed the wrist of the first Fallen Angel and sent him sailing through the air to slam into the second Fallen Angel.

Narrowing his eyes, he let his glamour fall away. "You want to fight? Well, bring it, 'cause you've just met your worst fucking nightmare." He drew Fae energy until the alley lit up from his glow. He was the fucking king of the Fae. Not much could withstand him. He threw a blast strong enough to maim or kill most beings and swore when a third Fallen Angel laughed. *The fucking Angel Assassin team.*

"You're interfering in something that does not concern you. My brother Abaddon was willing to let you go back to your safe island. I'm not." The Fallen Angel began to spin his sword like a master swordsman.

Baylen slammed up a shield of Fae energy as the Fallen Angel struck. The blow smashed into the golden energy shield and reverberated through his whole body. Fuck. Growling, he battered the assassin with Fae energy blasts, keeping the shield up. Another strike that almost drove him to his knees. He planted his feet on the ground determined that he was not going to be fucking moved. He wiped at the blood seeping from his lip with the back of his hand. His wings glowed with energy. His dark eyes were hard, incandescent with his fury. His entire being focused.

He launched himself forward in a rush of power, blast after blast of Fae energy slammed into the trio of former Angels. The air began to glow with the sheer amount of energy discharging in rapid succession. The third Angel shouted in fury driven back by the Fae energy bursting over his body and hurled an explosive blast of Angelic power at Baylen.

Twisting to avoid the blast, he gasped as fiery pain blazed through his side, warm blood spilling down his body. Fuck. He looked up into the eyes of the first Fallen Angel, his teeth clenched, a snarl erupting from his throat. "You die first."

The Fallen Angel shrugged. "The dagger embedded in you says differently."

Baylen drew Fae energy to him and slammed his fist into the ground, discharging the energy in a violent wave that knocked the three Fallen Angels from their feet.

"Enough." Caden Brody's voice rang out as he landed on the ground beside Baylen.

Fuck. *Why the fuck was the Guardian here?* "Why aren't you in Mystic Haven?"

"Saving you," Ali replied as she stepped into the light.

He blinked. What the fuck was she wearing? Fuck! He grabbed Aliora and shoved her behind him. "You can wear that for me later," he said in an aside voice, though his whole body was rigid, his heartbeat loud in his ears.

Ali rubbed her ear and took a deep breath. She was so angry she wanted to scream, but Gods, she'd never seen Baylen like this. *His eyes.* She swallowed. She couldn't let that dark thing she'd glimpsed have him.

"Caden, I may fucking kill you when we get back to Mystic Haven. You had no business bringing Ali here."

Caden looked at him and shook his head before focusing on the Fallen Angels. "You have three seconds to get out of here, before I take you apart."

"Just the two of you?"

Ali stepped away from Baylen, her eyes on the dangerous trio slowly rising to their feet between Baylen and Caden.

"The three of us against the three of you won't even be a workout." Caden's voice was icily calm as he ignored the Fae king's furious swearing. "You won't get another warning. If I ever see you back here, you won't live to tell the tale." Caden's runes suddenly flared with golden light.

Rough curses in the night air. "We have no war with you, Guardian."

"If you have a war with the Fae king, then you have a war with me."

Cold eyes assessed the situation. Measuring each opponent, lingering on the small plump woman the Fae king so carefully guarded. There was an unidentifiable element about her that made each of them hesitate. Finally, with an abrupt nod, the Fallen Angel Assassins shot up into the air, scattering in different directions.

"Why are you here, Baylen?" Ali asked, reaching out to push Fae healing energy into the wound in his side. Baylen grabbed her wrist. "Leave it." His voice was a rough snarl that made her narrow her eyes.

"Answer my question."

"Dispensing justice."

"Justice?" Ali tilted her head. "Or vengeance?"

Baylen growled. "Why the fuck are you here?"

"I'm saving your life."

"The threat is gone. You can go home now."

Dismissed. She raised her eyebrow. "The threat is not gone. You're just looking in the wrong direction."

Baylen turned and realized that Ali was right.

Caden hovered in the air, a deadly Fae Guardian, runes glowing brightly. And in his eyes, Baylen read death.

"Choose well, Baylen Knight, King of the Fae. I will not tolerate any more of these—excursions. If you wish to die, let us be done with it."

"Oh, I'm up!" Aliora stepped between the two men. "Baylen, Aurora was just telling me that she's hoping you will come and tuck them in at their grandparents, when you get home."

Baylen glared at her. "Why are you talking to my daughter in the middle of the night?"

"She mind linked me and asked if I knew where her daddy was. She had a bad dream."

"She just randomly mind linked you?"

Sarcasm at its finest. "Baylen, children often 'path me. They know I'm safe and that I care."

Baylen growled and turned to glare at Caden, Fae energy flaring bright, and Ali held her breath.

The next second he was gone, soaring high into the sky toward Mystic Haven.

Chapter One Hundred Thirty

EARTH DIMENSION THREE
Mystic Haven, B.C., Canada

CADEN PAUSED AS THEY approached Aliora's home. "He's on your beach."

"I sense him."

"I'll talk to him."

"No, Caden. Thank you. I can handle Baylen."

"He's angry, Aliora, and he's dangerous."

Ali smiled. "Ever the protector, Caden. Baylen won't hurt me. The fact that he comes to me is important. Even now when he's so angry, he still comes to me. I wanted to have a look at that wound anyway. Go home to your kids. I'll contact you if there are any problems."

Caden watched her for a moment, before nodding. There was another situation he had to deal with, and with the deadly Wards around her home, he knew that even the powerful Fae king would be knocked on his ass if he tried anything stupid. "Be careful. 'Path me if you have the slightest concern."

Ali landed on her front step, opened the door, and walked through the house. Her clothes changed into a golden medieval gown as she walked out onto her back deck. Baylen stood watching the ocean, and she was struck by his aloneness. "Baylen." She made her way to him, her bare feet sinking into the coolness of the sand.

"Part of it is vengeance." He stared at the moon as she tucked her hand into the curve of his elbow. "Jadeah didn't deserve to die because of the extremist views held by a small, twisted fringe group. They blew her shop up because she was an 'alien.' Fuck them. I hope they are rotting in the most horrifying hell that anyone could imagine. At least I know that they will not harm anyone else." He turned to face her. "I'm the Fae king. It's my job to protect my people."

"But it's not your job to be judge, jury, and executioner. What if you killed an innocent person?" She reached up and smoothed a strand of his hair back.

"My cyber security team is the best in the world. My threat hunters are second to none."

"Mistakes can still happen, Baylen. The justice systems are in place for a reason."

His jaw clenched, and he stared down at her. "They didn't protect Jadeah or Charli." He turned back to the ocean. He wasn't surprised that she knew about Jadeah and Charli. He knew about the rumors. Exhaustion suddenly swept over him, and he swayed.

"Baylen, come inside. I'll make coffee and take a look at that wound for you."

"I haven't slept in days."

"How come?"

"Nightmares. I can never save them." He looked at her. "Or you. I can't risk your life, Aliora."

She stepped forward and slid her arms around him. "I'm here, Baylen. I'm safe." He stood stiff in her embrace, but she kept holding him, and after a few moments, he wrapped his arms around her and held her tightly, his head coming to rest against her neck. When he let her go, she took his hand and led him into her house and tended to his wounds. "Stay with me tonight, Baylen. No strings attached."

He stared into her eyes wanting to stay with everything that he was but knowing that the risk was too great. If Wisteria ever returned, he could not have his name linked with Ali's.

He opened the door and stepped out. Closing it softly behind him. For a moment, he leaned his head against the solid wood, regret filling him. Stepping back, he soared up into the air knowing that he could never let himself come this close to her again. He had to fucking protect her, and if the only way to do that was to push her way, that is exactly what he would do.

Chapter One Hundred Thirty-One

EARTH DIMENSION THREE
Mystic Haven, B.C., Canada

BAYLEN LANDED AT HIS parents' house. He should have gone home and showered first, but he'd needed to make sure his daughter was okay.

"Daddy, is that you?" Aurora's voice clear over their mind link.

"It's me. You should be sleeping, Ladybug." He walked through the Security Wards and up the steps. Opening the door, he stepped into the silent house, and Aurora flew around the corner heading straight for him. He opened his arms and caught her, holding her close. Her arms wrapped around his neck, and she clung to him. *"Daddy, I had a bad dream. I dreamed that three black birds were hurting you. I tried to scare them away, but they wouldn't stop. Then a ginormous white tiger and Aliora came and saved you!"*

His chuckle was rough and edged with unspeakable sorrow. *"Thank you for trying to save me, Aurora."* His heart ached with the knowledge that he held his fierce little daughter to him with hands covered in dried blood.

"Can we go home, Daddy? I want to cuddle with you and Jewel and Falcon." Her little nose wrinkled. *"But first you need to have a shower. P-hew!"*

Baylen laughed. He couldn't help it. Gods what would he do without his children? His mom stepped into the living room, and her eyes caught his. He knew she saw him, saw the state he was in, and in her eyes, he saw the same question that Aliora had asked him. Justice? Or vengeance?

"Take your little ones home, Baylen. A night of cuddling is just what you all need. Always choose love."

Chapter One Hundred Thirty-Two

EARTH DIMENSION THREE
Mystic Haven, B.C., Canada

CADEN SIPPED ON A LARGE black coffee and listened as Riley, Finn, and Jett filled him in on the attack they'd managed to stave off. Striker leaned back in his chair not saying anything, and honestly, Caden got it. They were way past fatigue and heading into flame-out.

"It's a good thing, the ancient Fae held onto their tech and ships," Striker finally commented. "It would have been a helluva lot harder without them."

Finn nodded. "Do you think they might be open to sharing the technology with us? Or possibly teaching us to manufacture our own?"

"I'll speak to Ryder, Finn. I'm sure something can be arranged," Caden said as he stood up. "I'll be in touch."

Jett and Striker stood up too, waving off Riley and Finn's thanks. "We'll talk to Baylen about a formal alliance."

Chapter One Hundred Thirty-Three

THE KNOCK ON THE DOOR, early the next evening, had Aliora looking at the front door with a glare. She was deep into a sexy fantasy novel and in no mood for company. She considered not answering, but she could feel Baylen's energy.

She uncurled from the sofa and walked over to open the door. Baylen leaned against the door jamb looking totally disreputable especially with that black eye.

"That looks sore. How's the knife wound?"

He shrugged. "Nothing I couldn't handle. Striker insisted on healing the worst of the damage."

Her eyebrow rose. She'd seen how he'd been handling that situation. "Looks like those Fallen Angels got in some good shots."

"So did I." His voice was a low growl as he stepped forward backing her into the foyer. The door slammed behind him, and she heard the lock click. "You've been working on your telekinesis."

He snorted and put his hand on the wall behind her, leaning in close. "Wanna kiss me better?"

Shaking her head, she ducked under his arm and moved into the living room. "I was reading a good book, Bay. You are not exactly in my good graces right now."

"How about if I pay for my stupidity by making the scene you're reading a reality."

Ali gaped at him. "It could be a murder scene!"

His grin was slow and lazy. "I can sense your arousal, Ali. There is no way that would happen if you were reading about someone dying."

Her eyes widened. "You cannot!"

"And your nipples are hard."

She crossed her arms, her cheeks heating.

"Give me the book, Aliora. Let me read that scene. I'll make it happen."

She bit her lip, tempted.

"I promise, I'll make it so good for you."

"It'll have to be very good after last night." She lifted her chin, still angry that he'd almost gotten himself killed.

Baylen grinned. "Understood."

Hesitantly, she picked up her book, turned to the scene she'd been reading and handed it to him.

He read the first few lines and his eyebrow raised. He looked up at her and raised an eyebrow. "Sometimes I get the feeling that I really don't know you at all. Why don't you get us something to drink? Wine, beer. Something alcoholic."

She looked suspiciously at the man reading her book. "I thought Fae were not affected by alcohol?"

He shrugged. "Adult drinks for an adult evening."

Ali nodded as he sat down on the couch. Turning she walked into the kitchen, the skirts of her dress swirling around her ankles. Oh, my gosh. What had she agreed to? She opened the fridge and took out two bottles of the beer she had stocked for him and held one to her warm cheek. Was she really going to do this? She turned and walked back into the living room, and he patted the sofa beside him as he read. She sat down and he looked up from the book a devilish expression written all over his face. "Aliora, you naughty girl." He took the beer and winked at her, before taking a long drink, setting the bottle on the end table beside him and starting to read again.

Ali took a drink of her beer and shuddered. Not her favorite drink. She took another one, longer this time before setting her bottle safely on the other end table.

Baylen closed the book and set it beside his beer. Then he slouched on the couch. "So, Ali, my innocent little halfling. If I am reading this right, you are about to get ravished. Consensually ravished, of course. Do you consent?"

Ali laughed. "Only if you're going to tear off my dress and have your wicked way with me."

"Consent means you have to say yes you want to have me ravish you."

Ali rolled her eyes, but some part of her was pleased that he was a man who took care to make sure she wanted this. "Yes, I consent to ravishing me as per our agreement regarding your atonement for stupidity." She held up a finger when he looked like he was going to say something. "Actually, you also owe me for the last time you were here and pushing me to have a threesome with you and your buddy."

Baylen laughed. "It was pushy and you're obviously not ready for that kind of kink. So, I shall re-enact this book scene as atonement for the sin of pushing something you weren't ready for. *and* for last night's risks. Also known as stupidity. What's your safe word?"

Ali bit her lip, as butterflies soared in her stomach. "Red."

"I don't have a pirate costume, you're going to have to settle for a disreputable looking biker dude who's traveled back in time to ravish a medieval fairy princess."

She laughed and nodded. "Deal." She could feel the heat building between her legs. "One more thing. I have limits, Baylen, don't push me too far."

He looked at her seriously, knowing full well what she meant. "I won't be going on anymore middle of the night flights."

She searched his eyes and finally nodded.

"Ready?"

"Yes."

Baylen stood up and pulled her to her feet in front of him. He scowled but added a wink, so she knew he was playing. His hands fisted in the neckline of her dress, and he tore it right down the middle. She gasped. He stripped the ruined dress from her and wrapped a muscular arm around her waist, taking her down onto the couch.

Her hands rose to clench on his shoulders, and he looked into her eyes. "Okay?"

She nodded—her eyes wide. He winked and swooped in for a hard kiss. His tongue swept into her mouth, and she moaned, her hand fisting in his hair. He rose, kneeling over her and fisted his hand in her pretty lace bra, she was shocked at the ease with which he tore it off her. The look in his eyes. A fluttery feeling in her stomach. Her nipples hardened even more, and she could feel the heat growing between her legs. Gods, she wanted him.

He groaned as he saw her pretty coral nipples. Reaching out, he cupped her breast, his thumb brushing over her nipple. She gasped and arched as pleasure zinged through her. "Perfection. I want to suck on those pretty nipples." He settled against her again, his mouth on hers, his hands moving over her body. She moaned softly against his lips as he tugged at her nipples.

"Do you like that?" He asked as he lifted enough to stare into her eyes.

She swallowed and nodded.

"More?"

She licked her lips and he groaned.

"Yes." She whispered.

Leaning forward, he took her nipple into his mouth, sucking and licking, before nipping gently. His other hand moved down her body, gliding over her skin and she swore she could feel Fae energy trailing from his hands. He let go of his glamour and she blinked her eyes open. He was staring at her with a roguish twinkle in his eyes. "Improvising. I'm a disreputable Fae biker dude from the future. Touch my wings."

She lifted trembling fingers and reached out to stroke his wings. He groaned and she did it again. He tugged on her nipple, rolled it between his fingers. She arched and moaned softly. Letting go of her nipple, he came to his knees. "Let go of your glamour." His hands moved to her hips, and he tore her panties off, his tongue slicking over his lip as he stared at her pussy. He lifted his eyes and she stared back at him, completely enchanted by the power of his lust, and the unparalleled beauty of a Fae with no glamour. Swallowing, she let go of the first layer of her glamour allowing him to see her.

He watched her change, everything about her became more. Her hair color, her eyes, her ears. He reached out and traced the gentle point and she inhaled. *She was such a sensual little creature.* He eased her up to her knees in front of him. "I want to fuck you."

She laughed softly. "I want you to fuck me."

"That's not in the book." He winked at her. *But by the ancients he was tempted.* He reached out and stroked her wings, enjoying her gasp and the soft sexy sounds she made. His mouth quirked up on one corner. He was going to improvise again because the writer had no idea what a real Fae could do. He sent Fae energy wrapping around her nipples and smiled crookedly when she gasped and writhed before him. He moved his hand to her hip and slid it down until he cupped her soft pussy. She bit her lip and her hips arched. With his other hand, he fisted her hair tugging her head back until she met his eyes. "I want to see your eyes while you come." He slid his finger between her folds and stroked.

"Oh!" She gasped and squirmed, her hands moving up to stroke his chest. The energy encircling her nipples was like tiny sparks of electricity and fire. And it tightened and released. Tugging as if it was his fingers. Her wings fluttered behind her as her eyes stared into the heat of his gaze.

"Touch my wings, Ali."

She licked her lip and lifted her hand to his wing, her fingers trailing over the exquisitely sensitive energy that formed his wings.

"Fuck. Again."

A small thrill ran through her at his words. Confidence rising, she did it again.

"Just. Like. That." He wanted her hands on his fucking cock. His dick was fucking hard enough to pound nails. He could feel his zipper pressing hard against the stiff length of his cock. He was going to be wearing those marks for a while, he suspected. He also knew he would never survive if she got her hands on his cock. He was playing with disaster, but he fucking couldn't stop. He slid two fingers inside her tight sheath, his thumb working her clit. Her hips arched and an inarticulate cry left her lips. "Please," she whispered.

He sent more Fae energy to tease her nipples and stroke over her wings. She cried out, her head tipping back, her eyes closing.

"Open your eyes, Aliora." He needed to see the pleasure that held her in its grip. He needed to see her caught up in ecstasy. He needed to see the moment she came for him.

Ali blinked her eyes open, her body writhing. Oh, gods. Her body flooded with pleasure. She needed to come. Her nipples tingled, her wings.... She moaned, "Baylen."

"Look in my eyes, Ali." It was a command, and he didn't give a fuck. Book or no book, he wanted to see her go over. He wanted to see her face twisted in ecstasy. He kept thrusting his fingers deep inside her, feeling her pussy tightening, and feeling the tiny convulsions starting. "Aliora!" His voice was sharp.

She blinked and locked her eyes with his. "Good. Just like that, my wild little halfling. Come for me. Now."

Her body bowed, a cry leaving her lips, the intimacy of The Fae King staring into her eyes, seeing her pleasure was both staggering and deeply personal—And something she'd never shared with anyone else.

Gods, he could watch her come forever. It was one of the most erotic moments of his life. He ignored the rock-hard condition of his cock. His thumb rubbed harder on her clit and her body locked as a soft scream left her mouth, convulsions tearing through her again and again. *Fuck she was beautiful!*

She couldn't have torn her gaze away from his, even if her life had depended on it. Her heart thumped wildly, and her breath caught as waves of pleasure slammed through her. Finally, the convulsions slowed, and she inhaled with a gasp, her body slumping.

Baylen lifted a hand and cupped her face. "Beautiful." He eased his fingers from her pussy and brought them to his lips, sucking her essence off them before he eased her down onto the sofa and stroked his hand over her throat, closing gently. The corner of his lips tugged up in a sexy smile as he heard her catch her breath.

Slowly, he stood up, his eyes moving over her relaxed body. This was a memory he intended to keep forever. Resisting his body's demands that he take what she offered, he stepped back. He had to get out of there before he did something he would regret. Before he did something that would risk her life.

"Baylen?" Her voice was soft, questioning, the edge of hurt entering it. He heard her but he turned and walked out the door. If last night had taught him anything, it was that Ali was far to willing to walk into danger. So, yeah, he was a fucking asshole, but at least, she would live. Hopefully with a good memory of the last time they were together.

Chapter One Hundred Thirty-Four

ALIORA WALKED DOWN the street toward The Dark Moon restaurant owned by Stone Zeyev. She didn't feel like her own cooking tonight and the emptiness of her house had driven her out. Opening the door, she took two steps in and almost bumped into Baylen, with his arm around a pretty woman with black hair and deep green eyes. Baylen wore black jeans and white dress shirt, and the woman wore a dress that threatened to spill her significant bosom out for everyone to see.

"Baylen." She forced a smile to curve her lips, while all the ways she could kill him filtered through her mind.

"Aliora." He nodded. "This is Desiree. I convinced her to come visit from the mainland."

Ali nodded. *The bastard!* "Have fun."

"Oh, we are, aren't we, Desiree?" The woman giggled and Baylen looked down at the woman's cleavage with a roguish smile on his lips.

Ali started to turn, wanting nothing more than to get away from the stupid Fae king, when a hard hand closed over her arm and drew her against a large male form. She blinked up at Stone Zeyev. She could feel the anger he was keeping banked. "Excuse me, Baylen. I've been waiting for my date. I'm going to close the restaurant now." The big Wolf Shifter alpha turned from Baylen, his voice gently scolding. "You're late, Ali." He leaned down and kissed her. She was still blinking when he lifted his head and winked at her. "Sit over here, Ali, I've got to lock up so we can have the evening to ourselves." He turned and looked at Baylen who stood staring at them, his date seemingly forgotten.

"I'm sure you understand, Knight," Stone said as he walked toward them. "Looks like you have plans of your own."

Ali wasn't sure she'd ever seen the Fae king looking so angry.

"Aliora."

Even his mindlink was angry. She ignored him and sat down at the table that Stone indicated.

"Aliora. We are going to talk."

She heard the threat in the Fae king's mindlink.

"No. We're not."

The restaurant door opened, and she heard Desiree's voice asking if they were going to the castle now. The door closed behind them, and she heard the lock engage.

Stone dimmed the lights, turned on the closed sign, grabbed a bottle of wine and sat down across from Aliora. "Hey. What's up with King Jackass?"

Ali shrugged. "Thank you."

He smiled. "Ali, you have been great with my pack's cubs. You're one of the sweetest people I know, and he was being an ass. Doesn't he know that shifters can smell a mating?"

Ali paused mid-reach for her wine glass. "Uhm." She blushed and took a sip from the wine he poured her. "The Fae king is not in the market for a mate."

"Idiot." Stone shook his head. "Do you want a steak? And I've got a delicious cheesecake for dessert."

Ali smiled. "Yes, please. You don't have to close your restaurant."

"The Fae king might be a blind idiot. But I sure as hell am not. No way I'm turning down an evening with a woman as beautiful as you."

Chapter One Hundred Thirty-Five

ALIORA CROUCHED TO pet little Aspen McJames' new puppy when she noticed Baylen coming out of the coffee shop with a lovely brunette. The woman clung to his arm, and his hand covered hers. Ali froze for a moment, her eyes narrowing. *The asshole Fae king*. She rose to her feet forcing her eyes to move away from the couple and back to Aspen. She smiled gently at the little girl. "Captain Jack Sparrow is a lovely puppy, Aspen."

The little girl nodded her head, her long blonde ponytail bobbing up and down. "I'm going to call him Sparrow for short."

Ali laughed softly. "Sparrow is a good name."

"Oh, I hear my mommy calling me. I better go." Aspen skipped off down the sidewalk toward a blue minivan that a heavily pregnant bear shifter was loading groceries into. Ali watched for a moment to make sure that Aspen got safely to her mother before turning toward the bookstore. She pondered if she should buy a science fiction romance or a romantic comedy when she heard her name. Forcing a smile to her lips she turned to face Baylen and the woman with him. "Hello, Baylen." *I mean dick.*

"Aliora, it's nice to see you. This is Suzette. She's considering a move to our little sanctuary island. I'll be showing her around this weekend."

Ali smiled sweetly—as she thought about biting the dick king, hard, and maybe zapping him with Fae energy. "It's nice to meet you, Suzette. Make sure you stop by the wharf. There are a lot of artisan shops there and the best ice cream." She looked over at Baylen and forced another smile. "Have a nice weekend." Crossing her fingers behind her back as she spoke, because she really hoped his weekend was a three-ring circus of catastrophes.

She watched as they started to walk away, waited until they were past her before she turned back toward the bookstore. Forget romcom, she was going to find the darkest romance book she could find. One with the dirtiest sex ever. And she wasn't going to think about the Fae king at all. A wicked smile curved her lips, and she sent a mindlink. *"Baylen, I forgot to mention that those toys we ordered came in. I'll give them a test run this weekend."*

The answering growl left her feeling much better.

Chapter One Hundred Thirty-Six

EARTH DIMENSION THREE
Mystic Haven, B.C., Canada

BAYLEN GOT OFF HIS motorcycle, strode to Ali's door and knocked. He glanced at the sun and winced. It was early. Shit. He should have waited a few more hours. It was the fucking dream's fault. Yeah, he'd expected them to get worse when he stopped fooling around with Ali, but he had not expected this never-ending lust for her. He could barely stand to even casually touch the women he'd been parading around, and he certainly could not fuck them.

He didn't want to fuck them. His goal was to push Ali away. That was it. He had not expected to end up as a fucking eunuch in the process.

The door opened and a sleep rumpled Ali stood there in a thin white tank top that clearly showed her tight coral nipples and black pajama bottoms with silver stars and moons scattered over them. His cock instantly woke from its hibernation and shot to attention. *Of course, it did.*

"What do you want, King of the Fae?"

He handed her a package. "I'd ordered this for you a while ago."

Her eyebrow rose. "I need coffee." She turned and walked through her house to the kitchen, not caring if he followed her or not. She tossed the package onto the island and waved her hand sending golden sparkles through the air. The coffee maker turned on and began to brew. The cupboard opened and a mug flew out and floated down to sit in front of her. Baylen reached around her and picked up the coffee cup. 'Have a nice day.' He read. *Hmm.* Setting it back on the island he went to grab a mug for himself. By the time he set his cup down, she'd already poured her coffee and was sipping it. His eyes narrowed as he saw the bottom of her mug when she took a drink. The fucking cup was giving him the finger. He reached for the coffee and poured himself a cup. "Are you going to open that package?"

"Nope."

"Why not?"

"I don't need you to buy me things."

"We're still friends aren't we, Ali?'

"Mm, I don't think so."

"Why not?"

"Don't you think you should have said something if our friends with benefits agreement was over?"

"It's not over."

Ali's eyebrow rose, and she rubbed her left ear. "Yes, Baylen, it is."

"Because I fucked someone else?" *And now I'm a gods-damned liar. If there was a hell for Fae, he was heading straight for it.*

"See, I knew you were smart."

He growled and took another sip of his coffee. This is what he'd wanted. This was exactly what he'd planned that she would think. So why did it feel so shitty? He set the mug down on the island. "I'll see you around, Ali."

Chapter One Hundred Thirty-Seven

ALI STEPPED OUT OF the liquor store, a bottle of expensive Fae whiskey tucked into her backpack. Tonight, she was going to binge watch Bridgerton and get drunk. Shirina had told her that the Duke of Hastings was super hot. Maybe he would inspire a few fantasies for her. *Fantasies that did not involve that bastard Fae king.* Oh. She'd almost forgotten. Micah wanted her to stop by the tattoo shop and look at a tattoo he thought she might like. She turned abruptly and started across the street, her mind on her plans for the evening.

A horn blared and she jumped, her eyes wide. Maverick Fiain stepped out of his police cruiser and shook his head. "Aliora Aurelius, I should write you a ticket for jaywalking."

"Sorry, Maverick. I should have looked."

"I've got her." Micah said, his arm wrapping around her as he cursed silently. "There's no need for a ticket, I plan to spank her ass as soon as we get into the shop."

"Micah!"

"That was dangerous, Ali." He'd fucking lost a century of his life when he saw her about to absentmindedly step out onto the street. It was a damn good thing that he'd gone out for a coffee.

Maverick shook his head, watching them as they crossed the road, still arguing like brother and sister. "Hold up."

Ali turned to see the tall dark haired Dragon shifter crossing the street toward her. "Ali." He gave her a slow crooked grin. "Would you go to the movies with me tonight?"

Her eyes widened, and she gave him a tentative smile. "I was going to watch the Bridgerton series tonight." She bit her lip. "But sure."

Maverick grinned. "If you prefer, I could bring Chinese food over and we could watch the series together."

Her cheeks grew warm. "Uhm, have you seen the Bridgerton series?"

Maverick nodded, a sexy teasing light in his eyes. "Yes, ma'am. And I would love to watch it again. With you."

"Wait a damn minute," Micah muttered as his eyebrow rose. *What the fuck?* He glanced from Ali to Maverick, and it occurred to him that it might do Ali good to go out with someone who looked at her like Maverick was looking at her. He fought to hide his smirk. *It certainly wouldn't hurt to get her mind off his asshole friend, who didn't know a good thing even when it was right in front of him.*

Ali laughed, shaking her head at Micah. "Shh, you're not my brother."

"Bridgerton?" A dark male voice entered the conversation and Ali clenched her fists. "Isn't that the show with all the fucking in it?"

Ali turned to Baylen and smiled sweetly, taking note of the blonde on his arm. She sniffed. *He wasn't even worth biting.* "Why yes, I believe it is." She stepped closer to Maverick.

Micah crossed his arms and muttered something about blind idiots and just desserts.

Maverick's arm settled over her shoulders. "What's it to you, Fae?"

Baylen scowled. The blonde watched them all with interest. "It's a great show, Baylen. Don't be a prude."

Ali's lips tilted into a smile. She might like this lady. She stepped forward and held out her hand. "Hi. I'm Aliora Aurelious."

The blonde smiled back at her and gave her hand a gentle squeeze. "Lacey Raven."

"Oh! Of Raven Design?"

Lacey nodded, smiling.

"Oh, my gosh! I've been wanting to order some lingerie from your store for the longest time!"

Lacie dug into her bag and handed Ali a card. "Here. This is a discount for your first order. I've also started stocking some sexy time items. Have a look at my website."

Ali grinned from ear to ear. "I will. I'm so excited!"

Micah smirked. "I'm going to be late for my next client, I better get into the shop. Don't forget to come and see me. I want to show you that new design, Ali." He turned and headed into the tattoo shop.

Baylen crossed his arms, ignoring Micah, and glared at Maverick as he sent a mindlink to Ali. *"What the fuck are you doing, Ali?"*

Her eyebrow rose and she resisted the urge to rub her ear. *"Asshole."*

"I'll help you look, Ali," Maverick said, a wicked grin on his face.

"Scoundrel." She laughed thinking that this dragon shifter had a gleam in his eyes that surely spelled trouble.

"Honestly, I vote that you let him look with you." Lacey spoke up. "My site is great for getting to know the inner workings of the male mind."

Ali and Maverick both laughed, and Baylen growled. They all turned to look at him. Baylen glanced at the sun, "It's getting late. I should get you home, Lacey."

Lacey paused and studied the Fae king. "Weren't we going to have our own evening together?"

Baylen adjusted his shirt sleeve. "I'm planning to take you to the opera on the mainland. I thought you might want to change."

Lacey studied him some more, then turned to Aliora and Maverick. "Want some company? I love Bridgerton and I'd love to show you guys my website. And, Ali, I would love to design some lingerie for you." She walked closer to Ali and Maverick as Baylen stared after her. "I'm bi and not averse to a sexy threesome, if you two are interested."

Maverick moved closer to Ali as she gave him a wide-eyed look and slid her hand around his arm. Mostly 'cause she didn't want to fall down. This had taken the strangest turn. "You're welcome to come and watch Bridgerton with us and show us your website," she said hesitantly.

Maverick adjusted her hold so he could lace his fingers with hers. "I've got to finish my shift. I'll bring Chinese. Alright?" He sent Ali a mindlink. *"Wow, this escalated quickly. No, we are not going to have a threesome, so don't worry. And how did you manage to steal the Fae king's date, Wild Thing? Do you always attract this much trouble?"*

Ali stared at him totally dumbfounded. She finally cleared her throat. "Lacey, I need to pop into the tattoo shop here for a minute. We can go to my house after that."

Lacey smiled and looped her arm through Ali's then glanced over at Baylen. "See you around."

Ali glanced from Baylen back to Lacey, feeling kind of shell shocked, and turned to walk to the tattoo shop, Lacey chattering away at her about the fun they were going to have.

Maverick drove off, and Baylen was left standing in the street. *What the fuck just happened? Had Ali stolen his date? What the fuck!*

Chapter One Hundred Thirty-Eight

EARTH DIMENSION THREE
Mystic Haven, B.C., Canada

BAYLEN WOKE UP WITH a jerk and cursed at his never ending hard on. His fucking life was going to shit, and he regretted that he'd allowed himself to give into the temptation that was Aliora Aurelius.

At first, the more he'd fucking played with Ali the more the dream walking abated, but the nightmares fucking escalated. He couldn't kill the monsters that tore Ali apart every night in his dream, and as the past had proven, he couldn't protect her in the real world either. Just as he couldn't protect Jadeah or Charli.

He arrived at her house after he took the kids to school. No point in tempting himself with her sleepy pajama-clad body.

She was up, dressed and working on her laptop when he arrived. *Much better.* He poured himself a coffee and sat down across from her. "How are you?"

Ali leaned back in her chair and frowned at him. "Not happy with you."

"I figured."

He reached into his pocket and set a small package on the table. "For Micah."

"Give it to him yourself."

Baylen grinned, a flash of white teeth. "It's not the kind of present he would like from me, but he will love it from you. I was also thinking that since you have jumped into the world of threesomes—with my date." He glared at her. "That it's time for us—you, me, and Micah—to get around to fucking." *Not that he believed for one second that she'd participated in a threesome or that he had any plan of ever sharing her with anyone. He'd fucking kill any bastard who even dared to suggest a threesome to him.* But the facts remained, staying with him would only get her killed and this was the ideal way to make sure she wanted nothing more to do with him. He raised an eyebrow bracing for her answer, knowing with everything inside him what it would be.

Aliora glared at Baylen. "Get out."

Chapter One Hundred Thirty-Nine

EARTH DIMENSION THREE
Mystic Haven, B.C., Canada

ALIORA TOOK A SIP OF her extra-extra-large Arianna's Secret Brew coffee, *guaranteed to keep you awake after a sleepless night*, and she'd had way too many of those lately. Every single time she fell asleep she was plagued by this infernal Fae dream walking business. It was all Baylen's fault. Yes, she was blaming him. He had to be doing it on purpose. The bastard. Her dreams had changed from sensual to flat out wicked. The things he did to her in those dreams shocked her and left her wet and trembling with no relief in sight.

Why was she thinking about this again?

She forced her mind back to the elegant medieval dresses on her laptop screen. This online shop was her favorite. It catered to all things geek and cosplay. The dresses she was looking at were high quality and not easy on the pocketbook. At this moment, that didn't matter. She was immersed in dress buying therapy. She added the rich deep purple with the small train, and the sunny yellow with no train. She clicked over to the next page and smiled a tired smile as she saw the accessories.

The bell jingled a happy sound as the door to the coffee shop opened and she glanced up. Baylen Knight and a redheaded woman. A woman snuggled much too close to Baylen to be a casual acquaintance. Ali's eyebrow rose. That asshole.

She rose from her chair, adjusted her forest green dress, and swept up the aisle between the tables.

Marching up to Baylen and his... his... person, she poked him in the chest repeatedly. "Stay out of my dreams!" Her voice was loud enough to carry throughout the busy morning crowd. A crowd of superhumans, many of whom knew the Fae mating signs, and dream walking was certainly one of those signs.

Ali felt the surprise that rippled through the coffee shop. She sensed them staring at her, staring at Baylen, staring at the redhead, and she didn't care. She was exhausted from Baylen's interference with her dreams, fed up, and here he was with this... this... person. She was done.

Baylen stared in shock at Aliora. *What the fuck?* The woman who'd been happily clinging to his arm, narrowed her eyes, and he recognized that something fucking unpleasant was about to occur.

Ali glanced around at the room and lifted an eyebrow, her arms crossing over her chest as her fangs slid out. She was going to bite him so hard!

"What the fuck, Aliora!"

She stabbed him in the chest again with her finger. "Stay out of my dreams! Especially if you are screwing someone else!"

Baylen growled. "You stay out of my dreams!"

"Oh, no, boyo!" *Was she channeling her grandfather Edge?* "I'm not the one invading your dreams." She sniffed in disdain. "I certainly would not join in the dreams of any man who doesn't know where his dick belongs."

Baylen growled furiously. "I'm not your mate."

"That's right, and I'm not the one glowing, Fae. That's all on you. Stay. Out. Of. My. Dreams!"

"All on me? The fuck you say! No one goes into mating alone!" He glared at Ali, baring his teeth, and with a wave of his hand the room became still, people frozen in the moment, as he created a time shift.

"I'm your king!" Baylen snarled furiously. "You will fucking obey me or suffer the consequences. There will be no more discussion of this. Especially in public."

"You're not my king."

Baylen took a step forward. The look on his face had Ali backing up warily. "You keep saying that Aliora, yet I'm the fucking King of the Fae. That means I'm your king too."

Aliora stubbornly shook her head, and he moved closer, backing her against the wall. His hand braced by her head, and he leaned down to speak quietly, his authority rolling off him in waves. "If I'm not your king, what the fuck am I?"

"Apparently, my mate."

Baylen growled, furious, and he kissed her. Hard. In control. He wasn't going to let this woman interfere in his plans. His tongue slid between her lips, and he tasted her unique flavor, and the coffee she'd been drinking. The kiss became more heated. He couldn't get enough. *Gods. Just this moment. This one moment. No one would ever know.* His arms came around her and he gathered her against him, groaning into the wildfire of her kiss.

Ali kissed him back just as passionately. She wanted to get lost in his arms—Lost in this moment. But she was done with his game playing. Her arms wrapped around his neck, and she simply lifted one finger. The time shift shattered, and she nipped his lip. Startled, he growled, as something in the silence around them changed. He lifted his head and looked around. The Saturday morning coffee crowd all gaped at him. At him kissing Aliora. *Fuck.* Kissing the fuck out of Aliora. While glowing. *Fuck.*

Ali tore herself away from Baylen, grabbed her laptop and rushed out the door. He took a step after her and someone stepped into his path. He raised his eyes, fury in every line of his body, and froze as his eyes met the determined gaze of his father. *Oh, shit.* He glanced past his father to see his mother standing just behind him. The look on her face. *Fuck.*

Chapter One Hundred Forty

BY THE TIME HE GOT outside, all he saw was a glimpse of Aliora's skirt as she disappeared into Micah's tattoo shop. Growling, he stormed across the street. Shoving open the door, he stepped inside just in time to see Ali pull the small package he'd given her for Micah from her backpack. She slapped it down on the front desk in front of Micah. "This is for you, from the Fae king. I have no idea why he couldn't deliver it himself. I suspect, from our brief conversation, that he wants to fuck you."

Everyone was gaping at her until a low growl drew all their attention. Micah, fury in his eyes, was already around the counter. A burst of speed put him right in front of the Fae king. His fist plowed into Baylen's jaw with enough force to send Baylen crashing to the floor. "You're not my effing type, Baylen. Keep your gifts and quit using me to hurt Aliora!"

Baylen rose to his feet, his hand rubbing his jaw. Fuck. He glared at Micah and stalked over to the front counter, picked up Aliora and tossed her over his shoulder. "Not a fucking word!" He snapped at Micah and walked out the door as his friend flipped him the bird.

The asshole Fae king shot up into the air with her still draped over his shoulder and flew her back to her house. Not that it was fucking easy, she fought like a fucking wildcat. Landing, he stalked into her kitchen. He set her on a chair and glared down at her. "Stop pushing me, Ali!"

She jumped to her feet, hands on her hips, arms akimbo. "You stop pushing me! How dare you flaunt your conquest's in my face!"

"I'm not fucking flaunting anything!"

"You are and I'm warning you right now that, if you do it again, there will be consequences!" Ali didn't know when she'd ever been this angry. She was shouting, something she never did, and frankly she didn't care.

Baylen stepped closer. "What the hell do you call what you did? You think you're the only one who can hand out consequences?"

A rush of heat surged through her, her fangs dropped, and she sank her teeth into his neck.

"Fuck!" His hand closed over the back of her neck, and he hauled her back. "Fuck! You bit me!"

She growled at him like a little feral thing, and by the creators, he'd had fucking enough. His hand closed over her arm, and as he sat on the nearest kitchen chair, he pulled her facedown over his lap. Yanking her long skirt up, he brought his hand down on her lace covered ass hard enough to make her yelp. He smacked her gorgeous ass twice more before he realized that she'd stopped struggling. *Oh fuck. He was a total asshole. Shit.* He lifted her and set her between his legs. He didn't even know what to fucking say. "I'm sor—" Her mouth crashed into his, her tongue sliding between his lips. Her hands slipped through his hair, and she kissed him. Her fangs nipped his bottom lip, and he pulled back, eyeing her. Her eyes were bright, her cheeks pink, her nipples hard, and fuck, he could sense her arousal. *Fuck.* His cock surged to attention. Fuck. "Ali—"

"You're in my dreams every night!" She yelled. "I'm aroused all the time, and there you are parading your latest pickuparound!"

He growled. She yanked her dress off over her head. Her pink lace underwear set left nothing to the imagination. He swallowed and the wrong head took over. He picked her up, laid her on the table, and tore her panties from her. She planted her feet flat on the table and drew up her knees until she was spread open before him, the scent of her arousal filling his nostrils. His hands caught her hips, and he drew her to the edge of the table, his tongue swiped his lower lip, and he raised his eyes to hers.

"Please, Bay." Her voice was a siren's whisper he couldn't resist. He leaned forward and licked through her folds. She jerked and her hands settled in his hair. He couldn't stop, he couldn't get enough of her sweet taste, he couldn't get enough of her gasps and her cries. He feasted. Making her come over and over again until she begged him to stop. Rising, he leaned over her, his hand on the table by her head. His breathing just as harsh as hers. His gaze locked with hers, wildness glittering in the darkness of his eyes. She heard his zipper release, and his cock nudged her entrance.

"Aliora."

"If you stop, I will kill you." Her voice filled with such fierce demand that a half smile quirked his lips. He filled her in one thrust. She gasped, her hands clenching on his shoulders. What followed was frantic, driving, and as wild and dark as the man she dared to love. Her heart stuttered with her realization, and he closed the breath of distance between them, his lips moving over hers, demanding a response. Her hands rose to clench in his hair, fisting the strands as she pressed closer. A harsh masculine groan as her nipples brushed against him. His kiss turned voracious as their movements became more frantic. He pressed his big body against hers, and she clutched at him. "Baylen."

His eyes opened and the heated sexuality in his gaze made her toes curl. His hand moved between them, his finger stroking her clit. Her whole body tightened, and she couldn't tear her eyes from the fire blazing in his. In the next instant, her orgasm swept over her, made all the more powerful by the knowledge that he couldn't hold back either. The warmth of his seed filled her as they both groaned, their bodies convulsing as wave after wave of ecstasy rushed over them.

She had no idea how long they lay there. Finally, Baylen moved off her and lifted her into his arms. He carried her into the bedroom, laid her on the bed, crawling in after her and pulling the thick comforter over them. His hand found hers and squeezed. She turned to look into his face.

"I can't offer you much, Aliora. I can't offer you forever, I can't offer you a mating. I can't offer you marriage or even to move in with me. I'm not capable of love anymore and even if I was,—I won't risk your life. Do you understand?"

Ali studied the man beside her. *Would he try so hard to protect her if he had no feelings for her?* "Can you be faithful to me?"

He nodded. "I haven't been with anyone since I met you, Ali."

Her eyebrow rose but inside she heard the ring of truth in his words. She also knew that if he'd actually fucked another woman, it would have affected the dream walking and the mating call, they were both experiencing. She stared at him still angry. Still hurt. "The redhead?"

He shrugged looking sheepish. "My cousin. Thank goodness she was there though, because she ran interference with my parents so I could go after you."

Ali's eyes widened. "Your parents?" A horrified whisper.

Chapter One Hundred Forty-One

EARTH DIMENSION THREE
Mystic Haven, B.C., Canada

BAYLEN PACED HIS STUDY. *Fuck. Fuck. Fuck.* Why was he so worked up? Sex with Ali had been fucking amazing. *That's why.* It hadn't been fine. It hadn't been boring. It hadn't been good. It had been fucking amazing.

He should be sleeping. He should be planning the next time he had her in his bed. *No, no, no.* Not in his bed. In her bed. Or on the couch. Maybe outside. Hell, he could do her anywhere except his bed. He winced. *Okay, I can't 'do' her.* That was wrong. *Okay. Okay. Baylen. Breathe. Just Breathe.*

His mind drew blanks on this situation. Situation? There wasn't a situation. He was fucking Aliora Aurelius. Sweet, gentle, kind Aliora. *Fuck.*

He groaned and shoved a hand through his long hair, pushing it back. He wanted to thoroughly corrupt her. He wanted to tie her to his bed and touch her for hours. He wanted her to beg for his cock. He wanted to hear her pleading with him to fill her. He wanted to see those pretty nipples of hers stiff and hard for him. He wanted to be rough and hard with her. He wanted to be soft and gentle with her. He wanted to laugh with her and make her blush.

He wanted her screaming his name. *Fuck. What the hell am I thinking?*

This was just supposed to help get rid of all the fucking dream walking. This was supposed to ease the mating signs, not make them worse. Not turn him into a crazed sex maniac. *I'm so fucked.*

Chapter One Hundred Forty-Two

EARTH DIMENSION THREE
Mystic Haven, B.C., Canada

ALRIGHT, he tossed back his glass of whiskey. *I'm obviously going about this the wrong way.* Quickies. That's the answer. *I need to keep things quick. Fuck her and get out.* Back up plan. *I need a back up plan.* He stalked around his study, pausing to pour himself another whiskey. *I could open the playroom in the castle dungeon.* Not his personal one of course, but the one that had come with the castle. *The fucking Ancient Fae were pervs.* There is nothing remotely emotional there. No soft fuzzy feelings. Yeah, that could work.

Chapter One Hundred Forty-Three

BAYLEN TILTED THE WHISKEY bottle to his lips and had a long drink. Did that woman bring soft and fuzzy wherever she went? Fuck. He would never look at that playroom the same way again. *But it would make a really nice secret library for her.* He stopped, horrified by the direction of his thoughts. *Fuck.* He took another drink from the whiskey bottle, but he made a note to have construction started immediately.

I can't fuck her again. That's all there is to it. The thought crushed him.

He lifted the bottle to his lips again. *Fuck.* Distance. *I have to create distance while I fuck her.* But how the fuck was he supposed to do that? She was like the cuddliest, softest person he'd ever met. She was a superhuman pillow, and her glow-in-the-dark skin was so damn cute. *Cute?* His eyes widened, and he turned and grabbed his phone.

"Micah? I'm fucked. I can't be fucked. I am the King of the Fae. No fucked up kings are allowed."

"What the hell?" Micah took the phone from his ear and stared at it. "Do you know what time it is, Baylen?"

"It's Aliora's fault."

"Have you been drinking that special blend of whiskey that can actually get Fae drunk?"

"Yes." He took another swig from the bottle.

Micah paused. "What's going on, Baylen?"

"Look, Micah. You're my best friend. You must help me."

"Sure. How can I help?" Micah shook his head, hoping Baylen would start to make sense.

"We have to have a threesome."

Micah opened his mouth. Closed it. A bark of laughter slipping free. "Last time we did that we were in the military. Remember that gorgeous blonde with the big—"

"Micah. I'm serious. I thought about never fucking again. But we both know that isn't practical."

Micah started to laugh.

"Listen. Just listen. If I fuck Ali with you there will be no soft fuzzy feelings. She wouldn't be able to bring them into that kind of situation, right? I could get my perspective back. Stop laughing Micah."

Chapter One Hundred Forty-Four

EARTH DIMENSION THREE
Mystic Haven, B.C., Canada

BAYLEN WALKED INTO the tattoo shop, and into the back directly to Micah's studio. He flung himself down in the chair by Micah's desk and glared at his friend.

Micah raised an eyebrow.

"I can't see Aliora anymore."

"Why?"

"I'm getting in too deep."

"Dude, I'm the guy you are calling every day to talk about Ali."

"See. Too deep." His phone pinged and he opened it up. "Fuck."

"What?"

Baylen started typing.

Micah walked over to look at Baylen's phone. Aliora in sexy lingerie. *Whoo man!* He started to laugh as he saw Baylen's reply.

You have no idea what you just started.

Baylen stood up. "Gotta go, Micah. I have a date with Ali."

Micah shook his head, laughing so hard he could barely lift his hand in farewell.

Chapter One Hundred Forty-Five

BAYLEN'S EYES SNAPPED open. *Fuck.* He'd fallen asleep. Ali cuddled up to him all soft and warm, her head on his chest, her hand curled over his heart. He fucking didn't want to move. Except this damn instinctive chronometer that told him the first rays of the sun would touch the earth in thirty-seven minutes. He had to be gone long before then.

Gently, he shifted Ali over, his lips quirking at her grumpy complaint. Easing off the bed, he found his jeans and t-shirt. He was zipping his jeans when he realized she was watching him.

"It's only a little while before dawn. You should come back to bed."

Baylen tugged on his t-shirt and ran a hand through his long hair.

"Baylen?"

"Go back to sleep, Ali."

She sat up and frowned at him. "I can make you a coffee."

"No."

"What's going on?"

"Nothing, Ali. I need to go."

Her head tilted. "Are you—"

"Let it go, Ali!" He growled. "Just fucking let it go!"

She watched him silently as he stalked from her room, and moments later heard the front door close. His motorbike roared to life a few seconds later. Climbing out of bed, she walked into the kitchen and started the coffee maker, as she heard his bike racing away.

She drank her coffee as she watched the sun crest over the ocean. Sighing, she set down her cup. Walking out onto her private beach, the first rays of the sun moved over her with its life-giving energy. She inhaled deeply and continued across the sand and waded into the ocean that lapped gently at the shore. Instantly scales rippled over her arms.

She'd been going to tell Baylen about her Mer side this morning. She wrinkled her nose and fought the tears stinging her eyes. A few more steps and the gills opened behind her ears. She kept walking. Sure, swimming in her pajamas was weird, but she didn't feel like magicking a swimsuit.

When she was out far enough, she swam for a while before moving to her back and floating in the morning sun. She knew she had to let this go. Baylen had been clear about this only being an affair. He'd been clear about no sleepovers. Yeah, he'd been staying later and later, and okay, she'd wanted to read into that.

"Aliora." Baylen's voice in her mind.

"Hello, Baylen."

"What are you doing?"

"Swimming."

"This early? That's got to be cold."

"I'm fine."

"Look Ali, I'm sorry for being a dick this morning."

She was silent, trying to figure out what to say. *"Yeah, being a dick is not okay with me. You want to tell me what was going on?"* Silence greeted her question.

"I don't want to talk about it, Aliora."

"Okay. If you don't want to come here anymore—"

"I'll be there tonight, and I'll be fucking you."

"That's more than a bit arrogant, Baylen." She could almost see him grin.

"You know it's kind of an intimate thing for a Fae to share the morning sun with someone."

"More intimate than having your cock inside my pussy?"

"Aliora!"

She heard his shock and frankly she didn't care. *"I need the morning light too, Baylen. It's not that shocking. Does something happen to the Fae king that doesn't happen to any other Fae? Do you grow horns or turn purple?"* She sank under the water and sat on the sandy bottom. *"You know what? Never mind. Don't bother coming over tonight. I need to wash my hair."*

"Wash your—? You little brat." There was a clear warning in his voice.

She shrugged. *"I've got to go. I have things to do."* She ended the conversation. She sat on the ocean bottom for another hour thinking about this morning. When she finally rose to the surface, she still didn't have any answers but the gut feeling that Baylen was hiding something from her persisted.

A head popped up a few feet away from her and she gasped.

"Sorry, didn't mean to startle you. I'm Riley Muirgheal. I was watching you. What are you?"

Ali frowned. "It's kind of rude to watch people."

Riley grinned. "I'm Mer and I was worried when I saw you sitting on the bottom of the ocean like that. You don't have a tail, and as far as I know the only human type of water breathers are the Mer."

"I'm Aliora Aurelius. My great grandfather Breaker Murchadh is Mer."

"Breaker Murchadh? That scallywag is your great grandfather? The stories about that man are legendary. Would you like to go for a coffee? I'd love to get to know you, and I can tell you about the Mer here in Mystic Haven."

Ali smiled. "I would like that."

Chapter One Hundred Forty-Six

EARTH DIMENSION THREE
Mystic Haven, B.C., Canada

ALIORA ADMITTED SHE was grumpy as she walked up to the Fae Ward that guarded the Castle. She hadn't slept well last night, after their argument.

She really needed to understand why he'd been so upset. It was weird that Baylen had freaked out over something as small as catching a few rays of sunlight with her. Her Fae instincts were going crazy. He was hiding something.

The Ward shimmered in front of her, and she turned her thoughts from Baylen and his strange behavior and focused on the Castle Ward. This Ward was different, and she didn't want to upset it. Comprising three kinds of Wards, it was sentient, capable of learning and extremely powerful. It had the ability to render the Fae castle totally invisible. In fact, the only people who got into the Fae castle were those escorted by the King, his family, his Trium, or the castle guards. This particular Ward was fully capable of detecting good and evil and could create an impenetrable barrier to prevent evil from entering the castle grounds. If evil ignored its warning, it could and would destroy it. It also had the interesting ability to move people through time and space, if it sensed danger to one of the ones it protected.

Which was all fine and dandy, except today, when she wanted to sneak into the castle unseen. She stopped in front of the Ward, and it swirled around her. She laughed. *"Hello, Castle Ward."*

"Greetings Mate of the Fae King."

"You recognize me?"

"Of course, Aliora Aurelius. This is your home."

"My—" She stopped herself and considered her plan. *"Castle Ward, may I walk around the castle? I would like to greet the sun."*

"Of course, you may go anywhere you wish on the castle grounds."

"Uhm, what about Baylen?"

"Baylen has access to the full castle grounds as well, but he's in his room right now. Would you like to go to his room?"

Aliora blinked. *"No. no. I just wanted to see the sunrise."*

"The best vantage point is from the king's balcony outside his bedroom. Would you like me to transport you there?"

"No. I don't wish to disturb his rest."

The next moment she found herself on the east side of the castle in a majestic garden. "Oh!" She gasped. "Thank you, Castle Ward."

The Ward vanished and Ali looked around. The castle rose in front of her facing east. She could see a large balcony stretching along one stone wall and she assumed that was the king's bedroom. A few seconds later she heard a sound and Baylen stepped through sliding glass doors onto the balcony.

She ducked behind a flowering tree and peeked around it to watch. Swallowing, she stared up at him, entranced by all his naked male glory, as the sun was about to rise. She bit her lip in anticipation hoping he would drop his glamour. She longed to see him in all his Fae splendor.

The first rays of the sun crept across the land banishing the darkness. She held her breath. Eagerly watching as the light touched his body. She gasped trying to make sense of what she was seeing, shaking her head back and forth, her trembling fingers covering her mouth as he stiffened, agony delineating every muscle. The cords of his neck stood out in grim display as his head fell back. His teeth bared in a grimace of untold pain as blisters erupted across his body.

Creators! What was happening! His human form wavered, disappeared, leaving him a Fae starkly beautiful even as he burned. Yet the immensity of his power was enough to overcome the destruction. Golden Fae energy spread over him. Healing every blister. Every burn.

He stood panting his hand clenching the stone railing of his balcony, his head bowed, long hair tumbling around his face.

"Baylen." A bare whisper of sound torn from her heart.

His head jerked up, his eyes wild and dark as they connected with hers. Fury burned in their depths and his muscles bunched as he leapt over the balcony railing. She inhaled sharply, his primitively chiseled Fae features clearly defined by the early morning light. His beauty was dark and terrifying, and sent heat rushing through her veins.

She turned but it was far too late. He was on her. His hands turning her to face him. A growl filling the air.

She was the light. Glowing in unearthly splendor. Revealed in the most unexpected way. Long curling hair that reflected the sunrise, eyes that spoke of the mysteries of their world, wings that shimmered in the morning air. Her voice was an exotic seductive wisp gliding over him, wrapping around his cock. His cock that had been rock hard from the moment he saw her watching him.

"I see you, Baylen Knight."

It was such an Elf thing to say that he paused. A grimace crossed his face. Acceptance, fucking acceptance of a darkness that could get her killed.

"You weren't supposed to see that. You were never supposed to see my darkness!"

She smiled as the sun glowed all around her. "Darkness cannot hide you from me."

"The darkness wants to consume you!" his voice a harsh growl.

Her smile became mysterious, a seductive invitation. Darkness could never consume her. She spread her arms wide, her clothes vanishing. Her eyes met his. She saw the naked need that rode him hard. "Then give the darkness what it wants."

His hand closed around her throat, a dark snarl curled his lips, echoing in the morning air. Backing her against the broad trunk of the flowering tree his eyes never left hers.

Creators, there was such fury in his gaze. She lifted her hands, her fingers lightly grazing his chest.

He grabbed her wrists, pinning them with one hand, above her head against the rough bark of the tree. He stepped forward, crowding her, his body pressing into hers.

Her nipples rasped against his chest, his cock a hard ridge against her stomach. His mouth crashed down onto hers, his tongue thrusting into her mouth. A rough moan as he took the kiss deeper, harder. As if he couldn't get enough of her.

She kissed him back, opening for him, her tongue sliding against his, accepting his invasion. Arousal rushed through her veins, heat gathering between her legs. Her nipples peaked as he tore his mouth from hers and nipped his way down her neck, forcing her head to the side until he could bite the area where her neck and shoulder joined. She gasped, and he bit harder, not enough to break the skin but hard enough to leave a mark.

His hand fisted in her hair as he came back up to her lips. His eyes met hers, glittering, wild, dark. "I'm going to fuck you so hard." His voice a guttural growl that sent a fluttery feeling soaring through her stomach. Her tongue slicked over her bottom lip, and he leaned down, nipping the plump curve. She jerked and he licked the tiny hurt, their breath became one as he ghosted his lips over hers, a barely there tease before his kiss became hard and demanding again.

His hand released her hair and moved down her body in a rough caress, he palmed her breast. A low rumble of satisfaction between hard fast kisses, as his thumb rubbed over her nipple. His head lifted, his eyes searching hers as he pinched the sensitive tip. She gasped and arched, as erotic pleasure flooded her senses. A hard half smile curved his lips. He ducked down and his mouth closed over her nipple. He sucked hard as his hand clasped her hip tightly enough that she suspected she'd wear his marks for a while, and she didn't care because this was so good. This was so wild.

His teeth grazed her nipple and she cried out. He bit down, just hard enough that an electric zing burst through the tender nub. A shocked moan spilled from her lips. He lifted his head, his eyes feral as they met hers. His hand closed over her breast, and he growled, shifting closer his cock smearing a warm trail of precum over her stomach. She flexed her hands, and he tightened his grip, his other hand moving to her thigh, sliding up to clasp her ass. His touch rough and possessive, she bit her lip and arched into him. He lifted her leg and urged it around his hip, his hand sliding back to her ass, and he lifted her.

She gasped, shocked by his strength. His cock pressed against her entrance, and he thrust hard, filling her in a single stroke. Crying out, she wrapped her other leg around him. His buttocks flexed with every fast heavy thrust, as he fucked into her pussy with a determination that shocked and aroused her. Brutal strokes, which left her feeling invaded in the most erotic of ways. "Please." her breath panted out of her. "More."

Her breasts bounced against his chest, her nipples rasping against his. "Baylen!" Her voice was a shocked breathless gasp, as he wedged his hand between them, his fingers sliding through her folds to rub over her clit.

"Come for me, Ali." His voice was a dark command. His fingers spilling Fae energy over her swollen clit. She arched helplessly at the tingle and sharp sparking bite of his magic.

Her breath caught as her whole body tensed, and a surge of Fae energy slid over her whole body, every sensitive nerve springing to life as hard convulsions rocked through her. Her pussy clamped down on the hard cock pistoning in and out of her, and she cried out, her voice mingling with the rough shout that left his lips as his seed jetted from him, splashing deep inside her.

He collapsed against her, his weight pushing her back against the tree. His head rested on the trunk beside her ear. His breath warm against her. After a moment, he eased from her and swung her into his arms. His wings easily carried them both up to his balcony and into his room. He laid her on his bed, tugging blankets over her, and crawled in after her, wrapping his arms around her. "Sleep, little slayer of darkness."

Chapter One Hundred Forty-Seven

WISTERIA STEPPED OUT of the vortex and into the castle garden and stared around. It hadn't changed much from the last time she'd been here. She looked to the east, and there in the distance, she could see a small cottage almost completely covered in brambles. She allowed the memories to surface, and a cruel smile touched her lips. Though her time had been cut short, she'd still accomplished a great deal.

Most importantly, she'd established a nest long enough for her to make a trip back in time to the moment The Ward was being created. From there it had been a simple matter to imprint her presence on the newly created Ward. Not the younger rage fuelled creature she had been when she first discovered the Fae living on this world. No, she'd imprinted this older, wiser, scarred version who had barely survived her encounter with Baylen Knight. The version of herself that The Ward had never met.

She'd been so close to claiming her consort. Until her rebellious pet managed to destroy her nest. It had taken her years to find her way back to this dimension. Her pet would pay for that. Wisteria smiled. There were some things in life that brought true pleasure.

She could feel time moving forward and knew that she needed to establish a new nest as soon as possible, but she had time to check on her consort.

As she made her way through the garden a noise caught her attention. A low moan and a man's growl. Her eyebrow arched. Was she about to catch someone in flagrante delicto? The idea was delicious. She moved closer to the sounds, and as she rounded a large shrub, she saw a feminine leg wrapped around a very masculine ass as it flexed. Definitely in flagrante delicto. The male was pounding into the female with such aggression that she had to see who it was. She moved to another shrub, where she would not easily be seen, and peered out.

Her features tightened and she pressed her lips together. Her consort! Having sex with a naked woman in the garden, in broad daylight! She considered joining him, *what a delightful surprise that would be*, until she noticed the glow around him. *That bitch was his mate!*

A low, dangerous growl rumbled through her. How many mates was she going to have to kill? She was outraged with the Creators. How dare they interfere with her plans! She shrugged. Creators plans or not, she would kill every woman who made a claim on her consort. It was one thing for Baylen to fuck his servants, or her pet. It was quite another for him to take a mate.

He could use Ciara in whatever manner he pleased. It would only strengthen the darkness she'd planted in him. The darker Baylen Knight became, the more power she'd gain. She had glorious plans to tempt him to do things he would never consider doing on his own. She smiled. Every time he gave in to temptation, the darkness would grow. She looked forward to the day, her consort's heart was as black as hers. She watched for another minute, formulating her plans. This mate would have to die of course, but first things first. She needed to find her pet and re-establish her nest.

Chapter One Hundred Forty-Eight

EARTH DIMENSION THREE
Mystic Haven, B.C., Canada

WISTERIA LEFT THE ROYAL gardens and stalked through the forest. When she was several miles from the Fae castle, she stopped and let her senses sweep out, seeking her pet. Her rage was a blood red wash of color in her mind. Finding Ciara would help her to regain control. This was not a time when she could make mistakes. There were more Fae here than the last time she had been on this island. Far more than she alone could defeat without having an established nest. She smiled coldly. She would feast when the time was right.

A different signature appeared in her scan. It was close, very close, and it did not have the natural shields of a Fae. She moved silently through the forest, pausing occasionally to spin energy webs to trap her prey. A cry drifted to her on the breeze, and she turned and strode back to the web that tugged at her. A young woman was tangled in the fine gossamer energy strands. "You poor dear." She said, and she smiled, letting her glamour go.

The woman screamed and began to struggle frantically, hopelessly entangling herself further in the sticky energy.

Wisteria laughed, a brittle, harsh sound. Her sharp teeth flashing in the coolness of the forest. "You are a lovely Elf."

Wisteria began to move slowly and deliberately toward the young woman caught in her web. "You'll have to excuse my poor manners. I've had a dreadful morning. My consort is once again banging someone I've not approved. Fortunately, you can help relieve my stress." She tore the woman's clothing from her body, her movements violent and purposeful. "I firmly believe in playing with my food before I devour it."

Chapter One Hundred Forty-Nine

EARTH DIMENSION THREE
Mystic Haven, B.C., Canada

CADEN WALKED INTO THE Mystic Brew pub and looked around. Janie Valeska, the owner of the pub, waved and lifted a coffee pot. He grinned and shook his head. A man had to change it up once in a while. He was about to slide into a booth when he saw Ciara at the bar. She had a pink drink in front of her and was staring at the surface of the bar as a man spoke earnestly to her. He noticed that her fingers were clenched tightly around her drink, and she nodded but did not say anything. He frowned. He'd never seen Ciara at the pub by herself and certainly hadn't seen her with a man since the father of her child had left the island and never returned.

He'd known they hadn't been mates, but it was ice cold to abandon your woman when she was pregnant with your child. Turning, he walked over to the bar. "Hey, Ciara."

Ciara looked up at the sound of her name, tears pricking her eyes at seeing Caden. She smiled a shaky smile and let out a breath she hadn't realized she'd been holding. It had been a bad idea to come here. She blamed it on hormones. Fae hormones. "Caden."

The relief was so plain in her eyes that Caden was glad he'd followed his instincts. "Let's get a booth. This is too noisy." He nodded at the man, who looked dismayed, and put his hand on Ciara's back to usher her over to a booth along the back of the pub.

Once they were seated Ciara spoke, "Thank you, Caden."

He grinned. "Rescuing damsels is in my job description."

Ciara laughed. "You might have been rescuing him. I was thinking of zapping him if he touched me one more time."

A waitress approached and took their order.

"Is one of your friends going to join you here this evening?"

Ciara shook her head as the waitress returned and set Caden's cola and her tea on the table. "I, uhm...." She bit her lip and glanced at Caden from under her lashes.

He raised an eyebrow.

She took a breath as her cheeks warmed. "I haven't, you know, been interested in... uhm... men. Since Kelby left."

Caden watched her intently. "You are now?"

She took a drink of her tea and shrugged. "I—"

When she didn't finish, he spoke, "It's been about three years?"

She nodded.

"You think you're ready to dip your toes in the water again?"

She stared down at the table. Caden frowned, troubled by her quietness. The Fae were by nature, sensual creatures.

For her to have gone three years without a lover was unusual. "Was being with Kelby a good experience after everything that happened?"

Ciara picked up her tea and took a sip. The waitress returned and set their food on the table. She took a few moments to nibble on a French fry and gather her courage. "It wasn't bad, Caden."

Wasn't bad? This woman deserved a helluva lot better than wasn't bad. "What do you want?"

Ciara looked at the cop, puzzled and a tiny bit distracted by his gorgeous face. The whole package was frankly amazing. She loved it when he'd started to let his hair grow. He was gorgeous with his short hair, but now? Wow. Shoulder length, curly, sun-streaked dark brown hair, hazel eyes that could turn green in an instant. A beard touched with white. He was so damn masculine that she always felt a little bit nervous around him. And she would never admit to anyone that she'd entertained more than one sexy fantasy about this man. "What do you mean?"

Caden chuckled. "Do you want a single hook up? Dating? Do you want a love relationship? Friendship? A cuddle buddy? Only sex?"

Her eyes widened and she quickly took another drink of her tea. Scalding her tongue.

"Ciara." Caden chided. "We've been friends for years now. Hell, we sat on the beach the other night and talked for hours. You don't have to be shy with me. You know damn well I've got your back, and I'm not going to judge you."

Ciara stared at Caden as if she'd never seen him before. This had to be one of the weirdest conversations she'd ever had. She was talking about sex and relationships with the cop—The Fae Guardian. The man you never wanted to piss off. The man who handed out speeding tickets like they were going out of style. She reached over, picked up his glass of cola, and took a drink.

"Tea was hot, huh?"

She nodded and took another sip. "I'm not giving it back."

Caden laughed. "Okay." He glanced over at the waitress, pointed at the glass that Ciara had confiscated, and held up a finger. The waitress nodded and within a few seconds set another glass of cola on the table.

"I want—" she nibbled her lip. *Oh, my gosh, am I really going to discuss my lack of a sex life with the cop?* "I don't know, Caden." *Apparently, she was.* "To have a friend, to be held, sex. I miss sex. Does that make me a terrible person?"

Caden shook his head. "Of course not, Ciara. You're not a robot. Friendship, touch, and even sex are all perfectly normal things to want, to need."

Ciara shrugged again. "I, uh...." She swallowed. "I have scars." She hunched her shoulders and stared down at her hands. "Not everyone is okay with that."

Caden watched her carefully for a moment, an ugly feeling in the pit of his stomach. "Ciara, you're one hell of a courageous woman. You fought a monster and survived. If anyone has a problem with the marks of your courage, they can get fucked." He reached over and lifted her chin until she looked him in the eyes. "Please tell me that Kelby wasn't like that."

She shrugged and glanced away.

Caden had an overwhelming urge to hunt Kelby down and knock some sense into him. Maybe it was a good thing the man had done a runner. Caden leaned forward and stared into her eyes. He'd always had a thing for her eyes. That shade of teal was real pretty. "You want some rules?"

Ciara swallowed. "Rules?" she asked faintly.

"You know, if you find someone you would like to take the risk with."

"Uh. I guess I haven't thought that far ahead, Caden." She laughed and turned the glass of cola in front of her.

"Let's see. Privacy? Is that important to you?"

"Yes." She nodded. "I have Sophia and my grandparents."

Caden chuckled. "Your grandparents are wild as hell. They wouldn't even blink. But I agree with you that discretion is important."

Ciara laughed. "My gramma has been hinting for me to go 'have some fun' for a while. My gramps has flat out told me to find someone to get wild with. Fae." Her voice sounded lovingly exasperated.

Caden grinned. "Guess that is a perk of not aging."

Ciara shook her head. "I've been scarred for life by those two and their shenanigans."

"I caught them in the library once." Caden laughed. "I've never been able to go into the cookbook aisle again."

Ciara groaned, but she couldn't stop the laughter from spilling out.

"How often would you want to see this person? Do you have people you would keep informed for your own safety? You're going to have to talk about sex and what you are okay with and what you aren't."

She laughed. "What are you, my big brother?"

Caden stared at her, and the intensity in his eyes stopped her laughter. She swallowed.

"Hell no, Ciara. Hell no. But I am available."

Her eyes shot to his, and he winked at her. "I promise that I can do a damn sight better than 'it wasn't bad,' and you know me. You know that I'm safe. I'm fully on board for friendship, cuddles, and sex."

"Together?" Her voice was a high-pitched squeak.

Caden smirked. "That's usually how it's done."

Ciara blinked. Oh. My. Goddess. Caden had just suggested that they—She swallowed—That they have sex. Together. Her and the cop.

Caden reached out and lifted her chin until her eyes met his. "Think about it."

His phone beeped, and he picked it up, frowning a little as he read the text. "I've gotta go. My kids have gotten into some shenanigans with their aunt." He started to pocket his phone, paused, and looked up at her, a slow half smile curving his lips. He was not going to just walk out of here and leave it like this. He wanted her to consider his offer. He wanted her thinking about him. Taking his work phone out of his pocket, he scrolled through it until he found her number. He sent her a text from his personal phone.

Ciara's phone immediately beeped. She picked it up.

This is my private number. Text me back.

Ciara glanced from her phone to the man sitting across from her. His private number? He had a look in his eyes that she didn't know what to make of. He raised his eyebrow.

She bit her lip and texted back.

This will make it easier for me to invite your kids to Sophia's birthday party.

He read the text and chuckled. *Naw, he was not going to let her get away with that.* He stood up, tucking both phones away in his pocket. Placing one hand on the table, the other on the back of the booth where she sat, he leaned down and spoke quietly in her ear. "That's not the invitation I want, Ciara. Think about what I said. I sure as hell will be." And He left.

Chapter One Hundred Fifty

EARTH DIMENSION THREE
Mystic Haven, B.C., Canada

BAYLEN WOKE TO THE soft neon blue glow of a feminine figure standing beside his bed. He blinked sleepily. "Ali? What are you doing here?"

"I need you, Baylen." She reached out and took his hand, tugging.

He reached for her, but she stepped back, and he heard her soft laugh. Growling, he sat up, his eyes adjusted enough to see that she was naked. Glowing and beautifully naked. "Ali, don't tease me before I've had my coffee."

She grinned and took his hand, setting it on her breast, her hard nipple rubbing against his palm. "I need you." She stepped back again.

He stood up, his cock hard and took a step toward her. "Maybe I'll paddle your ass."

"Sounds kinky."

He laughed. She was sweetness and light, but there were times when he wanted nothing more than to corrupt her. He reined in that thought. "Are you trying to seduce me, Ali?"

"Yes." She stepped back. "I want you to fuck me."

He blinked. "Swearing, Ali?" *Creators that fucking made his cock hard.*

"I want you to take me hard, Baylen Knight, King of the Fae."

He smirked and followed her as she led him out onto the balcony. "I might have to punish you."

She bent over the balcony railing and glanced back at him over her shoulder. "Here. Fuck me here."

His mouth dropped open. *Fuck.* He glanced at the star-studded sky. The night was quiet around them. "I'm going to fuck you alright, but I want to play first." His hand curved over her ass, and he stroked the silken skin, squeezed gently. "You have a filthy mouth tonight."

She laughed a gentle husky sound on the faintest breeze of the night. "Are you going to punish me, King of the Fae? Do you want me to suck your cock?"

Whoa—She was—Holy shit. He swallowed. "Yes, and yes."

A sassy little smirk lifted the corners of her mouth, as she looked at him over her shoulder, and he couldn't take his eyes off it. "What are you waiting for Fae king?"

He swallowed. *Was she daring him?* He raised his eyebrow and dark lust rose like a wave inside him. His fingers slid down the curve of her ass and stroked plump pink feminine folds. He heard her small gasp and smiled as his fingers moved between her folds, gliding through the silky wetness of her arousal. "You're wet, Ali." He circled her clit before stepping closer and gently kicking her feet further apart. "Hmm, should I spank you first, or should I make you suck my cock." He nudged her up against the cold stone of the balcony railing, and his other hand closed over her breast, tugging her nipple. Her moan was soft, and he smiled. "You like that. Do you want more?"

"Yes." Her reply was breathless.

He leaned over her, pressing his hard cock against her ass, as he slid a finger deep inside her pussy. "You have to earn more, Ali." A dark whisper in the night.

She moaned and he squeezed her nipple. A breathless cry. He smiled, letting go of the dark lust he tried to control around her. He stepped back and she moaned her disappointment as his hands slid from her body. He caught her hands and set them on the balcony railing, spreading her arms out. "Stay there." He nudged her feet further apart. "Beautiful." He brought his hand down on her ass in a sharp slap. She jerked and gasped. "Stay still." His voice was hard, dark with lust. Another heavy slap, and another. He rubbed the warmth of her glowing flesh, easing the sting as he thought that having a woman that glowed in the dark was an interesting addition to his little games. He tweaked her nipple and tugged on the other one. His fingers glided through the folds of her pussy, and he circled her clit, rubbing over it. "You're so lusciously wet. Want more?"

"Yes."

He smiled. "Get down on your knees. Suck my cock first."

Ali slowly straightened. Her heart raced, her ass stung, and her nipples were hard as the cold stone she had been spread over. Turning, her eyes met his and she could see the darkness of his lust. This is what he'd been holding back from her. She swallowed and knelt. She wanted all of him, and she was willing to do whatever it took. He stroked her cheek as he lifted his cock to her lips. She opened her mouth, and he nudged the head inside. Her hands came up and he shook his head. "Uh uh. Hands behind your back." She met his gaze and reached behind her, her fingers closing over the stone slats. His hips flexed and he moved deeper into her mouth. She slid her tongue over his velvet flesh, relishing the hardness.

"Suck me." It was a hoarse command.

She began to suck, and he bucked against her, almost gagging her before he gained control. His hips moved back and forth, a slow, easy, relentless thrusting that made butterflies soar in her stomach as she began to learn what he liked.

Growling, his thrusts faster, less coordinated, he suddenly jerked back pulling his cock from the warmth of her mouth. Her lips were swollen and red, and he could see the excitement in her eyes—The knowledge that she had the power to reduce him to his knees. He helped her to her feet and took her mouth in a wild, hard kiss, filled with tongue and rough nips. Lifting his hand, he fisted her hair and drew back, his breath panting out of him as he fought for control. Their eyes met and held. He turned her, kicked her feet apart and bent her over the balcony, her arms again spread along the stone railing. Gods, she was beautiful. His fingers closed over her nipple again, and he milked it as his fingers found her pussy. Warmth, liquid heat, he plucked at her clit and smiled as she squirmed. "I promised you more." His hand moved from her pussy back to her ass. He squeezed and rubbed. Lifting his hand, he stopped. "How many?"

"What?" she sounded breathless, aroused, dazed.

"I owe you a spanking. How many?"

"I don't—"

He smiled at her confusion. "One? Three? Five?"

Silence. He pinched her nipple and she jumped. "Answer me." He began to tug and roll the sensitive tip between his fingers.

She moaned. "One."

He smirked. "You sucked me more than once, Ali. Let's be fair about this."

She swallowed. "I—"

"Five, sweet Aliora."

"Oh, gods." Her voice was breathless, aroused.

He smiled a dark smile, and began to spank her, his other hand playing with her nipples. Her cries were music on the breeze. Her moans made his cock harder and harder. The smell of her arousal filled the air around him. "Five." He said out loud on the last one, and he plunged his cock into her wet pussy.

She gasped as he filled her, the sting on her ass only adding to the pleasure of his cock sliding deep. She bucked against him, and he clasped her hip, steadying them as he began to relentlessly shaft into her. He played with her nipples, he toyed with her clit. She was sensation, and rapture—and she could feel the sun beginning its ascent. She bucked back against him and squeezed her inner muscles. He groaned and she did it again.

That Cosmo article was right.

He went wild, slamming into her, and she clung to the railing, her breasts bouncing. His fingers closed around her clit, tugging, pinching gently. She groaned. *Not yet.* She panted, trying to control the massive orgasm that was rushing toward her. *Not yet. The sun. The sun had to rise first. Oh, gods. Oh, gods.* She struggled to hold on, the pleasure all but overwhelming her. His harsh pants in her ear triggered shivers running up and down the length of her spine.

He could feel his darkness rising, his lust burning through him in a wild wave of erotic possessiveness. His hand found her breast again and his fingers tugged on her nipple, pinched, and her pussy squeezed tight around his cock again. The groan that broke from his chest was rough, wild. He would not come before her. He growled and began to rub and circle her clit. She cried out and he did it again and again until her voice grew hoarse with her pleasure. Nuzzling her neck, he nudged her head to the side and his teeth closed gently over the slope of her pointed little ear.

"Oh!"

Gods, she was liquid fire, burning him alive. Catering to his darkness. Filling him with her light. He clenched his teeth, his hips jerking hard as her sweet pussy squeezed him. She went wild against him, her hips moving, her breasts bouncing. He wouldn't survive another minute.

"Come, Ali!" It was a command. A harsh demand. The order of the most powerful Fae king to ever live. The plea of her lover.

She could not resist. Her inner muscles clenched, her whole body tensed, she went up on her tiptoes, and as the sun broke over the horizon, she came apart in his arms, as his roar broke the silence of the new day.

Slowly, he came back to himself, his breath panting in her ear and a sudden horrifying realization came upon him. The sun! He jerked out of her, stepping back terrified that she would share his fate. She turned and smiled at him, sliding down to sit on the floor of the balcony. Silently she watched him and waited. That's when he realized she'd done it on purpose. "Aliora!" His bellow was rage induced, and still she smiled.

"You're alright. You're safe."

He stared at her bracing for the pain, preparing for the inevitable. Nothing. No burn. No blisters. After a minute he swallowed. "How?"

"Your darkness needs an outlet."

"An outlet?"

She nodded. "Think of it as a new fun way to start your mornings."

Chapter One Hundred Fifty-One

EARTH DIMENSION THREE
Mystic Haven, B.C., Canada

CADEN STARED AT THE body hanging from the tree in a tangle of foreign energy. There was no doubt that the victim was a female Elf. Her body was a wizened corpse. A husk of the vital young woman she had once been. Grimly, he pulled his phone from his pocket and called in the forensics team. He studied the scene a little more before making a second call. That energy field worried him. He couldn't let the forensics team go near it until he knew it was safe. "Shirina, Caden here. I need you to attend a crime scene. There is something here I don't understand. He gave her the coordinates and turned to Kit Calloway, the blond, blue eyed leader of the Elves on Mystic Haven. He stood with his High Warriors and Caden could see their fury. "Which one of you found the body?"

Navarre stepped forward. "We were on patrol here because we sensed something different in the forest. We spread out, and I found her."

Caden nodded. "Did you touch the body or that energy field?"

"No way. That energy field is strange. I thought at first that she'd become entangled in it and her struggle to escape made it worse." He swallowed. "But then I saw she was naked. I'll kill the bastard that did this to her."

Caden stared at the Elf, understanding his anger. He was pissed too. "I'll handle that, Navarre."

"What kind of sick asshole does this?" Kit clenched his fists. "Where was the effing Ward? Is it not protecting Elves anymore?"

"I don't know where The Ward was, Kit, but I intend to find out. I assure you that The Ward will always protect every citizen on this island. I've called Shirina. She'll be here soon, and hopefully, she can give us some answers."

"Caden, there are more of these energy fields scattered throughout the forest."

Caden stared at Kit. "How many? Show me!"

Kit nodded. "Follow me. I've stationed my warriors at each of them. We did a thorough search."

Shirina parked Rosie close to Caden's SUV and shrugged a backpack over one shoulder. Climbing out of her van she began the trek into the forest. She pulled a sophisticated scanning device out of her backpack and turned it on. *"Caden, I'm almost to you. I'm getting some strange readings."*

"Stop, Shirina! I'm on my way to you. Remain exactly where you are."

By the light. What if she'd walked into one of those energy fields? Caden looked at Kit. "Shirina is here and picking up some strange readings. I told her to stay where she is. Come on."

A few minutes later they found Shirina in a small clearing, her scanner sat on a rock beside her, and she'd used her tablet to open a holo-screen. She was frowning and moving through information at a rapid pace.

"Shirina."

She looked up. "Hello, Caden. Hello, Kit. I've got some readings here that are deeply concerning." The men walked over to her.

"I'm sure they are. Here's the situation. Kit had his men patrolling this area of the forest last night because they were sensing something was off. One of his men came across the body of a young female Elf. She'd been caught in some kind of energy field. His men also found several other energy fields scattered around the woods."

Shirina frowned. "The energy was powerful enough to kill her?"

Kit was shaking his head. "No. She was murdered."

Shirina's eyes met Caden's. "Take me to her."

As they came into view of the crime scene. Shirina gasped, shaking her head back and forth in denial. "No. Oh, no." She pressed her hand against her chest and took a shaky breath. "Oh gods, Caden." She forced herself to move forward. "Oh Gods. They've found us."

"Who? Who has found us, Shirina?"

She stared up at him, trembling so much that he wrapped an arm around her. He exchanged a grim look with Kit. "Shirina. Take a breath. Tell me who has found us."

"We—" She took a shuddering breath. "We need Ryder and his Trium. Hurry."

Caden stilled. He gave an abrupt nod and sent a mind link. *"Ryder, I need you and your Trium here on an urgent matter. Shirina insists you need to be here."* He sent the coordinates with the mind link.

"On our way, Caden." Ryder's voice was powerfully clear and Caden could almost hear the unasked questions the ancient Fae had.

"Can you tell me what this is, Shirina?" Caden turned his attention to the Ward Expert.

She nodded. "It's—" She swallowed. "AV'ran energy web."

Caden took a deep breath. So. "Wisteria."

Kit frowned. "Caden, the victim was naked. She'd been tortured and possibly sexually assaulted. Shouldn't we be looking for a male?"

Caden shook his head. "No. Wisteria has managed to get on this island twice. One of her victims was a female Fae, whom she held captive, tortured, and sexually assaulted numerous times. The death toll from both of those encounters was high." He walked over to the energy web and swore. "We're going to have Ryder have a look though. In case we've missed something. They know more about the V'ran than any of us." His phone buzzed, and he looked at it. The Forensics team had arrived. He had them wait in the parking area. No way was he risking anymore lives. Moments later, Ryder, Maxen, and Blade landed in the clearing. The moment they saw the energy web with the body they stiffened.

"Do you know how to neutralize the webs?" Caden asked, his expression grim.

Blade nodded. "Yeah. Though we learned it much too late to save our people. How many are there?"

"My warriors found eight plus this one," Kit replied, watching all the Fae carefully.

Ryder swore and stared at the crime scene, his hands on his hips. "Blade, get Nerys here. You know what to bring back. I know she was experimenting with a new type of energy dispersion unit for the possibility of mass webs. See if she's ready to test it."

Blade nodded and shot into the sky as Maxen walked over to Shirina and spoke quietly to her.

Ryder looked at the Elf leader, and Caden and shook his head. "You weren't here when Baylen was attacked by what we believe is the last of the V'ran, Wisteria Abital."

"I've read the reports, and I was here when she managed to get on Mystic Haven the second time," Caden replied. "There were none of these energy webs then."

Ryder nodded. "It's probably why she managed to stay hidden so long. The first time she was here, she almost killed The Ward. She murdered several shifters and came very close to killing Baylen as well. What that man did to survive and protect The Ward was nothing short of a miracle." Ryder clenched his jaw and stared at the web and the body entangled in it, before looking at Kit. "We will get her down as soon as Nerys gets here. She has the equipment we need. I'm sorry Kit."

Kit nodded gravely.

"Caden?" Ryder looked at the cop. "We need to let Baylen know."

"I will. I want the body removed first. There is no need for him to see that."

Ryder nodded, knowing full well how deeply this would hit the man. "Agreed."

"Give me a minute." Caden said and walked away from everyone so he could send a private mind link. *"Ciara. Where are you?"*

"I'm having an ice cream with Sophia."

"Go to your grandparents. Now."

"Caden?"

"Trust me. Go now. Please."

"On my way."

Caden walked back over to the crime scene. He rubbed his neck and considered next steps. First, they had to dismantle those energy webs. After that it was imperative to find out how the young Elf female had been killed, and, he frowned, how the hell Wisteria had gained access to the island again. He turned and walked over to Shirina and Maxen. "Shirina, can you check on The Ward? We need to know how she is able to get past our best defenses."

Shirina nodded. "I'll start on that right away. I honestly am puzzled by this." She shook her head. "Technically, she shouldn't be able to get on this island. Within days of The Ward's creation, we input all the information we had on the V'ran. After each of the two incursions in the last years, we updated the Wards on her methods." She began to pace back and forth, shoving her hands through her hair, and gripping the white-blonde strands before letting go and shaking her head.

"Just talk to the Wards, Shirina. Let's take this one step at a time. There is always the possibility that this is not Wisteria."

"If it's not Wisteria, we're in deep trouble, Caden. She claims to be the last of her kind."

Caden nodded. "Let's get the facts first. Talk to the Wards."

Blade and a slender woman with long brown hair landed in the clearing. They each carried a small handheld device and had some kind of weapon strapped to their backs. Caden squeezed Shirina's shoulder and walked over to join Blade and Nerys. "Tell me about those weapons and that device."

Nerys demonstrated the weapon. "It's a weapon that utilizes sunlight to disrupt the natural energy that surrounds the V'ran. These creatures are from a star system that orbits a pulsar. I know, it sounds impossible. But there are still many things we do not know about the multiverse." Next, she explained how the small handheld devices could read the wavelengths of the energy web and counteract them. In effect neutralizing their cohesiveness. Within a few minutes, the forensics team was helping Kit and his men, carefully lower the Elf female into a body bag resting on a gurney.

Chapter One Hundred Fifty-Two

EARTH DIMENSION THREE
Mystic Haven, B.C., Canada

BY THE TIME CADEN GOT home, it was late, and his kids were all in bed. He thanked his mom and watched her drive away, with firm instructions to message him when she got home. He grabbed a beer and went out and sat on his deck, staring up at the star filled night sky.

What a day. There was a monster loose on his island. A monster that, so far, no one had been able to defeat. Why wasn't the Guardian side of his nature awake? He should be out hunting that monster. His phone dinged, and he looked at the screen. His mom was home. He let out a breath and replied, suggesting she increase the strength of the protection Wards around the farm. A few seconds later, his phone rang. His father. "Hello Da."

"What's going on, son?"

For a moment, a split second, Caden was struck by the danger to everyone he loved. His kids. His sisters. His parents. *How the hell was he going to save them?* Gods. *Ciara.* Who'd already faced the monster once. The world spun. Darkness edged his vision. His heart began to race as adrenalin flooded his system. A lump settled into his throat. He squeezed his eyes shut. Shit. *He couldn't catch his breath.* He couldn't have answered if his life had depended on it.

"Caden?"

He could hear the concern in his father's voice. He swallowed. *What the hell was happening to him?*

"Caden, take a breath. I'm on my way."

Fuck. Fuck. Fuck. He stood up in a rush, his phone falling to the ground. Two strides took him to the massive tree in his backyard. The one his kids loved to climb. The one he'd built a treehouse in for them. *Gods.* He shut his eyes again trying to get the images of death and destruction out of his mind. *Shit.* He slammed his fist into the tree. Again. Again. Again. Blood flowed, the scent rich and coppery. His skin took on the stripes of his tiger. His breath rasped out of his chest in hard pants. *Fuck.* He pressed his head against the cool bark, inhaling the woodsy scent desperately trying to control the urge to shift. His glamour fell away. *Godsdamnit! Get some fucking control damnit!*

"Caden." His fathers voice.

What the hell? He hadn't even scented his approach.

"Son." His father's hand on his shoulder. "I've got you."

Caden turned and stared at his father, his eyes bright with the tears he fought to keep from falling. He shook his head, still not able to find his voice.

"Breathe, Caden. It's a panic attack. Breathe. That's it. You've got this, son. Another breath." Daniel took Caden's hand wincing at the bloody mess, turned it and pressed it palm down against the tree. "Focus on how the bark feels. There are frogs out tonight. Can you hear them? Take another breath."

Caden could feel himself shaking, but he forced himself to concentrate on what his father was saying. *A panic attack? Shit*. He took a breath, another. The rough bark beneath his fingers helped to ground him. "Fucking frogs." He managed to say.

His father chuckled. "Correct. It's mating season and they want the world to know. The stars are amazing tonight."

Caden glanced up at the majesty of the universe and took another breath. "Sorry, Da."

"Nothing to be sorry about. You have an extremely hard job. You are one of the strongest men I know, Caden, but you're also human."

"Superhuman."

Daniel laughed. "Yeah, we're superhuman, but that doesn't mean that we're invincible. We have emotions. Things get to us. That's normal."

Caden swallowed. "Wisteria is back."

Daniel stilled. He took a deep breath and looked his son squarely in the eye. He knew his son. He knew that Caden would do everything possible to stop that creature. Even at the cost of his own life. "That just might be the stupidest move she's ever made."

Caden laughed, the sound a rough, hoarse rasp.

"Caden, you don't have to do this by yourself. There are a whole lot of superhumans on this island that are going to want to help you take that bitch down. Work with them. Talk to them. She does not stand a chance on this island."

Caden searched his father's eyes and nodded. "Thanks for coming, Da."

"Always, son. Now, let's go inside so I can look at your hands."

Chapter One Hundred Fifty-Three

CADEN PULLED UP IN front of The Dark Moon restaurant and parked his SUV. Officially, The Dark Moon did not open until later in the afternoon, but he knew that Stone would feed him. After all, they'd been friends since they could both toddle around and get into mischief. Their mothers were fast friends, so it was inevitable, and once they'd gone to school, they'd met Maverick and his twin brother, Chasin. After that, the four were inseparable.

He opened the door and stepped in. "Hey."

Stone looked out from the kitchen. "Caden. What the hell are you doing here?"

"I was hoping for lunch."

Stone studied him for a moment. "I've got some lasagna from last night."

"Great. Got any coffee on?"

Stone just looked at him. "Have I got coffee on? Seriously?" He walked out of the kitchen and over to the state-of-the-art coffee machine. He poured Caden a cup and brought it over to him. "I'll heat up the lasagna. Want garlic bread?"

Caden nodded. "Thanks, Stone."

Stone looked at him for another moment before heading back into his kitchen. Something was wrong. He got the lasagna heating and made the garlic toast then headed back out with glasses of water that he set on the table. "Be right back."

He walked over and made sure the closed sign was showing and locked the door. Heading back into the kitchen, he plated the lasagna, and put the garlic toast into a basket. Balancing the two plates and the basket he brought it all to the table Caden was sitting at. He set it all out and sat down with his friend. "What's going on, Caden?"

Caden watched Stone for a moment. "I'd like to tell you nothing is going on, but—" He took a breath. "I have reason to believe that Wisteria is on the island."

Stone sat back, his eyes going the ice blue of his wolf. "Eat." He motioned to Caden's plate. "I vote we kill the bitch this time."

Caden took a bite, chewed, and swallowed before shaking his head. "No arguments there."

Stone watched Caden for a moment. "How do you know she's here?"

"We found a body. A female Elf. She was tangled up in some kind of energy web. I had some of the Ancients come and have a look."

Stone nodded, taking in how grim Caden looked. "Where did you find the body?"

"In the forest, a few kilometers to the south of the Fae Castle."

"Bet the Fae king was not too happy about that."

"Haven't told him yet. That's my next stop."

"Who do you have patrolling the area?" He knew Caden. There was no way he would not have a hunt already going on.

"The Elves."

"What happened to the Ward?"

Caden shook his head and took a sip from his glass of water. "I've no clue. Shirina's on it. Hopefully, she'll have some answers soon."

With a deep inner shock, Stone noted the bruised, torn up condition of Caden's hands. It only took him a second to understand his friend had been punching something solid and unmoveable. "My pack will patrol tonight." Caden started to shake his head. Stone stared at him, his eyes hard. "My damn pack is going to patrol tonight. I know you, Caden. You're going to try to save us all. That's not going to work this time. This is the third time this alien monster has found us. It's time for this whole island to work together. It's going to take all of us to defeat her."

"Your pack is vulnerable to her, Stone." Caden's voice betrayed his agony.

"We're all vulnerable to her, Caden. It's not just your responsibility to protect Mystic Haven. That job belongs to all of us. To every superhuman on this island."

Caden watched the wolf shifter for a long moment, indecision written all over his face. Stone leaned forward. "Are you okay?"

Caden's jaw clenched, and he swallowed, his eyes washed to a brilliant green, and stripes began to show on his face. Stone noted the changes and the fine tremble in Caden's hands. Something sure as hell was wrong. "Caden, what's going on man?"

Picking up his glass of water, Caden took a drink before he answered. "I—" He paused and studied his friend. Shit. He did not want to tell Stone about last night. He rubbed his neck. *He'd had a fucking panic attack. What did that make him?*

"Caden. We've been friends since we were in diapers. We've gotten into enough shit together that someone could write an epic fantasy adventure tale about us. We've always had each other's backs. Tell me what's going on."

"I had a panic attack last night."

"Damn. Why didn't you call me?"

"I was on the phone with my dad when it hit. He came right over. Guess it pays to have a doctor in the family."

Stone studied him. "You carry a load that no one else would even think of attempting. This can't continue. You're going to break man, and that's not okay. You, me, Maverick, and Chasin made a pact. We would always be there for each other. We're a brotherhood. A fellowship. We are the Swords of Mystic, and if there has ever been a time for our fellowship to gather, it's now. Caden, let us help."

Caden shook his head and picked up his coffee, taking a long sip. "You know, Stone, this is hard. I should be able to—"

Stone cut him off. "No, Caden. No. You need to look after your mental health. This island needs you. Your kids need you, and I need you. So, no. You don't get to keep carrying this load all by yourself. Just effing no! I've already messaged Maverick and Chasin. They are on their way."

Hell. Caden stared at Stone, seeing the wolf in his eyes. *Ah, hell.*

A knock on the door and Stone rose to let Maverick and Chasin in.

"Look, guys, I appreciate your coming, but Stone has to open soon, and I need to—"

"This is my restaurant, and I'll decide when I need to open," Stone snarled.

Caden's eyes narrowed. "You need to quit interrupting me."

Chasin took a seat. Maverick grinned and pulled out the chair across from his twin. "Sorry, Caden, but this gathering of The Swords of Mystic is now in session. I figured something was up this morning when you walked in without your coffee. Not to mention your hands. Did you beat up one of those giant boulders out in Black Sands Cove?"

Caden leaned back in his seat and scrubbed a hand over his face. "Creators of Light! What the hell? I gotta call into the station and let them know I won't be in for a while."

"Already took care of it."

Caden glared at Maverick. "I also need to go and talk to the Fae king and Ciara."

"Ciara was fine this morning. I saw her on the beach with her little girl," Chasin spoke up, then with a wicked grin, he leaned forward. "Or did you want to speak to that sexy woman alone?"

Caden folded his arms over his chest and simply watched the dragon shifter.

"We'll go with you to talk to Baylen and Ciara," Maverick said, knowing how important that was. "But we're all going to talk first."

"Right." Caden didn't move, his arms still crossed.

Maverick shook his head. "Right now, Caden, your eyes are green, you are stripped, and you have wings. Now, you want to tell me nothing is wrong?"

Caden stood up and walked away. Staring out the big front window he fought to get some control back. What was he doing? What the hell was he doing? Finally, with a sigh he turned back to his friends. "Things have gotten pretty stressful lately. I had a panic attack last night after I got home from dealing with the whole Wisteria shitshow."

"Honestly, Caden, I'm not surprised. This year has been hell, and you're always the one leading the charge." Maverick rested his crossed arms on the table. "I know it's not easy to talk about this kind of stuff. Hell, we're males, and we're superhumans, and you're a fucking hero. So yeah, talking about anything that could possibly make us look like we don't have complete control, or are weak is not something we like to do." Maverick stood up and walked over to pour himself a coffee. "Listen man, if it helps to know this, I've been talking to Dr. Esteban for a few months now. Juan's been great. He's really easy to talk to. This job, being a cop, it's tough. We see some terrible shit, and we can't fix everything. We can't protect everyone."

Caden swallowed and nodded. "I guess this Wisteria thing, after all the other things that have gone down this year, it just hit me. I don't know how to protect everyone. I don't even know if I can protect the people I care about."

"That's why we're here." Stone said. "We made a pact when we were teenagers, and that promise included being there for each other. Hell, I remember Chasin adding 'hiding bodies' to our official pact back in the day." They all chuckled before Stone continued. "We're all going to stand together. We can help Caden. Let's talk about what needs to be done."

Chapter One Hundred Fifty-Four

EARTH DIMENSION THREE
Mystic Haven, B.C., Canada

BAYLEN SAT HELPING his kids with their homework. Not that there was much homework when your kids were only in third grade, but there were the usual math and reading assignments. One of the guards stepped into the doorway of the family room, and Baylen paused.

"Caden Brody is here." The guard said quietly. "Would you like me to escort him and the others to your office?"

The others? Baylen nodded. "Sure, my office will be fine. Have the kitchen send up coffee, and please let the nanny know that I need her to finish helping the kids with their reading."

A few minutes later, Baylen strode down the corridor that led to his office. He entered to find Caden, along with Stone, Maverick and Chasin seated on the couch and easy chairs that made up an informal meeting area. He eyed them curiously, before taking a seat with them. "Hello, Caden, Maverick, Stone, Chasin." He nodded at each one as he said their name. "What brings you to my home this evening?"

"I'm afraid I've come with news you aren't going to want to hear." Caden said.

Baylen nodded. "What's going on?"

"We believe Wisteria is on the island."

Baylen froze. *Fuck!* "Why do you think she's here?"

"The Elves' found the body of one of their females trapped in an energy field. I had Shirina come and have a look at it. She insisted on bringing in some of the Ancients. It was an energy web and could only have been created by the V'ran."

Baylen looked at Caden with hard eyes. "Why was I not notified immediately?"

"It's an ongoing investigation, Baylen. I needed more information before I came to you."

Clenching his fists, Baylen forced himself to speak calmly. "Every second that bitch is on this island, we risk lives."

Caden nodded. "I agree with you. I've had my officers searching since we knew it was most likely Wisteria. I stationed some of the Ancients around Ciara's home and around the Castle last night."

"The fuck, Caden? You didn't think I needed to know about this?"

"And have you go off on your own vengeance seeking mission that would have, most likely, resulted in your death or capture by that creature?" Caden's eyes met the Fae king's furious gaze. "That would have only added to the problems, Baylen."

"Fuck!" Baylen shot to his feet. "You don't get to make that kind of decision for me, cop. I'm the fucking Fae king!"

Caden stood up. "And I'm the Guardian of this island."

The door to the office opened and Jett strode in followed by Striker. "What's going on?"

Baylen looked at The Protector and growled. "Wisteria is back." He dropped his glamour. "I'm fucking going hunting."

"Hell no, you're not." Caden stepped forward.

"I'd like to see you try to stop me."

Caden shrugged easily, his glamour falling away and the Guardian runes that covered his arms, chest, and back lighting up with a golden glow. "That's my job, Your Majesty. I'm the only one who can stop you, and I will. Your death would be a blow we could not recover from before Wisteria decimated this island and everyone on it. At that point, who could possibly stop her from taking over the Earth?"

"Don't fucking call me that," Baylen growled. "Fuck!" He turned toward the balcony and took a step.

Stone, Chasin, and Maverick stood up and glanced at Striker and Jett. Jett shook his head. "Baylen, Caden is right. You can't go off half-cocked." His voice was hard. "Not this time. You can't afford to let your anger control you."

Baylen turned, a snarl curling his lip. "Fuck you, Jett. My fucking anger doesn't control me."

"Your need for vengeance does, and the darkness you embrace."

Baylen stiffened, his eyes turning cold.

"What about Aliora, Baylen?" Stone asked. Everyone looked at him. "She's your mate," Stone said quietly. "She needs you."

"Fuck! Mind your own damned business, Wolf."

Stone noticed everyone staring at him, and he shrugged his massive shoulders. "What? I'm a wolf. Her scent is all over him."

Everyone looked back at Baylen. "I—Fuck!" He started pacing. *Could no one keep a fucking secret on this island?* Stone was fucking right. Aliora, his kids, and family would all need his protection. Along with the whole fucking Fae species. "Alright. What the fuck are we going to do? I assume you have a plan, Brody."

Caden nodded. "It was pointed out to me earlier today that I can't possibly save everyone on my own. As much as that infuriates me, it's correct. This is the third time Wisteria has found a way to get on this island. It's time for all of us to work together. We need all the superhumans to help. Stone, Maverick, and Chasin are going to speak to the leaders of the Superhumans on Mystic Haven.

"The wolf pack is going to patrol tonight. They have tracking skills that we don't. My hope is that will get us close enough to her that we can take her out.

"I also think we need to get Shirina, Aliora, and Ciara working together with the Wards because somehow the Wards are not able to see her.

"We also need to consider an evacuation plan."

Jett nodded slowly. "I think you're right, Caden. I think we should consider finding a way to push her into a remote location. I think, at that point, if the current royal Trium, the former royal Trium, and the Guardian all attack, we have a good chance of killing her."

Striker shook his head. "I don't think it will be that easy based on what history we have from the V'ran attack on the Tuatha Star System. I think it's going to take more than the Fae."

"We have a host of Angels guarding Mystic Haven now. I know we can count on their assistance," Caden said.

"You know, there are some deities that guard Earth. Maybe the Angels would know how to contact them. They might be of assistance," Chasin spoke up.

Plans made, Baylen walked toward the patio doors.

"Where are you going?"

Baylen glanced back at Jett. "To pick up Aliora. She'll be safer here at the castle than anywhere else."

He should have known that she would never simply do as he told her.

Chapter One Hundred Fifty-Five

EARTH DIMENSION THREE
Mystic Haven, B.C., Canada

CIARA FINISHED PAYING the cashier and wheeled her cart out of the store. Sophia bounced in the seat and chattered excitedly about the swim they'd had last night with her grandparents. Ciara smiled and smoothed her daughter's dark curls back. "You liked Gramp's surfboard?"

"Yes!" Sophia clapped her little hands. "I loves it."

"I had fun to, Babygirl." A shiver ran down her back and a sense of foreboding filled her. Ciara glanced around the parking lot but didn't see anything. Frowning, she unbuckled her daughter and lifted her onto her hip. "I'm going to put you in your car seat."

"Okay." Sophia peered over her mom's shoulder. "We go now."

"As soon as the groceries are in the trunk." Ciara unlocked her car and opened the rear door. Quickly, she buckled Sophia in, still feeling that sense of wrongness. "Mama's going to put the groceries in the trunk."

"Hurry, Mama." Sophia's eyes were serious.

Ciara smiled and touched her daughter's cheek. "I will." She closed the door, relocked it, and moved to the back of the car, popping open the trunk. She glanced around again, before quickly loading the bags of groceries. Closing the trunk, she paused long enough to take a good look around and note the exits. Her heart pounded so hard, she wondered if it was going to explode. She took a deep calming breath, even as her stomach tightened. Something wasn't right. At that moment, an electrical charge passed through her, her skin prickling in reaction. *Oh, gods.* Her hands shook so bad, she could hardly unlock the door of her vintage '69 Camaro. She yanked open the door and got into the car, slamming it behind her. Hitting the lock, she put her key into the ignition. The car started with a roar, and she reversed out of the parking spot. Putting the car into first, then shifting quickly into second, she drove much too fast across the parking lot. A few seconds later she pulled out of the parking lot, and turned onto the main street, tires squealing.

"Mama go fast!" Sophia cheered from the back.

Ciara jumped when she heard the chirp of a siren behind her. She looked into the rear-view mirror, and sure enough, there were red and blue flashing lights. She pulled over, still shaking. A moment later a knock on her window. She quickly wound it down, her eyes meeting Caden's.

"Are you alright, Ciara? You came out of that parking lot like the bats of hell were after you, and you're not wearing your seatbelt."

Ciara glanced down. Oh, heck. She *wasn't* wearing her seatbelt. She lifted a shaking hand and pushed a long curly lock behind her ear. "I—I'm sorry, Caden. I thought—"

"Hey." Caden crouched down by the car and reached in, his fingers catching her chin to gently turn her face to him. "What's going on?"

"Hi. Hi. Dakota's Daddy." From the backseat.

Caden glanced back and smiled at the little girl. "Hi, Sophia."

"Tiger. Rawr."

Caden chuckled. "Dakota tells me you have a tail."

Sophia nodded. "It's blue. I show you when we go swimming."

"Deal. I'll show you my tiger then too."

Sophia grinned and Caden winked at her before he turned his focus back to Ciara. "Talk to me."

"This is going to sound silly. I thought someone was watching me. I got scared." She shook her head embarrassed.

Caden stood up quickly and looked back at the grocery store parking lot, searching the cars parked there. He keyed his radio. "Josef, can you do a flyby of the grocery store parking lot?"

Ciara blinked, and turned in her seat, leaning out the window. A second later a blue dragon dropped out of the clouds and swooped low over the grocery store parking lot. *What the heck?* "Caden?"

"I'm not seeing anything Caden." Josef's voice carried back over the radio.

"Ten four. Catelyn, Marcus, bring your K9's to the Apples and Oranges grocery store parking lot. Do a thorough search. Report back to me with your findings." Caden crouched down beside her car again. "Ciara, I'm going to follow you home."

Ciara stared at him. "You're scaring me."

"You're safe. I'll be right behind you."

"Mama go fast. Zoom!" Sophia said from the backseat.

Caden laughed. "No. Mama's going to go slow. She doesn't want a ticket." He opened the driver's door and leaned in to fasten Ciara's seatbelt. Lowering his voice so that only Ciara could hear him, he said. "Though I wouldn't mind handcuffing you." He winked.

Ciara gasped, and blushed. Oh gods, was he reading her mind? She'd had a dream last night of him and his handcuffs. "I, uh, I'll just—"

"Drive slow and safely," Caden finished for her. He shut her door, patted the top of her car, and walked back to his SUV.

Chapter One Hundred Fifty-Six

EARTH DIMENSION THREE
Mystic Haven, B.C., Canada

WISTERIA PACED IN THE shadows of a patch of large trees a couple houses down from her pet's home. Would the police never leave? She'd stayed far enough back, as she followed the cherry red Camaro, that she hadn't been noticed, or so she thought. Until the police issued SUV pulled up behind her pet. Shortly after that two more police officers arrived.

She debated cutting her losses when two huge Fae with dark hair pulled up. She watched them talk to the police officers and take up positions at the front and back of the house.

She wanted to scream. Cursing under her breath she backed further into the trees and silently opened a vortex. She would be back. Soon. Very soon. When she came back, she would punish her pet.

She stepped into the vortex and back out of it in the middle of a dark forest on the other side of the island. Cursing under her breath, she clenched and unclenched her hands as she looked around. The forest was quiet, but she noticed a light shining through it. She smiled, a grotesque pulling back of her lips to reveal her jagged teeth.

Cracking her neck from side to side, she took a deep breath. Adrenaline rushed through her body, along with an edgy twitchy feeling. So be it. She would find other prey for now. She glided silently through the forest, a deadly predator intent on making a kill. The house she came to was small with none of the Fae Wards to protect it. She moved to a side window and peered in. A young man sat on the couch, watching a TV show. Not a Fae, but he would still fill her stomach. Silently she moved to the other windows and checked for more people. He was alone. With a smile, she drew on the glamour of a beautiful woman. After that she carefully spun energy webs over all the windows and the doors. Going to the front door, she knocked.

A moment later the door opened. "Hello." The young man smiled.

"Hello, I'm lost. Can you help me?"

"Of course. Come in."

She stepped in and dropped her glamour.

There was no one to hear his screams. No one to hear him beg. No one to save him.

Chapter One Hundred Fifty-Seven

EARTH DIMENSION THREE
Mystic Haven, B.C., Canada

THE PHONE RANG, WAKING Caden. He picked it up off the bedside table. "Brody."

"Caden." Stone's voice. "We've got a body. Other side of the island. You're going to need your forensics team."

"Give me the coordinates."

The wolf pack alpha sent him the information immediately. "Caden, this is bad. I've never seen so much blood. I think it was a Sprite. We've found a wing. The body is so torn apart that I can't tell anything else."

"Don't contaminate the crime scene."

"We haven't. We never went in. The door was wide open. My patrol smelled blood and contacted me. We followed the scent."

"I'll be there as soon as I call in the team. Where is The Ward?"

"No sign of it."

"Damn it! Thanks, Stone."

Chapter One Hundred Fifty-Eight

EARTH DIMENSION THREE
Mystic Haven, B.C., Canada

"CIARA. MY PRETTY LITTLE pet."

Ciara's eyes snapped open, her heart racing. She sat up and flung her hand out. Immediately several Fae Orbs lit up the room. She looked around as she moved from her bed, her breath panting out of her.

"Let me in, Pet."

Slamming up shields, and more shields around her mind, she grabbed her cell phone from the bedside table and ran from her room to Sophia's. Gathering her daughter's sleeping little body close, she made sure to take Sophia's favorite blanket. Moving through the house she began to check on the Wards that protected her home. There were definite signs of stress that were worsening before her eyes. Where were the warriors that Caden had assigned to watch her house? She swallowed. Carefully she reached out with a tentative mind link, seeking one of the ancient warriors that should have been standing guard.

"There you are, Pet. Let me in."

Creators! Ciara slammed up the shields again. It was Wisteria. *No, no, no!* Wisteria had found her, again. Tears stung her eyes. Deep inside she started to shake. *No. No.*

Calm. She had to protect Sophia. That bitch was not going to harm her daughter.

The best way out was the skylight over her living room. That had always been her planned escape route if Wisteria ever returned. Wisteria could not fly. Though she had the ability to climb at horrifying speeds. So, that meant she must shore up her Wards. She could not let Wisteria break through that barrier to her home. Once she burst through that skylight, she had to have enough power to shoot high into the sky and wrap herself and Sophia in an invisibility glamour.

Gently setting Sophia on the couch, she took a deep breath and spread her arms wide. A breath out and she let her glamour go and began to draw Fae energy to her. As the golden energy flowed into her, she began to add power to the Wards around her home. Immediately, she could tell that Wisteria had done something to the Wards. They were slowly being poisoned, and the more Fae energy she poured into them the faster the poison was spreading. She snapped off the flow of Fae energy and instead sent out a gentle seeking thread. As it touched the Ward, information began to trickle back to her. She swallowed, pressing her hand to her neck. Her whole house was surrounded with an energy web. That's what was poisoning the Wards. *How long would it take for that Web to destroy her Wards?* Not long.

She stared around her living room, her mind desperately trying to figure out a way out of this trap. Every time she'd tried to send a mind link, Wisteria intercepted it and had a channel back to her. She could not allow Wisteria even the smallest thread into her mind. She could not allow Wisteria to control her again. She picked up the phone she'd set beside Sophia and dialed 911. Nothing. She bowed her head, tears sliding down her cheeks. It had to be that energy web. On the remote chance that the signal was getting through, she put it on speaker and set it on the coffee table. "This is Ciara Walker. The warriors protecting my house are missing. Wisteria has an energy web around my house. I have to get Sophia out."

She thought about how she'd destroyed Wisteria's nest years ago. It was the best chance and it had to be done quickly before Wisteria found a way into her mind. Once again, she began to pull Fae energy into herself while she crouched down beside her sleeping daughter. "Sophia, wake up, Babygirl. Mama needs you to do something important."

"Mama?" Little hands patted her cheek and sleepy teal eyes so much like her own peered at her. "You's crying. Do you need my blankie?"

Ciara smiled and shook her head. "Thank you but you are going to need your blankie." *Where was the safest place for Sophia?* "Our house has an icky web around it."

Sophia's eyes widened and she sat up and peered around her mother. "Is there a big spider?"

Ciara nodded. "Yes. I'm going to make a hole through the web, and I want you to wrap Mer energy around yourself. Only Mer energy, not any Fae energy. Understand?"

Sophia tilted her head, her black curls falling around her shoulders. She blinked at her mom. "Only Mer?"

"Yes, Babygirl. Show me."

Sophia concentrated and neon blue began to glow around her. "Good girl." Ciara smiled at her. "When I make the hole, I need you to crawl through it. Don't let it touch you, and keep your pretty blue energy really bright, okay?"

Sophia drew back, her little nose scrunched. "Ew, mama. I don't want to crawl through a spider web."

"I know, Babygirl. But I need you to find Dakota's daddy and tell him I'm stuck here. After you're through the hole, run to the park. When you get there, you must fly high in the sky and send a mind link to Dakota's daddy. Can you do that?"

Sophia frowned. "You can come through the hole with me."

"No, baby. I have only Fae energy. I will get tangled in the web if I try to go through the hole."

"I share."

Ciara smiled and stroked Sophia's hair. "You are such a kind girl, Sophia. I'm proud of you. Thank you for offering to share your Mer energy with me, but you will need that energy for yourself. Now, what are you going to do for Mama?"

Sophia sighed. "Mer energy and crawl through an icky spider web. No Fae. Run to the park. Fly up up up. I need to be Fae to fly Mama." She stared at her Mama in exasperation.

Ciara laughed. "Yes, you do Babygirl. But not until you get to the park, okay?"

Sophia nodded. "Then I talk to Dakota's daddy through my mind."

"Yes. Do you remember how?"

Sophia laughed. "'Course, Mama. Don't be silly. I talk to Dakota all the time, and the Ward. But not to strangers."

"Good girl!" Ciara pressed a kiss to Sophia's forehead. "I'm giving you permission to talk to Dakota's daddy."

"I think I need to talk to Gramps and G'ma."

Ciara smiled. "Gramps is helping to guard the Fae castle tonight and G'ma is too."

"I could talk to the king."

Ciara tilted her head. "You can talk to the Fae king?"

"'Course Mama, I always see a bright and shiny mind line to him."

Ciara nodded, tears burning her eyes. Of course, Baylen would have created an emergency line to the Fae children. He was a father. He would think of the children. He was also massively powerful and maintaining that line would be a simple thing for him. "Sophia, try to talk to Dakota's daddy first, if you can't reach him, try to talk to the Fae king."

"Okay, Mama."

"It's time to go." She picked up her daughter and took her to the front door. Whispering a prayer to the Creators, the Ancients, and The Ones Who Had Gone Before, she opened the door and stepped out onto her doorstep. From outside she could see all the protection Wards around her house were activated. They shimmered with golden Fae energy streaked with the blackness that was poisoning them. Beyond them she could see the strange glow of the energy web. She could not see past that web. She walked down the steps and across the lawn to her protection Wards. The night air was cool against her bare legs, the short purple silk night slip she wore was not designed for warmth.

"I don't like this, Mama."

"I don't either, Sophia."

"Can we go back inside, Mama?"

"No, Babygirl. I'm sorry. I need you to be brave and do what I asked."

Sophia nodded solemnly. Ciara set her daughter on the ground and watched her tiny toes curl into the cold grass. Carefully, she tied the corners of Sophia's soft pink blanket together, so it formed a cape that fell down her daughters back. "There. Now your blankie won't get lost."

"Mama!"

Ciara jerked to her feet, pushing Sophia behind her. She could see Wisteria climbing the energy web. Creators, she even moved like a spider. Turning, she crouched down in front of Sophia. "Shh, Babygirl. It's alright. I need you to be quiet. Don't mind link Mama. Now, see the secret fort we made from the vines last week? That is where I'm going to make the hole. Come on."

Carefully she wrapped them both in an invisibility glamour, and they walked over to the flower garden that bordered her property. The Wards crackled and shimmered against that small fort, and she was thankful that she'd ensured the Wards were extra strong there, even though it was going to make it impossible for her to make more than a small hole. Crouching down, she ushered Sophia into the little flowering fort. "Wait till Mama says go. Understand."

Sophia nodded her eyes huge.

Carefully, she placed her hands against the Ward and assessed the strength she would need to blast a hole through her protection. When she had a clear reading, she swallowed and blinking away her tears, she pressed a kiss to her daughter's soft cheek. "I love you, Sophia."

"I love you too, Mama."

Ciara backed out of the fort, stood up and stepped back. She took a deep breath, dropped the invisibility glamour, and spread her arms, opening herself wide to the stream of Fae energy that surrounded this planet. It rushed into her, and she gasped. The golden glowing coming off her as she drew that stream of energy drove the night's darkness back.

"What are you doing, Pet?"

Ciara ignored the voice seeking entrance into her mind. More and more Fae energy poured into her.

"I am going to enjoy punishing you. Do you remember how I used to do that, Pet? How I used to bring you to your knees, begging."

Her hands trembled, knowing she could hear Wisteria so much clearer even through her mental shields because her Wards were failing. Focusing on where she knew the hole needed to be. She carefully targeted the area just on the other side of the fort and forced the massive amount of energy into a narrow channel. An intense flash of golden energy slammed into the protection Ward. The Ward began to disintegrate beneath the onslaught. The strange energy of the energy web showing through. Ciara twisted her hands, and the Fae energy twisted with her movement, becoming a complex, spiraling tempest of immense power eating away at both Ward and energy web. A hole opened and grew. Oh, Creators, just a little more. She had to hold it for a little longer, and suddenly there it was. "Go, Sophia! Go!" She screamed. The failure of her Wards was sudden, and she reeled as Wisteria's power slammed against her mental shields. A small blue glow moved through the hole and Ciara dropped to her knees, forcing the hole to remain open until the glow was completely through and moving away. Teeth gritted, she twisted and slammed what remained of the tempest into the creature that dropped to the ground behind her.

Wisteria hit the ground with a scream of rage. Panting, Ciara staggered to her feet, as the monster that had haunted her dreams for years rose.

"You will pay for that, Pet."

Chapter One Hundred Fifty-Nine

EARTH DIMENSION THREE
Mystic Haven, B.C., Canada

SOPHIA RAN AS FAST as her little feet would carry her. A blue glow moving much faster than a human child of three could ever manage. Tears trembled on her lashes, for she had seen the bad spider lady that had broken through her Mama's Wards. She saw the swing set and turned into the park, releasing the death hold she'd had on her Mer energy—she let her glamour fall away and became the tiny Fae child that was her other half. Her energy wings fluttered behind her as she stared back toward her house. "Mama?" She could see the energy web around her home, and she started to cry. She didn't want to leave her Mama, but she had promised to find Dakota's daddy. She drew Fae energy and began to move her wings like Mama had taught her. She lifted off the ground, and with a last tearful look at her home, she turned and using the energy stream that she normally used to talk to Dakota, as a beacon, she began to fly. *"Dakota's Daddy! Dakota's Daddy!"* She was crying so hard that she couldn't 'member his name. *"I'm scared, please answer me."*

Caden shot to his feet as a frightened little girl's voice came across his mind link. Damnit. He'd fallen asleep on the couch. *"Sophia? What's wrong little one? Where's your mama?"* He was already in the air. The Guardian runes glowing. He sent a mind link to his oldest son. *"Ben, call your grandfather to come over."*

"Mama needs you! There's a bad Spider lady!"

Caden locked on to the mind link and soared through the air. *"I'm on my way, little one. Are you hurt?"*

"No. I'm tired. I don't flies this far by myself."

There. He spotted a tiny golden glow. She was much higher than he'd expected. He adjusted his trajectory. *"I see you, Sophia. Do you see me?"*

"Yes." Her little voice wavered. *"I want my Mama."*

His heart hurt at the fear he heard. *"You're so brave, Sophia. Mama's going to be so proud of you. I'm close to you, Little One."*

Every second was a thousand years, the closer he got the more tired her little voice sounded. He could see that she was having a hard time staying on course, her little wings moving slower and slower. He poured on a burst of speed and swept her into his arms, just as she dipped. Holding her tight against his chest, his heart pounding, he was relieved when she wrapped her little arms around his neck.

"Thank you, Dakota's Daddy. Can we go help my Mama now?"

"I think I better take you to my house first. You can have a sleepover with Dakota, and I'll go help your Mama, okay?"

"K."

He could feel her tears against his neck. *"You're safe, Sophia. I promise. Dakota's grandma and her grandpa are at my house. They will look after you while I go help your Mama."*

He landed in the yard and moved swiftly into the house. His mom and dad were coming in the front door. He saw their surprise at the tiny girl with black curls clinging to him. "Da, Mom, this is Sophia Walker, Ciara's daughter. She flew all the way over here so I could help her Mama. I told her she could have a sleepover with Dakota."

Sophia peeked up from Caden's neck.

"Hello, Sophia, I'm Dakota's grandmother. Would you like a warm chocolate to drink?"

Sophia sniffled and nodded. "You're Fae like my Mama."

Ariel Brody smiled. "Yes, I am, sweetie."

Caden gently put Sophia on a kitchen chair and crouched down in front of her. He brushed her long curls back out of her face. "Can you tell me what happened, Sophia?"

"Mama said there was a big spider web over our whole house. She told me to put on my Mer energy only. No Fae. She broke a hole through our Ward that keeps us safe, and through that icky web. I crawled through and ran away to the park. But I saw the scary spider lady. She was being mean to my Mama." Sophia's voice trembled and tears shimmered on her lashes. "Please help my Mama."

"I will Sophia." Caden's gut tightened, and he rose to his feet. He turned to his parents. "I've gotta go."

His father nodded. "Go son."

Chapter One Hundred Sixty

AS CADEN FLEW TOWARD Ciara's house, he reached out to the ancient warriors that he'd had guarding the house. There was only silence. Grimly he sent a mind link to Josef Drake, his second in command. *"Josef, I need you to get our officers to Ciara's house, I believe Wisteria is there."*

"We're already on our way there Caden. There was a 911 call placed from that residence."

"There were supposed to be two ancient Fae watching her house. I'm not getting any response to my mind links to them."

"Acknowledged." Josef replied. *"Extreme caution relayed to my team."*

"I'm about two minutes away. Do not approach the house. Set up a safe perimeter."

"Acknowledged."

Caden hit the Swords of Mystic mind link that his idiot friends insisted they needed. *"Wisteria has Ciara. I'm just arriving. My officers have set up a perimeter. Let the Ancients know and tell them the watchers are silent. We are going to need that web neutralizing device they have. Someone let the Fae king know so he doesn't blow a gasket."*

Caden landed and strode toward the perimeter, a dangerous, determined Fae glowing with the runes that marked him as the Guardian. His eyes swept over Ciara's home, and he noted the presence of a massive energy web, and the absence of the powerful security Wards that normally guarded the small house. He fought his need to charge into battle and walked over to Josef. "What have you got, Josef?"

"Not a lot. We found the two Ancients. They are going to need a healer. I've got an ambulance on the way. I suspect that Wisteria was in a hurry, or they would have been dead."

Caden nodded. He looked over at the house again, a muscle ticking in his jaw. He knew what Ciara had survived the last time that creature had her. "I need to get in there."

"I'm going with you," Josef said.

"Josef—"

"Caden. I'll shift into my dragon, but I am going with you."

Their eyes met, and Caden nodded at his partner. "Have you heard from Maverick or Molly?

"They're on their way."

Caden nodded. That would make three dragons—One ice, two fire. Surely, even a V'ran couldn't survive a Guardian and three dragons.

Sam Walker and his wife Genna landed beside Caden. Their faces were determined and the power they contained massive. They were Ancients, part of the original Fae who'd come to earth over a thousand years ago. Sam met Caden's gaze. "We've finished reconnaissance of the perimeter of the house. Ciara's Wards are gone. Nothing remains of them. The energy web around her house is massive and powerful. We're going to need that thing neutralized before we can go in. I've sent for the former Trium and some of our people who know how to deal with these things."

"Sam, we can't wait."

"But we will." The blond man's face was hard. "If we are going to save my granddaughter and her baby, we must have that web neutralized."

"Sophia is safe."

Genna closed her eyes. "Thank the light!"

"Ciara sent Sophia through a hole she made in the Wards and told her to come to me."

Sam nodded. "That's why those Wards collapsed so completely then. She made those Wards near indestructible, and she would have known what putting that hole in them while they were surrounded by that web would do."

Caden nodded remembering the night, several years ago, that he'd helped her to escape from Wisteria. "Sam, I've got three dragons. We need to try to take that web down. She could be—I can't wait."

Genna's hand closed around his arm, and he looked at her. "Caden, I know you want to get in there. I know. Believe me. Everything that I am is screaming at me to rush that web, but we must wait. We survived the V'ran, and we've learned how to deal with them. Trust me, you don't want to get caught in an energy web. We will get Ciara back." Her eyes searched his. "I need you to try to contact Ciara. Sam and I can't get through to her on a mind link.

Please? Any information she could give to you would be helpful."

Caden growled, stripes rising on his skin, but he nodded. He walked a short distance away fighting with his urgency to get into that house. "I'll try."

"Ciara. It's Caden. Can you hear me?"

A low pain filled message. "Caden. Sophia?"

"Safe."

A broken sob. "Thank you."

"Talk to me Ciara. Where is Wisteria?"

"Here."

"We're going to get you out of there."

"I don't—" A scream filled the mind link.

"Ciara! Ciara!" Caden brutally fought against his instinct to run into that house and kill. His eyes met Sam's, claws erupting from his fingertips. A ferocious growl rumbled from his chest.

Ryder landed, his eyes taking in the scene. He'd been in constant contact with Sam and understood the situation. He strode over to Caden and set his hand on his shoulder. "Caden. We've got this. Come on, let's get this web neutralized."

The Ancient Fae who'd arrived with Ryder spread out around Ciara's house. Caden stood beside Ryder and his Trium. He'd already ascertained the best entry point, and he was bloody going in the second that web came down.

"It might interest you to know that we based this technology on what Ciara did to destroy Wisteria's nest the first time that creature took her."

Caden glared at Ryder. "Then why is this the first I've heard of it?"

Ryder looked at him. "Indeed."

Blade, Nerys and Asterine flew to the top of the house, hovering in the air above the roof. Nerys fiddled with her device and glanced at the house. A frown crossed her lovely face. She looked at Caden and signaled him to join them.

Caden flew up and Nerys pointed at the large skylight over Ciara's living room. Caden looked into it and saw the horror that being captured by Wisteria meant. He lifted rage-filled eyes to Nerys. She signed for him to be ready. Blade, Nerys and Asterine all lifted the small handheld devices and pointed them at the skylight. Nerys glanced at Caden and pointed up. He soared straight up into the air and turned as golden light erupted from the devices. A horrendous shriek reverberated from the house and Caden saw the web retreat from the skylight. He dove, arrowing straight down, his wings streamlined against his body. Crashing through the skylight, he somersaulted, landing on his feet beside Ciara. A terrible roar filled the air, and he ripped Wisteria off her. Flinging the creature across the room where she slammed into the wall. She rose to her feet, grey skinned and jagged toothed. "How dare you!"

Caden growled and placed himself between her and Ciara. "You are dead."

Wisteria laughed, her eyes drifting over him. "By you? I don't think so."

Caden stalked her, his eyes the brilliant green of his tiger. A soft hand touched his back. Ciara. She moved to his side. "By both of us, Wisteria."

The front and back doors burst open The Royal Trium and the former Trium. Several Fae warriors dropped down from the skylight.

Caden sent a powerful blast of Fae energy at the creature. Fae energy lit up the room as Ciara and the rest of the Fae joined in.

Wisteria shrieked and opened a small vortex, the wormhole, hidden by the massive burst of Fae Energy directed at her. She jumped into it, and it winked out of existence.

Chapter One Hundred Sixty-One

EARTH DIMENSION THREE
Mystic Haven, B.C., Canada

WISTERIA PACED IN THE remote forest she'd landed in the night before, feeling every second that ticked by. Her time grew shorter to establish a nest. Eventually, the Fae would figure out what she'd done, and the Wards on this island would begin to hunt her. She stared around the forest and screamed her frustration to the air. She'd been so close. She took a breath of the foul air of this world and froze as a small noise reached her. Wrapping the glamour of a beautiful human, with brunette hair and big brown eyes, around herself, she called out. "H— Hello? Is someone there? Please. I need help."

A man's voice replied. "Wait right there, I'm on my way. I heard you scream. Are you hurt?"

Her lips curved into a smile. "N—No. I was frightened by a noise."

"What are you doing so far out? This is a very remote area."

"I was camping with my boyfriend. He got angry with me, and he left me here." She ended the sentence with a sob that any actress would be proud of. Her glamour changed, her hair becoming messy, a dusty smudge on her cheek, and scrapes on her knees. Dirt stained her t-shirt and shorts.

The man stepped into view. Tall, muscular, and delicious. Wisteria let a tear escape.

"He left you? What the hell? We'll make sure Caden knows about this. That was damned dangerous. How long have you been out here?"

Wisteria's hand trembled as she lifted it to push back her hair. "Two nights. I've walked and walked but I think I'm lost."

"It's okay. I'll get you back to Mystic Haven. It's a good thing I decided I needed more supplies. You could have been wandering around here for days and never seen anyone. I was hiking down to my assigned parking spot in the park tourist information area."

"You live up here?"

The man grinned. "Yes, ma'am. I'm a biologist studying the cougar population on the island."

"You're not a Fae?"

The man shook his head. "Nope. I'm a Pixie, and you're a human. How do you know about Superhumans?"

"I grew up in Mystic Haven."

He offered her a drink of water, but she shook her head. "I found a stream a few minutes ago."

"Alright, let's get going then. It's a long way. We'll reach the parking area by nightfall."

He turned and Wisteria threw an energy web around him. He struggled furiously, and she smiled. "I do love it when my dinner resists. It works up my appetite." She let her glamour go. His look of horror only made her laugh.

"Let's play a game, shall we?" She strode up to the man caught in her web and began to tear his clothes from him. "Go ahead and use your powers. I've never encountered a Pixie before, I'm sure you must have a way to defend yourself."

The small amount of energy she was able to absorb from the man was not enough to sustain her for any length of time, but she was pleased by how long it took him to die. His screams echoed through the forest for hours while she'd dined on his flesh.

Donning her glamour, she opened a vortex and stepped in and out into the town center. Seeing a coffee shop, she entered, ordered a coffee, paying for it with the money she'd taken from the man's backpack. Finding a table at the back of the crowded little cafe, she sat down and took the man's phone from her pocket. He'd been most cooperative in giving her the code. She opened the phone to find contact information for the Fae castle. It took a few minutes, but eventually, she was connected to the Fae king. It was truly amazing how much power her name had on this world.

"Knight here."

"Hello, Consort."

"What do you want, Bitch."

"Uh uh. That is no way to talk to your lover." She stood up and walked out of the cafe. "Do you remember the last time we made love?" Crossing the street into the small park, she waved at a driver who stopped for her. "It was glorious. I held you down and fed from your Fae energy while

I rode you." No one was around so she sat on one of the benches. "You came so hard, and so did I."

She waited, enjoying the silence—the silence that overflowed with fear, disgust, and even his hatred. "One of my favorite memories."

"Nightmares don't you mean? After all, I defeated you soon after that."

"Why would that make it a nightmare? The fact that you were strong enough and clever enough to defeat me only proves why you are my consort. I learned from that experience, my love. Just as I learned from my pet. The next time I take you, you will not escape."

"Fuck off, Bitch."

She laughed. "Such colorful language. I'm enjoying our call, lover, but my time is precious." Her voice hardened. "Bring me my pet."

Baylen jerked. *What the fuck?* "You want me to bring you Ciara?"

"Yes, Consort."

"You think I would surrender myself and Ciara to you?"

"At this time, I only require my pet. You can bring her to me and leave."

"There is absofuckinglutely no chance of that ever happening."

"I'm sitting across from your children's school. They will be out soon, won't they? In exchange for their safety, you will bring me my pet." She got up and moved deeper into the little park. A smile curving her lips as seconds later she saw Fae Warriors landing around the school's perimeter. "Tsk, tsk, Baylen. I have many ways of getting to your children. Do not make me demonstrate. You will retrieve my pet and bring her to me at midnight." She adjusted her glamour and walked across the park and into the school yard.

"Why do you want Ciara so badly?"

"That is not your business at this time, Consort. I'll call you later and tell you where to bring her." She stood with a group of mothers and gave them a friendly smile, the phone at her ear indicating she couldn't talk at that moment, watching for Baylen's children.

"I'll come. We'll leave Ciara out of this. After all, I'm the one you want to fuck."

She laughed gently. "I enjoy my pet too, Consort. She is the one I want tonight. But don't worry, I will happily share her with you when the time is right." Seeing the triplets, she moved closer and used the phone to take a picture of them. "Such pretty children, Baylen. They look like you." She sent the picture and walked away, adjusting her glamour subtly as she went. The phone, she dropped into a trash receptacle as she walked by, now a pretty blonde in a soft dress. She kept walking, again adjusting her glamour as she went around a corner. By the time she entered the small electronics store she appeared to be a blond male in jeans and t-shirt. She purchased a cheap phone and loaded it with a short number of minutes, flirting with the young woman behind the counter, as she paid. From there she walked across town and into the garden center. In the middle of that lush oasis, she found a private seating area and opened a vortex and stepped into it. The vortex closed and

Wisteria was instantly transported back to the remote forest.

Chapter One Hundred Sixty-Two

EARTH DIMENSION THREE
Mystic Haven, B.C., Canada

"HEY, ALIORA. HOW ARE you? What can I do for you today?"

"Hi, Gin!" Ali smiled at the school receptionist.

"Oh, my gosh." Gin began to flip frantically through her date book. "Were you booked with one of the classes today? Did I forget to write it down?"

"Just finished actually," Ali laughingly reassured the grey-haired wolf shifter. Not that Gin was old. Far from it, but she did shift into a grey wolf.

Gin stopped her frantic page turning and looked at Ali. "I didn't even see you come in."

Ali shook her head. "You were on your lunch break. Helen signed me in. How've you been, Gin? We haven't had coffee in ages."

Gin smiled and closed her date book. "I've been great. We need to have a coffee soon. I have so much to tell you." She peeked around the office. "Aliora, Cree asked me out!"

"What? Oh, my goodness!" Ali rushed around the desk to hug Gin and they both squealed. "When? How? I need details!"

Gin laughed and shook her head. "We need to have coffee. Saturday morning? 'Cause you've been holding out on me, and I've been hearing rumors. A lot of crazy rumors."

Ali laughed. "Which rumors?"

"I think you know, Aliora. Rumors that involve a certain Fae king."

Ali couldn't stop the grin that spread over her face. "Saturday morning. My house?"

Gin nodded. "I'll bring the coffee and the chocolate."

"Deal."

The end of day bell rang, and Ali waved to Gin as she headed out before the masses descended. Kids called out happy greetings to her as they walked by, and Aliora waved and sent showers of golden sparkles.

She glanced up and saw the three Fae warriors Baylen had following her standing beside a large rugged black SUV. She waved, and her instincts went on high alert. She glanced around. A slender dark-haired woman moved toward her. Was she a threat? Creators, she was on edge. Which, considering everything that had gone on in the last few days, made total sense. The dark-haired lady smiled and continued past. Ali breathed out in relief.

A middle-aged woman stepped out of a vehicle parked by the sidewalk, and Ali glanced at her. Every part of her suddenly went to high alert, and she threw up a shield of pure sunlight. The woman shrieked, and Ali was horrified to see a strand of gossamer energy moving toward her.

"Run!" She heard one of the Warriors shout, but there were children spilling out onto the sidewalk. Their happy chatter made a discordant sound to the pounding of her heart. She turned, slamming a barrier between the woman and the kids.

The energy strand snapped on her arm, and she almost went to her knees as agony sliced through her.

The woman growled and grabbed her arm.

Ali shoved the woman.

"You are not going to enjoy what I do to you. "The woman lifted her hand and black wisps of energy began to spin from her fingertips.

Ali shrugged. "Ditto, bitch." She punched a blast of pure light into the female, dodging the black wisps of energy. One of them slid across her face and she gasped at the sharp sting.

The woman staggered, shrieking as the light slammed into her. She rose to her feet, black blood dripping from her nose, her glamor falling away to reveal the monster. Grey skin, jagged teeth, and eyes of pure black. Wisteria clenched her fists as she stared at the woman who thought she could steal her consort. The woman standing in her way. Slowly, she began to draw back on the web that had encircled the woman's arm. Her death would be slow and cruel.

The energy web tightened on her arm, and Ali cried out, stumbling forward a step, dragged off balance as the creature began to wind in her web.

One of the Fae Warriors wrapped an arm around her waist and slashed a sword charged with Fae energy down across the web. It snapped and the creature fell back. Turning the Warrior sprinted for the SUV, as the others began to fire Fae energy blasts. The Warrior tossed Ali into the vehicle and climbed in after her as sirens began to scream. The other two Warriors continued to blast the creature with Fae energy as they backed into the SUV. Police cars raced up the street toward them. The driver stomped on the gas and the SUV shot out onto the road. Ali caught a pain-filled glimpse of the woman running with several officers chasing her as they raced away.

Chapter One Hundred Sixty-Three

EARTH DIMENSION THREE
Mystic Haven, B.C., Canada

CADEN SWORE AS THEY burst out of the alley. Turning around in a circle, he looked at Maverick who shook his head. "Where did she go? Anyone have eyes on her?"

Josef shifted into his dragon and launched into the air.

Catelyn leaned over, her hands on her knees, as she gasped for air. "How fast was that thing running? Did you see the way she scurried over that fence back there?"

Caden shook his head. "Hell, if I know how fast that was."

"I can't see her Caden." Josef said over their mind link.

"Fuck!" Caden shoved his hair back. "Get the K9 units in here. Let's see if they can pick up a scent."

Chapter One Hundred Sixty-Four

EARTH DIMENSION THREE
Mystic Haven, B.C., Canada

BAYLEN, JETT, AND STRIKER were waiting when the SUV roared into the portico at the castle's main doors. Baylen ripped open the back door and reached for Ali, gently tipping up her face. Blood had colored the whole side of her face red. "Fuck, Ali! I'm going to kill that bitch."

He started to lift her from the vehicle, and she cried out. "Slowly and painfully." He muttered darkly and paused as she carefully moved her arm from where it had pressed against him. Black welts encircled her arm, and her skin was red and inflamed around them. Striker stepped up beside Baylen.

"We have a gurney." When Baylen shook his head, he sighed. "Let me look at her as we go."

"Hey, Aliora. Bet that cut hurts like a bitch." His voice was calmly professional. "Let me look at that arm." She winced when he touched it. He took her pulse, as they hurried down the hall. They turned into the medical area and Striker directed them to a bed. "Jett, get Maxen here. He's got the most experience with injuries caused by the V'ran. I don't like the looks of those welts." He opened a cupboard and took out the items he needed to clean the wound on her face. "This might sting, Aliora, but I've got to get a better look at this cut."

"Maxen is on his way."

"Thanks."

Baylen held onto his fury by the finest thread. Crossing his arms, his legs braced apart he swore on his crown that he would kill that bitch this time.

Chapter One Hundred Sixty-Five

EARTH DIMENSION THREE
Mystic Haven, B.C., Canada

MAXEN AND STRIKER CONTINUED examining her arm when Ali's phone rang. She fumbled it out of the pocket in her dress with the hand that wasn't injured. Caller unknown. With a sigh she hit the speaker icon. "Hello."

"I'm going to kill you, bitch. Baylen is mine. Your death is going to hurt, badly. Your screams will be music to my ears."

Baylen, who'd been lounging against the wall, straightened and grabbed the phone from Ali's hand only to have Jett reach out and take it from him and give him a look. Jett opened his own phone and punched in a code as he walked out of the medical bay and into the hall, the woman's voice still screaming obscenities and threats.

Baylen squeezed her shoulder. "You're safe here, Ali"

She nodded, but she couldn't stop trembling.

"Jett will handle that. I suspect he's hoping to get a trace. He's got some fancy high-tech security programs on his phone, and I have no doubt that he's on his way to our cyber security techs."

A moment later two big scary-looking warriors walked into the med bay and took up positions along the wall. Ali eyed them suspiciously. "I'd like to go home. I need some chocolate." Her voice broke. Baylen stroked back her hair fighting his need to wrap his arms around her. "I've got you." His hand closed over her uninjured one. He gave Striker and Maxen a hard look.

"We're almost done here, Ali." Maxen's voice was warm. "I'm going to hook you up to an IV and get some meds started. Striker has ordered the sunroom to be set up for you. You're going to need sun therapy and rest.

Jett stepped back into the med bay and signaled Baylen to come with him. "I'll be right back, Ali, and I'll bring chocolate." He winked at her, and she had to laugh.

Striker stepped back. "Alright, I've done what I can here. I'm going to make sure the sunroom is ready, while you get that IV started, Maxen."

Maxen waited for the king and Striker to leave before continuing. "I've also ordered that a warm saltwater bath be drawn. You have some Mer in you." His eyes met hers. "How many species are in your lineage?"

Did he suspect? How much should she tell him?

Maxen silently inserted the IV needle and taped it securely to Ali's arm. "You're being really quiet." He looked at her, his dark eyes serious. "Did you know that I'm Unseelie?"

Aliora shook her head. "No. I didn't." She smiled. But I guess maybe I should have. I can see there is something different about your energy.

Maxen nodded. "As you probably know, there are three races of Fae. Seelie, which is the most prolific. They need only sunlight to keep their energy stores high. Then there is the Unseelie like me. My race is rare, and few of us escaped the carnage of the Tuatha war. We need the moon and the sun to stay at our peak, and finally, there was the Changeling Fae. We were unable to rescue any before the ships left the Tuatha star system. Recently though the Angels brought Caden his new daughter Safire the lone survivor of a planetary war. . A newborn Changeling. Now, there is you."

Aliora's eyes met his and she swallowed. He smiled at her and inclined his head. "Doctor-patient confidentiality. It would be helpful in your treatment though if you could tell me your lineage."

"Baylen doesn't know." She shook her head. "No one has ever guessed before."

"That's because they're not an Ancient Unseelie Fae healer who took genetics in his medical training. We've lost much of our history, much of our knowledge, but I can give you a brief history of the Changeling Fae if you're interested."

"I would love to know more about my heritage. My grandfather had limited knowledge of the beginnings of the Changelings."

Maxen smiled. "The origins of the Changeling Fae were unique. Generations of species from many different worlds mixed and mingled freely until one day a woman of mixed heritage mated a Fae. Their son was the first Changeling Fae. His name was Ajani Bodhi. Ajani retained the essence of all his ancestors. He was a being with powers that no one had ever seen before. A re-mingling, a combining. Power added to power, and frankly he was thought to be an anomaly. Until it happened again many years later. Over the years our scientists figured out that it was the addition of Fae genetics that created these unique beings. But still, it was extremely rare and no two were alike. They came from a hugely varied background. The one common thread was always a Fae mating. They weren't considered a race of Fae until one day a Changeling Fae mated another Changeling Fae and they had children. Those children were pure Changeling Fae. They'd bred true. Another branch of Fae was added to our people. Of course, they were all lost in the battle against the V'ran. It seems we've come full circle, Aliora. The Changeling Fae have appeared again. The chances of that were thought impossible."

Aliora smiled. "That's incredible. Thank you, Maxen."

He smiled and squeezed her hand. "Of course. Now, what are we going to do about this secret of yours?"

"Will you keep it?"

Maxen watched her for a moment. "Why is this a secret you feel necessary to keep from the Fae king?"

"My grandfather is Edge de Fae."

Maxen nodded. "I know Edge. He's one of the greatest heroes of our people. He's also a total rogue."

Ali laughed. "Yes, he is. He said the Changeling home world, Aelrindel, was the first planet in the Tuatha star system to fall. As far as he knew they never got a ship off the planet to join the convoy. The satellite footage and drone footage they recovered showed a bloodbath. He thinks the

Changelings were targeted because their unique genetics created such a powerful energy that the V'ran feasted on it and were strengthened to the degree that they were almost invincible when they went after the rest of the Fae home worlds. My family decided it was important to keep what I am a secret. I'm not ready to reveal what I am."

"Baylen is your mate."

Ali smiled sadly at Maxen. "He refuses to take another mate. He refuses to see me as anything other than a gentle woman who could not survive his enemy. With a V'ran loose on our world, I could become a bigger target, and heaven help us if she got her hands on me and realized what I am. Or worse if she got her hands on Baylen and me."

Maxen nodded, his face grave. "For now, I will keep your secret. I agree the risks are too high, at this time, for you to reveal who and what you are."

Chapter One Hundred Sixty-Six

EARTH DIMENSION THREE
Mystic Haven, B.C., Canada

BAYLEN STEPPED INTO the corridor to speak to Jett and his phone rang, he answered hoping for an update on Ali.

"I am going to kill her, Consort. I promise you that. No more mates!"

Jett took one look at his face and the phone in his hand, and he snatched it away and held it up to his ear.

"If you want to fuck around, you can fuck around with my pet." Wisteria's voice was ice cold with her fury.

His eyes met Baylen's and he lifted a finger to his lips. Getting out his phone he tapped in the same code he'd accessed a short while ago. Then he hit the speaker icon on Baylen's phone and signaled Baylen to keep her talking.

"You should have brought Ciara to me. You have only yourself to blame, Consort."

"I'm not giving Ciara to you."

With a 'follow me' jerk of his head, Jett led the way to their tech department.

"That is not an option, Consort."

"I don't follow your orders. Stay the fuck away from my family."

Wisteria laughed. "I thought you'd learned who was in control from our first meeting. I shall enjoy demonstrating my power over you again."

Baring his teeth, blood red fury washed over him. He met Jett's eyes and got the signal to keep talking. "You have an active imagination, Wisteria."

"Poor King of the Fae, you know you will kneel before me again. The only question is how brutal the lesson will be. Kill this Aliora, and bring me my pet, and the lesson will not be too harsh. Fail me again and I will turn your castle into the site of the bloodiest massacre on this godsforsaken island." The phone went dead, and Baylen looked at Jett, fury in every line of his body.

"We got enough triangulation to give us some idea of where she is calling from. I'm sending the information to Caden."

"Just give me the fucking information, Jett."

Jett shook his head. "Hell, no. You are already walking a dangerous line. If something goes wrong and she gains control of you, this island would be fucked. The information goes to Caden."

Chapter One Hundred Sixty-Seven

EARTH DIMENSION THREE
Mystic Haven, B.C., Canada

BAYLEN PACED, HIS BLOOD pounding in his ears. He struggled with the overwhelming urge to do his own search for that bitch who was hurting the people he cared about. He fucking knew that if Ali had not been laying in the sunroom, healing he would have forced her to leave this island. He fucking still should.

A knock sounded on his study door. He turned and glared. "What the fucking hell does someone want now? Fuck! This had better be fucking important!" He yanked open the door.

Shirina arched her eyebrow. "It is." Her three large-ass dogs wandered into his private study and lay down in front of the fireplace. He glared and started to turn when he noticed the mouse peeking out of the pocket on her flowing red skirt. He looked up at Shirina and raised his own eyebrow. "You brought a rodent to the Fae castle?"

"What?" Shirina glanced down and gasped. "Gus-Gus! You little sneak." She scooped him into her hand and lifted him up until he was nose to nose with her. "You were not invited to my meeting with the Fae king. You better curl up in my pocket and go to sleep, so he doesn't feed you to a cat. Excuse me, a fucking cat." She tucked the small striped mouse back into her pocket and gave the Fae king a bland look. "I have news that I believe you are going to want to hear. I've asked Caden to join us."

"Sure, just make yourself at home and invite whoever the fuck you want."

Shirina reached into her bag and pulled out a brown paper bag. She set it on the coffee table, gave him a glance and sat down on the couch. "Those are for sharing. Do you have coffee?"

"Fuck!" Baylen glared at the calm woman, before snatching up the phone and calling down to the kitchen. "A large pot of coffee and three mugs please." He hung up and turned to the woman who was smiling serenely at him. "Fucking hell, Shirina. How long before that fucking cop gets here?"

Shirina met his eyes. "How long has it been since you got laid, Your Majesty?'

"Are you fucking volunteering?"

Shirina laughed. "I would, but I happen to like Aliora, your mate."

Baylen eyed her. "She is not my fucking mate."

Shirina shook her head. "She is, Your Majesty. You just haven't mated her yet. What is the hold up?'

"None of your fucking business."

Shirina laughed again, not at all insulted by his colorful language. "Is she here at the castle? She might be interested in this meeting. I can have a word with her about fucking you if you need me too."

Baylen stared at the slender woman. He didn't know whether to laugh or throw her out. "Creators, Shirina. You are a hell of a lot of trouble."

She grinned. "I know."

He threw himself into the big armchair and leaned forward to open the paper bag. Cookies. Freshly baked too. He grabbed two and sat back in the chair. Another knock at the door. He eyed the door for a moment before saying "Come in."

A servant pushed in a cart with a large coffee urn, several cups, and cream and sugar containers. Right behind the coffee cart, Caden walked into the room.

The servant left, and Baylen waved the cop into a chair. "Shirina has called this impromptu meeting so she can explain what's going on." Baylen stood up and poured them each a coffee and brought the steaming hot beverages to the coffee table. "The chair is yours, Shirina."

Shirina smiled a faint half smile. "I've been studying the Wards trying to understand why none of our protection Wards recognize Wisteria. Well, except for the ones that were around Ciara's house. I have an interesting theory."

Caden took a sip of his coffee. "Go ahead."

"You know how Wisteria can vanish into thin air when she is being chased."

"Yeah, that's a fucking pain in the ass," Baylen muttered.

Shirina grinned, "What if she is able to summon vortexes like the angels do?"

"That would be a problem," Caden said. "Do you think she can do that? Were the V'ran capable of that?"

Shirina shook her head. "Not that we know of, Caden. I have no evidence to support the theory I'm about to throw at you, but it's the one thing that would make sense." She looked at both men before continuing. "Wisteria has always been different from any other V'ran we have encountered. I'm not saying she wasn't part of that attack force. I have no idea how long lived her species is. I can tell you, that the V'ran that attacked the Tuatha star system, were never interested in any kind of relationship with the Fae. They considered themselves superior and they considered us food. You don't fuck your food."

Caden winced. Baylen shook his head. "You're saying the insane bitch who keeps hunting me is, in fact, insane."

Shirina nodded and helped herself to a cookie. "From a V'ran point of view I'm sure they would consider her mentally unstable."

"I could've told you this years ago. The woman's insane. Do you have any other *important* information?"

Shirina sipped her coffee. "What if there are other things different about Wisteria? The only races that can vanish into thin air are, the Fae with an invisibility glamour, Nymphs but differently, as they simply go noncorporeal, becoming whatever they're associated with, like part of a river, or tree, or even the sunset. Then there are Angels." She glanced at the two men. "Now, Angels are the ones I think are most pertinent to what we are discussing. They can open vortexes that take them to different dimensions or even different times. They can also use those vortexes to travel through space. I'd lay odds that's what Wisteria has been doing."

"How?" Caden asked.

"That's the question I don't fully have an answer to, but I would suggest that there is possibly some connection between Wisteria and Ash Morana."

Baylen rubbed his shoulder. "I don't know how we can prove that."

Caden looked thoughtful. "Do you have a holo-screen in this study, Bay?"

"Sure." He leaned forward and touched the coffee table. A holo-screen appeared.

"Thanks. Computer, show us the data we have on Angels."

The screen filled with glowing words. They all began to look through the list. "Shit." Caden said.

"What?"

"They really can go back in time or forward into the future."

"How would that pertain to Wisteria?" Baylen asked, frowning.

"Wisteria had Ciara for months the first time. We know she had some form of mind-control over her. Ciara told me once that Wisteria raped her mind before she ever raped her body.

We know that Ciara builds crazy powerful Wards. I would bet that Ciara knows how the original Ward on this island was created. Not just book knowledge, but with a depth of understanding that few people have."

Shirina nodded. "That makes sense. Wisteria could have found that information in Ciara's mind. It's probably one of the main reasons that Wisteria kept her alive."

They exchanged grim looks. Shirina sighed. "If Wisteria went back in time to within a few days after The Ward was created. Before we'd introduced the information on the V'ran, and before we'd taught it the history of the Fae, she might have been able to imprint herself on The Ward, as a safe entity."

Caden frowned. "But if that's the case, then the first time she came to the island and attacked The Ward and Baylen, shouldn't The Ward have learned from that?"

Shirina nodded. "Yeah, that means this theory doesn't work"

"Wait." Baylen leaned forward. "She didn't know how The Ward worked until after she had Ciara. If she simply imprinted on The Ward, she would get stuck in an endless time loop that would never succeed beyond that first encounter. But she did succeed, she came later and captured Ciara. What if she went back in time and imprinted this older version of herself on The Ward?"

"The Ward wouldn't recognize her. When the earlier version of herself showed up on the island, The Ward would have done what it was trained to do. The past would have played out undisturbed."

"But why didn't The Ward learn from Ciara's experience? It's like The Ward doesn't even recognize Wisteria's existence."

Shirina nodded thoughtfully. "Computer, please display all the information we have about the encounter Ciara Walker had with the V'ran named Wisteria Abital"

The information appeared and they began to look through it. "There," Baylen said. "Look at that."

"Wisteria used Ciara to hide her presence while she created a nest in Ciara's home. From then on, with Ciara secured in her prison, Wisteria could use her physic signature as her own." Shirina's voice grew more and more horrified. "My creators, Caden, what happened to Ciara was a living nightmare."

Caden shook his head. "The Ward doesn't even see Wisteria because it never encountered her doing anything evil. The safe imprint remains untouched. The nest she made while she was using Ciara's physic signature hid her actions, and it hid Ciara herself from The Ward. Hell." He looked at Baylen. "I bet, after what you and The Ward did to her the first time, that she's scarred and that helps to disguise her from The Ward as well."

"I don't understand why The Ward didn't kill Ciara when Charli's body was discovered. Ciara was no longer hidden, and she'd destroyed Wisteria's nest. Shouldn't The Ward have thought Ciara did it?" Shirina spoke up, reaching over to gently squeeze Baylen's arm.

"No." Caden shook his head. "I think Wisteria thought she could move freely and kill freely as long as she could disguise herself as Ciara. But I don't believe that Wisteria has ever understood Ciara's strength. Ciara resisted Wisteria every step of the way. Wisteria brutally tortured her. Yet

Ciara knew what Wisteria planned. I believe Ciara fought desperately to save Charli that day.

When I got into the house that Wisteria used to hold her, Ciara was already free. I just got her out of the house. She was badly injured, but all she could think about at that moment was saving Charli and Baylen. She mentioned Baylen and Charli right before she destroyed Wisteria's nest.

I also think that Wisteria wanted Charli to see her. We have evidence that she wanted all of us to know it was her that killed Charli. Wisteria might have thought she could hide back in Ciara's physic signature after the kill. Unfortunately, for her, Ciara destroyed her anchor to Mystic Haven. It tore Wisteria from this dimension, I believe.

Baylen walked away to stare out the window that overlooked the gardens, and a bramble covered cottage in the distance, his heart aching. "Now, I know why she's so desperate to gain control of Ciara again." Baylen muttered. "Fuck, I want to kill that bitch."

Caden nodded, his eyes hard. "How do we fix this Shirina?"

Shirina pushed her long silvery blonde hair back over her shoulder, her face a study in concentration. "First, I think we have a bigger problem. All the main Wards on this island learn from The Ward." She looked at the two men. "That means that the castle is not protected, and neither are the emergency caves." She shook her head, "The schools, our hospitals, the police station, the fire station, even the Mer Wards. My Creators, Caden. This is a disaster!"

Baylen turned back to face them. "That's why she said she'd seen me fucking Aliora. She's been close to the castle."

"Solutions. Now." Caden snapped.

"Ciara, Aliora, and me, plus Baylen and you Caden." We need to go to The Ward first and teach it every form of Wisteria and V'ran we know of. Ciara must let it into her mind to see what Wisteria did. But once it knows, it's going to start hunting her. We are going to have to go to each high security place and teach each Ward because The Ward is going to be hunting."

Caden swore. "There is too much room for Wisteria to be able to keep moving around the island from one place to another if we do it that way. The carnage would be horrific. Heaven help us if she is able to gain control of Ciara again. We're not going to start with The Ward. We're going to start right here with the Castle Ward. She's after Baylen, and we cannot afford to lose the Fae king or those he loves." Caden gave Baylen a look. "It will also create a safe place for our people. The Castle Ward is powerful, it can help us to teach the other Wards."

"Next, we fix the Wards that guard the emergency caves." Baylen said quietly. "That way we can evacuate the island population if we need to."

"The castle grounds go to the ocean do they not?"

Baylen nodded. "Yeah, this whole mountain and down to the ocean from the west."

"Okay, so, as soon as the Castle Ward is updated, it will reach out to the Wards that protect the Castle lands and they in turn will end up reaching the ocean and the Mer Wards." Shirina nodded. She pulled up a map on the holo-screen. Computer mark all the lands connected to the Fae Castle."

"The emergency caves also connect to the ocean so they will help with that too." Caden said.

"After we get the emergency cave Wards updated, we can concentrate on the Wards that protect the schools."

"Yes." Shirina touched the schools marked on the map. "Color red please." The computer complied.

Caden studied the map. "After the schools, we need to go to The Ward. I don't think we can leave it longer. It's going to be agitated and confused by the conflicting information the finished Wards are now projecting. That makes it dangerous. After that, we still have the hospitals, police station, and the fire station to do. Hospitals next."

"Then the police station and finally the fire stations. Fuck, Caden, I don't like leaving the police station without a reliable Ward that long." Baylen frowned and stared at the map.

"Baylen, we're the police. We are the best equipped to handle any kind of attack. We must get our most vulnerable protected first. Fire stations and the Police station last. I'll alert my officers. One good thing about all of this is the fact that as the Wards are updated, they will naturally spread that update to the smaller private security Wards." Caden stood up. "I'm going to get Ciara, is Ali here?"

Baylen nodded. "She was hurt in that attempt by Wisteria today."

Caden frowned. "You didn't tell me that."

Baylen shoved a hand through his hair. "Honestly, Caden, I've been a fucking mess. Ah, hell. We should've had Jett in this meeting."

"Can Ali help us with the Wards?"

"I think she might do me serious harm if I try to stop her."

Caden laughed. "Alright, I'm heading out to get Ciara. I'll be back soon."

Shirina stood up too. "I'm going to alert Ryder and his Trium. If he can get the Ancients standing guard over our vulnerable until we can sort these Wards out it will help."

Baylen nodded. "I'm going to brief Jett who will raise holy hell for not being part of this meeting. I'll see you when you get back here. Shirina, feel free to use my study to contact the Ancients."

Chapter One Hundred Sixty-Eight

EARTH DIMENSION THREE
Mystic Haven, B.C., Canada

THEY GATHERED IN THE great foyer of the Fae castle, The Fae King, The Protector, and The Healer, The Ward Expert, The Guardian, two women of great power and a former Royal Healer. This is where they would begin the hunt for an evil that could destroy them all.

Baylen set his hand on the stone wall, understanding that this place was more than just a castle. It was a living, breathing Ward, designed to protect the ones who lived within its walls.

"Castle Ward, we must speak of danger."

A stirring in the air, a shimmer of golden light, and The Castle Ward swirled around Baylen. *What danger exists that I cannot defeat?*

Caden raised his eyebrow. Shirina laughed. "Castle Wards do tend to take on the personality of the current king and Trium."

Ali smiled. "Indeed."

Baylen ignored them and focused on the sentient being. "Wisteria Abital."

"I am aware of that being, but she was destroyed. Her image and history have been recorded to prevent further destruction by any of her species."

"Wisteria Abital lives. She has returned more than once to this island and has caused great harm."

"Immediate update required. I will contact The Stratagem Ward and update my knowledge."

"No." Baylen spoke up. "We will update you ourselves. The Forest Stratagem Ward is currently unaware of the problems."

"Please remove your glamours so I can verify your identities."

A moment later, eight Fae stood fully revealed, and one secret Changeling partially revealed. The Castle Ward swirled around them, touching each one in turn. *"Greetings Baylen Knight, King of the Fae. Greetings Protector, Jett Sidhe. Greetings Healer, Striker Barron. Greetings Guardian, Caden Brody. Greetings Shirina Sítheach of Erendrial, in the Tuatha Star System, Creator, Healer, and Protector of Wards. Greetings Healer, Maxen Ransom. Greetings Ciara Walker of the Tiên lineage. Greetings Aliora Aurelius of the de Fae lineage.*

"Baylen Knight, King of the Fae, you may proceed."

"Castle Ward, I need you to scan Ciara Walker's memories. She will think of how the incident began. Please scan the whole incident, after that look at her memories in the last few weeks for a recent incident. Please be aware that these are traumatic incidents for Ciara."

The Castle Ward swirled around Ciara, and when Caden stepped closer the Ward spoke. *"Do not be concerned,*

Guardian, I can assure you that no harm will come to Ciara. Ciara of the Tiên lineage, I will only access what you permit, and I will do so in a way that you will not be forced to relive the incidents. It will only take a moment."

Ciara took a breath and nodded. The Castle Ward swirled around her in iridescent gold. A few seconds later, it backed away. Hovering in the midst of the Fae, its colors changing, after a few moments it swirled over The Guardian, then Aliora, and finally The Fae king.

"Ciara's memories have led it to Caden, Aliora and Baylen. It's almost done." Shirina said quietly.

"This is most disturbing." The Castle Ward spoke into all their minds. *"This Wisteria Abital is far more dangerous than we understood. I believe her to be mentally unstable which makes her erratic."*

"We have a theory, Castle Ward." Shirina stepped forward. "We believe she had capabilities beyond her species. Would you like to see?"

"Yes." The Ward swirled around Shirina. *"Ah, I see. Yes, I believe you are correct. All the Wards on this island must be updated! It is imperative."*

"Castle Ward."

"Yes, Fae King?"

"Wisteria Abital is currently here in Mystic Haven. Do you detect her presence?"

"She's not in the castle, your Highness. I can assist with the update to the Guard-Stratagem-Defense Ward that protects the castle lands."

"Thank you, we will attend to that in a moment. Are you fully able to protect everyone within these walls, and prevent her from attaining entrance to the castle?"

"I am."

"Thank you, Castle Ward." Baylen looked around at everyone gathered. "That's one. Let's get the castle grounds secured."

Long into the night they worked, aware that with every Ward they updated, they also pushed Wisteria further and further away from her prey. It was only a matter of time before she retaliated.

Chapter One Hundred Sixty-Nine

EARTH DIMENSION THREE
Mystic Haven, B.C., Canada

WISTERIA OPENED A VORTEX onto the beach a few meters in front of the woman standing in a patch of sunlight, her hair glowing reds and golds in the light. The woman who dared to claim her consort. She would pay for that. It was mere days after her consort had sent his Wards hunting her. She was furious and she was hungry. She'd warned him of the harsh lessons he would learn if he forced her hand. Today was lesson one.

A sneer curved her lips as she took in the woman's gown that spoke of a long dead era. *She was,* Wisteria's eyes traveled over the woman, *short and plump.* She shook her head, scoffing at the idea that someone like her could possibly hold Baylen's attention. A cold smile. *Honestly, she was doing her consort a favor by freeing him from this unnecessary burden.* She looked forward to his gratitude. Even if she had to force him to see it.

Ali looked up as the Wards appeared, their power rippling over her. *'Danger!'* The Wards sent the word whispering through her mind, their defensive stance behind her clearly conveying that something was wrong. She touched the beings' minds with calm reassurance as she studied the V'ran standing several feet away.

"You should leave this planet while you still can, Wisteria. There is no place for you to run now." She frowned. *Why aren't the Wards attacking?* Opening a mind link she sent the image of Wisteria to Caden, Baylen, and Shirina.

Baylen's voice blasted through the mind link so clearly that she knew he was already in the air flying towards her. *"Aliora, she can't fly. Get in the air! Now! Where are the fucking Wards!"*

Caden's voice. *"Aliora, get the hell out of there! I'm on my way! Don't engage! Don't engage!"*

"Aliora. Are you alone? You have to get away! Fly! Run! Why haven't The Wards engaged her?" She could hear the urgency in Shirina's mind link.

"The Wards are here but not engaging. I don't know why." Wisteria was almost to her. *"Wards, now would be a good time to get involved."*

"Do you know who I am?" The woman's smile could draw blood.

Ali looked at the woman. *"Wards! This is the woman from the update!"*

"I know who you are. Your name is Wisteria. You're a murderer."

"I'm going to kill you, so yes, I am a murderer. Your murderer." The woman's voice was the whisper of evil.

Aliora looked her up and down, her eyebrow raised. *"Wards! What the heck? You are slacking! Get her!"* Nothing. *"Fine, I'll take care of this myself!"* She dropped her glamour allowing the creature before her to see her for the first time. Allowing the world to see her. A being unique in the multiverse. Genetics combined and reformed. Stardust multiplied, mingling with all the powers of each of her ancestors. Powers transformed and refined by fragments of an ancient code, multiplied in infinite combinations.

"Wisteria." Her voice was gentle. A hushed hum of beauty and purity. "I'm your worst nightmare. The being you should fear above all others." Ali struck. A blast of pure light slamming into the creature before her. Wisteria's glamour dissolved as she screamed, flying backwards to crash into a massive rock formation that rose out of the ocean.

The Wards sent her a cheer. She eyed them for a moment. *Figures.* A crooked smile and a wink changed Ali's clothes from the long flowing blue princess dress to black leather pants, tank top and knee high flat soled boots. "Do you like the light, Wisteria?" She walked closer. "The problem is that light reveals the things you hide. Every lie, every manipulation, every vile thing you have done, murderer."

Wisteria rose to her feet, black blood trickling from her lip, her glamour burned away by the light. A split second later she stood on the beach. "You will die. Baylen is mine. He's *my* consort. I will rule this paltry world with him by my side."

In the distance Ali could see several Fae flying toward her. The Guardian and The Royal Trium. All she had to do was hold off Wisteria until they got there. She could do that. *Right?* She glanced at the Wards. *Right.* Yes, that was sarcasm. She took a breath, muttered something not very polite about the Wards, and looked at Wisteria. "No.

Baylen is mine. I won't allow you to harm him, nor will I allow you to bring harm to my world."

"Wards!" Ali hissed. *"Now would be a really good time for you to get involved!"* Still nothing. She gave them an irritated look before focusing back on the monster in front of her. *Be tough. Be scary. Be mean.* "Ah, Wisteria. How deserving of death you are, and you have met the one who can mete it out." Okay, a little drama worked too.

Wisteria snarled and flung herself at Ali, and Ali caught her by her throat and lifted. *Oh, those self defense lessons her father had insisted upon had paid off.* "Uh uh, Wisteria." Ali tossed the creature aside as she slammed her hand down. Light exploded! Wisteria screamed and another bolt of pure light lit up the sky.

Silence.

Wisteria rose to her feet, skin burned in several places, her hands spinning energy webs out of thin air. She cast them out, so they hovered between her prey and the would-be rescuers.

Ali glared at the Wards. *I'm going to tell the Fae king that you did nothing to help!* She lifted her hand, golden sparkles spilling from her fingertips, neutralizing the webs as they came into contact with the sticky energy strands.

Wisteria laughed. "I don't need my webs to kill you."

"It would probably make it easier though." Ali smiled grimly.

Wisteria shook her head. "No. You're easy prey." Her gaze flicked over Ali dismissively. "The webs were to prevent anyone from being foolish enough to attempt to help you."

Ali nodded. "I see. Let's dance then." Golden magic sparked from her hand, and she held a dagger. Casually, she tossed the glowing dagger up. Light began to gleam from the blade that tumbled through the air. Ali caught it easily. Expertly. Wisteria was on her, claws extended, jagged teeth bared in a horrifying grimace. Ali hadn't grown up on a farm, in the wild Canadian west for nothing. She fisted her left hand and punched the bitch as hard as she could. Wisteria went down, and Aliora stepped back. *Ouch.* She opened and closed her hand a few times, before transferring the dagger to her left hand, as she waited for the monster to rise.

"You will pay for that!" An evil shriek.

Ali met Wisteria's eyes as they circled each other, and when claws slashed out, Ali whipped the dagger across Wisteria's cheek. Blood flowed. But Wisteria had also managed to carve out deep furrows along Ali's arm. She ignored the pain and focused on the alien creature in front of her. Wisteria kicked out, caught Ali in the chest knocking her back. She hit the sand with an oof and saw Wisteria rushing toward her. Knowing she would die if that bitch got her claws on her she flung the dagger. The weapon streaked through the air in a flash of light and embedded deeply in Wisteria's shoulder. An explosion of light and smoke filled the air, and Ali rose to her feet as several beings of power appeared out of nowhere. "Angels, and—" Ali paused, her eyes studying the newcomers. "Deities?"

The dark-haired deity dressed in a perfectly fitted black suit, with a dark smoldering sexuality crossed his arms over his chest. The second one, with long blond hair and muscles that would make most women swoon, spoke. "I'm Etan Llewellyn and this is my brother, Adler. What are you doing, Lass? You've caused quite a disturbance."

Ali rolled her eyes and sent another cross look at the Wards. She heard a choked sound and glanced over as the Royal Trium arrived. Baylen clenched and unclenched his fists. His face filled with dark fury. "Ali, move away."

"I'm pretty sure I've got this now!" She snapped and turned back to the blond deity. "Taking out the trash. Could you open one of those vortex thingys" She lifted her hand and a bubble of light floated out of the smoke. Wisteria trapped inside it. "Goodbye, Wisteria." *And good riddance.*

"Aye." That was the dark haired one. His eyes moved over her searchingly. "Levi."

A disreputable looking Angel nodded his head. "Of course. Anywhere in particular, Adler?"

The dark-haired deity shrugged. "Our Creators might be interested in her."

The vortex opened and Ali flew to the bubble, reaching out.

"Don't!" Baylen shouted, tendons standing out on his neck, his fists clenched so tightly that his knuckles showed white.

Ali glanced at him and back at the air pocket her eyebrow raised. Wisteria pounded on the bubble, and slashed at it with ugly claws, screaming silent threats of gross evil.

Ali gently touched the sphere with one finger. It streaked across the sky like it had been shot from a jet fighter, hit dead center on the vortex and snapped the twisting maelstrom out of existence.

Levi's eyebrow rose. "I would have done that."

Ali smiled sweetly while inside she was planning to have a few harsh words with the Wards. "I was already here."

"Why didn't you kill her!" The guttural roar came from Baylen, his lips pulled back, teeth bared.

Ali stared at him, her eyebrow arching. "Excuse me? I sent her to the Creators. Nothing is powerful enough to stop that vortex. Except maybe an Angel." She shrugged, irritated by Baylen's reactions. Why the heck was he mad now?

"Or a Fallen Angel." Levi's voice was quiet. Everyone turned to look at him. His face was grim. "Whatever that creature was, she is nothing created by Rune or Eliana. The only other being in the multiverse capable of creating new lifeforms is Ash Morana. His secret experiments and the resulting creation of demons were part of his fall. We must report this incident, and that creature to the Creators." Levi looked to Etan and Adler. The two deities looked at each other and nodded. Levi went to Ali. "Thank you. You prevented a tragedy today."

The Angel lifted his hand and a great vortex opened. The three powerful beings stepped into the violently swirling phenomenon of air, clouds, and space, and instantly the vortex disappeared.

Chapter One Hundred Seventy

EARTH DIMENSION THREE
Mystic Haven, B.C., Canada

ASH STOOD IN SPACE observing the blue planet called Earth. The brutal cold of space suited his mood right now. Many people considered rage to be an emotion of fire and heat, and he had experienced that, at times, but for him the deepest rages were often colder than ice.

The problems with the genetics experiments were mounting. There were anomalies that could not be accounted for. The majority of soldiers selected worldwide had not reacted well to the serum. There was something missing, some element that had been overlooked. What the experiment had produced were disfigured, half human half something else creatures, most of them not even recognizable as human. They were nightmarish creatures of horror who could not wield the superhuman magic of the Elves. Totally useless for his plans. He'd ordered his scientists to put them down. At this rate, the promises he'd made to the world governments would not be fulfilled. That was unacceptable. These failures could not be revealed. He'd also ordered his men to round up more Elves and any other superhuman they could find. These experiments would produce the results he sought—His thoughts cut off abruptly as he saw a vortex, containing a ball of light, streaking away from the earth.

His eyebrow rose and he spread his mighty wing. A vortex? How interesting. What was that small host of Angels up to now? Soaring through space, he intercepted the vortex and ripped it open. What he found both irritated him and made him laugh. "Hello, Wisteria." The highly decorated soldier had once been one of his top assets in the destruction of the Fae on Erendrial, in the Tuatha Star System.

She screamed for him to release her from the light bubble that she was trapped in, and he understood why. Her skin was turning black and covered with huge blisters as she reacted to the light that the bubble was made of. *Foolish female.* He had too many of his men out looking for her and here she was, on his stronghold, interfering with his plans. "I see that your light immunity needs to be updated. I did send for you when your vaccination expired. But don't worry, Wisteria, I will take care of you."

Ash created a new vortex and stepped into it with the light bubble in tow. Her screams finally easing the fury that had been consuming him. He was tempted to slow the vortex down, to enjoy her suffering a little longer, but he had pressing matters he needed to resolve.

Stepping out of the vortex and onto Aracsna, home world to the V'ran in the Dark Flame Star System, he ordered his servant to bring a hover gurney. When the floating cot arrived, he ripped open the light bubble and watched dispassionately as Wisteria fell out onto the ground. He was irritated. That female was a loose cannon.

He nodded to his servants to put her on the gurney. Was it possible that she'd suffered some kind of brain injury? He'd been told that she considered a Fae to be her consort. A Fae! He shuddered. The Fae were food for the V'ran. Not playmates.

He followed the gurney into the medical ward of his castle on this cold little world in the deep reaches of the multiverse. The medical staff quickly removed her clothing and transferred her to a clear med pod. He stepped forward, lifting his hand to stop them from beginning treatment. "I've been wondering where you'd gone too."

Wisteria turned her head slowly to face the Fallen Angel who had created her kind. "You had no assignments for me, I took a couple of personal days."

Ash raised an eyebrow. "Personal days? Who've you been hanging out with?"

Wisteria shrugged, and he wondered how she'd survived to this point. The Fae who'd managed to escape his trap, made it to the planet Earth and discovered the V'ran's weakness, their fatal flaw. They were deathly allergic to the light from a white dwarf star.

Those Fae then made the trip to the original Aracsna home world and poisoned their pulsar sun with the light of a white dwarf star. Most of his creations died that day. He'd managed to create a vaccine antidote that saved a remnant and brought them to this secret world. He'd tasked them with scientific discoveries and reproduction. He would not lose his army. He still had a foe to destroy.

He eyed the female. "Wisteria, have you engaged in reproductive activities at all?"

A sly smile tilted her lips. "Perhaps."

Shaking his head, he walked up to her. "Not with your food. You cannot reproduce with a Fae."

"I don't wish to reproduce with anyone but my consort."

"Your consort?"

Wisteria looked at him with open defiance. "My consort is the Fae king."

"While I am certain that you would enjoy eating the Fae energy he produces, he cannot be your consort. First, a consort implies you are a Queen. You are not. You are a decorated soldier. Second, the V'ran are dying. It's your duty to help prevent that. Having sex with your food will only remind me how crazy you are."

Wisteria lifted her chin. "I did my part for your war, Morana. I'm done. Now, I will conquer my own worlds."

Ash stared at her. "You're interfering with my plans. I believe, Wisteria, that consequences are in order."

He looked at the medical staff. "Give her the antidote for the sun poisoning, but allow her to heal naturally, and do not give her any medications for the pain."

Wisteria screamed at him, and he looked at her with a raised eyebrow. "Consequences, remember?"

Wisteria shook her head, her eyes wild with pain. "Please, Master. The pain is too much."

Ash considered her. "Tell me, Wisteria. How did you get to Earth, Dimension Three?"

"V—Vortex."

"One of my Fallen Angels opened a vortex for you?"

"I—don't need anyone to—open vortexes for me."

Ash paused. His eyes sharpened and he leaned closer to her, observing everything about this creature he'd created. "Doctors, please send blood samples to my lab immediately." He held out his hand and a slender metal collar appeared in it. "Open the pod."

The medical staff complied, and he leaned over Wisteria and fastened the collar around her neck. Stepping back, he signaled the medical staff to reseal the pod. "Proceed with accelerated healing and immediate pain relief." He watched as a blue mist filled the pod and settled over her. Her skin began to heal. A yellow mist filled the med pod, this one a pain reliever. He waited until she was breathing easier to begin his questioning.

"You said the Fae king is your consort? How did you access that island? It's protected by highly advanced Ward technology."

"I'm more intelligent than their pathetic technology."

"You've found a way to destroy their Wards?"

Wisteria shook her head. "I found a way to deceive it. I can go anywhere on that island. Do anything I want. The Ward does not recognize me."

Ash pulled up a chair and sat down by her med pod. "How were you trapped in that light bubble then?"

Wisteria's eyes filled with rage. "That bitch, Aliora, did it."

"What bitch? Is she a Fae?"

"Yes. No. I have no idea what she is, but she is powerful."

"Tell me everything, Wisteria—From the beginning."

RISING FROM THE CHAIR, Ash smiled at the woman in the med pod. "Rest, Wisteria. You have done well."

"May I have another light vaccine?"

"Of course."

"Thank you. I'll return to my consort as soon as the vaccine is updated."

Ash turned to look at her, a faint smile crossing his face. "You are needed here, Wisteria. Your genetics are needed to bring diversity in the reproduction efforts to save your people. You will need to mate with at least three males of your species and produce offspring from each union."

"I cannot! I must get back to my consort!" She tried to open a vortex. Nothing happened, and she turned horrified eyes to Ash. "What have you done?"

Ash smiled. "I've merely ensured that you remain home and help your people. The collar, unfortunately for you, can only be removed by me personally. When the time is right, I will bring you with me to defeat that island and those that think they can protect it. Until then, be a good V'ran, and help your own people. Who knows, you might find that you enjoy sex with your own kind better than the perversions you are currently fascinated with."

Chapter One Hundred Seventy-One

EARTH DIMENSION THREE
Mystic Haven, B.C., Canada

BAYLEN PICKED UP ALI, and she gasped and wrapped her arm around his neck. "What are you doing? I can walk!"

"I'll carry you." Baylen's voice was hoarse, his hands tight around her.

She narrowed her eyes. "You need to have a word with the Wards."

Caden studied Baylen for a long moment. "Are you hurt, Aliora?"

She looked at Caden and smiled. "I'm fine."

Baylen made a choked noise and shot up into the air. Ali clung to him for dear life and frowned.

"Are you okay, Aliora?" Caden sent her a mind link.

"I'm fine. Baylen seems to be a little shaken up. Listen, can you check out those Wards. They didn't help me at all."

"I'm on it, and I'm only a mind link away if you need me," Caden replied. *"Come into the station tomorrow, and we'll file a report."*

She thought that, by the time they were done with the healers, Baylen would have calmed down, but no. The look on his face only showed that he'd grown angrier.

"Ali." His voice was dark as he strode into his bedroom and dropped her on his bed.

She scooted off the massive bed. "Baylen."

"I'm going to spank your ass."

She paused, and her eyes narrowed. "The hell you are."

He stalked her and she backed up. "I don't know why you are being such a jerk. It wasn't like I had a choice. The Wards weren't doing anything! I couldn't just stand there."

A dark growl rumbled from his chest. "I told you to get the hell up into the air!"

She stared at him for a minute, shook her head, and lifted her hand, golden magic spilling from it and the black leathers she wore were replaced by a navy-blue medieval gown covered in sparkly crystals. "The Wards were not engaging."

"You fucking let that bitch live! She can find you!"

Ali's mouth dropped open. "Excuse me?"

He grabbed the neckline off her dress and tore it in two. She gasped. "Baylen!"

"You can call me king, or my lord, or master, but by the Creators, you are fucking going to learn to obey me."

"Oh, I don't think so."

He'd never known such fury in his life. His mind kept stuttering over the knowledge that Wisteria knew how to find her. *Oh, gods. No. No. No.* He clenched his fists in the torn edges of her dress and pulled her closer. "You could have been killed! What do you think would have fucking happened if you'd died?"

Ali stilled and watched Baylen, she could see the darkness growing in him, and it struck her that he was terrified. For her. The darkness inside him was feeding off his fear and his anger. She could not allow that to happen.

"Get on your knees, Aliora!" He fisted her hair.

She went to her knees, not because she was afraid, she wasn't. She was determined. The darkness would not steal him from her. There were many ways to fight battles for the soul, and her light was more than capable of vanquishing the darkness that sought to destroy Baylen. That seed of darkness Wisteria had placed in him would not prevail. Not ever. How many mornings had she fought the darkness with him? This was no different.

He tilted back her head, his eyes hard. "Never has a mate tried me so fucking hard. I won't lose you too, Ali."

"I'm here, Bay."

He reached over and touched something on the wall behind her and it slid away. She twisted to look. "You have a secret room? Is it a library?" Her voice was excited, but she couldn't help it. She'd always wanted a secret library!

Baylen growled, and the next thing she knew, he'd yanked her to her feet and tossed her over his shoulder. She gasped and his hand landed hard on her uptilted ass. "Ow!"

The hidden door slid closed behind them, and Fae orbs began to float all around them. Baylen moved confidently down the stairs and into a room filled with things that she'd only ever read about. When he set her on her feet, her eyes werehuge. "Uhm, this doesn't look like a library."

His eyes met hers and she could see he was still angry. *Light. Light. She was light.*

"Take off the dress, Aliora Aurelius."

She wrinkled her nose. Dang it, he'd used her full name. She shrugged out of the ruined dress. "You owe me for that."

"That sass is only going to get you into more trouble."

She almost shrugged, but the look on his face stopped her. She decided it might be wise not to push too hard.

"Take off the rest."

She tilted her head, maybe it was a good thing to learn how deep his darkness went. She stripped off her bra and panties.

"On your knees."

Wow, he was going to get the 'go fuck yourself' mug for a long time. She knelt.

"In here, you will call me my king."

Her eyebrow rose. "You're not my—"

His fingers closed over her nipple, and he pinched hard enough to make her gasp. *She wasn't going to bake him brownies this week!*

His hand reached out and tilted up her chin, his voice hard. "Do you understand?"

She nodded.

"That's not going to do. You've racked up another punishment for yourself."

She inhaled and let her breath out slowly, rubbing her ear. "I understand."

"Biting will add more to your punishment. You understand what?"

She flashed her fangs. "I understand, my king."

His eyes stared into hers, his face cut from stone. Reaching down, his hand under her elbow he helped her to stand and walked her over to a chain dangling from the ceiling with a pair of leather cuffs attached to it. Silently, he buckled them around her wrists and began to pull the chain back until her arms were stretched above her and she was on her tiptoes. She could easily have gotten free, such were her powers, but she remained. "It's a little cold in here."

Baylen nodded and strode over to the fireplace. A little zap of Fae energy and a fire lit up the darkness. A few more Fae orbs floated around her.

He walked over to a large shelving unit and opened the doors. Interior lights flickered on, and she could see all kinds of things that she had never seen before, but possibly read about. "Don't we have to sign a contract or something for this?"

He turned to look at her, his eyes hard. "That's another one."

"My king." She swallowed. *Man, he was taking this seriously.*

"This isn't fifty shades. This isn't some fictional fantasy. How many times am I going to smack your ass, Aliora?"

She blinked. "Uhm? Once?"

His eyebrow rose. "You just added another smack so let's count. "One for just now." He gave her a dark look.

She blinked. Oh, damn, she'd forgotten to say *my king* again. She wrinkled her nose.

"Two is for the minute before when you forgot to say my king, three is for your first stubborn refusal. You also have three swats coming for the danger you put yourself in. The total is six smacks on your ass." He turned to look at her, something sparkly dangling from his fingers. "That total is fluid. If you keep defying me, the total will go up. You will keep score. If you fib to me when I ask, the total will go up by two for every single missed number. Do you understand me, Aliora?" He picked up a paddle.

Aliora swallowed, her eyes huge. "Yes, my king."

"How many times am I going to smack your ass?"

"Six." Her eyes got even bigger as she hastened to add. "My king."

"What's your safe word?" He started back towards her.

"Red, my king." her voice was quiet. Her determination, stronger. No matter how deep the darkness that drove him, it would never be able to extinguish the light.

He circled her, his hand trailing over her body. She bit her lip, her breath catching as his fingers gently tugged on her nipple. A second later, his fingers trailed over her mound and slipped between her feminine folds to circle her clit. She moaned softly, and he looked into her eyes a dark half smile playing over his lips.

She shivered, recognizing the darkness in his eyes. He moved behind her, and she cried out at the loss of his touch. A moment later, his hand trailed down her back, his hands smoothing over her ass. "You have a beautiful ass, Aliora." A whisper in her ear. "Remember, this is about obedience."

Her eyebrow rose and she wanted to rub her ear so badly. *No, no. She was fighting battles, not running.* His fingers traced her ear as if he'd heard her thoughts, a shadow caress over the slope, a barely there touch to the tip.

"Let me see you, Aliora."

She closed her eyes and let go of the first layer of her glamour.

He stroked her energy wings. "Very pretty, but you added to your punishment."

Her eyes flew open. "Why?"

"That's two."

She took a deep breath. "Why, my king."

"You feel that is unjust?"

Aliora blinked. "I let my glamour go, my king."

He circled back around to face her, and she could see the fury in his eyes. His hand closed around her throat, a firm reminder of his control. "You fucking have been hiding yourself from me this whole time. I saw you! I fucking saw you when you were facing off with that psycho bitch. Now, let go of your fucking glamour."

She swallowed, hyper aware of his hand around her throat. He wasn't hurting her. In fact, she was certain he was being very careful. This was a show of dominance. She was surprised to feel herself responding to it. *Am I aroused by this? No. I can't be.* Her nipples were hard, and she really, *really* wanted his fingers back on her clit. Her eyes widened. *I am!*

"Three Aliora"

"Are we up to nine?" She squeaked.

His eyes glinted, his hand tightening a fraction.

"I—"

"Careful."

She swallowed against the warmth of his hand and let her glamour fade. His eyes moved over her, everything clicking into place, every species that had contributed to her DNA. Long curly hair the true colors of the sunset, deep purples, oranges, reds, gold. Nymph. Eyes that spoke of her Mer and Elf heritage, water, and earth, aquamarine with striated bronze and gold rings,glowing sparks filling their depths. The delicately pointed ears could be Elf or Fae or even Pixie, but those fangs with that temper were pure Sprite. Fae energy wings that shimmered with brilliant colors, purple, blue, gold, every other color in between, and the darkness of the universe lit by tiny sparkles of golden light. Her skin was the pale blue of a Pixie, her nipples a deep navy. His gaze moved down over her curvy body, his cock twitching as he noticed the tight curls that hid her sex were the same rich color as her hair. Deep purples, oranges, reds, gold. He liked it. He lifted his eyes to her face again and noticed her features had taken on a decidedly Fae cast and she smelled like fucking heaven. He leaned in and growled as her scent wrapped around him. She was his mate and by the fucking creators he was hers. This utterly unique woman belonged to him, and she'd lied to him about that too.

His eyes wandered over her one more time, and he paused as it all came together in his mind. Ali was a Changeling Fae. A race of Fae thought to be extinct.

"Aliora, am I your mate?"

She swallowed, her eyes large.

"Remember, sweet little Changeling, that anything but the truth is going to add to your punishment."

He knew. She could see it in his eyes. He knew what she was, and he knew that he was her mate. Her secrets were revealed to The King of the Fae. She licked suddenly dry lips. "Yes, my king."

"Yes, what?"

Her heart was beating hard in her chest. "Yes, you are my mate, my king." Her words were a quiet whisper in the darkness, a light shining in the cold blackness of his life.

He released her throat and stepped back. His eyes were dark and unreadable, and he turned to pick up two sparkling objects before turning back to her. "Punishment, then pleasure. How many times am I going to smack your ass, Aliora?"

She swallowed and nibbled her bottom lip. "Nine times, my king?"

He shook his head. "Eleven Aliora. You've lied about who you are to me, and what you are."

"Bay—"

His hand closed around her neck again. "Do. Not." This time she saw his rage. "I am your king and you have denied me for far too long." He stepped back. Her heart ached, but she was a warrior fighting for her mate. She knew that, as angry as he was, Baylen would never harm her.

A moment later he tugged on her nipple, and something pinched down on it. She cried out and his hand closed around her throat. Not hard, but enough to remind her that he was in control.

"Shh, Aliora." His fingers moved to her other nipple. The pinch came a moment later, and she tried not to cry out, but damn it, that hurt.

"Shh." His thumb rubbing over her bottom lip. "First punishment, then pleasure. Understand?"

She swallowed. "Yes, my king."

His hand moved down her body, a slow sensual caress that made her catch her breath. He parted her folds, his eyes holding hers, and began to circle her clit. She gasped, her hips arching. His tongue swept over his lower lip, and her eyes tracked the movement. A soft cry spilled from her lips when he gently pinched her clit. His finger circled again, and again, taking her right to the brink before he stepped back.

Her chest heaving, she groaned, staring at him in dismay. His expression betrayed nothing as he watched her grapple with the thought of begging him to touch her again. He moved behind her, his hands stroking over her exposed flesh. She inhaled sharply as pleasure surged through her veins. The hard slap of the paddle against her ass was both shocking and painful. She cried out.

"Count, Aliora."

"One, my king." The paddle struck again. She scrunched her eyes closed, her muscles tensing. "Two, my king."

His hand moved over her burning flesh. "Relax, Aliora."

The paddle connected with her ass again. Her cry was louder this time. "Three, my king." His hand stroked the red mark and she gasped. Another hard slap against her burning flesh "Four, my king."

His fingers clasped her hip and moved around her and lifted her chin. "You're alright." He cupped her pussy, his fingers parting her folds and seeking the dampness within. "You're wet." He circled her clit. "Open your eyes."

She lifted her eyelashes, knowing he could see the threatening tears. His dark eyes searched hers. "You risked your life, Aliora. As your king, I will not allow that." The fingers on his other hand traced over her clamped nipples, tugged gently as he circled her clit again and again until her cries filled the room. Pain and pleasure all tangled up together. He stopped and studied her for a moment. "I'm not seeing remorse, Aliora."

To be honest, what she was feeling had nothing to do with remorse, but she didn't think she better say that to him. He turned away for a moment, and when he turned back to her, there was a look in his eyes that left a fluttery feeling in her stomach. He reached for her nipple, and she felt him do something to the clamp. She looked down but his hand covered what he was doing. She glanced back up into his eyes, as he fiddled with the second clamp. Then his mouth was on hers, his tongue surging into her mouth as he let go of the clamps. A pained cry burst from her lips only to be swallowed up by the voracious kiss. His hand fisted in her hair, and he slowly ended the kiss. "Look." His voice was a sinful whisper. She glanced down as he stepped back. He'd attached tiny weights to the clamps. She whimpered and he lifted her chin. "You risked your life, Aliora. When you risk your life, you risk mine. You risk the Fae." His hand went back to her pussy. He stroked her, circled her clit. Pushing two fingers into her, he curved them, and she gasped as he hit a spot she'd hadn't even known existed. He rubbed it and she started to shake. "Punishment before pleasure." He whispered against her lips and took a step back, his fingers leaving her body. She gasped. "No! my king."

His lips quirked up. "Good save. If you need me to stop, use your safe word." He moved around behind her.

Did she want him to stop? The paddle landed hard, and she jerked, causing her breasts to bounce and the clamps to pull against her tender flesh. She cried out and his voice whispered in her ear as his breath ghosted over her neck. "Count, Aliora."

"Five, my king." a tear escaped, but at the same time she wanted nothing more than to come. She wanted his fingers back inside her, she wanted him to touch her clit. She could feel the dampness between her thighs. The paddle struck again. Her breath caught at the fiery sting and a second later, the sharp bite of the nipple clamps as the weights bounced. Another tear sliding down her cheek. "Six, my king." *Maybe she was a deviant?* Baylen's hand smoothing over her back and her burning ass. She wanted those fingers somewhere else. Her hips arched.

"The next two are going to be fast and hard." His voice was a dark breath against her ear, his fingers trailing a light caress over her wings. She shivered, her nipples hardening impossibly more. He delivered two fast hard smacks that tore a short scream from her lips. "Seven, my king. Eight, my king." she couldn't prevent the tears or the hoarseness of her voice.

He moved around her, his fingers gently lifting her chin. "Good, Aliora. Only three more to go." He kissed her, a soft slide of his lips over hers. "Open your eyes." His thumbs wiped her tears away as he studied her. She wanted to beg him to touch her. She wanted to beg him to let her come. His fingers moved between her legs, cupping her damp swollen pussy, before sliding between her folds. "You're so wet, Aliora." His voice was rough. She stared into his eyes, her tongue slicking over her bottom lip. He tilted his head. "Safe word?"

She shook her head. "No, my king." The look in his eyes sent shivers over her body.

"I don't think stubborn has ever looked so sexy." He eased two fingers inside her and curved them, she gasped, and he smiled, the look in his eyes burning with lust. His fingers slid over that spot again and she cried out, her hips jerking forward. "Easy. We're not done yet." He stroked again, her breath caught, her whole body shaking. "Easy." He eased his fingers from her and stepping back he circled her, slowly. Unable to help himself, he slid his hand into her hair and kissed her hard, his fingers toying with her clit, then sliding back inside her. She gasped, her voice a high-pitched little cry as he found that spot again. "That's it, Aliora. That's it. Hold on. Just like that. Don't go over." His eyes burned into hers as he slowly removed his fingers from inside her and moved back. She stared at him, her breasts heaving, the bite of the weighted nipple clamps and the burning sting of her ass only adding to the overload of sensations rioting through her. "Do you want to say your safe word?"

"No." Her voice was a raspy whisper.

"Remember, no coming, Aliora." He moved behind her and she heard a soft buzz just before he pressed something deep inside her. She stiffened, going to the tips of her toes. "Baylen!" Her voice was a wail of shocked pleasure. His arm wrapped around her waist and pulled her back against him. She could feel the hard on he was sporting pressing against her.

"No coming, Aliora. Punishment first. That's our agreement." His voice was a harsh rough demand.

She whimpered as his fingers pushed the object against that spot. "Oh, gods! Oh, gods! Oh, gods!"

He eased his fingers from her, leaving her panting and fighting to control the orgasm that was threatening to burst over her.

The paddle struck and she cried out. The pain and pleasure so incredibly twisted together that she didn't know one from the other. "Nine, my king!" Her voice was a high wavering moan. The next followed swiftly. "Ten, my king!" a shriek. The third one landed across the last two and she screamed. "Eleven, my king." Tears were running down her face, her nipples felt as if they were on fire, and that damned thing inside her was buzzing away against that spot, and she desperately needed to come. "Please, my king! I can't—I need to—"

"Do. Not. Come. Aliora." His voice hard, giving no mercy.

She fought for control. "Please! I need to come! Please!" Dimly in the back of her mind she heard the paddle hit the floor. Baylen's arm wrapped around her waist again and his fingers slid easily into her wet pussy. She whimpered and jerked against him.

"Do not come, Aliora." His voice was strained, spoken between his teeth. "Do not fucking come."

He eased the toy from inside her, letting it drop to the floor, and in the next moment his cock slid deep, and she screamed.

"Come!" A hard command against her neck, his arm a band of steel around her hips as he thrust wildly. His cock pistoning in and out of her pussy. His other hand curved around her throat, and she shattered, her whole body convulsing over and over as his seed jetted hot and hard deep inside her.

When it was finally over, she leaned limply against him gasping for breath. He straightened, his arm still wrapped around her. "I'm going to remove those clamps. It's going to sting." He worked quickly, and hell yes it stung. Then he swung her into his arms and climbed the stairs with her.

Once back in his bedroom, he laid her on his bed and crawled in behind her. He turned her to face him and brushed the tears still dampening her face away. "You're incredible, Ali. Are you alright?" He lifted her chin and stared down into her beautiful eyes.

Ali laughed. "That was amazing, and you're still not my king."

"Why?"

"Finally, you ask." She reached up and brushed a lock of hair back that had fallen over his cheek. "Baylen, you are the Fae king. You hold an incredible amount of power, but in our relationship that power cannot exist. We both must have the ability and safety to be ourselves, and to communicate openly and honestly with each other. We both must have the right to say no. If you pull the king card, I am left with no choices. That's not safe for either of us. I want you to have the freedom to be fully yourself, and I want the same freedom for me. We won't always agree and that's okay. Respect for each other's thoughts, feelings and opinions is essential though. I need to feel safe with you in all areas and I want to give you the same safety.

Baylen watched her silently for a moment. "What about what we just did in my playroom?"

Aliora smiled. "I liked that walk on the wild side, but it's not something I am going to agree to everyday. Variety is the spice of life."

Baylen laughed. Her eyes were already drifting closed. He held her close, gently stroking his hand down her back. "Sleep. Just sleep now."

Chapter One Hundred Seventy-Two

LEVI STOOD WATCHING the ocean, a light breeze blowing his long blond hair. He watched as a couple gave him wary looks, before walking well around him, and he knew why. The hardness of his eyes, the scars that marked him, and his shimmering white wings, heavily marbled with the black feathers that warned of his dangerous dance with the darkness. Not that he cared what anyone thought. He'd survived his battles.

Caden arrived first, and seconds later The Fae King. Levi nodded to them both. "I have news that you need to hear."

Caden nodded. "What's the news Levi."

"The vortex that we used to send Wisteria to the Creators never arrived."

"What do you mean?" The Fae King's voice was tight.

Levi looked at him and knew him to be a man who stood on the razor's edge of good and evil. Light and darkness. The unimaginable power this man contained could decimate the world.

"The vortex was intercepted before it could reach the In-Between, where the Creator's reside. Neither Rune nor Eliana saw it."

Caden swore.

"Wisteria is alive and free?" Baylen forced the words out as if a great stone lay on his chest. Nightmare images of Jadeah and Charli's broken bodies filled his mind.

Levi watched him silently for a moment before inclining his head. "My host is searching for any lingering energy that could tell us where she went."

"Baylen. We will find her. I swear we'll find her." Caden met the Fae king's eyes.

"No. She will find us. Find me. As she's always done." Baylen shot up into the air, his powerful wings carrying him rapidly from their sight.

"Fuck! Fuck! Fuck!" Caden grabbed a huge drift log from the beach and slammed it into the ocean.

Levi touched his arm. "We will find her." He launched into the air, streaking straight up. His host awaited him, and they had much to do.

Caden stood alone on the beach, the wind blowing his hair, and he wondered if any of them would survive.

Chapter One Hundred Seventy-Three

EARTH DIMENSION THREE
Mystic Haven, B.C., Canada

THEY DROPPED THE CHILDREN off at school, and Baylen drove them here to her home. She made them coffee and they sat at the table drinking it. Ali was all too aware of how quiet Baylen had been since the day he'd met with Caden, and the shadows in his eyes that he refused to talk about, but he'd stayed close to her. They'd played games with the kids, and after the kids were asleep, he'd taken her in so many ways, and he'd woken her up over and over again all through the night. There'd been an urgency to him that she hadn't understood.

"Is everything alright, Bay?"

He looked up at her and gave her a half smile, but she could see the darkness in his eyes.

"Would you like to sit in the sunlight?"

He shook his head but stood and walked over to stare out her patio doors at the ocean.

She rose to her feet and went to him, knowing that something was wrong. "Baylen. Talk to me. What's wrong?"

He turned to her and drew her into his arms, his mouth settled over hers in the most tender kiss he'd ever given her. Drawing back, his eyes met hers and he stroked his hand across her cheek. She tried to understand the churning emotion in the depths of his eyes, but he leaned his forehead against hers, his arms tight around her.

"Baylen. Please. What's wrong?"

He started backing her towards her bedroom. "I can't get enough of you, Ali." He pulled her dress off and dropped it on the floor, her bra went next, by the time he picked her up and set her on the bed, he'd stripped her naked. His clothes quickly followed. His hands moved slowly over her. His touch gentle, as he pressed kisses over her entire body. Slow and easy, he brought her to orgasm after orgasm, showing her erogenous zones that she'd never known of. Loving her gently, as if she was the most precious person on the planet. As the day passed, his loving became more urgent, more intense. At one point, she rolled on top of him and stared into his eyes, her finger stroking over his cheekbones, love swelling in her heart. Tingles moved through her finger and found a mysterious circuit directly to her clit, and he rolled with her. She ended up underneath him, his weight pressing her into the mattress as his cock slid deep into her pussy. "I need you, Ali." His eyes stared into hers with such intensity that a shiver worked its way over her body.

"Have me, Baylen," she whispered. "Have all of me." She let her glamour go, hiding nothing from him.

"My beautiful little Changeling. I don't deserve you." But he let his glamour go too. The passion burned bright, a conflagration that nothing could stop. The mystery of two Fae loving each other in their natural state when all things were possible, when claims could be made, when hearts could be bound. She'd never seen Baylen like this. The urgency, the passion, and his determination to take it slow. It was killing her. "Baylen! Please. Please. my king."

His eyes glinted with sudden humor, and he nipped her lip. "Now, you voluntarily say it." He grew serious, his eyes dark and tormented as he took her mouth in a tender kiss. She could almost touch his emotion, it was so thick in the air. His Fae magic moved over her body, and she cried out, arching helplessly. His fingers eased between her folds, and he stroked her clit. She shattered in an explosive orgasm that swept him up in its ecstasy, his cries echoing hers as his seed splashed deep inside her. With a final kiss, he rose from the bed and dressed. Ali sat up. "Is it time to pick up the kids?" She started to move off the bed but his hand on her shoulder stopped her.

"No, Ali."

"No?" She tilted her head.

He took a deep breath and started to walk toward the door. His hand was on the doorknob when he spoke again. "You need to leave this island, Ali."

"What?" She froze staring at his back.

"Leave Mystic Haven. Find a man to love and have babies with him."

She started to shake. "Baylen? You're my—"

He shook his head, not looking at her. "No. I'm not. I can't be. This is over." And he walked out of her life.

Chapter One Hundred Seventy-Four

EARTH DIMENSION THREE
Mystic Haven, B.C., Canada

THE TEARS WOULDN'T stop. She couldn't stop crying. She couldn't stop the grief. It hurt to move. She felt like she was a million years old. And she was alone.

Everything inside of her was empty. The darkness was all around her. How long had it been since she'd seen the light? How long since she'd been warm? She moved through her home in silence, a ghost that still lived. Haunted by her memories.

She stood in front of her patio doors and saw the first rays of dawn's light begin to break through the darkness and she longed to feel the warmth, but she was terrified to step outside. If she went into the sun, if she swam in the sea, the pain would continue. She wanted it to stop. She needed it to stop.

"Aliora?" A voice in the darkness of her house. She ignored it, staring out at the dawn.

"Ali, what's happened?" Warm hands on her shoulders turning her around. She found herself staring into Caden's concerned face. He tried to brush away the tears that she couldn't stop from flowing. Then he swung her up into his arms and walked out onto her patio, sitting down on her porch swing with her still in his arms. "Ali, we're going to sit here in the sunlight together. Tell me what's happened. Did someone hurt you?"

Did it count when your heart had been torn out of you? She shivered violently. Caden grabbed the soft blanket on the seat beside them and wrapped it around her. "I think I better get you to a healer."

She began to shake her head back and forth. "No! No. I can't."

"Shh." He hugged her close, his arms wrapped around her. "It's okay, Ali. I'll call Baylen."

She began to sob, shaking her head. "He—He told me to leave."

"Leave?" Caden frowned. "Did you have a fight?"

"No. He said it's over."

Caden could feel fury begin to burn inside him. "When did this happen?"

Ali looked at the cop who had always treated her like a little sister. "Monday."

"Creators, Aliora, it's Friday. Have you been alone all this time?"

She nodded, lifting a shaking hand to push her hair back.

"Have you eaten anything?"

Another shake of her head.

"Have you called anyone?"

She huddled against him and didn't answer. He sent out a mind link. *"Shirina, I need you to come to Aliora's right away."*

He stood up and set Aliora on the porch swing. "I'm going to make tea and get you something to eat. Stay here in the sun." But when he got up to go into the kitchen, she followed him like a little lost waif. *He was going to kill a Fae king. He was going to fucking kill him.*

He saw Aliora's laptop sitting on the island, and he opened it. "Login for me, Ali." He turned the laptop, so it was in front of where she stood silently watching him.

After getting the tea water started, he checked the laptop and was relieved to see that she'd logged in. He clicked on the video chat icon and pulled out a stool, picked Ali up and set her on the stool. Then he got a mug out of the cupboard and found her stash of tea. Tea bag in the cup, sugar, and he poured in the boiling water. He set the tea in front of her and scrolled through her contacts until he came to her family's chat. It was a godawful time to call anyone, but that couldn't be helped. He hit the connect icon.

"Don't."

He looked at Ali, her messy hair, her too pale face, her tear swollen eyes. "You need your family, Aliora."

The computer rang and a blonde Elf answered. "Hello Al—You're not Ali. Who are you? You're a police officer?" Her eyes moved over Caden taking in his uniform. "Why are you on my granddaughter's laptop? Is she alright?"

"Caden Brody. I'm the chief of police. Ali is safe but I think she needs her family." He looked over at Aliora. "Ready?"

She was shaking her head, but he turned the laptop anyway.

"Aliora." It was the grandmother's voice, deeply concerned. "What's happened?" She glanced away from the screen for a moment at the sound of a door closing. "Edge, we need to go see Aliora, right away. Make the arrangements." Looking back, she gave her granddaughter a gentle smile. "Talk to me."

A knock sounded on the front door and Caden went to answer it. Shirina stepped inside and Caden explained what was going on. They went to the kitchen and Shirina introduced herself to Ali's grandmother and hugged Aliora. "I'm going to make you something to eat, Ali."

Caden nodded to Shirina. "I'll be back."

Chapter One Hundred Seventy-Five

CADEN STALKED UP TO the Fae castle, and with a wave of his hand slammed the massive, Ward protected, door open. He walked into the majestic entryway and when Fae guards came running, he knocked them flying with a roiling surge of Guardian empowered Fae energy. His senses led him through the castle and out into the backyard. Not that it could be called a yard. It was hundreds of acres in size. Baylen stood watching the sunrise, his arms crossed over his chest.

"Knight." Caden's voice carried across the space, and Baylen turned as Caden moved faster than any super ever could. He grabbed Baylen by the collar and slammed him back into a massive tree.

"What the Fuck! Back the hell up cop, or I'll tear you apart."

Caden laughed, the sound filled with a dangerously hard edge. "You have never seen the day when you could tear me apart. I am the Guardian, and my purpose is to take you out if you ever step fully into that darkness you play with—And I fucking will."

Baylen punched him.

Caden simply planted his feet apart and hit back. Two hard punches to the face. Baylen staggered as Jett and Striker came running out, and Caden flung out a blast of Fae energy that sent them both flying backwards.

He picked up Baylen by the throat. "You hurt her! You hurt the gentlest person on this island. After all that she has done for you! I want to kill you right now!" He flung Baylen down on the ground and sent another wave of Fae energy to block the Trium and guards.

"It's not your fucking business!"

"The hell it isn't! Aliora is my friend."

"Then protect her, Guardian." Baylen rose to his feet barely keeping his temper in check. "Keep her the fuck away from me. You fucking know that I have powerful enemies who will destroy her."

"You're a fool, Baylen. You don't see what is right in front of you."

Baylen touched the back of his hand to the cut on his cheek. He could already feel his eye swelling. "I may be a fool, but at least she's alive."

"For how long?"

Baylen's eyes met Caden's. "Longer than if she was with me."

Caden shook his head. "Until one of your enemies discovers she's your mate, and you are not there to protect her. Until one of them see's that you love her."

"They won't discover anything. I'm not going near her again."

"You carry her mark. Even with your glamour, I can see it."

Baylen swore and stormed into the house. Yanking open the nearest bathroom door, he stalked inside to the mirror. Fuck. Light clung to him in the form of tiny stars trailing across his cheekbone. They shimmered iridescent gold in the light, and he'd never seen anything like it. His mind went to the last time he'd seen her, the last time he'd made love to her. Her finger ghosting along his cheek. He knew she hadn't done it on purpose. She'd been as caught up in the intensity of the moment as he'd been. He turned and walked back into the yard to face Caden.

"Wisteria will destroy her."

"She already dealt with Wisteria. Too bad you don't see that. You hurt her again, Baylen, and I'm coming for you." It was a warning given by the Guardian, and Baylen knew he was deadly serious.

"Get her off this island, Caden."

Chapter One Hundred Seventy-Six

EARTH DIMENSION THREE
Mystic Haven, B.C., Canada

THE ROYAL TRIUM STOOD silently and listened as the massive wooden door of the castle slammed shut behind Caden. Before any of them could say anything, they saw a shift in the air and before them Edge de Fae appeared. He was a massive man, standing well over six feet tall, and heavily muscled. His long red hair hung in a straight sheet to his waist. Power clung to him like a second skin. Beside him, his wife, Ciska. The richness of her Elven magic was like an intoxicating scent in the air.

Jett growled. "What the hell has happened to the Wards around this Castle!"

Edge raised his eyebrows. "This is a private meeting, Protector."

Baylen crossed his arms and glared at the couple before looking at Jett and Striker. He nodded once. They turned and stalked away, Jett muttering that he was going to phone Shirina to come back and run another check on the bloody castle Wards.

"What can I do for you de Fae?" Baylen was fucking done.

"We came to check out our granddaughter's—man?"

Baylen knew he'd been insulted. They were not acknowledging him as their king, they were not acknowledging him as a Fae, and they were not acknowledging him as Aliora's mate. Fuck, that question mark at the end of the sentence even cast aspersions on his manhood. His eyes met Edge's, and after a long cold stare, he turned his gaze on Ciska. "You came to the wrong place."

"No." Ciska walked over to him. "That's her mark. An Elf only marks for love. Not like you Fae who glow at the moment you even get in the near vicinity of your mate."

Ouch. That was a lot of disdain. Baylen shifted uncomfortably

"Or bond them to you the first time you have sex." Ciska threw a look at Edge.

Edge frowned. "She's never going to let me live that down."

"Why are you here? You're not her parents." Baylen was feeling pissy. *Fuck this shit. He'd done what he needed to do.*

"Of course not, Boyo." Edge said. "We're her grandparents. Be thankful that it's us that showed up, because if her father knew, he would do everything in his power to destroy you." Edge shook his head. "Caden contacted us, and we caught a ride with an Angel that owed me a favor. You hurt our girl."

Baylen crossed his arms.

"It's not Edge you'll be dealing with." Ciska spoke up, and Baylen jerked his gaze to her. "You're his king, but you sure as hell are not mine. You will answer to me."

Baylen glared. "I answer to no one."

Ciska laughed. "You sure about that? I would say that Guardian can make you answer." She waved at his cut and bruised face. "I've never seen a Fae king, or a Guardian, like the two of you. But I know that there are always checks and balances. That's how the Creators do things. You're a dangerous, dangerous Fae, Baylen Knight. You're black as sin, and your power is off the charts. The damage you could do is unfathomable, but that Guardian?" Ciska shook her head. "He's your balance, the check if you go to the darkness that you like to hide in. The risk is great. But—may the Creators help us if he ever goes bad. Who stops a Guardian?"

Baylen stared down at the small Elven woman before him filled with a sense of shock that someone who was not a Fae could see what he was, that she could see what Caden was. "I guess you've put me in my place."

Ciska shook her head. "Baylen, you need the light. You will self-destruct if you don't open your heart to the light. A Fae cannot survive in darkness."

Baylen looked away. "Sometimes there's no choice."

"There's always a choice, Baylen."

"I need the darkness to stop evil. I need the darkness to protect my people."

"A lie told by the evil one. Do you embrace it? Is it worth your soul? What of your children? What of my granddaughter? Would you be their destroyer?"

Baylen gave her a look of utter anguish and shot up into the sky.

Ciska sighed and turned to her husband. He wrapped his arms around her, holding her close. "He needs our Ali."

"Desperately."

Chapter One Hundred Seventy-Seven

EARTH DIMENSION THREE
Mystic Haven, B.C., Canada

A BARE SLIVER OF MOON hung in the velvet night sky surrounded by an untold number of stars and Baylen didn't know where he was flying, or even how long he'd been flying. He didn't know what to do. *Had he embraced the darkness that was inside him?* He knew he'd welcomed the darkness when he killed those wizards, just as he knew that he should've involved Caden and the police. Yet, as the Fae king, it was his call to make. He had the power to sentence death to any evil being that came after his people. He had the power to enact that sentence. But he hadn't even considered anything beyond his pain and his need to avenge Jadeah. *What did that make him? Was he a murderer?*

His heart stuttered. He slowed to a hover and stared down at the earth beneath him. He knew his power was vast. The darkness in him tempted him daily to use his powers. If he turned to the darkness completely, would Caden be powerful enough to stop him? Could The Ward stop him? If he turned to the darkness, would his Trium also turn?

His heart pounded in his chest he flew to The Ward, knowing it could detect evil. He landed and started walking through the forest The Ward inhabited, knowing full well that he could be walking to his death, and maybe that was a good thing.

He walked for a few minutes before he saw the shimmering gold of The Ward and the iridescence of the strange new Mist Ward that Ali had created. He hesitated. *Maybe he shouldn't do this?* His heart thudding in his chest, he took a step forward. Risk or not, he had to know.

Another step, he could hear his breathing. Sweat broke out on his forehead. His mouth grew suddenly dry. He took another step and the two Wards swept around him. *How long had it been since he communed with The Ward?* His breath left him. Not since before Jadeah's death. So many years. Yes, he'd opened the Season of Light and taken his kids. Yes, he spoke to The Ward during dangerous situations, but he'd avoided the deep communication his people had with the Wards.

His eyes teared up, and he bowed his head. *Gods.* The Ward had saved him, had connected with him, had helped him to defeat Wisteria the first time.

Images began to tumble through his mind. The Ward communicating with him, though he did not deserve it. The image of a dark night sky filled with stars. "Baylen, King of the Fae, glory of the night sky."

Baylen laughed quietly and sent The Ward an image of Ali.

The Ward returned an image of light. "The light that cannot be defeated."

"Yeah. She is light. She's good, and gentle, and kind." He tried to send images of all those things.

The Ward urged the other iridescent Ward forward. A mist shimmered in the air and reached out to him. As it touched him, he heard words in his mind.

"Wherever there is light, darkness takes flight. To remain, would only lead to its destruction. The darkness has no power over the light. Light must be your source, Baylen Knight, King of the Fae. It's your power and your heart, it's justice and forgiveness, it's now and the future. Love, faith, and hope. It's your vanguard. Light advances before you and shows you the way. Light seeks out your enemies and secures the land. No matter how deep the darkness, Baylen Knight, light will prevail."

As the Wards retreated, the forest filled with the ancient lullaby that had once saved his life.

If the darkness should arrive,
Let the light be your guide.
Even one small glimmer of light
Pierces the blackest night
When there is only darkness,
we will be the light.
Light remains.
Seek the light,
Find your way.

Chapter One Hundred Seventy-Eight

EARTH DIMENSION THREE
Mystic Haven, B.C., Canada

BAYLEN STOOD IN THE darkened woods after the Wards left, completely numb. The darkness was so deep without even the moon to bring light. He lifted his hand and couldn't even see it. He hated these particular woods. The place where Wisteria had poured her foul magic. The place where he'd lost his soul, the place where The Ward, a creature of light and goodness had almost died.

"The place where you almost died." A richly feminine voice spoke, and he whirled around, Fae energy cloaking him. "Show yourself!"

A laugh filled with gentleness—and a power so terrifying it caused his glamour to fail. "Perhaps, Baylen Knight, it is you who should show yourself."

He shifted, alert for any movement, a dangerous primal being searching the darkness for the danger hidden in its depths.

"That is the problem with darkness, Baylen. You think you can hide in it. That it protects you. But the longer you remain in the darkness the more it consumes you."

The voice was closer. He turned, and out of the darkness a woman began to appear, her hair glowing with all the colors of the universe. Her eyes black and mysterious yet filled with the wonders of space. Colorful mists swirled in their depths. Baylen inhaled sharply. "Creator?"

"Eliana Aezorwyn."

Baylen stood very still. "What do you want? The Fae have no part of you."

"Many things, but nothing from you. Do not fear, though the Fae have abandoned us, we have not abandoned you."

"Why are you here?" His voice was hard, filled with an impotent fury. Eliana smiled and it was a smile so gentle that he felt a terrible rage.

"To help you, Baylen."

"I don't need help."

"I am aware that you don't believe you need help. You did reject the gift we sent you."

Baylen froze. "Gift? You sent me the gentlest being that could ever exist. You sent me someone so vulnerable that I could never protect her. You sent fodder for Wisteria."

Eliana shook her head. "We sent you light, Baylen. The light that will save you."

"Why? Why send me light? My life was created in the depths of hell. People have died because of me." His voice was a furious growl of rage and agony.

Eliana shook her head, her eyes filled with such love that he could not comprehend it, he just knew to the depths of his soul that this Creator knew everything he was. Everything. Nothing was hidden from her gaze. Every thought, every action —private or public— was revealed to her. He wanted to hide from the power of a love that saw the unvarnished, imperfect, reality of who he was, and yet, still remained.

"Has everything been hell, Baylen? Has there been no good? Has there been no sweetness, no pleasure, no love?" She tilted her head and studied him before turning and looking up at the star-studded sky. "I've studied the multiverse. I've watched the galaxies. I was there when stars were born, and planets surrounded them like a beautiful necklace that paid homage to their glory. I came to this world, and I looked upon the mountains. I saw the lakes and streams that nourish this land. I walked among its misty forests and the heat of the golden desert sands. I heard the songs of the wind and the roar of the oceans. I watched as civilizations rose. Yet there was something that this world needed desperately.

"You.

"This world needs you.

"Baylen, you are not the darkness that tried to destroy you. You're not the darkness you survived. You are not the darkness that you dared to stare in the eye and refused to submit too. You are the light that could not be defeated. You are the light that refused to surrender."

Chapter One Hundred Seventy-Nine

EARTH DIMENSION THREE
Mystic Haven, B.C., Canada

ASH CIRCLED THE BLUE planet, a smile curving his lips. Today was the beginning of the end for that cursed island that defied him. Today he knew exactly how to overcome the Fae Wards that protected that piece of land and the people who lived there.

He opened a vortex and traveled back in time to The Ward creation date. He changed his eye color, adjusted his hair color, and left it loose. He left his wings their glorious black and he stepped out of the vortex to meet the young Ward. The best part of this deception was the deception itself. Something that he excelled at. He laughed softly. Excelled was perhaps too modest. He was the master of deception, the father of lies, the beginning and end of deceit. He drew the aura of a good but hard man around himself. He painted himself as a warrior and protector. He drew in the essence of one who had given his life to protect his people, and he approached The Ward with confidence.

His goal accomplished, he returned to the present. Hovering in space he stared again at the blue planet. "Aliora, I'm coming for you."

Opening a vortex, he stepped into it and zeroed in on the woman he planned to make his queen. Seconds later he stepped out onto a beach lit with sunlight, and the woman that he sought. He studied her. She was... average he supposed. But he was a man who had a deeply personal understanding of the fact that beauty could easily hide evil. He wondered what she would look like without her glamour, but in the end he didn't care. He was not there for her beauty, he was there to take her to his most secure stronghold, far from this planet and this dimension. Where he would fuck her until she conceived his child. His son. The information he'd gleaned from Wisteria and her memories had told him much about the small woman standing in the sunlight. She was a powerhouse. An anomaly. Something that Rune and Eliana could not possibly know about. Her genetics blended with his would produce beings unstoppable by any known species. She was worthy of his seed. He watched the sunlight glitter around her and decided that he needed many sons, a whole army of sons. "Hello, Aliora."

Ali turned, startled and her mouth fell open as she stared at the beautiful being before her. He was gorgeous with his shoulder length blond hair, his ice blue eyes, and those obsidian black wings. He winked at her and she tilted her head. "What happened to you?"

"Bad things."

She saw the calculation in his eyes. "Hmm. Bad things you embraced?"

Ash grinned. This woman was intelligent. "Of course." He took her hand in his. "I'm Ash Morana, Aliora." His voice was a beautiful song of enticement. "Would you like to fly in space? It's an experience you will never forget." His voice wrapped around her with seductive intent, conjuring powerful images of sensuality and eroticism.

Chapter One Hundred Eighty

EARTH DIMENSION THREE
Mystic Haven, B.C., Canada

THE WARD SWIRLED AROUND Baylen, and he almost fell from the sky. *What the fuck?*

"Come. The Dark One has arrived."

Baylen frowned. *"Could you be any more cryptic, Ward?"*

"Ash Morana."

Baylen looked at the sky around him, scanning for any sign of the evil bastard who'd already taken one run at Mystic Haven. *"I don't see him, Ward."*

"He's here to take your mate."

"What—? What does that bastard want with Aliora?"

"Sons. An army of sons."

"What? Where the fuck is he?"

"Aliora must choose."

Baylen turned slowly and stared at The Ward. *"Choose?"* A growl rumbled through the air. *"Did you allow that fucker on this island?"*

"Of course. I've been waiting for him since my creation."

"Report to Shirina for an immediate emergency evaluation!"

"I am functioning within parameters, King of the Fae. The being Ash Morana attempted to deceive my youngest self in the same way as Wisteria Abital did. I have learned much. He is dangerous beyond most of our Warrior's abilities. At this moment he does not attack. He seeks to find a woman to bond with."

"Aliora is not that woman! She is mine!"

"You rejected her. She's free to choose another."

"No, she fucking isn't! She would never choose that evil son of a bitch! Take me to her. Now. He will kill her!"

"I have read his intent. He will not kill her. That I will not allow. Aliora must make her choice."

Fuck this shit! Baylen turned towards Mystic Haven and swept out his senses. There. She was on the beach by the wharf. Why the fuck hadn't Caden got her off this island? With a mighty sweep of his wings, he shot through the air. *"Aliora!"* Nothing. It was like his mind link bounced. *"Are you fucking blocking my mind link, Ward?"*

"Yes."

"Fuck!" He shouted and drew in his wings tightly to his body, arrowing down to the beach below him.

He landed mere feet away from Aliora and the Fallen Angel, close enough to hear the bastard's seductive words. *Fuck!* Caden and Levi landed beside him bare seconds later.

Aliora ignored Baylen and arched a delicate brow at Ash as she gently disentangled her hand from his.

"Don't you go near him, Aliora. Don't you fucking go near him." Baylen's voice was a dark growl that demanded obedience.

Men. Aliora frowned, ignoring both compulsions. "As lovely as a flight through space sounds." She glared over at Baylen for a second. "I believe the price for it would be far too high."

Ash laughed, a low masculine sound that sent shivers through her. She shook her head at him, aware that he was doing it on purpose. "Come, Aliora, a night in my bed wouldn't be a 'price to be paid.' It would be... pleasure—ecstasy." His voice sounded sinful, the look in his eyes shockingly erotic.

Baylen growled. "No. Fucking. Chance."

Ali laughed and thought hard about zapping the Fae king. "I do like darkness." She paused, glancing at Caden and Levi and winked. A low curse and a dangerous shift in Fae energy had her rolling her eyes. She stepped back and shook her head at Ash. "But I have no interest in evil."

"Good. Evil. Those are mortal constructs. Neither exist."

Ali stared at this beautiful being who exuded charm and magnetism, and she knew that, whatever else Ash Morana was, he was indeed the embodiment of evil. No matter how he disguised it. "I will not go with you, Ash. My place is here."

Ash sighed but kept his voice gentle. "What you do not understand is this is not a request. This is a fact. You are coming with me. Now, I can either make your experience pleasurable or I can make it your worst nightmare. That is the only choice you have, Aliora."

"Hold that thought. How do you know about me?"

Ash raised an eyebrow at her impertinence. "Have you met Wisteria? She's one of my creations."

Aliora's eyebrows rose. "Wisteria! She told you about me?"

"She's rather angry with you, or maybe it's more with the man who hasn't mated you yet. Her 'consort.'"

"When did she give you this information?"

"A few days ago. When I intercepted the vortex that was taking her to the 'Creators.' The light bubble was a nice touch, by the way. A fitting punishment from my queen."

Ali stared at Ash. Of course, he was the one who noticed her moment of petty vengeance. "You're saying that she never reached the Creators?"

Ash smirked at her. "I am, and of course, the Angelic host here would have reported that fact back to The Guardian and The Fae King."

Her fangs slid out. She held up a finger. "Just, uh, hold on a minute. I need to deal with something." She turned her back on Ash and marched over to Baylen. "Did you know this? Did you know Wisteria had not made it to the Creators?"

Baylen looked at her warily. "Yes."

She shed her glamour and moved so fast that he didn't have time to do more than jerk as her fangs sank into his jaw.

"Fuck! Shit!" Baylen stumbled back a step, his hand rising to cover the small bleeding puncture wounds.

She stabbed him on the chest with her forefinger. "You knew and that is why you broke up with me?" Her voice rose as she poked him again. "Answer me!"

"She'll be back, Ali. She will always come back."

"What the fuck!" Ali felt everyone's shock and she didn't care. She poked him again, harder. "I'm fully capable of dealing with Wisteria!"

"No." Baylen growled. "No fucking way will I risk your life."

"That's not your decision to make!"

"It sure the fuck is! I'm your fucking king and your fucking mate!" He shouted.

Ali drew herself up to her full five foot four inches and glared up at the man in front of her. "You are *not* my king! How many times do I have to tell you that? The decisions made about our life together and Wisteria should've been decisions we made together. But since you've abdicated your role as my mate, I will be making that decision on my own." She turned away from Baylen, so furious that she was sure she'd lost all control of her glamour.

Baylen grabbed her arm and turned her back to face him. "This is not your fucking decision. She is fucking after me."

"She's after the whole Earth! You are just the toy she's amusing herself with! When she tires of you, she will kill you! Your life is at risk as much as mine!"

"I will fucking destroy this whole fucking planet if she harms you!"

Aliora glared at Baylen. "Yes, you are the big bad Fae king. I'm sure that, now you have gotten me out of the way, you will continue on your path of self destruction!"

Caden exchanged glances with Levi and Ash. It was the weirdest moment he'd ever been in. They all turned and walked a little further away.

"I'm going to fucking spank your ass, Ali!" Baylen roared.

"Oh, no. No, you're not! You gave up all rights to me so you could wallow in the darkness."

"The fuck I did! I was protecting you!"

"You were protecting yourself! Not me! I don't need that kind of protection, Baylen. I don't need a knight in shining armor! I need a partner. I need a friend. I need someone who recognizes me for who I am and respects that. I need someone who sees me and loves me—Exactly as I am. Someone who will do whatever it takes to make our relationship work. I need someone who chooses me!"

Aliora turned away from Baylen and marched over to the three males. "Ash Morana. Go home. I'm not going with you, and if you try to force me, I will make you sorry you were ever created!"

Ash grinned, a flash of white teeth and a roguish glint in his eyes. "I choose you. I'm not a fool like others who shall remain nameless. I can hold him down for you if you wish to torture him." He rubbed his hands together. "I do love a woman with fire in her soul. You could help me rule Hell. I have no doubt you would keep us all in line."

Ali rubbed her ear. "Please keep your pet spider on a leash in the future. I will only say this once. If she comes back, I will end her."

"You better not fucking bite him, Ali!" Baylen growled. Ali flipped him the bird behind her back and continued to glare at Ash.

Ash stared at the short curvy woman before him and was shocked by his lust for her. "You are worthy to carry my children—To be my queen."

"No."

"None of them...." He waved at the three males who stood ready should he make any wrong moves. "...can stop me if I decide to take you."

"You overestimate yourself. I could stop you, and I would," Ali said quietly. "Beyond that, I think it would be unwise for you to take on The Guardian."

Ash grabbed her arm. "You must understand that I'm going to take you. I don't wish a war between us, but you will be my queen."

A growl and Baylen leapt between them, all wild primal Fae, his eyes glittering with his rage. He grabbed Ash and threw him. "Do not touch my mate!"

Ash rose to his feet, an angry glint in his eyes. "You rejected her, King of the Fae. She's fair game now."

The Fae king never said a word. His long hair blew in the wind. His eyes had gone eerily cold as he drew massive amounts of Fae energy. In the next instant he blasted all that energy into the Fallen Angel who ruled the darkness. Blast after blast slammed into the creature who dwelt in the blackest of nights. He stumbled back and threw up a shield of black energy that absorbed the next explosion of Fae magic.

Caden and Levi moved forward, and The Ward surrounded Ali as her glamour fell away. *"Choose, Aliora."*

"Stop that!" She swatted at the shimmering iridescent Ward. "I need to help Baylen!"

"Even though he has rejected you?"

Aliora huffed. *"You don't know anything about men. Does that look like rejection to you?* She waved at the Fae king, fighting a being of immense power to protect her.

An Angelfire sword appeared in Ash's hand. Its normal blue light corrupted into an inky black that absorbed the light around it. He swung it at Baylen and advanced as the Fae king dodged to avoid the blow. Levi drew his swords from their crisscrossed scabbards on his back and threw one to Baylen. The Fae king snatched it out of the air and swung it hard to crash into the blade that was slicing toward him.

Ali tried to skirt The Ward as she heard the harsh metallic ring of sword slamming against sword. *"Get out of my way!"*

"You choose the Fae king?"

"Yes! Get out of my way!"

"No, Aliora. He must fight for you."

No! I can defeat Ash! Let me go! Let me help him!"

"It's not your power that is in question, Aliora. It is his. Baylen must learn to trust in his own power."

Ali looked at The Ward with tears in her eyes. *"He fights all the time! His power is unimaginable! Please. I can help him!"*

"He believes the darkness is his power. Darkness can not defeat darkness. Only light can do that. He is a Fae. A being of the light. He can only protect you with the power of the light."

"I'm his light!" Ali cried, tears streaming down her face.

"Yes. Now, we will see if he understands that—If he will step away from the darkness to protect the only one who can save him."

Chapter One Hundred Eighty-One

EARTH DIMENSION THREE
Mystic Haven, B.C., Canada

SWEAT TRICKLED DOWN his temple, but Baylen ignored it. His focus solely on the Being of Evil that wanted to steal Ali from him. Their swords clashed again and again.

"Aliora will be mine." Ash's words were vicious punches to Baylen's heart. "I will use her to breed my sons, and I will use my sons to destroy your kingdom!"

Baylen fought to control the rage that beat at him, fought to ignore the images of Ali brutalized by this Fallen Angel. His sword slammed into Ash's, the crash resounding through his bones.

"What kind of lover is she, Fae king? Not that it matters overly, I'm as comfortable with rape as I am with seduction."

Nausea rolled in Baylen's stomach. "The only thing you're going to be comfortable in is fucking death, Asshole!" He deflected a blow and advanced, slamming his sword over and over against Ash's.

Ash moved closer and their swords locked, the metal screeching as the blades slid against each other. They turned close enough that he could see the sweat on Ash's skin, the grim lines carved into his face as he strained to break the lock. "She is mine, Baylen. Recognize the truth. You cannot overpower me. I am the Ruler of Darkness, and you are my subject. A pathetic being who hides in the deepest night. A man who has snuffed out his own light. Did you enjoy what Wisteria did to you?"

Baylen roared his fury and slammed a sudden punch into Ash's face. They both stumbled and went to their knees as Baylen jerked his sword free of Ash's. They rose to their feet, Ash's face dark with fury as he pressed the back of his hand to his lip, where blood flowed freely. "You will pay for that."

"Less chitchat, more fucking." Baylen growled as he sent Fae energy flowing into the sword he wielded. The blade began to glow, and he swung hard. Metal clashed against metal, again and again and again. Creators! He needed more. He reached out and drew on the energy of the Fae, and still it was not enough. They danced, they parried, they thrust their swords. The clang of metal was loud in the air, and he could sense the darkness growing. *Fuck! Fuck! Fuck!* His rage, his hatred grew, and still, it was not enough. It was not fucking enough! He bared his teeth and swung again with all the power in his body. There was a great ringing as the metal of their weapons slammed into each other. The muscles corded in Baylen's throat, his teeth clenched in a fearsome snarl as he fought to retain his footing, to push back the sword that was steadily pushing him down. He went down to one knee, an ancient Fae war cry leaving his lips, even as an equally ancient lullaby whispered around him. This time he understood. This time he didn't hesitate. He reached for the light, that agonizing pure light that rushed into him revealing all his flaws, all his sins, the light that burned away the darkness as it mingled with his energy. He still didn't fully understand what Ali was, but he fucking knew to the depths of his soul that she belonged with him. That she was his light and that she was the only one who could save him. That he was her protector as much as she was his.

The roar of a thousand Fae warriors filled him as he surged to his feet, glowing brighter and brighter until the energy detonated outward along the blade in his hands. Ash screamed in agony, and a moment later The Ward catapulted him through the air, his wings trailing smoke as he spiraled through the atmosphere. A vortex opened and he flew into it. It snapped closed and vanished.

Baylen stood, the tip of his sword resting against the sand. He breathed heavily, blood trickling from cuts he hadn't even been aware of. He looked over and his eyes met Ali's. She stared at him for a moment, and he saw the emotions washing over her face. A moment later she disappeared.

He took a deep breath. Her message was clear. He would have to go to her.

Chapter One Hundred Eighty-Two

EARTH DIMENSION THREE
Mystic Haven, B.C., Canada

BAYLEN LANDED AT THE ranch that was owned by Ryder dé Danann. He'd never been here before. Never once had he sought out the former king. He'd done everything on his own, learned from his mistakes and carried on.

Except—after he'd lost Jadeah—he should have reached out. He should have asked for help. He'd been fucking broken with no idea how to go on, surviving only for his kids.

For the life of him, he couldn't understand why the fuck he hadn't reached out after Charli was murdered by that monster. Why was it so fucking hard to admit he couldn't control the whole fucking world? He couldn't save the world.

He turned slowly seeing the barns and corrals, all well kept. Horses ran in a large pasture, a couple of ancient Fae were repairing something over by a large garage, and there were flower gardens surrounding the big ranch house. It all seemed very idyllic, he paused and shoved his hand through his hair. Somehow, he'd never pictured any of this for Ryder, but the man fucking deserved some peace after over a thousand years as the Fae king.

"Hello, Baylen."

He turned as Ryder stepped from the barn. The man was even wearing a godsdamned cowboy hat.

"Ryder." He rubbed his neck, knowing that he looked like shit. "How did you do it, Ryder?"

Ryder raised an eyebrow. "Do what?"

"Survive being the Fae king for over a thousand fucking years. Fight a war against monsters, save our people, get everyone to earth, start over. Fucking survive—without losing yourself?" Baylen swallowed. *Fuck.*

"Ah." Ryder walked up to Baylen and set his hand on the younger man's shoulder giving it a squeeze. "Sounds like we need to have coffee for this conversation. I've been hoping you'd come, Baylen."

Chapter One Hundred Eighty-Three

EARTH DIMENSION THREE
Mystic Haven, B.C., Canada

BAYLEN STOOD STARING at the small cottage. It was nearly overgrown with blackberry bushes and roses. He wanted to blast it with Fae energy. He wanted to watch it burn. He had not returned to this place of death since he'd carried Charli's body from it—And he acknowledged that some part of him had died here when he found her.

The message written on her body in blue paint had set him on a course that he'd never deviated from. He was a man marked by evil. A man destined to be alone.

He'd gone to all the Ancients, and he'd learned everything he could about the V'ran, the ancient enemy of the Fae people. The enemy they could not defeat. He'd had sophisticated satellite technology created and launched. Detection and protection, cloaked in the less sophisticated technology of this time. He'd thought they would have warning if a V'ran ship ever approached the Sol System. But Wisteria had found a way to infiltrate his world a third time.

He had no concept how Ali survived that meeting, but she had, and now she was a target. Everything inside him raged at the unfairness, at the horror he could already feel creeping into his life.

Which was why he stood here now. This is where Charli had died. He needed to see if there were answers here. He stepped forward and the Ward he'd set to protect this place of death, shimmered into view. He lifted his hand and the grey shimmer faded as it recognized him. Reaching out he grabbed the brutally thorned canes and ripped them from the door, ignoring the blood that flowed from his hands.

Opening the door, he stepped into the silent darkened interior as his Fae energy healed the wounds. With a thought, several Fae glow orbs floated in the air, providing enough light for him to see. Dust lay heavy over everything. Spiderwebs hung from the corners of the ceiling and gathered in the white spindles of the antique wrought iron bed he'd loved his mate on. His hand lifted to his chest, clenching over his heart as he saw the smear of blue paint on the fluffy white duvet.

Stepping forward, he touched a pillow, his fingers trailing across the softness as he was bombarded with memories of Charli. Her long brown hair spread across the pillow as she cried out in pleasure. Her back arched and her breasts lifted, nipples hard as he thrust into her. He swallowed. Her laughter filled his memory, as she threatened to do that *thing* he loved. He closed his eyes. *Fuck.*

Taking a breath of the stale air he forced himself to turn away from their bed and scan the rest of the room. The last painting she'd been working on stood on an easel before a window that normally let in copious amounts of sunlight. He walked over to it, more Fae glow orbs appearing. Their light shining on the picture. It was the interior of this cottage. Light streamed through dirty windows, but he could see the brambles that lay across their glass surface. He frowned. There was the table that they'd shared lunch at so often... a fragile teacup sitting there as if waiting for her to take a sip from it, and it was all covered in dust.

With a sense of surrealness, he glanced over to the table and his heart stilled as he realized it looked exactly the same as the table in the painting. Right down to the teacup and the patterns of light falling over the dust.

"Charli. What the hell?" His voice broke. Swallowing the sick feeling rising in his throat, he forced himself to look at the painting again. All her art supplies were covered in dust and cobwebs. The bed was made but there was a blue paint smear. *Oh, gods.* On the far side of the bed, on the small oak bedside table was a wooden box that he'd never seen before. He turned. The box was there. He shoved back his long hair with a trembling hand and looked back at the painting. There in the corner was the full-length mirror, that they'd often made love in front of. A tear fell as he saw her reflection in the glass, holding out the very same box that sat on the small table by their bed. He fell to his knees. *Oh, gods! Charli!* A harsh sob broke from his chest. *She'd known she was going to die.* The thought destroyed him. An agonizing cry of such pain, tore from him, that the Fae worldwide gasped.

Forcing himself to stand, he made his way to the bed and the box on the little table. He stared at it for the longest time before finally sitting down on the bed. In his mind burned the image of Charli's reflection in the mirror holding out the box. She wanted him to have whatever was inside that box. His hand trembled as he reached out and opened the lid. Stones. Memory stones. Some silver and some bronze, and over them lay a yellowed note with his name written in Charli's handwriting. She'd even turned the y into a heart with tiny heart-shaped flowers curling all around it. He picked up the note and carefully opened it. 'For when the darkness consumes you.'

He closed his eyes, a terrible sense of loss filling him. Gods, how she had known him. How he missed her.

Picking up a silvery stone he set it on the table and watched as it activated. A three-dimensional image of Jadeah appeared, she wore her wedding dress and laughed looking up into his face at their wedding. He blinked away the tears stinging his eyes. The image wavered and Charli's voice spoke softly. "I gathered these from your friends and family, Baylen. They all loved Jadeah and were happy to share their memories. I've come to love her, too, through these memories. She's a part of you, Falcon, Aurora, and Jewel. She's a part of me now too. I see why you love her so much. I see why you miss her. Keep going, there are so many beautiful memories here."

He carefully reached for another stone, and another. Memories and more memories surrounding him, filling him. Until he'd worked his way through the silvery stones and the bronze stones that memorialized his Charli. Until there was only one bronze stone left. He set it on the table. Charli appeared. "I've tried to put everything here. All our memories." She smiled and he could see the tears in her eyes. "There is nothing you could have done, Baylen. I

know you will blame yourself. I know you will seek to erad-
icate the one responsible for this. As you did with the cult
that took Jadeah from you. I know your darkness will grow.
I know you'll hold on to it. I know you will hold it dangerously close. But we are people of the light, Baylen." A
tear slipped down her cheek. "It's the light that has always
saved us, and it's the light that will save you. When the light
comes, Baylen," her voice grew fierce, "embrace it—Embrace *her* with all the wild power that is yours. Most importantly forgive yourself. Love is not done with you yet,
mate. For that I am grateful. Whoever she is, Baylen, love
her with everything you are. Have more babies. Laugh, argue, make up, do all those wild sexy things you used to do
with me and add more to your repertoire. Don't hold back.
Build an amazing life together. Jadeah and I, we want you
to have a love so powerful it changes your world. We want
to hear whispers, even past this veil that separates us, of the
legends they will tell of you and your queen. Goodbye, my
love."

Baylen slid to his knees by the bed as great sobs
wracked his body.

Chapter One Hundred Eighty-Four

EARTH DIMENSION THREE
Mystic Haven, B.C., Canada

ALI SAT CURLED UP ON her porch swing, staring out over the ocean, as she had all night. The stars had faded into the beauty of the sunrise, and the majestic colors of the sunrise had faded into the blue of the sky and still there was beauty in that.

A cup of tea floated out and sat on the small table beside the swing. She sighed and reached for the dainty China cup. Taking a sip, she closed her tear dampened eyes as the warm tea slid down her throat. He'd made his choice, and she had to accept it. She took another sip blinking away the tears that had no end.

There was a sudden shift in the energy, and she looked up at the sky feeling the power of The Fae King long before she saw him. He landed, and she thought he looked like hell, especially with that black eye and the cut on his cheek. He walked over and sat down beside her, the swing rocking gently. They both stared out over the ocean. He reached out and took her hand, his fingers sliding between hers, and she was shocked by how he was trembling.

"I fucked up, Ali."

"Yes, you did."

White clouds moved across the sky, hiding the sun for brief moments.

"I'm not a man to surrender, Ali."

"I know."

"I don't know if I ever told you this, but Jadeah was an alien. She had the prettiest soft pink skin and these big silver-grey eyes. When I met her, she had dark hair but somewhere along the line she decided I liked blondes." He laughed, and Ali heard the tears. She blinked away the moisture that threatened to fall from her own eyes. "One day, I came home and she's a stunning platinum blonde. She had that ability. To change her appearance. I miss her, Ali. I love her. Still." He shrugged.

"I know you do, Bay."

"That's never going to change. She was my mate."

Ali nodded, her heart aching.

"She had no chance. There were these Wizards. They were some kind of cult. They believed that aliens did not belong on Earth. They believed Earthlings were superior. Whether Supers or just your garden variety of humans. They hated the Fae too. Cause, you know, we're aliens, even though we've been here over a thousand years. They sent a suicide bomber into her shop. A young human man who suffered from a mental illness. He was a child really."

Ali wiped the tears that flowed down her face. "Creators. Baylen. I'm so sorry."

"I couldn't protect her, but I avenged her." He looked at Ali and his eyes were hard, his voice cold and broken. "I killed them all. Every single one of them."

So that was the darkness. "I would have too."

Baylen laughed, a harsh disbelieving sound. "You are light, Ali. Beautiful light." He took a deep breath as her hand tightened on his for a moment. He squeezed back. "Charli was a whole different story. She was a wild child. An incredible artist. She was Fae. Long brown hair, and beautiful brown eyes, and usually, a smudge of paint on her face somewhere. A second chance, Ali. After I'd lost my world. She brought me back to life. I thought we had forever. Creators help me, but I loved her. Since I'd killed the Wizards, I thought I could protect her. But my past caught up with me."

"Wisteria."

Baylen nodded, his eyes haunted as he looked at her. "Wisteria is the one who put that sliver of darkness in me."

Ali smiled faintly. "Wisteria—and you."

Baylen looked out over the ocean. "I've embraced that darkness."

"I see you, Baylen."

Acceptance. An acceptance he did not deserve. "I could not protect Charli. Wisteria came when I wasn't there, and she killed Charli. Mere hours afterwards, I found out about Ciara. One of my Fae, captured and tortured by that evil bitch. She'd had her for weeks, Ali. Why didn't I know? I should have known. I should have saved her and Charli. I'm the fucking Fae king, the most powerful Fae in existence, and I failed them."

Ali closed her eyes, feeling his pain.

"I need to tell you something, Aliora, something I've never spoken about with anyone. Something I never told Jadeah or Charli." He stared down at their clasped hands.

"You can tell me anything, Bay." Ali squeezed his hand, stunned by the depth of trust he was placing in her.

He took a deep shuddering breath, bracing for rejection. "The first time I encountered Wisteria, I was twenty-six years old. I was a hotshot pilot, and I thought the world was my fucking oyster. He glanced at Aliora. "She wore a human glamour. I didn't see through it. I spent the night with her and met her the next day at one of the island hot springs. That's when she took hold of my mind. She—" He fought to say the word. The ugly word that he'd never said out loud. "She raped me." He started to shake.

Tears burned Ali's eyes, and so many things fell into place. She turned, her eyes meeting his, her hand lifting to rest against his cheek. "I've got you, Baylen." Her fingers stroked over the mark she'd left on him. "You don't have to go through this alone. I'm here."

He took a deep breath and stared into her eyes. He didn't know what the hell he was searching for, but something deep inside him stilled. She'd always seen him. She'd always seen his brokenness, even if she hadn't known the cause. The brokenness he tried so desperately to hide.

"Thank you for telling me. I know that had to take a lot of courage." She smiled through her tears and his heart ached. Those tears were for him.

"You know this isn't your fault, right? You didn't deserve this."

"I should've seen what she was. I don't understand how I didn't recognize the enemy of our people." His voice sounded agonized.

Aliora moved to her knees and wrapped her arms around him. "We all thought they were dead, Baylen. Ryder and his Trium thought they'd destroyed the V'ran. You couldn't have known."

And there she was. Lighting his way. "Would you go with me to speak to Dr. Esteban? I—I need help."

Ali smiled, her eyes meeting his. Her love a healing balm to his ravaged soul. "Of course, I will."

Baylen took a deep shuddering breath. He'd known she would be there for him, but he'd let his fear rule him. It was time to step into the light.

"Every time I've loved, I've given my all. I'm not the kind of man who holds back. I loved Jadeah and Charli. I always will. Do you understand?"

"Yes." Her voice broke. What she wouldn't give for him to love her like that.

"I would not survive losing another mate." His eyes met hers and she saw the grim awareness in them. "Thank the Creators for Caden, because he is the only one who could stop me if I gave in to this darkness. He would have to. I would lose my soul. I would destroy everything. Everyone. There would be nothing to stop me if you were not in the world, Ali."

Her eyes widened.

"I'm in love with you, Ali, and I always will be."

Tears spilled down her face. "Baylen?"

His dark eyes stared into hers, and he let go of his glamour. She could see the glow even in the light of day. Her breath caught. She lifted a trembling hand and touched his face. "I love you too."

"I know you do, Ali. I don't deserve you. I don't deserve another chance. I'd tell you to run, but creators help me, I would find you. You deserve light and gentleness. Everything you are, you deserve back a hundred times or more. All I can offer you is my darkness."

"Baylen." She took his face in her hands. "How many times have we conquered your darkness together? How many mornings did we burn together? I am light. Your light."

Baylen stared at her. "That's what that female creator and Charli said."

Ali tilted her head, and the whole story poured out of Baylen. The Wards, Eliana in the woods, the cottage with the painting. Everything.

Reaching out, Ali brushed his dark hair back and tucked it behind his pointed ear. "What do you say?"

Baylen stared at her. "You're my light. I won't survive losing you, Ali. The darkness would devour me. I would destroy the world."

"You're still kind of stuck on that point aren't you. Baylen, I need you to know—" she paused, her eyes holding his intently, "to understand that I will always fight to stay with you. I will fight for us."

Baylen reached for her. "I'm no fucking knight in shining armour, Ali. I've been to war. Fuck that, I've been to hell and returned with part of it still burning in my soul.

My armor is tattered and dented and scraped. But by all the fucking deities, I am the man you want to have at your side in a war." His voice was low and hard and dangerous. Yet, in this moment. In this place. It was the most intimate thing he'd ever said to her. She studied his face, met his intense gaze. "Do you promise?"

"Yes." A single word, but the very timber of his voice made it a solemn promise. His dark eyes held hers. The moment lingering between them, and she understood she had the vow of The Fae King. But more than that, she understood that the man had given her an oath that he would sacrifice his life's blood to keep. He would fight for her—for them. Her heart thumped hard in her chest. She swallowed and took a shaky breath.

"Mate with me. Marry me. Be my light, Aliora. For all eternity."

She touched his cheek, tracing over the mating mark she'd already left on him. Her eyes met his. "Yes. For all eternity."

Epilogue

ASH LOOKED UP FROM his desk. "Yes?"

"Cordelia is ours, though I suspect the Mer will make an attempt to take it back."

Abaddon stood beside his brothers, Akuma, and Asani, the infamous Angel Assassin Team. Ash leaned back in his chair and studied them. "You let the Fae king live."

Abaddon crossed his arms, a hard smile touched Akuma's lips, and Asani narrowed his eyes. "Don't mistake us for your lackeys, Morana. We've agreed to aid you in taking over this planet because it suits our purposes. The Fae king's time will come, but first, we need to establish a stronger base. One underwater city is useless. Which sanctuary city do we take next?"

"Everborough. Start your planning. I want the Unicorn leader, Thea Valeska, taken alive."

The three Fallen Angels turned and started walking toward the door.

"Asani."

They turned as one, and an Angelfire blade slammed into Asani's cheek. Ignoring the cursing, Ash fixed them with a hard stare. "That's going to leave a nasty scar." His voice hardened. "Do not presume that you will survive me."

He opened a vortex and stepped into it. A moment later he stepped out, into the office of Drace Aphelion. "Report."

The End

Cast of Characters

ALPHABETICAL ORDER by first name.

Mystic Haven Dimensions takes place in Dimension Three unless otherwise stated.

Adler Llewellyn

- Deity
- Planet: Earth, Ireland, Dimension Four (Locked)
- Dragon Warrior
- Etan Llewellyn (Brother)

Aliora Aurelius (Or-el-eeus) (32)

- Changeling Fae
- Planet: Earth, Dimension Three
- Children's Party Entertainer
- Ciska de Fae (Grandmother)
    - Elf
- Edge de Fae (Grandfather)
    - Seelie Fae
- Breaker Murchadh (Great-Grandfather)
    - Mer

Amara Zayas

- Angel
- Angelic Realm, Earth, Dimension Three

- Owner of Another Dimension Book Store
- Part of Levi's Host

Angel Assassin Team

- Fallen Angels
- Brothers
    - Abaddon
    - Akuma
    - Asani

Arianna Tyrrell:

- Halfling golden eagle shifter/Phoenix
- Planet: Earth, Dimension Three
- Owner of the Chicco di Caffe

Ash Morana (Moor-ana)

- Fallen Angel
- Leader of the Ashes of Death Crime Syndicate
- Member of G.E.N.E.T.I.C.S.
- Access to all Dimensions

Asterine Skyfire

- Seelie Fae (Ancient)
- Planet: Uskara, Dimension One, Earth, Dimension Three
- Engineer
- Asterine Skyfire (Friend)

Baylen Knight: (36)

- Seelie Fae (Ancient)
- Planet: Earth, Dimension Three
- Fae King & Part of The Royal Trium
- Pilot & Part owner of Skyward Air
- Aurora Sky Knight (8) (Daughter, Triplet to Jewel & Falcon)
    - Nickname: Ladybug
- Jewel Fae Knight (8) (Daughter, Triplet to Aurora & Falcon)
    - Nickname: Warrior Princess
- Falcon Ender Knight (8) (Son, Triplet to Aurora & Jewel)
    - Nickname: Ace
- Jadeah Knight (Mate 1—Deceased, Mother to Aurora, Jewel, and Falcon Knight)
- Charli Knight (Mate 2—Deceased)
- Zander Knight (Father)
- Mia Knight (Mother)
- Riot Knight (Brother, Triplet to Baylen & Jarek)
- Jarek Knight (Brother, Triplet to Baylen & Riot)
- Rhys Bjorn (Friends & Partners in Skyward Air)
- Micah Thallan (Friends)

Blade Maddox

- Seelie Fae (Ancient)
- Planet: Erendrial, Dimension One, Earth, Dimension Three

- Former Royal Protector
- Warrior
- Maxen Ransom (Friend)
- Ryder dé Danann (Friend)

Caden Brody (35)

- Halfling Seelie Fae/White tiger shifter
- Planet: Earth
- Fae Guardian
- Widower
- Caden's Brood
  - Benjamin Brody (Bear shifter)
  - Gunnar Brody (Twin to Chance) (Tiger Shifter)
  - Chance Brody (Twin to Gunnar) (Tiger Shifter)
  - Pandora Brody (Seelie Fae)
  - Macen Brody (Twin to Marisol) (Pixie)
  - Marisol Brody (Twin to Macen) (Pixie)
  - Dakota Brody (Coyote Shifter)
  - Safire Brody (Changeling Fae)
- Caden's siblings
  - Samara Brody (32)
  - Bashaya Brody (31) (Second in command, Fireman)
  - Kiera Brody (30)
  - Tori Brody-Hudson (28) (Police Dispatcher)
    - Wilder Hudson (Mate to Tori, Eagle Shifter)

    ◦ Catelyn Brody (25) (Police Officer)
    ◦ Nathan Brody (3) (Twin to Brighid)
    ◦ Brighid Brody (3) (Twin to Nathan)

Chasin Fiain (35)

- Dragon Shifter
- Planet: Earth, Dimension Three
- Fire Chief
- Maverick Fiain (Twin brother)
- Caden Brody (Friend)
- Stone Zeyev (Friend)

Ciara Walker

- Seelie Fae
- Planet: Earth, Dimension Three
- Writer
- Sophia Walker (Daughter)
- Genna Walker (Grandmother)
- Sam Walker (Grandfather)

Ciska de Fae

- Elf
- Planet: Earth, Dimension Three
- Mated to Edge de Fae
- Grandmother to Aliora

Daniel Brody

- White tiger shifter
- Planet: Earth
- Mated to Ariel Brody (Fae)
- Doctor
- Children
  - Caden Brody (35) (Mystic Haven Chief of Police, Guardian)
  - Samara Brody (32)
  - Bashaya Brody (31) (Second in command, Fireman)
  - Kiera Brody (30)
  - Tori Brody-Hudson (28) (Police Dispatcher)
    - Wilder Hudson (Mate to Tori, Eagle Shifter)
  - Catelyn Brody (25) (Police Officer)
  - Nathan Brody (3) (Twin to Brighid)
  - Brighid Brody (3) (Twin to Nathan)
- Hawke Brody (Brother)
- Travis Brody (Nephew)

Dagger Marrok

- Human
- Planet: Earth, Dimension two
- King Author's bodyguard & Knight of the round table
- Children: two sons
- Lady Aalis (Spouse, deceased)

Drace Aphelion (uh-FEE-lee-uhn)

- Althanean, Dimension Two
- Planet Althanea (El-thane-ee-uh)
- Wife: Havyn Aphelion
- Scientist
- High ranking member of the Sacred Ways Sect

Edge de Fae

- Seelie Fae (Ancient)
- Planet: Erendrial, Dimension One, Earth, Dimension Three
- Ciska de Fae (Mate/Wife)
- Warrior
- Grandfather to Aliora

Eliana Aezorwyn (Ay-zor-win)

- Creator
- Rune's younger sister
- Access to all dimensions
- Lives in the In-Between

Etan Llewellyn

- Deity
- Planet: Earth, Ireland, Dimension Four (Locked)
- Dragon Warrior
- Adler Llewellyn (Brother)

Finn Gallagher

- Merman
- Planet: Earth, Dimension Three
- Second in Command of the Mer

Genna (Genevieve) Walker

- Seelie Fae (Ancient)
- Planet: Erendrial, Dimension One, Earth, Dimension Three
- Sam Walker (Mate/Husband)
- Ciara Walker (Granddaughter)
- Sophia Walker (Great-Granddaughter)
- Mega Corporation owner (Greenhouse Empire)

Gin Monroe

- Wolf Shifter
- Planet: Earth, Dimension Three
- School Secretary

Helio MacConaill

- Horse Shifter
- Planet: Earth, Dimension Three
- Tattoo Artist

Janie Valeska

- Mixed Genetics Shifter (Unicorn/pegasus/Horse shifter)
- Planet: Earth, Dimension Three

- Owner of Mystic Brew (Pub)

Jett Sidhe

- Seelie Fae
- Earth, Dimension Three
- The Royal Protector, Part of The Royal Trium

Josef Drake

- Ice Dragon Shifter
- Planet: Earth, Dimension Three
- Second in Command Mystic Haven Police
- Cassandra Drake (Mate)

Juan Esteban

- Leopard Shifter
- Planet: Earth, Dimension Three
- Psychologist
- Jazmin Esteban (17) (Niece)
    - Ricardo Esteban (Deceased. Mate to Emilia, Father of Jazmin, Brother to Juan)
    - Emilia Esteban (Deceased. Mate to Ricardo, Mother of Jazmin, Sister-in-law to Juan)
- Khiiral Darkfire (19) (Juan is legal guardian)

Keir

- Angel
- Angelic Realm

Kit Calloway

- Elf
- Planet: Earth, Dimension Three
- Leader of Mystic Haven Elves (Clan Name: Mae'r Dewr - The Brave)
- Seismologist, Warrior
- Kit's High Warriors
  - Aien
  - Paeris
  - Braern
  - Navarre
  - Jhaeros

Lavender Wildstone

- Sheline
- Planet of birth unknown, Nephara, Dimension 9,700,241
- Servant of Ash Morana
- Mate to Rome Amberfire

Levi Hariel

- Angel
- Angelic Realm, Earth, Dimension Three
- Leader of a small covert Angelic Host

Marcus Smith

- Cougar Shifter
- Planet: Earth, Dimension Three
- Police Officer

Maverick Fiain (35)

- Dragon Shifter
- Planet: Earth, Dimension Three
- Police Officer
- Chasin Fiain (Twin brother)
- Caden Brody (Friend)
- Stone Zeyev (Friend)

Maxen Ransom

- Unseelie Fae (Ancient)
- Planet: Ilrune, Dimension One, Earth, Dimension Three
- Former Royal Healer
- Doctor
- Blade Maddox (Friend)
- Ryder dé Danann (Friend)

Micah Thallan (36)

- Seelie Fae
- Planet: Earth, Dimension Three
- Owner of Mystic Ink & Tattoo Artist
- Sniper

- Baylen Knight (Friends)

Nerys Daenala

- Seelie Fae (Ancient)
- Planet: Uskara, Dimension One, Earth, Dimension Three
- Engineer
- Asterine Skyfire (Friend)

Rabia

- Angel
- Angelic Realm
- Zerachiel (Mate)

Reef

- Seelie Fae
- Planet: Earth, Dimension Three
- Tattoo Artist

Rhys Bjorn

- Bear Shifter
- Planet: Earth, Dimension Three
- Part owner of Skyward Air & Pilot
- Baylen Knight (Friends & Partners in Skyward Air)

Riley Muirgheal

- Mermaid
- Planet: Earth, Dimension Three
- Leader of the Mer

Rome Amberfire

- Zallaphan
- Planet of birth unknown, Nephara, Dimension 9,700,241
- Servant of Ash Morana
- Mate to Lavender Wildstone

Rune Aezorwyn (Ay-zor-win)

- Creator
- Eliana's older brother
- Access to all dimensions
- Lives in the In-Between

Ryder dé Danann

- Seelie Fae (Ancient)
- Planet: Erendrial, Dimension One, Earth, Dimension Three
- Former Fae King & part of the Royal Trium
- Horse Rancher
- Blade Maddox (Friend)
- Maxen Ransom (Friend)

Sam Walker (Tiên lineage)

- Seelie Fae (Ancient)
- Planet: Tarathiel, Dimension One, Earth, Dimension Three
- Undercover agent for the Former Fae King
- Undercover agent for the Current Fae King
- Surfer
- Genna Walker (Mate/Wife)
- Ciara Walker (Granddaughter)
- Sophia Walker (Great-Granddaughter)

Sariel

- Angel
- Angelic Realm, Earth, Dimension Three
- Part of Levi's Host

Shade

- Seelie Fae
- Planet: Earth, Dimension Three
- Tattoo Artist

Shirina Sítheach

- Seelie Fae (Ancient)
- Planet: Erendrial, Dimension One, Earth, Dimension Three
- Ward Expert by Royal appointment to the Former Fae King & Trium
- Ward Expert by Royal appointment to the Current Fae King & Trium

Striker Barron

- Seelie Fae
- Earth, Dimension Three
- The Royal Healer, Part of The Royal Trium
- Doctor

Stone Zeyev (35)

- Wolf Shifter
- Planet: Earth, Dimension Three
- Alpha Mystic Haven Wolf Pack
- Owner & Chef of The Dark Moon restaurant
- Caden Brody (Friend)
- Chasin Fiain (Friend)
- Maverick Fiain (Friend)

Thea Valeska

- Unicorn Shifter
- Planet: Scotland, Earth, Dimension Three
- Alpha Unicorn herd, Everborough Sanctuary City
- Leader of Everborough
- Member of the Superhuman Counsel
- Janie Valeska (Daughter)

Wisteria Abital

- V'ran
- Planet: V'ran, Dark Flame Star System,

Dimension One

Glossary

ANGELFIRE BLADE: Sword or Dagger used by Angels. These weapons are incredibly dangerous.

Creators: Beings who exist out of time and space. The last two surviving Creators, created the Multiverse

Energy Web: an energy field spun by a V'ran. It is a type of web. It's capable of trapping and entangling any beings who walk into them.

Energy neutralizing devices: small handheld devices could read the wavelengths of the energy web and counteract them. In effect neutralizing their cohesiveness.

Fae: There are many myths, legends, and stories in Irish culture regarding The Tuatha Dé Danann. These beings are said to be a magical race that possessed supernatural powers. It is also said that they did not come from earth. Of course, Irish culture, folklore, and mythology is very rich, diverse, and complex. It contains far, far more than the simple explanation I give above. My interpretation is purely fictional and sparks from the wonderful idea that The Tuatha Dé Danann may have originated from beyond our little planet and corner of space. The Fae of Mystic Haven Dimensions are the product of my imagination, and they are unique.

- The three branches of the Fae of Mystic Haven Dimensions
  - Seelie Fae
    - Need the energy of the sun

- have always been the most numerous race and can be traced back to the beginning of the Fae species.
  - Unseelie Fae
    - Unseelie Fae are rare since the Tuatha War
    - Predominantly Dark Haired
    - Need the energy of the sun *and* moon
    - resulted from a small mutation that caused them to need both moonlight and sunlight to regenerate.
  - Changeling Fae
    - The Changeling Fae were thought to be lost in the Tuatha War.
    - Need the Sun.
    - A changeling Fae is an extremely rare and unique Fae born of mixed blood. Not simply a halfling. A Changeling occurs when genetics have been mixed and remixed for generations.
    - Their powers are incredibly vast. They are *not* the blending of a halfling nor are they a typical Fae halfling with all the powers of both species. They are unique. Their abilities and powers

combined and reformed.

- Their appearance is Fae with features from the other species.
  - They always have Fae wings, but those wings can vary in color.
  - Their skin color could be from any of their ancestral genetics.
  - Their ears are always pointed.
  - Their eyes always have sparks of color (similar to an opal), but the iris color of the eyes can be any eye-color.
  - No two Changeling Fae are alike.

Fae Energy/Fae Magic: What the humans call Fae Magic the Fae know as energy manipulation. Fae are creatures of energy. They have an instinctive knowledge of how energy works and how to manipulate it.

Fae Orb: A Fae Energy created light source in the form of an orb. All Fae have the ability to create Fae Orbs.

Flame-Out: The Fae are susceptible to a condition they call Flame-Out.

- Flame-Out is a dangerous fatigue that could kill

if not treated. Basically, it means that they expended so much energy that they must recharge to survive. Sleep and sunlight recharge them. The amount they need will be in direct proportion to the level of energy they exert.

- Sunshine: The Fae are creatures of light and energy. They need the sun. Too many days away from the sunlight will weaken them.

Glamour: For superhumans that are not shifters, glamours are a necessity.

- **Glamour** is the ability for superhumans to use their powers to hide their true appearance, so they blend with the human population.
- Shifters are either human or their specific animal in appearance.
- The Fae have the ability to project a glamour that is so beautiful it entrances people.
    - Invisibility is another form of glamour for the Fae.

Godsdamned: A common swear word throughout the multiverse. There are two Creators, so this particular expression is plural.

Hologram Technology: Holograms are three-dimensional images generated by interfering beams of light that reflect real, physical objects

Holo-screen: A Holographic screen/computer

In-between: The in-between is the place where the creators existed. It is a place out of time and space, existing between nothingness and the Multiverse.

Mating:

- **Dream Walking:** One of the most important Fae signs of mating. A fae can enter the dreams of their mate. Those dreams are usually romantic or erotic in nature.
- **Mate Call:** The mate call is a little-known phenomena that occurs when the mating is recognized. A Fae can suddenly glow if they come into close proximity with their destined mate. Especially the first time.
- **Fae Soul Bond:** When two Fae are mates, if they both are in Fae form during sex, the male can create a soul bond with the female.

Millennia: The plural form of millennium. A period of a thousand years.

Mind link: a telepathic connection between superhumans

Multiverse: A multidimensional universe.

Sanctuary Cities and boroughs:

- Each leader of the Sanctuary Cities and Boroughs are part of the superhuman Counsel
- The Sanctuary Cities and Boroughs are a network spread across the globe.
- A Sanctuary City is a refuge, a safe place for

Superhumans. They are carefully warded and guarded.

- A Borough is a smaller refuge community, providing goods and services for superhumans. They are also carefully warded and protected
- Boroughs are designed to also be used as temporary refuges in the event of a Superhuman disaster

Sanctuary Cities mentioned in The Ways of Light

1. Mystic Haven (Vancouver) - Run by Caden Brody - Refuge Island
2. Everborough (Edinburgh) - Run by Unicorns

Underground Boroughs mentioned in The Ways of Light

1. Elderrock (Calgary) - Run by Elves

Superhumans: A Superhuman is all of the other species that are not human. Fae, Shifters, Dragons, Aliens, Mer etc.

Sol Star System: The Star System that the Earth is part of.

Telekinesis: The ability to move objects by using mental powers or Fae Energy.

The Sacred Stardust Chalice: A mystical healing chalice made from an ancient meteorite embedded with stardust. First mentioned in Forsaken, Realm of The Forsaken, Book 1.

Time Shift: A Fae ability that takes considerable power and strength to master. A Time Shift is the ability to freeze time for a few minutes.

Vortex: chaotic wormholes, created & controlled by individual angels as a means of instantaneous travel through dimensions, time, and space.

- Wormholes are a type of bridge that connects two different points in space-time, theoretically creating a shortcut that could reduce travel time and distance.

Wards: Mystic Haven is protected by several different types of wards. These wards have different functions and different abilities. The Fae create energy wards, and the Mer create wards from the water. Wards are sentient beings

- **Simple Protection/Security Wards**
  - Generally speaking, these Wards surround a home or property
  - Warn the owners of danger and if something has passed through the Ward
  - Keep children and pets inside the boundaries of the property
  - Keep natural animals out of the yard or property

- **Guard Wards**
  - Renders the object it is guarding invisible
  - Usually connected to a hidden

activation device
- Difficult to create
- Mer and Fae have these kinds of Wards
- The emergency cave entrance is hidden by this kind of ward

- **Stratagem Wards**
  - The Ward & The Mist Ward
  - Dangerous to create
  - Can only be created by the most powerful Fae and The Fae King
  - Created to detect good and destroy it
  - Strengthen by good. The residents of Mystic Haven are encouraged to visit the Wards often.

- **Defense Wards**
  - There are five defense wards on Mystic Haven. The Fae created four that defend all sides of the island, and the Mer created one that defends the waters around the island.
  - The four created by the Fae are located at the emergency cave, until they are released.
  - The underwater ward created by the Mer is active all the time.
  - Dangerous to create
  - Capable of detecting & destroying evil

- **Guard/Stratagem/Defense Ward**

- The Fae Castle Ward
- A combination of the three Wards
- Extremely dangerous to create, Created by the King and his Trium & most powerful Fae
- Every Fae castle on the earth is one of these Wards
- Extremely powerful & fully capable of destroying evil
- Renders the castle invisible in times of danger, to everyone, unless they have been escorted through the Ward by a member of the Royal Trium, Royal Family, or one of the castle guards.
- Creates an impenetrable barrier, so that evil may not enter
- Capable of moving people through time and space if it senses danger to one of the ones it protects.

Wing Types: There are several different kinds of superhumans with wings in the Mystic Haven Dimensions Series. It is reasonable to assume that the wings of each being must be very large to carry the being they belong to.

- Dragon's wings look very similar to bat wings.
- Shifters have the wings of whatever kind of animal they are.
  - Eagle
  - Falcon

- ○ Hawk etc.
- The Fae have energy wings.
- The Sprites have wings that are similar to butterfly wings but on a much grander scale.
- The Angels have large, feathered wings.

Wildfires:

- Wildfires are a serious threat in many places in the world. British Columbia Canada is one of those places, along with all provinces in Canada. Please be mindful of the fire danger in your area and use the utmost care to help prevent these tragedies.
- 'Wildfires can rapidly burn millions of acres of land and can destroy everything—trees, homes, animals, and humans in their paths. Families and whole communities that live in rural, wildfire-prone areas are in danger of losing their homes and having to flee for their own safety.'

https://www.shelterboxcanada.org/

- Canadian Wildfire resources:
  - ○ https://firesmartcanada.ca/
  - ○ https://www.nrcan.gc.ca/our-natural-resources/forests/wildland-fires-insects-disturbances/17598

Don't miss out!

Visit the website below and you can sign up to receive emails whenever Arlie Sheelin publishes a new book. There's no charge and no obligation.

https://books2read.com/r/B-A-SLWO-TFQZB

BOOKS 2 READ

Connecting independent readers to independent writers.

Also by Arlie Sheelin

Codes of Creation - Realm of The Forsaken
Forsaken

Mystic Haven Dimensions
The Ways of Light

The Codes of Creation - The Zemyneah Experiment
The Way Maker

Watch for more at https://www.arliesheelin.com/.

About the Author

Writer, introvert, and a bit of a geek. **Favorite Authors:** Nalini Singh, Angela Knight, Sandra Hill, and Louis L'amour. I've raised my kids on a steady diet of **Star Trek** *and* **Star Wars,** which resulted in *them taking me* to sci-fi/ cosplay conventions. Bonus points! I'm also an Indie RP writer - which means I write short story fiction online as some of my favorite characters. My drink of choice is tea, Earl Grey, or Chai. But on cold days, I go for Hot Chocolate with the odd venture into Peppermint Mocha. Caffeine is the magic elixir that helps fuel the imagination. I have a New Media Production and Design Diploma. - Which is a fancy way of saying I have creative skills with computers, mainly graphics.

Read more at https://www.arliesheelin.com/.